H. G. Wells was born in 1866 and educated at a private school at Bromley, Midhurst Grammar School, and the Royal College of Science, where he studied biology with T. E. Huxley. He had two years' apprenticeship in a draper's shop, of which he made good use in *Kipps* and *The History of Mr Polly*. He then insisted on cancelling his indentures and tried teaching, before turning professional writer. He wrote more than a hundred books, including novels, essays, histories, and programmes for world regeneration. Wells, who rose from obscurity to world fame, had an emotionally and intellectually turbulent life. An apostle of socialism, science and progress, he was in Bertrand Russell's words, 'an important liberator of thought and action'. He outraged public opinion with his views on free love and the impermanence of marriage expressed in the novels *Ann Veronica* (1909) and *The New Machiavelli* (1911). Wells wrote a number of fantasies, among the most famous are *The Time Machine* (1895), *The Island of Dr Moreau* (1896), *The Invisible Man* (1897), *The War of the Worlds* (1898) and *The Shape of Things to Come* (1933). His novels about the world of the shabby genteel, with which he had personal experience, are among his best fiction; they include: *Love and Mr Lewisham* (1900), *Kipps* (1905), *Tono Bungay* (1909) and *The History of Mr Polly* (1910). He also collaborated in a series of modern educational works, *The Outline of History*, *The Science of Life* and *The Work, Wealth and Happiness of Mankind*. His *Experiment in Autobiography* (2 vols., 1934) reviews his world. He died in 1946.

H. G. Wells

# The New Machiavelli

Introduction by Melvyn Bragg

A closer examination . . . shows
that Abelard was a Nominalist under
a new name.

G. H. Lewes, *Hist. Philos.*

It suffices for our immediate purpose
that tender-minded and
tough-minded people . . . do both exist.

William James, *Pragmatism*

Penguin Books

Penguin Books Ltd, Harmondsworth, Middlesex, England
Viking Penguin Inc., 40 West 23rd Street, New York, New York 10010, U.S.A.
Penguin Books Australia Ltd, Ringwood, Victoria, Australia
Penguin Books Canada Ltd, 2801 John Street, Markham, Ontario, Canada L3R 1B4
Penguin Books (N.Z.) Ltd, 182–190 Wairau Road, Auckland 10, New Zealand

First published by The Bodley Head 1911
Published in Penguin Books 1946
Reissued 1966
Reprinted 1970, 1971, 1978
Reprinted with an introduction 1985

Printed and bound in Great Britain by
Cox & Wyman Ltd, Reading
Typeset in Linotype Times

# Contents

# Introduction

In *The New Machiavelli*, H. G. Wells moves from being a delightful, larky, trenchant social novelist whose writing could be compared with the more leisurely passages of Dickens, to being an urgent political educator whose thundering world views and ambitions seized on the novel as an ideal medium for propaganda. This split-level book is a key work in the life of a man whose experience as much as his writing is once again – and rightly – beginning to attract the wide attention he so vividly enjoyed during much of his professional lifetime.

*The New Machiavelli*, published in 1911, comes near the middle of that great flush of Wells's books which, from 1905 to 1915, included *Kipps*, *The War in the Air*, *Tono-Bungay*, *Ann Veronica*, *The History of Mr Polly*, *The Passionate Friends*, *Boom*, *The World Set Free*, *Mr Britling Sees It Through* and, though it is hard to credit, several other works as well as articles, pamphlets, speeches, letters, plans, feuds, and a private life that was anything but. This is a novel which can be read as a sharp chronicle of late-nineteenth-century suburban times, an essay in transparently transposed autobiography, a launching pad for notions of a Wagnerian grandeur, an exercise in personal revenge and a gauntlet thrown down before the most heightened aestheticism of the day. Sometimes it does indeed read as the outlines for several books, none of which would have lacked interest or intensity.

Here is H. G. Wells at his most pointed, as well as at his most expansive; the Wells who has as fair a claim to genius as no more than half a dozen other British novelists of this century; the Wells who went out a David of optimism to be a world shaper, as yet unclouded in his sporting scientific visions of a beautifully just, benevolently efficient and unmuddled universe.

*The New Machiavelli* tells the story of Remington, who recounts it as if it were his autobiography: a man in his early forties, in exile with his lover and their child, pondering over the reasons behind his decision to quit Britain, politics, his wife, his friends, and the undoubted possibility of power. The lofty comparison of himself with Machiavelli helps make the opening one of the weakest sequences in the novel. After that, Remington relates his story in several extremely roundabout ways.

This in itself is the prime giveaway. Had Wells wanted to write a handbook of politics, there is no doubting his capacity; there rarely was. He was one of the great autodidacts, and so confident in his self-acquired knowledge that he had neither hesitation nor qualms about pronouncing authoritatively. His justification was his generous urge to teach and warn: his redemption lay in a remarkably acute and far-seeing eye which his imagination lifted over the hurdles of a future bristling in present extensions to a new world of flying machines, space conquest, atomic power . . . Had he wished, he could have written a tract or an apologia; however, he was in the mood to write 'serious' and great novels.

This was a policy decision, the result of a 'plan'. Wells longed for the world to have a plan (his plan) and he began with – even experimented on – himself. Midway through the first decade of this century he seems to have begun to worry that his reputation was too 'confused'. He was a journalist, a trader in future fictions, a man of science entranced by that great adventure of the mind which was – and continues to be – ignored by most of the respected literary writers of the day. Like many another, alas, he thought that his joyful, brilliant early books which were so popular were also so easy as to be debarred from serious consideration. And Wells demanded serious consideration. One sure way to secure it was to acquire the reputation of a respected novelist – then sublime king of the artistic and social heap, following the great master-builders of the nineteenth century.

The artistic and the social both mattered. Wells was a competitor and, as an artist who had rocketed into the Establishment from the outside (a not uncommon path, but nonetheless rich in difficulties), he wanted to 'make it'. The fact that he had 'made it' with some of the freshest and most original books of their time – *The Island of Dr Moreau* (1896), *The Invisible Man* (1897), *The War of the Worlds* (1898), and the lovely social comedy of *Kipps* (1905) – indicated that he Must Try Harder and then he could succeed at the Highest Level. Highest, as always, meant most Serious, too often confounded with Solemn. Wells went for broke. And socially, too, it was far more comfortable to be regarded as the sage than the jester: jesters were forever outside the courtly dance; a sage could not only sit at the high table but could also be listened to, even reckoned with. Wells wanted all of that. His ambition was an ever-opening maw.

In 1910 he was still, thank goodness, too much the irresponsible story-teller adored by Henry James to let seriousness get him down entirely; hence one reason for the roundabout way. The first part of *The New Machiavelli*, supposedly Remington's upbringing in Bromstead but very like Wells's upbringing in Bromley, is a precisely convincing portrait of a muddled suburbia with the father as the wonderful example of muddled late-nineteenth-century man. (It must be obvious by now that 'muddle' is one of Wells's most respected terms of abuse: a most gentle censure.) He could have made his nouveau Machiavellian point in two or, at the most, ten pages – instead of which, he could not resist the luxury of recollection reconstructed as fiction, could not turn away from the chance to re-invent his father and mother, his sensual and intellectual childhood, his wild delight in memory. And fiction again breaks out in Staffordshire, where Remington goes to stay with an uncle whose character is far too much fun for Wells to let pass by swiftly. Once more we are given a five-course meal where, if he had been keeping the strict diet of his announced plan, a snack would have served.

Again, when Remington comes to London after a rather unsatisfactory meander around Cambridge, there was no need for him to attack and dissect the Baileys at such length and with such zest. But here Wells was on another tack: revenge. He had been hurt by the Fabian Society (he had, in short, not won them over to his point of view, due largely to the equally competitive but more practised skills of George Bernard Shaw) and he wanted to take it out on Sydney and Beatrice Webb, the driving force of that extraordinarily influential group. Once again, a digression – of a different variety to the Bromstead romp – gives an unexpected and in a way unnecessary length to the novel. In fact, although Wells had a plan for this book as he had a plan for the planet, the novel (like the planet itself) seems to thrive and often thrive best, unplanned.

Then there is Wells the practised politician. Here he falls far below the standard of Trollope and indeed well below many a lesser workaday political novelist in his ability to convey a sense of being there, inside the Palaces of Westminster or out on the electioneering streets. All mundane political life is sketched in strokes of charcoal so large as to be shapeless. The grit of political life – intrigue, hopes, late sittings, solitary slog – is absent. What interested Wells was the Grand sweep. He has his man elected; he has him creating committees and ruminating on Budgets; but that is not where the heart of the novel lies. Remington wants to save the world.

He has an old formula: to excite the clustering together of Exceptional People whose mental 'hinterlands' and belief in 'Love and Fine Thinking' (Wells's words) will progress the twentieth century on a scientifically righteous path. Not a single line of this long book gives any consideration as to how those Exceptional People will be discovered, nominated, selected, controlled or monitored. Wells's faith in the power of superior intelligence was benevolent. All the Clever People were, naïvely, assumed to be good.

It has to be faced that Wells's élitist ideas – Remington takes up the theme and indeed the party of the Aristocracy – imply a distrust of, if not a distaste for, the mass and that massively muddled form of political life, democracy. Even his benevolence cannot excuse his implicit degrading of most of humanity. On the other hand – and it does constitute some sort of reparation – he was an emphatic feminist, although his ideas on subsidized motherhood may not have appealed quite so keenly as his advocacy of the suffragette line.

On the whole, though, what one feels about his Great Views is that while they are quaint it is somehow marvellous that he should have held them with such sincerity, pursued them with such intellectual energy, and felt that he was able to engage the sympathies of his fellows on subjects which seem to us now unbearably remote. Who now seriously proposes an optimistic and positive pattern for the peaceful future of the world? Who can stand up and be counted as the visionary who convinces us that humanity can improve itself and its state? There is a melancholy

x

period flavour to it all, although, just perhaps, one of the reasons for the current Wells revival is a scarcely conscious renaissance of Utopian pacifist ideals.

As I write, however, the core of the Wells revival is sex and scandal. Anthony West, his son by Rebecca West, has published a portrait of his father which exalts and exonerates him but reveals him as no less controversial today than he was eighty years ago. Wells's own sensual autobiography – published fifty years after his death but breathing the fresh life of the man – has reawakened interest in someone thought buried and forgotten by the higher critics and academics, who had sided with Henry James in their Life versus Art struggle and placed Wells beneath the literary salt. He is back on the high table now. Not for the first time, an interest in sex has become an interest in the person.

Wells's own interest in sex is the most persistent and possibly the most distorting theme in this novel. It made it quite difficult for him to get the book published – incredible as that seems today; it lost him friends; more important, it caused a shift of ground among his serious admirers, which was felt sharply by Wells and, perhaps, propelled him away from truly serious, adventurous fiction, into downhill respectability and the final move away – to teaching.

*The New Machiavelli* was supposed to be fiction. It is, however, as was widely recognized at the time, a lightly disguised variation on the blazing affair Wells was having with the daughter of a professional acquaintance. The liaison resulted in a child. In life, the girl helped Wells by refusing to let him leave his second wife (portrayed here – only just sympathetically – as Margaret). In the book, Remington/Wells sweeps the girl abroad, leaving his career, and hence the country (such is the naïvety of his political vision), in ruins. For Wells posits the novel as a struggle between adventure and morality, between truth and convention, between the greatness of a powerful career and the honour of passion fulfilled. It is difficult to appreciate these balances: we are supposed to imagine Remington capable of reaching political heights; alas, we do not.

What do we see, however, is Wells's attempt to justify love outside marriage. We see Wells fighting against the hypocrisy surrounding public figures. Two years before *The New Machiavelli* he had published *Ann Veronica*, in which a young woman runs off with a married man, seduces him, is happy, glories in it, is a successful suffragette and gets away with the author's full support. The canting public was outraged. The *Spectator* campaigned against Wells, fuelled, as always, by its dislike of his lower-class origins, and he was denounced from pulpit and public library. The Mr Wells who had given them so much fun was excoriated for giving them so much trouble with their daughters. It was an extraordinary campaign which revealed – among many things – how far the English novel had become the English middle class at Art. Wells was out to change all that.

He was also fighting for his social life – (although on some levels he did not give a damn, convinced that his Brains would always see him through. His violent affair with Amber Reeves had rocked him, dismayed his friends and fed his enemies raw meat. So, in *The New Machiavelli*, open sex is not triumphant: it ruins a great man. Wells might think he had made amends.

But no – still the Establishment would not have it. Moreover, his literary skills were called into question by one or two of those he most deeply respected. Had he not brought out *Mr Polly* between *Ann Veronica* and *The New Machiavelli*, it is doubtful whether his reputation would have survived such a public outcry. *Mr Polly*'s comedy, wit, lightness, ease, social bite – all that Wells found most easy and thought least interesting – came in to save him, and so *The New Machiavelli* got its chance. It was published; sold well; received very mixed reviews; but, most aggravatingly of all for Wells, its views and its visions were largely ignored.

These occupied more and more of his attention. After *The New Machiavelli* he lost the heart or, more likely, the inclination, to meld the two – the spirit of imagination and the *gravitas* of Great Views. In *The New Machiavelli* itself there is no great melding: it is a patchy book, but patchy in the sense of a light fog – in this case the swirl of unusual solutions and speculations – which is there but is, after all, only light, and which lifts again and again to reveal the most wonderful Wellsian landscapes of character, place, incident and action.

*Melvyn Bragg, 9 January 1984*

# Book the First  The Making of a Man

## Chapter the First
## Concerning a Book that was never Written

### 1

Since I came to this place I have been very restless, wasting my energies in the futile beginning of ill-conceived books. One does not settle down very readily at two-and-forty to a new way of living, and I have found myself with the teeming interests of the life I have abandoned still buzzing like a swarm of homeless bees in my head. My mind has been full of confused protests and justifications. In any case I should have found difficulties enough in expressing the complex thing I have to tell, but it has added greatly to my trouble that I have a great analogue, that a certain Niccolo Machiavelli chanced to fall out of politics at very much the age I have reached, and wrote a book to engage the restlessness of his mind, very much as I have wanted to do. He wrote about the relation of the great constructive spirit in politics to individual character and weaknesses, and so far his achievement lies like a deep rut in the road of my intention. It has taken me far astray. It is a matter of many weeks now – diversified indeed by some long drives into the mountains behind us and a memorable sail to Genoa across the blue and purple waters that drowned Shelley – since I began a laboured and futile imitation of 'The Prince'. I sat up late last night with the jumbled accumulation; and at last made a little fire of olive twigs and burnt it all, sheet by sheet – to begin again clear this morning.

But incidentally I have re-read most of Machiavelli, not excepting those scandalous letters of his to Vettori, and it seems to me, now that I have released myself altogether from his literary precedent, that he still has his use for me. In spite of his vast prestige I claim kindred with him and set his name upon my title-page, in partial intimation of the matter of my story. He takes me with sympathy not only by reason of the dream he pursued and the humanity of his politics, but by the mixture of his nature. His vices come in, essential to my issue. He is dead

9

and gone, all his immediate correlations to party and faction have faded to insignificance, leaving only on the one hand his broad method and conceptions, and upon the other his intimate living personality, exposed down to its salacious corners as the soul of no contemporary can ever be exposed. Of those double strands it is I have to write, of the subtle protesting perplexing play of instinctive passion and desire against too abstract a dream of statesmanship. But things that seemed to lie very far apart in Machiavelli's time have come near to one another ; it is no simple story of white passions struggling against the red that I have to tell.

The state-making dream is a very old dream indeed in the world's history. It plays too small a part in novels. Plato and Confucius are but the highest of a great host of minds that have had a kindred aspiration, have dreamt of a world of men better ordered, happier, finer, securer. They imagined cities grown more powerful and peoples made rich and multitudinous by their efforts, they thought in terms of harbours and shining navies, great roads engineered marvellously, jungles cleared and deserts conquered, the ending of muddle and diseases and dirt and misery; the ending of confusions that waste human possibilities ; they thought of these things with passion and desire as other men think of the soft lines and tender beauty of women. Thousands of men there are today almost mastered by this white passion of statecraft, and in nearly every one who reads and thinks you could find, I suspect, some sort of answering response. But in every one it presents itself extraordinarily entangled and mixed up with other, more intimate things.

It was so with Machiavelli. I picture him at San Casciano as he lived in retirement upon his property after the fall of the Republic, perhaps with a twinge of the torture that punished his conspiracy still lurking in his limbs. Such twinges could not stop his dreaming. Then it was 'The Prince' was written. All day he went about his personal affairs, saw homely neighbours, dealt with his family, gave vent to everyday passions. He would sit in the shop of Donato del Corno gossiping curiously among vicious company, or pace the lonely woods of his estate, book in hand, full of bitter meditations. In the evening he returned home and went to his study. At the entrance, he says, he pulled

10

off his peasant clothes covered with the dust and dirt of that immediate life, washed himself, put on his 'noble court dress', closed the door on the world of toiling and getting, private loving, private hating and personal regrets, sat down with a sigh of contentment to those wider dreams.

I like to think of him so, with brown books before him lit by the light of candles in silver candlesticks, or heading some new chapter of 'The Prince', with a grey quill in his clean fine hand.

So writing, he becomes a symbol for me, and none the less because of his animal humour, his queer indecent side, and because of such lapses into utter meanness as that which made him sound the note of the begging-letter writer even in his 'Dedication', reminding His Magnificence very urgently, as if it were the gist of his matter, of the continued malignity of fortune in his affairs. These flaws complete him. They are my reason for preferring him as a symbol to Plato, of whose indelicate side we know nothing, and whose correspondence with Dionysius of Syracuse has perished; or to Confucius who travelled China in search of a Prince he might instruct, with lapses and indignities now lost in the mists of ages. They have achieved the apotheosis of individual forgetfulness, and Plato has the added glory of that acquired beauty, that bust of the Indian Bacchus which is now indissolubly mingled with his tradition. They have passed into the world of their ideal, and every humbug takes his freedoms with their names. But Machiavelli, more recent and less popular, is still all human and earthly, a fallen brother – and at the same time that nobly dressed and nobly dreaming writer at the desk.

That vision of the strengthened and perfected state is protagonist in my story. But as I re-read 'The Prince' and thought out the manner of my now abandoned project, I came to perceive how that stir and whirl of human thought one calls by way of embodiment the French Revolution has altered absolutely the approach to such a question. Machiavelli, like Plato and Pythagoras and Confucius two hundred odd decades before him, saw only one method by which a thinking man, himself not powerful, might do the work of state-building, and that was by seizing the imagination of a Prince. Directly these men turned their thoughts towards realization, their attitudes became – what shall I call it? – secretarial. Machiavelli, it is true, had some little doubts about the particular Prince he wanted, whether it was Caesar Borgia or Giuliano or Lorenzo, but a Prince it had to be. Before I saw clearly the differences of our own time I searched my mind for the modern equivalent of a Prince. At various times I redrafted a parallel dedication to the Prince of Wales, to the Emperor William, to Mr Evesham, to a certain newspaper proprietor who was once my school-fellow at City Merchants', to Mr J. D. Rockefeller – all of them men, in their several ways and circumstances and possibilities, princely. Yet in every case my pen bent of its own accord towards irony because – because, although at first I did not realize it, I myself am just as free to be a prince. The appeal was unfair. The old sort of Prince, the old little principality has vanished from the world. The commonweal is one man's absolute estate and responsibility no more. In Machiavelli's time it was indeed to an extreme degree one man's affair. But the days of the Prince who planned and directed and was the source and centre of all power are ended. We are in a condition of affairs infinitely more complex, in which every prince and statesman is something of a servant and every intelligent human being something of a Prince. No magnificent pensive Lorenzos remain any more in this world for secretarial hopes.

In a sense it is wonderful how power has vanished, in a sense wonderful how it has increased. I sit here, an unarmed discredited man, at a small writing-table in a little defenceless dwelling among the vines, and no human being can stop my pen except by the deliberate self-immolation of murdering me, or destroy its fruits except by theft and crime. No King, no council, can seize and torture me ; no Church, no nation silence me. Such powers of ruthless and complete suppression have vanished. But that is not because power has diminished, but because it has increased and become multitudinous, because it has dispersed itself and specialized. It is no longer a negative power we have, but positive ; we cannot prevent, but we can do. This age, far beyond all previous ages, is full of powerful men, men who might, if they had the will for it, achieve stupendous things.

The things that might be done today! The things indeed that are being done! It is the latter that give one so vast a sense of the former. When I think of the progress of physical and mechanical science, of medicine and sanitation during the last century, when I measure the increase in general education and average efficiency, the power now available for human service, the merely physical increment, and compare it with anything that has ever been at man's disposal before, and when I think of what a little straggling, incidental, undisciplined and unco-ordinated minority of inventors, experimenters, educators, writers and organizers has achieved this development of human possibilities, achieved it in spite of the disregard and aimlessness of the huge majority, and the passionate resistance of the active dull, my imagination grows giddy with dazzling intimations of the human splendours the justly organized state may yet attain. I glimpse for a bewildering instant the heights that may be scaled, the splendid enterprises made possible. . . .

But the appeal goes out now in other forms, in a book that catches at thousands of readers for the eye of a Prince diffused. It is the old appeal indeed for the unification of human effort, the ending of confusions, but instead of the Machiavellian deference to a flattered lord, a man cries out of his heart to the unseen fellowship about him. The last written dedication of all those I burnt last night was to no single man, but to the socially constructive passion – in any man. . . .

There is, moreover, a second great difference in kind between my world and Machiavelli's. We are discovering women. It is as if they had come across a vast interval since his time, into the very chamber of the statesman.

2

In Machiavelli's outlook the interest of womanhood was in a region of life almost infinitely remote from his statecraft. They were the vehicle of children, but only Imperial Rome and the new world of today have ever had an inkling of the significance that might give them in the state. They did their work, he thought, as the ploughed earth bears its crops. Apart from their function of fertility they gave a humorous twist to life, stimulated worthy men to toil, and wasted the hours of Princes. He left the thought of women outside with his other dusty things when he went into his study to write, dismissed them from his mind. But our modern world is burthened with its sense of the

13

immense, now half articulate, significance of women. They stand now, as it were, close beside the silver candlesticks, speaking as Machiavelli writes, until he stays his pen and turns to discuss his writing with them.

It is this gradual discovery of sex as a thing collectively portentous that I have to mingle with my statecraft if my picture is to be true, which has turned me at length from a treatise to the telling of my own story. In my life I have paralleled very closely the slow realizations that are going on in the world about me. I began life ignoring women, they came to me at first perplexing and dishonouring ; only very slowly and very late in my life and after misadventure, did I gauge the power and beauty of the love of man and woman and learnt how it must needs frame a justifiable vision of the ordered world. Love has brought me to disaster, because my career had been planned regardless of its possibility and value. But Machiavelli, it seems to me, when he went into his study, left not only the earth of life outside but its unsuspected soul. . . .

3

Like Machiavelli at San Casciano, if I may take this analogy one step further, I too am an exile. Office and leading are closed to me. The political career that promised so much for me is shattered and ended for ever.

I look out from this vine-wreathed veranda under the branches of a stone pine ; I see wide and far across a purple valley whose sides are terraced and set with houses of pink and ivory, the Gulf of Liguria gleaming sapphire blue, and cloud-like baseless mountains hanging in the sky, and I think of lank and coaly steamships heaving on the grey rollers of the English Channel and darkling streets wet with rain, I recall as if I were back there the busy exit from Charing Cross, the cross and the money-changers' offices, the splendid grime of giant London and the crowds going perpetually to and fro, the lights by night and the urgency and eventfulness of that great rain-swept heart of the modern world.

It is difficult to think we have left that – for many years if not for ever. In thought I walk once more in Palace Yard and hear the clink and clatter of hansoms and the quick quiet whirr of motors; I go in vivid recent memories through the stir in the lobbies, I sit again at eventful dinners in those old dining-rooms like cellars below the House – dinners that ended with shrill division bells, I think of huge clubs swarming and excited by the bulletins of that electoral battle that was for me the opening opportunity. I see the stencilled names and numbers go up on the green baize, constituency after constituency, amidst murmurs or loud shouting. . . .

It is over now for me and vanished. That opportunity will come no more. Very probably you have heard already some crude inaccurate version of our story and why I did not take office, and have formed your partial judgement on me. And so it is I sit now at my stone table, half out of life already, in a warm, large, shadowy leisure, splashed with sunlight and hung with vine tendrils, with paper before me to distil such wisdom as I can, as Machiavelli in his exile sought to do, from the things I have learnt and felt during the career that has ended now in my divorce.

I climbed high and fast from small beginnings. I had the mind of my party. I do not know where I might not have ended, but for this red blaze that came out of my unguarded nature and closed my career for ever.

# Bromstead and my Father

## 1

I dreamt first of states and cities and political things when I was a little boy in knickerbockers.

When I think of how such things began in my mind, there comes back to me the memory of an enormous bleak room with its ceiling going up to heaven and its floor covered irregularly with patched and defective oilcloth and a dingy mat or so and a 'surround', as they call it, of dark stained wood. Here and there against the wall are trunks and boxes. There are cupboards on either side of the fireplace and bookshelves with books above them, and on the wall and rather tattered is a large yellow-varnished geological map of the South of England. Over the mantel is a huge lump of white coral rock and several big fossil bones, and above that hangs the portrait of a brainy gentleman, sliced in half and displaying an interior of intricate detail and much vigour of colouring. It is the floor I think of chiefly ; over the oilcloth of which, assumed to be land, spread towns and villages and forts of wooden bricks ; there are steep square hills (geologically, volumes of Orr's *Cyclopaedia of the Sciences*) and the cracks and spaces of the floor and the bare brown surround were the water channels and open sea of that continent of mine.

I still remember with infinite gratitude the great-uncle to whom I owe my bricks. He must have been one of those rare adults who have not forgotten the chagrins and dreams of childhood. He was a prosperous west of England builder ; including my father he had three nephews, and for each of them he caused a box of bricks to be made by an out-of-work carpenter, not the insufficient supply of the toyshop, you understand, but a really adequate quantity of bricks made out of oak and shaped and smoothed, bricks about five inches by two and a half by one, and half-bricks and quarter-bricks to correspond. There were hundreds of them, many hundreds. I could build six towers as high as myself with them, and there seemed quite enough for every engineering project I could undertake. I could build whole towns with streets of houses and churches and citadels; I could bridge every gap in the oilcloth and make causeways over the crumpled spaces(which I feigned to be morasses), and on a keel of whole bricks it was possible to construct ships to push over the high seas to the remotest port in the room. And a disciplined population, that rose at last by sedulous begging on birthdays and all convenient occasions to well over two hundred, of lead sailors and soldiers, horse, foot and artillery, inhabited this world.

Justice has never been done to bricks and soldiers by those who write about toys. The praises of the toy theatre have been a common theme for essayists, the planning of the scenes, the painting and cutting out of the cast, penny plain twopence coloured, the stink and glory of the performance and the final conflagration. I had such a theatre once, but I never loved it or hoped for much from it; my bricks and soldiers were my perpetual drama. I recall an incessant variety of interests. There was the mystery and charm of the complicated buildings one could make, with long passages and steps and windows through which one peeped into their intricacies, and by means of slips of card one could make slanting ways in them, and send marbles rolling from top to base and thence out into the hold of a waiting ship. Then there were the fortresses and gun emplacements and covered ways in which one's soldiers went. And there was commerce; the shops and markets and store-rooms full of nasturtium seed, thrift seed, lupin beans and suchlike provender from the garden; such stuff one stored in matchboxes and pill-boxes, or packed in sacks of old glove fingers tied up with thread and sent off by waggons along the great military road to the beleaguered fortress on the Indian frontier beyond the worn places that were dismal swamps. And there were battles on the way.

That great road is still clear in my memory. I was given, I forget by what benefactor, certain particularly fierce Red Indians of lead – I have never seen such soldiers since – and for these my father helped me to make tepees of brown paper, and I settled them in a hitherto desolate country under the frowning nail-studded cliffs of an ancient trunk. Then I conquered them and garrisoned their land. (Alas! they died, no doubt through contact with civilization – one my mother trod on – and their land became a wilderness again and was ravaged for a time by a clockwork crocodile of vast proportions.) And out towards the coal-scuttle was a region near the impassable thickets of the ragged hearthrug where lived certain china Zulus brandishing spears, and a mountain country of rudely piled bricks concealing the most devious and enchanting caves and several mines of gold and silver paper. Among these rocks a number of survivors from a Noah's Ark made a various, dangerous, albeit frequently invalid and crippled fauna, and I was wont to increase the uncultivated wildness of this region further by trees of privet-twigs from the garden hedge and box from the garden borders. By these territories went my Imperial Road carrying produce to and fro, bridging gaps in the oil-cloth, tunnelling through Encyclopaedic hills – one tunnel was three volumes long – defended as occasion required by camps of paper tents or brick blockhouses, and ending at last in a magnificently engineered ascent to a fortress on the cliffs commanding the Indian reservation.

My games upon the floor must have spread over several years and developed from small beginnings, incorporating now this suggestion and now that. They stretch, I suppose, from seven to eleven or twelve. I played them intermittently, and they bulk now in the retrospect far more significantly than they did at the time. I played them in bursts, and then forgot them for long periods; through the spring and summer I was mostly out of doors, and school and classes caught me early. And in the retrospect I see them all not only magnified and transfigured, but foreshortened and confused together. A clockwork railway, I seem to remember, came and went; one or two clockwork boats, toy sailing ships that, being keeled, would do nothing but lie on their beam ends on the floor; a detestable lot of cavalrymen, undersized and gilt all over, given me by a maiden aunt, and very much what one might expect from an aunt, that I used as Nero used his Christians to ornament my public buildings; and I finally melted some into fratricidal bullets, and therewith blew the rest to flat splashes of lead by means of a brass cannon in the garden.

I find this empire of the floor much more vivid and detailed in my memory now than many of the owners of the skirts and legs and boots that went gingerly across its territories. Occasionally, alas! they stooped to scrub, abolishing in one universal destruction the slow growth of whole days of civilized development. I still remember the hatred and disgust of these catastrophes. Like Noah I was given warnings. Did I disregard them, coarse red hands would descend, plucking garrisons from fortresses and sailors from ships, jumbling them up in their wrong boxes, clumsily so that their rifles and swords were broken, sweeping the splendid curves of the Imperial Road into heaps of ruins, casting the jungle growth of Zululand into the fire.

'Well, Master Dick,' the voice of this cosmic calamity would say, 'you ought to have put them away last night. No! I can't wait until you've sailed them all away in ships. I got my work to do, and do it I will.'

And in no time all my continents and lands were swirling water and swiping strokes of house-flannel.

That was the worst of my giant visitants, but my mother too, dear lady, was something of a terror to this microcosm. She wore spring-sided boots, a kind of boot now vanished, I believe, from the world, with dull bodies and shiny toes, and a silk dress with flounces that were very destructive to the more hazardous viaducts of the Imperial Road. She was always, I seem to remember, fetching me ; fetching me for a meal, fetching me for a walk or, detestable absurdity! fetching me for a wash and brush up, and she never seemed to understand anything whatever of the political systems across which she came to me. Also she forbade all toys on Sundays except the bricks for church-building and the soldiers for church parade, or a Scriptural use of the remains of the Noah's Ark mixed up with a wooden Swiss dairy farm. But she really did not know whether a thing was a church or not unless it positively bristled with cannon, and many a Sunday afternoon have I played Chicago (with the fear of God in my heart) under an infidel pretence that it was a new sort of ark rather elaborately done.

Chicago, I must explain, was based upon my father's description of the pig slaughterings in that city and certain pictures I had seen. You made your beasts – which were all the ark lot really, provisionally conceived as pigs – go up elaborate approaches to a central pen, from which they went down a cardboard slide four at a time and dropped most satisfyingly down a brick shaft, and pitter-litter over some steep steps to where a head slaughterman (né Noah) strung a cotton loop round their legs and sent them by pin hooks along a wire to a second slaughterman with a chipped foot (formerly Mrs Noah) who, if I remember rightly, converted them into Army sausage by means of a portion of the inside of an old alarum clock.

My mother did not understand my games, but my father did. He wore bright-coloured socks and carpet slippers when he was indoors – my mother disliked boots in the house – and he would sit down on my little chair and survey the microcosm on the floor with admirable understanding and sympathy.

It was he gave me most of my toys and, I more than suspect, most of my ideas. 'Here's some corrugated iron,' he would say, 'suitable for roofs and fencing,' and hand me a lump of that stiff crinkled paper that is used for packing medicine bottles. Or, 'Dick, do you see the tiger loose near the Imperial Road? – won't do for your cattle ranch.' And I would find a bright new lead tiger like a special creation at large in the world, and demanding a hunting expedition and much elaborate effort to get him safely housed in the city menagerie beside the captured dragon crocodile, tamed now, and his key lost and the heart and spring gone out of him.

And to the various irregular reading of my father I owe the inestimable blessing of never having a boy's book in my boy-hood except those of Jules Verne. But my father used to get books for himself and me from the Bromstead Institute, Feni-more Cooper and Mayne Reid and illustrated histories ; one of the Russo-Turkish war and one of Napier's expedition to Abyssinia I read from end to end; Stanley and Livingstone, lives of Wellington, Napoleon and Garibaldi, and back vol-umes of *Punch*, from which I derived conceptions of foreign and domestic politics it has taken years of adult reflection to correct. And at home permanently we had Wood's *Natural History*, a brand-new illustrated Green's *History of the English People,* Irving's *Companions of Columbus,* a great number of unbound parts of some geographical work, a *Voyage round the World* I think it was called, with pictures of foreign places, and

20

Clarke's *New Testament* with map of Palestine, and a variety of other informing books bought at sales. There was a Sowerby's *Botany* also, with thousands of carefully tinted pictures of British plants, and one or two other important works in the sitting-room. I was allowed to turn these over and even lie on the floor with them on Sundays and other occasions of exceptional cleanliness.

And in the attic I found one day a very old forgotten map after the fashion of a bird's-eye view, representing the Crimea, that fascinated me and kept me for hours navigating its waters with a pin.

2

My father was a lank-limbed man in easy shabby tweed clothes and with his hands in his trouser pockets. He was a science teacher, taking a number of classes at the Bromstead Institute in Kent under the old Science and Art Department, and 'visiting' various schools; and our resources were eked out by my mother's income of nearly a hundred pounds a year, and by his inheritance of a terrace of three palatial but structurally unsound stucco houses near Bromstead Station.

They were big clumsy residences in the earliest Victorian style, interminably high and with deep damp basements and downstairs coal-cellars and kitchens that suggested an architect vindictively devoted to the discomfort of the servant class. If so, he had over-reached himself and defeated his end, for no servant would stay in them unless for exceptional wages or exceptional tolerance of inefficiency or exceptional freedom in repartee. Every storey in the house was from twelve to fifteen feet high (which would have been cool and pleasant in a hot climate), and the stairs went steeply up, to end at last in attics too inaccessible for occupation. The ceilings had vast plaster cornices of classical design, fragments of which would sometimes fall unexpectedly, and the wallpapers were bold and gigantic in pattern and much variegated by damp and ill-mended rents.

As my father was quite unable to let more than one of these houses at a time, and that for the most part to eccentric and undesirable tenants, he thought it politic to live in one of the two others, and devote the rent he received from the let one, when it was let, to the incessant necessary repairing of all three. He also did some of the repairing himself and, smoking a bull-dog pipe the while, which my mother would not allow him to do in the house, he cultivated vegetables in a sketchy, unpunctual and not always successful manner in the unoccupied gardens. The three houses faced north, and the back of the one we occupied was covered by a grape-vine that yielded, I remember, small green grapes for pies in the spring, and imperfectly ripe black grapes in favourable autumns for the purposes of dessert. That grape-vine played an important part in my life, for my father broke his neck while he was pruning it, when I was thirteen.

My father was what is called a man of ideas, but they were not always good ideas. My grandfather had been a private schoolmaster and one of the founders of the College of Preceptors, and my father had assisted him in his school until increasing competition and diminishing attendances had made it evident that the days of small private schools kept by unqualified persons were numbered. Thereupon my father had roused himself and had qualified as a science teacher under the Science and Art Department, which in those days had charge of the scientific and artistic education of the mass of the English population, and had thrown himself into science teaching and the earning of government grants therefor with great if transitory zeal and success.

I do not remember anything of my father's earlier and more energetic time. I was the child of my parents' middle years; they married when my father was thirty-five and my mother past forty, and I saw only the last decadent phase of his educational career.

The Science and Art Department has vanished altogether from the world, and people are forgetting it now with the utmost readiness and generosity. Part of its substance and staff and spirit survive, more or less completely digested into the Board of Education. . . . The world does move on, even in its government. It is wonderful how many of the clumsy and limited governing bodies of my youth and early manhood have given place now to more scientific and efficient machinery. When I was a boy, Bromstead, which is now a borough, was ruled by a strange body called a Local Board – it was the Age

22

of Boards – and I still remember indistinctly my father rejoicing at the breakfast-table over the liberation of London from the corrupt and devastating control of a Metropolitan Board of Works. Then there were also School Boards; I was already practically in politics before the London School Board was absorbed by the spreading tentacles of the London County Council.

It gives a measure of the newness of our modern ideas of the State to remember that the very beginnings of public education lie within my father's lifetime, and that many most intelligent and patriotic people were shocked beyond measure at the State doing anything of the sort. When he was born, totally illiterate people, who could neither read a book nor write more than perhaps a clumsy signature, were to be found everywhere in England; and great masses of the population were getting no instruction at all. Only a few schools flourished upon the patronage of exceptional parents; all over the country the old endowed grammar schools were to be found sinking and dwindling; many of them had closed altogether. In the new great centres of population multitudes of children were sweated in the factories, darkly ignorant and wretched, and the under-equipped and under-staffed National and British schools, supported by voluntary contributions and sectarian rivalries, made an ineffectual fight against this festering darkness. It was a condition of affairs clamouring for remedies, but there was an immense amount of indifference and prejudice to be overcome before any remedies were possible. Perhaps some day some industrious and lucid historian will disentangle all the muddle of impulses and antagonisms, the commercialism, utilitarianism, obstinate conservatism, humanitarian enthusiasm, out of which our present educational organization arose. I have long since come to believe it necessary that all new social institutions should be born in confusion, and that at first they should present chiefly crude and ridiculous aspects. The distrust of government in the Victorian days was far too great, and the general intelligence far too low, to permit the State to go about the new business it was taking up in a business-like way, to train teachers, build and equip schools, endow pedagogic research, and provide properly written school-books. These things it was felt *must* be provided by individual and local effort, and since it

23

was manifest that it was individual and local effort that were in default, it was reluctantly agreed to stimulate them by money payments. The State set up a machinery of examination both in Science and Art and for the elementary schools ; and payments, known technically as grants, were made in accordance with the examination results attained, to such schools as Providence might see fit to send into the world. In this way it was felt the Demand would be established that would, according to the beliefs of that time, inevitably ensure the Supply. An industry of 'Grant-earning' was created, and this would give education as a necessary by-product.

In the end this belief was found to need qualification, but Grant-earning was still in full activity when I was a small boy. So far as the Science and Art Department and my father are concerned, the task of examination was entrusted to eminent scientific men, for the most part quite unaccustomed to teaching. You see, if they also were teaching similar classes to those they examined, it was feared that injustice might be done. Year after year these eminent persons set questions and employed subordinates to read and mark the increasing thousands of answers that ensued, and having no doubt the national ideal of fairness well developed in their minds, they were careful each year to re-read the preceding papers before composing the current one, in order to see what it was usual to ask. As a result of this, in the course of a few years the recurrence and permutation of questions became almost calculable, and since the practical object of the teaching was to teach people not science, but how to write answers to these questions, the industry of Grant-earning assumed a form easily distinguished from any kind of genuine education whatever.

Other remarkable compromises had also to be made with the spirit of the age. The unfortunate conflict between Religion and Science prevalent at this time was mitigated, if I remember rightly, by making graduates in arts and priests in the established church Science Teachers *ex officio*, and leaving local and private enterprise to provide schools, diagrams, books, material, according to the conceptions of efficiency prevalent in the district. Private enterprise made a particularly good thing of the books. A number of competing firms of publishers sprang into existence specializing in Science and Art Department work ; they set themselves to produce text-books that should supply exactly the quantity and quality of knowledge necessary for every stage of each of five and twenty subjects into which desirable science was divided, and copies and models and instructions that should give precisely the method and gestures esteemed as proficiency in art. Every section of each book was written in the idiom found to be most satisfactory to the examiners, and test questions extracted from papers set in former years were appended to every chapter. By means of these last the teacher was able to train his class to the very highest level of grant-earning efficiency, and very naturally he cast all other methods of exposition aside. First he posed his pupils with questions and then dictated model replies.

That was my father's method of instruction. I attended his classes as an elementary grant-earner from the age of ten until his death, and it is so I remember him, sitting on the edge of a table, smothering a yawn occasionally and giving out the infallible formulae to the industriously scribbling class sitting in rows of desks before him. Occasionally he would slide to his feet and go to a blackboard on an easel and draw on that very slowly and deliberately in coloured chalks a diagram for the class to copy in coloured pencils, and sometimes he would display a specimen or arrange an experiment for them to see. The room in the Institute in which he taught was equipped with a certain amount of apparatus prescribed as necessary for subject this and subject that by the Science and Art Department, and this my father would supplement with maps and diagrams and drawings of his own.

But he never really did experiments, except that in the class in systematic botany he sometimes made us tease common flowers to pieces. He did not do experiments if he could possibly help it, because in the first place they used up time and gas for the Bunsen burner and good material in a ruinous fashion, and in the second they were, in his rather careless and sketchy hands, apt to endanger the apparatus of the Institute and even the lives of his students. Then thirdly, real experiments involved washing up. And moreover they always turned out wrong, and sometimes misled the too observant learner very seriously and opened demoralizing controversies. Quite early in life I acquired an almost ineradicable sense of the unscientific

25

perversity of Nature and the impassable gulf that is fixed between systematic science and elusive fact. I knew, for example, that in science, whether it be subject XII, Organic Chemistry, or subject XVII, Animal Physiology, when you blow into a glass of lime water it instantly becomes cloudy, and if you continue to blow it clears again, whereas in truth you may blow into the stuff from the lime water bottle until you are crimson in the face and painful under the ears, and it never becomes cloudy at all. And I knew, too, that in science if you put potassium chlorate into a retort and heat it over a Bunsen burner, oxygen is disengaged and may be collected over water, whereas in real life if you do anything of the sort the vessel cracks with a loud report, the potassium chlorate descends sizzling upon the flame, the experimenter says 'Oh! Damn!' with astonishing heartiness and distinctness, and a lady student in the back seats gets up and leaves the room.

Science is the organized conquest of Nature, and I can quite understand that ancient libertine refusing to cooperate in her own undoing. And I can quite understand, too, my father's preference for what he called an illustrative experiment, which was simply an arrangement of the apparatus in front of the class with nothing whatever by way of material, and the Bunsen burner clean and cool, and then a slow luminous description of just what you did put in it when you were so ill-advised as to carry the affair beyond illustration, and just exactly what ought anyhow to happen when you did. He had considerable powers of vivid expression, so that in this way he could make us see all he described. The class, freed from any unpleasant nervous tension, could draw this still life without flinching, and if any part was too difficult to draw, then my father would produce a simplified version on the blackboard to be copied instead. And he would also write on the blackboard any exceptionally difficult but grant-earning words, such as 'empyreumatic' or 'botryoidal'.

Some words in constant use he rarely explained. I remember once sticking up my hand and asking him in the full flow of description, 'Please, sir, what is flocculent?'

'The precipitate is.'

'Yes, sir, but what does it mean?'

'Oh! flocculent!' said my father, 'flocculent! Why –' he ex-

26

tended his hand and arm and twiddled his fingers for a second in the sir. 'Like that,' he said.

I thought the explanation sufficient, but he paused for a moment after giving it. 'As in a flock bed, you know,' he added and resumed his discourse.

3

My father, I am afraid, carried a natural incompetence in practical affairs to an exceptionally high level. He combined practical incompetence, practical enterprise and a thoroughly sanguine temperament, in a manner that I have never seen paralleled in any human being. He was always trying to do new things in the briskest manner, under the suggestion of books and papers or his own spontaneous imagination, and as he had never been trained to do anything whatever in his life properly, his futilities were extensive and thorough. At one time he nearly gave up his classes for intensive culture, so enamoured was he of its possibilities ; the peculiar pungency of the manure he got, in pursuit of a chemical theory of his own, has scarred my olfactory memories for a lifetime. The intensive culture phase is very clear in my memory ; it came near the end of his career and when I was between eleven and twelve. I was mobilized to gather caterpillars on several occasions, and assisted in nocturnal raids upon the slugs by lantern-light that wrecked my preparation work for school next day. My father dug up both lawns, and trenched and manured in spasms of immense vigour alternating with periods of paralyzing distaste for the garden, and for weeks he talked about eight hundred pounds an acre at every meal.

A garden, even when it is not exasperated by intensive methods, is a thing as exacting as a baby, its moods have to be watched ; it does not wait upon the cultivator's convenience, but has times of its own. Intensive culture greatly increases this disposition to trouble mankind ; it makes a garden touchy and hysterical, a drugged and demoralized and over-irritated garden. My father got at cross purposes with our two patches at an early stage. Everything grew wrong from first to last, and if my father's manures intensified nothing else, they certainly intensified the Primordial Curse. The peas were eaten in the

27

night before they were three inches high, the beans bore nothing but blight, the only apparent result of a spraying of the potatoes was to develop a *penchant* in the cat for being ill indoors, the cucumber frames were damaged by the catapulting of boys going down the lane at the back, and all our cucumbers were mysteriously embittered. That lane with its occasional passers-by did much to wreck the intensive scheme, because my father always stopped work and went indoors if any one watched him. His special manure was apt to arouse a troublesome spirit of inquiry in hardy natures.

In digging his rows and shaping his patches he neglected the guiding string and trusted to his eye altogether too much, and the consequent obliquity and the various wind-breaks and scare-crows he erected, and particularly an irrigation contrivance he began and never finished by which everything was to be watered at once by means of pieces of gutter from the roof and outhouses of Number 2, and a large and particularly obstinate clump of elder-bushes in the abolished hedge that he had failed to destroy entirely either by axe or fire, combined to give the gardens under intensive culture a singularly desolate and disorderly appearance. He took steps towards the diversion of our house drain under the influence of the Sewage Utilization Society; but happily he stopped in time. He hardly completed any of the operations he began; something else became more urgent or simply he tired; a considerable area of the Number 2 territory was never even dug up.

In the end the affair irritated him beyond endurance. Never was a man less horticulturally-minded. The clamour of these vegetables he had launched into the world for his service and assistance wore out his patience. He would walk into the garden the happiest of men after a day or so of disregard, talking to me of history perhaps or social organization, or summarizing some book he had read. He talked to me of anything that interested him, regardless of my limitations. Then he would begin to note the growth of the weeds. 'This won't do,' he would say, and pull up a handful.

More weeding would follow and the talk would become fragmentary. His hands would become earthy, his nails black, weeds would snap off in his careless grip, leaving the roots behind. The world would darken. He would look at his fingers with disgusted astonishment. '*Curse* these weeds!' he would say from his heart. His discourse was at an end. . . .

I have memories, too, of his sudden unexpected charges into the tranquillity of the house, his hands and clothes intensively enriched. He would come in like a whirlwind. 'This damned stuff all over me and the Agriculture Chemistry Class at six! Bah! *Aaaaaah!*'

My mother would never learn not to attempt to break him of swearing on such occasions. She would remain standing a little stiffly in the scullery refusing to assist him to the adjectival towel he sought.

'If you say such things –'

He would dance with rage and hurl the soap about. 'The towel!' he would cry, flicking suds from his fingers in every direction; 'the towel! I'll let the blithering class slide if you don't give me the towel! I'll give up everything. I tell you – everything!' . . .

At last with the failure of the lettuces came the breaking point. I was in the little arbour learning Latin irregular verbs when it happened. I can see him still, his peculiar tenor voice still echoes in my brain, shouting his opinion of intensive culture for all the world to hear, and slashing away at that abominable mockery of a crop with a hoe. We had tied them up with bast only a week or so before, and now half were rotten and half had shot up into tall slender growths. He had the hoe in both hands and slogged. Great wipes he made, and at each stroke he said, 'Take that!'

The air was thick with flying fragments of abortive salad. It was a fantastic massacre. It was the French Revolution of that cold tyranny, the vindictive overthrow of the pampered vegetable aristocrats. After he had assuaged his passion upon them, he turned for other prey; he kicked holes in two of our noblest marrows, flicked off the heads of half a row of artichokes, and shied the hoe with a splendid smash into the cucumber frame. Something of the awe of that moment returns to me as I write of it.

'Well, my boy,' he said, approaching with an expression of beneficent happiness, 'I've done with gardening. Let's go for a walk like reasonable beings. I've had enough of this' – his face was convulsed for an instant with bitter resentment – 'Pandering to cabbages.'

## 4

That afternoon's walk sticks in my memory for many reasons. One is that we went further than I had ever been before ; far beyond Keston and nearly to Sevenoaks, coming back by train from Dunton Green, and the other is that my father as he went along talked about himself, not so much to me as to himself, and about life and what he had done with it. He monologued so that at times he produced an effect of weird world-forgetfulness. I listened puzzled, and at that time not understanding many things that afterwards became plain to me. It is only in recent years that I have discovered the pathos of that monologue; how friendless my father was and uncompanioned in his thoughts and feelings, and what a hunger he may have felt for the sympathy of the undeveloped youngster who trotted by his side.

'I'm no gardener,' he said, 'I'm no anything. Why the devil did I start gardening?

'I suppose man was created to mind a garden. . . . But the Fall let us out of that! What was *I* created for? God! what was *I* created for?. . .

'Slaves to matter! Minding inanimate things! It doesn't suit me, you know. I've got no hands and no patience. I've mucked about with life. Mucked about with life.' He suddenly addressed himself to me, and for an instant I started like an eavesdropper discovered. 'Whatever you do, boy, whatever you do, make a Plan. Make a good Plan and stick to it. Find out what life is about – *I* never have – and set yourself to do – whatever you ought to do. I admit it's a puzzle. . . .

'Those damned houses have been the curse of my life. Stucco white elephants! Beastly cracked stucco with stains of green – black and green. Conferva and soot. . . . Property, they are!. . . Beware of Things, Dick, beware of Things! Before you know where you are you are waiting on them and minding them. They'll eat your life up. Eat up your hours and your blood and energy! When those houses came to me, I ought to have sold them – or fled the country. I ought to have cleared out. Sarco-

30

phagi – eaters of men! Oh! the hours and days of work, the nights of anxiety those vile houses have cost me! The painting! It worked up my arms; it got all over me. I stank of it. It made me ill. It isn't living – it's minding. . . .

'Property's the curse of life. Property! Ugh! Look at this country all cut up into silly little parallelograms, look at all those villas we passed just now and those potato patches and that tarred shanty and the hedge! Somebody's minding every bit of it like a dog tied to a cart's tail. Patching it and bothering about it. Bothering! Yapping at every passer-by. Look at that notice-board! One rotten worried little beast wants to keep us other rotten little beasts off *his* patch, – God knows why! Look at the weeds in it. Look at the mended fence! . . . There's no property worth having, Dick, but money. That's only good to spend. All these things. Human souls buried under a cartload of blithering rubbish. . . .

'I'm not a fool, Dick. I have qualities, imagination, a sort of go. I ought to have made a better thing of life.

'I'm sure I could have done things. Only the old people pulled my leg. They started me wrong. They never started me at all. I only began to find out what life was like when I was nearly forty.

'If I'd gone to a university; if I'd had any sort of sound training, if I hadn't slipped into the haphazard places that came easiest. . . .

'Nobody warned me. Nobody. It isn't a world we live in, Dick; it's a cascade of accidents; it's a chaos exasperated by policemen! *You* be warned in time, Dick. You stick to a plan. Don't wait for any one to show you the way. Nobody will. There isn't a way until you make one. Get education, get a good education. Fight your way to the top. It's your only chance. I've watched you. You'll do no good at digging and property minding. There isn't a neighbour in Bromstead won't be able to skin you at such-like games. You and I are the brainy unstable kind, top-side or nothing. And if ever those blithering houses come to you – don't have 'em. Give them away! Dynamite 'em – and off! *Live*, Dick! I'll get rid of them for you if I can, Dick, but remember what I say.' . . .

So it was my father discoursed, if not in those particular words, yet exactly in that manner, as he slouched along the

31

southward road, with resentful eyes becoming less resentful as he talked, and flinging out clumsy illustrative motions at the outskirts of Bromstead as we passed along them. That afternoon he hated Bromstead, from its foot-tiring pebbles up. He had no illusions about Bromstead or himself. I have the clearest impression of him in his garden-stained tweeds with a deer-stalker hat on the back of his head and presently a pipe sometimes between his teeth and sometimes in his gesticulating hand, as he became diverted by his talk from his original exasperation. . . .

This particular afternoon is no doubt mixed up in my memory with many other afternoons ; all sorts of things my father said and did at different times have got themselves referred to it ; it filled me at the time with a great unprecedented sense of fellowship, and it has become the symbol now for all our intercourse together. If I didn't understand the things he said, I did the mood he was in. He gave me two very broad ideas in that talk and the talks I have mingled with it ; he gave them to me very clearly and they have remained fundamental in my mind; one a sense of the extraordinary confusion and waste and planlessness of the human life that went on all about us ; and the other of a great ideal of order and economy which he called variously Science and Civilization, and which, though I do not remember that he ever used that word, I suppose many people nowadays would identify with Socialism – as the Fabians expound it.

He was not very definite about this Science, you must understand, but he seemed always to be waving his hand towards it, – just as his contemporary Tennyson seems always to be doing – he belonged to his age, and mostly his talk was destructive of the limited beliefs of his time ; he led me to infer rather than actually told me that this Science was coming, a spirit of light and order, to the rescue of a world groaning and travailing in the muddle for the want of it. . . .


5

When I think of Bromstead nowadays I find it inseparably bound up with the disorders of my father's gardening, and the

32

odd patchings and paintings that disfigured his houses. It was all a piece with that.

Let me try and give something of the quality of Bromstead and something of its history. It is the quality and history of a thousand places round and about London, and round and about the other great centres of population in the world. Indeed it is in a measure the quality of the whole of this modern world from which we who have the statesman's passion struggle to evolve, and dream still of evolving, order.

First, then, you must think of Bromstead a hundred and fifty years ago, as a narrow irregular little street of thatched houses strung out on the London and Dover Road, a little mellow sample unit of a social order that had a kind of completeness, at its level, of its own. At that time its population numbered a little under two thousand people, mostly engaged in agriculture work or in trades serving agriculture. There was a blacksmith, a saddler, a chemist, a doctor, a barber, a linen-draper (who brewed his own beer), a veterinary surgeon, a hardware shop, and two capacious inns. Round and about it were a number of pleasant gentlemen's seats, whose owners went frequently to London town in their coaches along the very tolerable high-road. The church was big enough to hold the whole population, were people minded to go to church, and indeed a large proportion did go, and all who married were married in it, and everybody, to begin with, was christened at its font and buried at last in its yew-shaded graveyard. Everybody knew everybody in the place. It was, in fact, a definite place and a real human community in those days. There was a pleasant old market-house in the middle of the town with a weekly market, and an annual fair at which much cheerful merry-making and homely intoxication occurred; there was a pack of hounds which hunted within five miles of London Bridge, and the local gentry would occasionally enliven the place with valiant cricket matches for a hundred guineas a side, to the vast excitement of the entire population. It was very much the same sort of place that it had been for three or four centuries. A Bromstead Rip van Winkle from 1550 returning in 1750 would have found most of the old houses still as he had known them, the same trades a little improved and differentiated one from the other, the same roads rather more carefully

33

tended, the Inns not very much altered, the ancient familiar market-house. The occasional wheeled traffic would have struck him as the most remarkable difference, next perhaps to the swaggering painted stone monuments instead of brasses and the protestant severity of the communion-table in the parish church – both from the material point of view very little things. A Rip van Winkle from 1350, again, would have noticed scarcely greater changes; fewer clergy, more people, and particularly more people of the middling sort; the glass in the windows of many of the houses, the stylish chimneys springing up everywhere would have impressed him, and suchlike details. The place would have had the same boundaries, the same broad essential features, would have been still itself in the way that a man is still himself after he has 'filled out' a little and grown a longer beard and changed his clothes.

But after 1750 something got hold of the world, something that was destined to alter the scale of every human affair.

That something was machinery and a vague energetic disposition to improve material things. In another part of England ingenious people were beginning to use coal in smelting iron, and were producing metal in abundance and metal castings in sizes that had hitherto been unattainable. Without warning or preparation, increment involving countless possibilities of further increment was coming to the strength of horses and men. 'Power,' all unsuspected, was flowing like a drug into the veins of the social body.

Nobody seems to have perceived this coming of power, and nobody had calculated its probable consequences. Suddenly, almost inadvertently, people found themselves doing things that would have amazed their ancestors. They began to construct wheeled vehicles much more easily and cheaply than they had ever done before, to make-up roads and move things about that had formerly been esteemed too heavy for locomotion, to join woodwork with iron nails instead of wooden pegs, to achieve all sorts of mechanical possibilities, to trade more freely and manufacture on a larger scale, to send goods abroad in a wholesale and systematic way, to bring back commodities from overseas, not simply spices and fine commodities, but goods in bulk. The new influence spread to agriculture, iron appliances replaced wooden, breeding of stock became systema-

34

tic, paper-making and printing increased and cheapened. Roofs of slate and tile appeared amidst and presently prevailed over the original Bromstead thatch, the huge space of Common to the south was extensively enclosed, and what had been an ill-defined horse-track to Dover, only passable by adventurous coaches in dry weather, became the Dover Road, and was presently the route first of one and then of several daily coaches. The High Street was discovered to be too tortuous for these awakening energies, and a new road cut off its worst contortions. Residential villas appeared occupied by retired tradesmen and widows, who esteemed the place healthy, and by others of a strange new unoccupied class of people who had money invested in joint-stock enterprises. First one and then several boys' boarding-schools came, drawing their pupils from London, – my grandfather's was one of these. London, twelve miles to the north-west, was making itself felt more and more.

But this was only the beginning of the growth period, the first trickle of the coming flood of mechanical power. Away in the north they were casting iron in bigger and bigger forms, working their way to the production of steel on a large scale, applying power in factories. Bromstead had almost doubled in size again long before the railway came; there was hardly any thatch left in the High Street, but instead were houses with handsome brass-knockered front doors and several windows, and shops with shop-fronts all of square glass panes, and the place was lighted publicly now by oil lamps – previously only one flickering lamp outside each of the coaching inns had broken the nocturnal darkness. And there was talk – it long remained talk – of gas. The gasworks came in 1834, and about that date my father's three houses must have been built convenient for the London Road. They mark nearly the beginning of the real suburban quality; they were let at first to City people still engaged in business.

And then hard on the gasworks had come the railway and cheap coal; there was a wild outbreak of brickfields upon the claylands to the east, and the Great Growth had begun in earnest. The agricultural placidities that had formerly come to the very borders of the High Street were broken up north, west and south by new roads. This enterprising person and then that

35

began to 'run up' houses, irrespective of every other enterprising person who was doing the same thing. A Local Board came into existence, and with much hesitation and penny-wise economy inaugurated drainage works. Rates became a common topic, a fact of accumulating importance. Several chapels of zinc and iron appeared, and also a white new church in commercial Gothic upon the common, and another of red brick in the residential district out beyond the brickfields towards Chessington.

The population doubled again and doubled again, and became particularly teeming in the prolific 'working-class' district about the deep-rutted, muddy, coal-blackened roads between the gasworks, Blodgett's laundries, and the railway goods-yard. Weekly properties, that is to say small houses built by small property owners and let by the week, sprang up also in the Cage Fields, and presently extended right up the London Road. A single national school in an inconvenient situation set itself inadequately to collect subscriptions and teach the swarming, sniffing, grimy offspring of this dingy new population to read. The villages of Beckington, which used to be three miles to the west, and Blamley four miles to the east of Bromstead, were experiencing similar distensions and proliferations, and grew out to meet us. All effect of locality or community had gone from these places long before I was born ; hardly any one knew any one ; there was no general meeting-place any more, the old fairs were just common nuisances haunted by gypsies, van showmen, Cheap Jacks and London roughs, the churches were incapable of a quarter of the population. One or two local papers of shameless venality reported the proceedings of the local Bench and the local Board, compelled tradesmen who were interested in these affairs to advertise, used the epithet 'Bromstedian' as one expressing peculiar virtues, and so maintained in the general mind a weak tradition of some local quality that embraced us all. Then the parish graveyard filled up and became a scandal, and an ambitious area with an air of appetite was walled in by a Bromstead Cemetery Company, and planted with suitably high-minded and sorrowful varieties of conifer. A stone-mason took one of the earlier villas with a front garden at the end of the High Street, and displayed a supply of urns on pillars and headstones and crosses in stone, marble, and granite, that would have sufficed to commemorate in elaborate detail the entire population of Bromstead as one found it in 1750.

The cemetery was made when I was a little boy of five or six ; I was in the full tide of building and growth from the first ; the second railway with its station at Bromstead North and the drainage followed when I was ten or eleven, and all my childish memories are of digging and wheeling, of woods invaded by building, roads gashed open and littered with iron pipes amidst a fearful smell of gas, of men peeped at and seen toiling away deep down in excavations, of hedges broken down and replaced by planks, of wheelbarrows and builders' sheds, of rivulets overtaken and swallowed up by drain-pipes. Big trees, and especially elms, cleared of undergrowth and left standing amid such things, acquired a peculiar tattered dinginess rather in the quality of needy widow women who have seen happier days.

The Ravensbrook of my earlier memories was a beautiful stream. It came into my world out of a mysterious Beyond, out of a garden, splashing brightly down a weir which had once been the weir of a mill. (Above the weir and inaccessible there were bulrushes growing in splendid clumps, and beyond that, pampas grass, yellow and crimson spikes of hollyhock, and blue suggestions of wonderland.) From the pool at the foot of this initial cascade it flowed in a leisurely fashion beside a footpath, – there were two pretty thatched cottages on the left, and here were ducks, and there were willows on the right, – and so came to where great trees grew on high banks on either hand and bowed closer, and at last met overhead. This part was difficult to reach because of an old fence, but a little boy might glimpse that long cavern of greenery by wading. Either I have actually seen kingfishers there, or my father has described them so accurately to me that he inserted them into my memory. I remember them there anyhow. Most of that overhung part I never penetrated at all, but followed the field path with my mother and met the stream again, where beyond there were flat meadows, Roper's meadows. The Ravensbrook went meandering across the middle of these, now between steep banks, and now with wide shallows at the bends where the cattle waded and drank. Yellow and purple loosestrife and ordinary rushes grew in clumps along the bank, and now and then a willow. On rare occasions of rapture one might see a rat cleaning his whiskers at the water's edge. The deep places were rich with tangled weeds, and in them fishes lurked – to me they were big fishes – water-boatmen and water-beetles traversed the calm surface of these still deeps; in one pool were yellow lilies and water-soldiers, and in the shoaly places hovering fleets of small fry basked in the sunshine – to vanish in a flash at one's shadow. In one place, too, were Rapids, where the stream woke with a start from a dreamless brooding into foaming panic and babbled and hastened. Well do I remember that half-mile of rivulet; all other rivers and cascades have their reference to it for me. And after I was eleven, and before we left Bromstead, all the delight and beauty of it was destroyed.

The volume of its water decreased abruptly – I suppose the new drainage works that linked us up with Beckington, and made me first acquainted with the geological quality of the London clay, had to do with that – until only a weak uncleansing trickle remained. That at first did not strike me as a misfortune. An adventurous small boy might walk dryshod in places hitherto inaccessible. But hard upon that came the pegs, the planks and carts and devastation. Roper's meadows, being no longer in fear of floods, were now to be slashed out into parallelograms of untidy road, and built upon with rows of working-class cottages. The roads came, – horribly; the houses followed. They seemed to arise in the night. People moved into them as soon as the roofs were on, mostly workmen and their young wives, and already in a year some of these raw houses stood empty again from defaulting tenants, with windows broken and woodwork warping and rotting. The Ravensbrook became a dump for old iron, rusty cans, abandoned boots and the like, and was a river only when unusual rains filled it for a day or so with an inky flood of surface water. . . .

That indeed was my most striking perception in the growth of Bromstead. The Ravensbrook had been important to my imaginative life; that way had always been my first choice in all my walks with my mother, and its rapid swamping by the new urban growth made it indicative of all the other things that had happened just before my time, or were still, at a less dramatic pace, happening. I realized that building was the enemy. I began to understand why in every direction out of Bromstead one walked past scaffold-poles into litter, why fragments of broken brick and cinder mingled in every path, and the significance of the universal notice-boards, either white and new or a year old and torn and battered, promising sites, proffering houses to be sold or let, abusing and intimidating passers-by for fancied trespass, and protecting rights of way.

It is difficult to disentangle now what I understood at this time and what I have since come to understand, but it seems to me that even in those childish days I was acutely aware of an invading and growing disorder. The serene rhythms of the old-established agriculture, I see now, were everywhere being replaced by cultivation under notice and snatch crops; hedges ceased to be repaired, and were replaced by cheap iron railings or chunks of corrugated iron; more and more hoardings sprang up, and contributed more and more to the nomad tribes of filthy paper scraps that flew before the wind and overspread the country. The outskirts of Bromstead were a maze of exploitation roads that led nowhere, that ended in tarred fences studded with nails (I don't remember barbed wire in those days; I think the Zeitgeist did not produce that until later), and in trespass boards that used vehement language. Broken glass, tin cans, and ashes and paper abounded. Cheap glass, cheap tin, abundant fuel, and a free untaxed Press had rushed upon a world quite unprepared to dispose of these blessings when the fullness of enjoyment was past.

I suppose one might have persuaded oneself that all this was but the replacement of an ancient tranquillity, or at least an ancient balance by a new order. Only to my eyes, quickened by my father's intimations, it was manifestly no order at all. It was a multitude of uncoordinated fresh starts, each more sweeping and destructive than the last, and none of them ever really worked out to a ripe and satisfactory completion. Each left a legacy of products – houses, humanity, or what not – in its wake. It was a sort of progress that had bolted; it was change out of hand, and going at an unprecedented pace nowhere in particular.

No, the Victorian epoch was not the dawn of a new era; it was a hasty, trial experiment, a gigantic experiment of the most slovenly and wasteful kind. I suppose it was necessary; I suppose all things are necessary. I suppose that before men will discipline themselves to learn and plan, they must first see in a hundred convincing forms the folly and muddle that come from headlong, aimless and haphazard methods. The nineteenth century was an age of demonstrations, some of them very impressive demonstrations, of the powers that have come to mankind ; but of permanent achievement what will our descendants cherish? It is hard to estimate what grains of precious metal may not be found in a mud torrent of human production on so large a scale, but will any one, a hundred years from now, consent to live in the houses the Victorians built, travel by their roads or railways, value the furnishings they made to live among or esteem, except for curious or historical reasons, their prevalent art and the clipped and limited literature that satisfied their souls?

That age which bore me was indeed a world full of restricted and undisciplined people, overtaken by power, by possessions and great new freedoms, and unable to make any civilized use of them whatever; stricken now by this idea and now by that, tempted first by one possession and then another to ill-considered attempts; it was my father's exploitation of his villa gardens on the wholesale level. The whole of Bromstead as I remember it, and as I saw it last – it is a year ago now – is a dull useless boiling-up of human activities, an immense clustering of futilities. It is as unfinished as ever ; the builders' roads still run out and end in mid-field in their old fashion ; the various enterprises jumble in the same hopeless contradiction, if anything intensified. Pretentious villas jostle slums, and public-house and tin tabernacle glower at one another across the cat-haunted lot that intervenes. Roper's meadows are now quite frankly a slum; back doors and sculleries gape towards the railway, their yards are hung with tattered washing unashamed; and there seem to be more boards by the railway every time I pass, advertising pills and pickles, tonics and condiments, and suchlike solicitudes of a people with no natural health or appetite left in them. . . .

Well, we have to do better. Failure is not failure nor waste wasted if it sweeps away illusion and lights the road to a plan.

## 6

Chaotic indiscipline, ill-adjusted effort, spasmodic aims, these give the quality of all my Bromstead memories. The crowning one of them all rises to desolating tragedy. I remember now the wan spring sunshine of that Sunday morning, the stiff feeling of best clothes and aggressive cleanliness and formality, when I and my mother returned from church to find my father dead. He had been pruning the grape-vine. He had never had a ladder long enough to reach the sill of the third-floor windows – at house-painting times he had borrowed one from the plumber who mixed his paint – and he had in his own happy-go-lucky way contrived a combination of the garden fruit ladder with a battered kitchen table that served all sorts of odd purposes in an outhouse. He had stayed up this arrangement by means of the garden roller, and the roller had at the critical moment – rolled. He was lying close by the garden door with his head queerly bent back against a broken and twisted rain-water pipe, an expression of pacific contentment on his face, a bamboo curtain-rod with a table-knife tied to the end of it still gripped in his hand. We had been rapping for some time at the front door unable to make him hear, and then we came round by the door in the side trellis into the garden and so discovered him.

'Arthur!' I remember my mother crying with the strangest break in her voice, 'what are you doing there? Arthur! And – *Sunday!*'

I was coming behind her, musing remotely, when the quality of her voice roused me. She stood as if she could not go near him. He had always puzzled her so, he and his ways, and this seemed only another enigma. Then the truth dawned on her ; she shrieked as if afraid of him, ran a dozen steps back towards the trellis door and stopped and clasped her ineffectual gloved hands, leaving me staring blankly, too astonished for feeling, at the carelessly flung limbs.

The same idea came to me also. I ran to her. 'Mother!' I cried, pale to the depths of my spirit, '*is he dead?*'

I had been thinking two minutes before of the cold fruit pie that glorified our Sunday dinner-table, and how I might perhaps get into the tree at the end of the garden to read in the afternoon. Now an immense tact had come down like a curtain and blotted out all my childish world. My father was lying dead before my eyes. . . . I perceived that my mother was helpless and that things must be done.

'Mother!' I said, 'we must get Doctor Beaseley, – and carry him indoors.'

# Chapter the Third

## Scholastic

### 1

My formal education began in a small preparatory school in Bromstead. I went there as a day boy. The charge for my instruction was mainly set off by the periodic visits of my father with a large bag of battered fossils to lecture to us upon geology. I was one of those fortunate youngsters who take readily to school work. I had a good memory, versatile interests and a considerable appetite for commendation, and when I was barely twelve I got a scholarship at the City Merchants School and was entrusted with a scholar's railway season ticket to Victoria. After my father's death a large and very animated and solidly built uncle in tweeds from Staffordshire, Uncle Minter, my mother's sister's husband, with a remarkable accent and remarkable vowel sounds, who had plunged into the Bromstead home once or twice for the night but who was otherwise unknown to me, came on the scene, sold off the three gaunt houses with the utmost gusto, invested the proceeds and my father's life insurance money, and got us into a small villa at Penge within sight of that immense façade of glass and iron, the Crystal Palace. Then he retired in a mood of good-natured contempt to his native habitat again. We stayed at Penge until my mother's death.

School became a large part of the world to me, absorbing my time and interest, and I never acquired that detailed and intimate knowledge of Penge and the hilly villadom round about, that I have of the town and outskirts of Bromstead.

It was a district of very much the same character, but it was more completely urbanized and nearer to the centre of things; there were the same unfinished roads, the same occasional disconcerted hedges and trees, the same butcher's horse grazing under a builder's notice-board, the same incidental lapses into slum. The Crystal Palace grounds cut off a large part of my walking radius to the west with impassable fences and forbiddingly expensive turnstiles, but it added to the ordinary spectacle of meteorology a great variety of gratuitous fireworks which banged and flared away of a night after supper and drew me abroad to see them better. Such walks as I took, to Croydon, Wimbledon, West Wickham and Greenwich, impressed upon me the interminable extent of London's residential suburbs; mile after mile one went, between houses, villas, rows of cottages, streets of shops, under railway arches, over railway bridges. I have forgotten the detailed local characteristics – if there were any – of much of that region altogether. I was only there two years, and half my perambulations occurred at dusk or after dark. But with Penge I associate my first realizations of the wonder and beauty of twilight and night, the effect of dark walls reflecting lamplight, and the mystery of blue haze-veiled hillsides of houses, the glare of shops by night, the glowing steam and streaming sparks of railway trains and railway signals lit up in the darkness. My first rambles in the evening occurred at Penge, – I was becoming a big and independent-spirited boy – and I began my experience of smoking during these twilight prowls with the threepenny packets of American cigarettes then just appearing in the world.

My life centred upon the City Merchants School. Usually I caught the eight eighteen for Victoria, I had a midday meal and tea ; four nights a week I stayed for preparation, and often I was not back home again until within an hour of my bedtime. I spent my half-holidays at school in order to play cricket and football. This, and a pretty voracious appetite for miscellaneous reading which was fostered by the Penge Middleton Library, did not leave me much leisure for local topography. On Sundays also I sang in the choir at St Martin's Church, and my mother did not like me to walk out alone on the Sabbath afternoon – she herself slumbered – so that I wrote or read at home. I must confess I was at home as little as I could contrive.

Home, after my father's death, had become a very quiet and uneventful place indeed. My mother had either an unimaginative temperament or her mind was greatly occupied with private religious solicitudes, and I remember her talking to me but little, and that usually upon topics I was anxious to evade. I had developed my own view about low-Church theology long before my father's death, and my meditation upon that event had

44

finished my secret estrangement from my mother's faith. My reason would not permit even a remote chance of his being in hell, he was so manifestly not evil, and this religion would not permit him a remote chance of being out of it. When I was a little boy my mother had taught me to read and write and pray and had done many things for me, indeed she persisted in washing me and even in making my clothes until I rebelled against these things as indignities. But our minds parted very soon. She never began to understand the mental processes of my play, she never interested herself in my school life and work, she could not understand things I said ; and she came, I think, quite insensibly to regard me with something of the same hopeless perplexity she had felt towards my father.

Him she must have wedded under considerable delusions. I do not think he deceived her, indeed, nor do I suspect him of mercenariness in their union ; but no doubt he played up to her requirements in the half ingenuous way that was and still is the quality of most wooing, and presented himself as a very brisk and orthodox young man. I wonder why nearly all love-making has to be fraudulent. Afterwards he must have disappointed her cruelly by letting one aspect after another of his careless, sceptical, experimental temperament appear. Her mind was fixed and definite, she embodied all that confidence in church and decorum and the assurances of the pulpit which was characteristic of the large mass of the English people – for after all, the rather low-Church section *was* the largest single mass – in early Victorian times. She had dreams, I suspect, of going to church with him side by side ; she in a little poke bonnet and a large flounced crinoline, all mauve and magenta, and starched, under a little lace-trimmed parasol, and he in a tall silk hat and peg-top trousers and a roll-collar coat, and looking rather like the Prince Consort, – with angels almost visibly raining benedictions on their amiable progress. Perhaps she dreamt gently of much-belaced babies and an interestingly pious (but not too dissenting or fanatical) little girl or boy or so, also angel-haunted. And I think, too, she must have seen herself ruling a seemly 'home of taste,' with a vivarium in the conservatory that opened out of the drawing-room, or again, making preserves in the kitchen. My father's science-teaching, his diagrams of disembowelled humanity, his pictures of prehistoric beasts that contradicted the Flood, his disposition towards soft shirts and loose tweed suits, his inability to use a clothes brush, his spasmodic reading fits and his bulldog pipes, must have jarred cruelly with her rather unintelligent anticipations. His wild moments of violent temper when he would swear and smash things, absurd almost lovable storms that passed like summer thunder, must have been starkly dreadful to her. She was constitutionally unadaptable, and certainly made no attempt to understand or tolerate these outbreaks. She tried them by her standards, and by her standards they were wrong. Her standards hid him from her. The blazing things he said rankled in her mind unforgettably.

As I remember them together they chafed constantly. Her attitude to nearly all his moods and all his enterprises was a sceptical disapproval. She treated him as something that belonged to me and not to her. '*Your* father,' she used to call him, as though I had got him for her.

She had married late and she had, I think, become mentally self-subsisting before her marriage. Even in those Herne Hill days I used to wonder what was going on in her mind, and I find that old speculative curiosity return as I write this. She took a considerable interest in the house-work that our generally servantless condition put upon her – she used to have a charwoman in two or three times a week – but she did not do it with any great skill. She covered most of our furniture with flouncey ill-fitting covers, and she cooked plainly and without very much judgement. The Penge house, as it contained nearly all our Bromstead things, was crowded with furniture, and is chiefly associated in my mind with the smell of turpentine, a condiment she used very freely upon the veneered mahogany pieces. My mother had an equal dread of 'blacks' by day and the 'night air', so that our brightly clean windows were rarely open.

She took a morning paper, and she would open it and glance at the headlines, but she did not read it until the afternoon and then, I think, she was interested only in the more violent crimes, and in railway and mine disasters and in the minutest domesticities of the Royal Family. Most of the books at home were my father's, and I do not think she opened any of them. She had one or two volumes that dated from her own youth, and she tried in vain to interest me in them ; there was Miss Strickland's

46

*Queens of England*, a book I remember with particular animosity, and *Queechy* and the *Wide Wide World*. She made these books of hers into a class apart by sewing outer covers upon them of calico and figured muslin. To me in these habiliments they seemed not so much books as confederated old ladies.

My mother was also very punctual with her religious duties, and rejoiced to watch me in the choir.

On winter evenings she occupied an armchair on the other side of the table at which I sat, head on hand reading, and she would be darning stockings or socks or the like. We achieved an effect of rather stuffy comfortableness that was soporific, and in a passive way I think she found these among her happy times. On such occasions she was wont to put her work down on her knees and fall into a sort of thoughtless musing that would last for long intervals and rouse my curiosity. For like most young people I could not imagine mental states without definite forms.

She carried on a correspondence with a number of cousins and friends, writing letters in a slanting Italian hand and dealing mainly with births, marriages and deaths, business starts (in the vaguest terms) and the distresses of bankruptcy.

And yet, you know, she did have a curious intimate life of her own that I suspected nothing of at the time, that only now becomes credible to me. She kept a diary that is still in my possession, a diary of fragmentary entries in a miscellaneous collection of pocket-books. She put down the texts of the sermons she heard, and queer stiff little comments on casual visitors, – 'Miss G. and much noisy shrieking talk about games and such frivolities and *croquay*. A. delighted and *very attentive*.' Such little human entries abound. She had an odd way of never writing a name, only an initial; my father is always 'A.', and I am always 'D.' It is manifest she followed the domestic events in the life of the Princess of Wales, who is now Queen Mother, with peculiar interest and sympathy. 'Pray G. all may be well,' she writes in one such crisis.

But there are things about myself that I still find too poignant to tell easily, certain painful and clumsy circumstances of my birth in very great detail, the distresses of my infantile ailments. Then later I find such things as this: 'Heard D. s—.' The 's' is evidently 'swear' – 'G. bless and keep my boy from evil.' And again, with the thin handwriting shaken by distress: 'D. would not go to church, and hardened his heart and said wicked infidel things, much disrespect of the clergy. The anthem is tiresome!!! That men should set up to be wiser than their maker!!!' Then trebly underlined: '*I fear his father's teaching.*' Dreadful little tangle of misapprehensions and false judgements! More comforting for me to read, 'D. very kind and good. He grows more thoughtful every day.' I suspect myself of forgotten hypocrisies.

At just one point my mother's papers seem to dip deeper. I think the death of my father must have stirred her for the first time for many years to think for herself. Even she could not go on living in any peace at all, believing that he had indeed been flung headlong into hell. Of this gnawing solicitude she never spoke to me, never, and for her diary also she could find no phrases. But on a loose half-sheet of notepaper between its pages I find this passage that follows, written very carefully. I do not know whose lines they are or how she came upon them. They run:

> And if there be no meeting past the grave;
> If all is darkness, silence, yet 'tis rest.
> Be not afraid, ye waiting hearts that weep,
> For God still giveth His beloved sleep,
> And if an endless sleep He wills, so best.

That scrap of verse amazed me when I read it. I could even wonder if my mother really grasped the import of what she had copied out. It affected me as if a stone deaf person had suddenly turned and joined in a whispered conversation. It set me thinking how far a mind, in its general effect quite hopelessly limited, might range. After that I went through all her diaries, trying to find something more than a conventional term of tenderness for my father. But I found nothing. And yet somehow there grew upon me the realization that there had been love. . . . Her love for me, on the other hand, was abundantly expressed.

I knew nothing of that secret life of feeling at the time ; such expression as it found was all beyond my schoolboy range. I did not know when I pleased her and I did not know when I distressed her. Chiefly I was aware of my mother as rather dull company, as a mind thorny with irrational conclusions and incapable of explication, as one believing quite wilfully and irritatingly in impossible things. So I suppose it had to be ; life was coming to me in new forms and with new requirements. It was essential to our situation that we should fail to understand. After this space of years I have come to realizations and attitudes that dissolve my estrangement from her, I can pierce these barriers, I can see her and feel her as a loving and feeling and desiring and muddle-headed person. There are times when I would have her alive again, if only that I might be kind to her for a little while and give her some return for the narrow intense affection, the tender desires, she evidently lavished so abundantly on me. But then again I ask how I could make that return? And I realize the futility of such dreaming. Her demand was rigid, and to meet it I should need to act and lie.

So she whose blood fed me, whose body made me, lies in my memory as I saw her last, fixed, still, infinitely intimate, infinitely remote. . . .

My own case with my mother, however, does not awaken the same regret I feel when I think of how she misjudged and irked my father, and turned his weaknesses into thorns for her own tormenting. I wish I could look back without that little twinge to two people who were both in their different quality so good. But goodness that is narrow is a pedestrian and ineffectual goodness. Her attitude to my father seems to me one of the essentially tragic things that have come to me personally, one of those things that nothing can transfigure, that *remain* sorrowful, that I cannot soothe with any explanation, for as I remember him he was indeed the most lovable of weak spasmodic men. But my mother had been trained in a hard and narrow system that made evil out of many things not in the least evil, and inculcated neither kindliness nor charity. All their estrangement followed from that.

These cramping cults do indeed take an enormous toll of human love and happiness, and not only that, but what we Machiavellians must needs consider, they make frightful breaches in human solidarity. I suppose I am a deeply religious man, as men of my quality go, but I hate more and more, as I grow older, the shadow of intolerance cast by religious organizations. All my life has been darkened by irrational intolerance, by arbitrary irrational prohibitions and exclusions. Mahometanism, with its fierce proselytism, has, I suppose, the

49

blackest record of uncharitableness, but most of the Christian sects are tainted, tainted to a degree beyond any of the anterior paganisms, with this same hateful quality. It is their exclusive claim that sends them wrong, the vain ambition that inspires them all to teach a uniform one-sided God and be the one and only gateway to salvation. Deprecation of all outside the household of faith, an organized under-valuation of heretical goodness and lovableness, follows necessarily. Every petty difference is exaggerated to the quality of a saving grace or a damning defect. Elaborate precautions are taken to shield the believer's mind against broad or amiable suggestions; the faithful are deterred by dark allusions, by sinister warnings, from books, from theatres, from worldly conversation, from all the kindly instruments that mingle human sympathy. For only by isolating its flock can the organization survive.

Every month there came to my mother a little magazine called, if I remember rightly, the *Home Churchman*, with the combined authority of print and clerical commendation. It was the most evil thing that ever came into the house, a very devil, a thin little pamphlet with one woodcut illustration on the front page of each number; now the uninviting visage of some exponent of the real and only doctrine and attitudes, now some coral strand in act of welcoming the missionaries of God's mysterious preferences, now a new church in the Victorian Gothic. The vile rag it was! A score of vices that shun the policeman have nothing of its subtle wickedness. It was an outrage upon the natural kindliness of men. The contents were all admirably adjusted to keep a spirit in prison. Their force of sustained suggestion was tremendous. There would be dreadful intimations of the swift retribution that fell upon individuals for Sabbath-breaking, and upon nations for weakening towards Ritualism, or treating Roman Catholics as tolerable human beings; there would be great rejoicings over the conversion of alleged Jews, and terrible descriptions of the death-beds of prominent infidels with boldly invented last words, – the most unscrupulous lying; there would be the appallingly edifying careers of 'early piety' lusciously described, or stories of condemned criminals who traced their final ruin unerringly to early laxities of the kind that leads people to give up subscribing to the *Home Churchman*.

50

Every month that evil spirit brought about a slump in our mutual love. My mother used to read the thing and become depressed and anxious for my spiritual welfare, used to be stirred to unintelligent pestering. . . .

## 2

A few years ago I met the editor of this same *Home Churchman*. It was at one of the weekly dinners of that Fleet Street dining club, the Blackfriars.

I heard the paper's name with a queer little shock and surveyed the man with interest. No doubt he was only a successor of the purveyor of discords who darkened my boyhood. It was amazing to find an influence so terrible embodied in a creature so palpably petty. He was seated some way down a table at right angles to the one at which I sat, a man of mean appearance with a greyish complexion, thin, with a square nose, a heavy wiry moustache and a big Adam's apple sticking out between the wings of his collar. He ate with considerable appetite and unconcealed relish, and as his jaw was underhung, he chummed and made the moustache wave like reeds in the swell of a steamer. It gave him a conscientious look. After dinner he a little forced himself upon me. At that time, though the shadow of my scandal was already upon me, I still seemed to be shaping for great successes, and he was glad to be in conversation with me and anxious to intimate political sympathy and support. I tried to make him talk of the *Home Churchman* and the kindred publications he ran, but he was manifestly ashamed of his job so far as I was concerned.

'One wants,' he said, pitching himself as he supposed in my key, 'to put constructive ideas into our readers, but they are narrow, you know, very narrow. Very.' He made his moustache and lips express judicious regret. 'One has to consider them carefully, one has to respect their attitudes. One dare not go too far with them. One has to feel one's way.'

He chummed and the moustache bristled.

A hireling, beyond question, catering for a demand. I gathered there was a home in Tufnell Park, and three boys to be fed and clothed and educated. . . .

I had the curiosity to buy a copy of his magazine afterwards, and it seemed much the same sort of thing that had worried my mother in my boyhood. There was the usual Christian hero, this time with mutton-chop whiskers and a long bare upper lip. The Jesuits, it seemed, were still hard at it, and Heaven frightfully upset about the Sunday opening of museums and the falling birth-rate, and as touchy and vindictive as ever. There were two vigorous paragraphs upon the utter damnableness of the Rev. R. J. Campbell, a contagious damnableness I gathered, one wasn't safe within a mile of Holborn Viaduct, and a foul-mouthed attack on poor little Wilkins the novelist – who was being baited by the moralists at that time for making one of his women characters, not being in holy wedlock, desire a baby and say so. . . .

The broadening of human thought is a slow and complex process. We do go on, we do get on. But when one thinks that people are living and dying now, quarrelling and sulking, mis-led and misunderstanding, vaguely fearful, condemning and thwarting one another in the close darkness of these narrow cults – O God! one wants a gale out of Heaven, one wants a great wind from the sea!

3

While I lived at Penge two little things happened to me, trivial in themselves and yet in their quality profoundly significant. They had this in common, that they pierced the texture of the life I was quietly taking for granted and let me see through it into realities – realities I had indeed known about before but never realized. Each of these experiences left me with a sense of shock, with all the values in my life perplexingly altered, attempting readjustment. One of these disturbing and illuminat-ing events was that I was robbed of a new pocket-knife, and the other that I fell in love. It was altogether surprising to me to be robbed. You see, as an only child I had always been fairly well looked after and protected, and the result was an amazing confidence in the practical goodness of the people one met in the world. I knew there were robbers in the world, just as I knew there were tigers; that I was ever likely to meet robber or tiger face to face seemed equally impossible.

The knife as I remember it was a particularly jolly one with all sorts of instruments in it, tweezers and a thing for getting a stone out of the hoof of a horse, and a corkscrew; it had cost me a carefully accumulated half-crown, and amounted indeed to a new experience in knives. I had had it for two or three days, and then one afternoon I dropped it through a hole in my pocket on a footpath crossing a field between Penge and Anerley. I heard it fall in the way one does without at the time appreciating what had happened, then later, before I got home, when my hand wandered into my pocket to embrace the still dear new possession I found it gone, and instantly that memory of something hitting the ground swam up into consciousness. I went back and commenced a search. Almost immediately I was accosted by the leader of a little gang of four or five extremely dirty and ragged boys of assorted sizes and slouching carriage who were coming from the Anerley direction.

'Lost anythink, Matey?' he said.

I explained.

' 'E's dropped 'is knife,' said my interlocutor, and joined in the search.

'What sort of 'andle was it, Matey?' said a small white-faced sniffing boy in a big bowler hat.

I supplied the information. His sharp little face scrutinized the ground about us.

'*Got* it,' he said, and pounced.

'Give it 'ere,' said the big boy hoarsely, and secured it.

I walked towards him serenely confident that he would hand it over to me, and that all was for the best in the best of all possible worlds.

'No bloomin' fear!' he said, regarding me obliquely. 'Oo said it was your knife?'

Remarkable doubts assailed me. 'Of course it's my knife,' I said. The other boys gathered round me.

'This ain't your knife,' said the big boy, and spat casually.

'I dropped it just now.'

'Finding's keepin's, *I* believe,' said the big boy.

'Nonsense,' I said. 'Give me my knife.'

'Ow many blades it got?"

'Three.'

'And what sort of 'andle?'

'Bone.'

'Got a corkscrew like?'

'Yes.'

'Ah! This ain't your knife no'ow. See?'

He made no offer to show it me. My breath went.

'Look here!' I said. 'I saw that kid pick it up. It *is* my knife.'

'Rot!' said the big boy, and slowly, deliberately put my knife into his trouser pocket.

I braced my soul for battle. All civilization was behind me, but I doubt if it kept the colour in my face. I buttoned my jacket and clenched my fists and advanced on my antagonist – he had, I suppose, the advantage of two years of age and three inches of height. 'Hand over that knife,' I said.

Then one of the smallest of the band assailed me with extra-ordinary vigour and swiftness from behind, had an arm round my neck and a knee in my back before I had the slightest in-timation of attack, and so got me down. 'I got 'im, Bill,' squeaked this amazing little ruffian. My nose was flattened by a dirty hand, and as I struck out and hit something like sacking, some one kicked my elbow. Two or three seemed to be at me at the same time. Then I rolled over and sat up to discover them all making off, a ragged flight, footballing my cap, my City Merchants cap, amongst them. I leapt to my feet in a passion of indignation and pursued them.

But I did not overtake them. We are beings of mixed compo-sition, and I doubt if mine was a single-minded pursuit. I knew that honour required me to pursue, and I had a vivid impres-sion of having just been down in the dust with a very wiry and active and dirty little antagonist of disagreeable odour and in-credible and incalculable unscrupulousness, kneeling on me and gripping my arm and neck. I wanted of course to be even with him, but also I doubted if catching him would necessarily in-volve that. They kicked my cap into the ditch at the end of the field, and made off compactly along a cinder lane while I turned aside to recover my dishonoured headdress. As I knocked the dust out of that and out of my jacket, and brushed my knees and readjusted my very crumpled collar, I tried to focus this startling occurrence in my mind.

I had vague ideas of going to a policeman or of complaining at a police-station, but some boyish instinct against informing prevented that. No doubt I entertained ideas of vindictive pur-

54

suit and murderous reprisals. And I was actually enraged whenever I thought of my knife. The thing indeed rankled in my mind for weeks and weeks, and altered all the flavour of my world for me. It was the first time I glimpsed the simple brute violence that lurks and peeps beneath our civilization. A certain kindly complacency of attitude towards the palpably lower classes was qualified for ever.

## 4

But the other experience was still more cardinal. It was the first clear intimation of a new motif in life, the sex motif, that was to rise and increase and accumulate power and enrichment and interweave with and at last dominate all my life.

It was when I was nearly fifteen this happened. It is inseparably connected in my mind with the dusk of warm September evenings. I never met the girl I loved by daylight, and I have forgotten her name. It was some insignificant name.

Yet the peculiar quality of the adventure keeps it shining darkly like some deep-coloured gem in the common setting of my memories. It came as something new and strange, something that did not join on to anything else in my life or connect with any of my thoughts or beliefs or habits; it was a wonder, a mystery, a discovery about myself, a discovery about the whole world. Only in after years did sexual feeling lose that isolation and spread itself out to illuminate and pervade and at last possess the whole broad vision of life.

It was in that phase of an urban youth's development, the phase of the cheap cigarette, that this thing happened. One evening I came by chance on a number of young people promenading by the light of a row of shops towards Beckington, and, with all the glory of a glowing cigarette between my lips, I joined their strolling number. These twilight parades of young people, youngsters chiefly of the lower middle-class, are one of the odd social developments of the great suburban growths – unkindly critics, blind to the inner meanings of things, call them, I believe, Monkeys' Parades – the shop apprentices, the young work girls, the boy clerks and so forth, stirred by mysterious intimations, spend their first-earned money upon collars and ties, chiffon hats, smart lace collars, walking-sticks, sunshades or cigarettes, and came valiantly into the vague trans-figuring mingling of gaslight and evening, to walk up and down, to eye meaningly, even to accost and make friends. It is a queer instinctive revolt from the narrow limited friendless homes in which so many find themselves, a going out towards something, romance if you will, beauty, that has suddenly become a need – a need that hitherto has lain dormant and un-suspected. They promenade.

Vulgar! – it is as vulgar as the spirit that calls the moth abroad in the evening and lights the body of the glow-worm in the night. I made my way through the throng, a little contemp-tuously as became a public schoolboy, my hands in my pockets – none of your cheap canes for me! – and very careful of the lie of my cigarette upon my lips. And two girls passed me, one a little taller than the other, with dim warm-tinted faces under clouds of dark hair and with dark eyes like pools reflecting stars.

I half turned, and the shorter one glanced back at me over her shoulder – I could draw you now the pose of her cheek and neck and shoulder – and instantly I was as passionately in love with the girl as I have ever been before or since, as any man ever was with any woman. I turned about and followed them, I flung away my cigarette ostentatiously and lifted my school cap and spoke to them.

The girl answered shyly with her dark eyes on my face. What I said and what she said I cannot remember, but I have little doubt it was something absolutely vapid. It really did not matter; the thing was we had met. I felt as I think a new-hatched moth must feel when suddenly its urgent headlong searchings brings it in tremulous amazement upon its mate.

We met, covered from each other, with all the nets of civili-zation keeping us apart. We walked side by side.

It led to scarcely more than that. I think we met four or five times altogether, and always with her nearly silent elder sister on the other side of her. We walked on the last two occasions arm in arm, furtively caressing each other's hands, we went away from the glare of the shops into the quiet roads of villa-dom, and there we whispered instead of talking and looked closely into one another's warm and shaded face. 'Dear,' I whispered very daringly, and she answered, 'Dear!' We had a vague sense that we wanted more of that quality of intimacy and more. We wanted each other as one wants beautiful music again or to breathe again the scent of flowers.

And that is all there was between us. The events are nothing, the thing that matters is the way in which this experience stabbed through the common stuff of life and left it pierced, with a light, with a huge new interest shining through the rent.

When I think of it I can recall even now the warm mystery of her face, her lips a little apart, lips that I never kissed, her soft shadowed throat, and I feel again the sensuous stir of her proximity. . . .

These two girls never told me their surname nor let me approach their house. They made me leave them at the corner of a road of small houses near Penge Station. And quite abruptly, without any intimation, they vanished and came to the meeting-place no more, they vanished as a moth goes out of a window into the night, and left me possessed by an intolerable want. . . .

The affair pervaded my existence for many weeks. I could not do my work and I could not rest at home. Night after night I promenaded up and down that Monkeys' Parade full of an unappeasable desire, with a thwarted sense of something just begun that ought to have gone on. I went backwards and forwards on the way to the vanishing place, and at last explored the forbidden road that had swallowed them up. But I never saw her again, except that later she came to me, my symbol of womanhood, in dreams. How my blood was stirred! I lay awake of nights whispering in the darkness for her. I prayed for her.

Indeed that girl, who probably forgot the last vestiges of me when her first real kiss came to her, ruled and haunted me, gave a Queen to my imagination and a texture to all my desires until I became a man.

I generalized her at last. I suddenly discovered that poetry was about her and that she was the key to all that had hitherto seemed nonsense about love. I took to reading novels, and if the heroine could not possibly be like her, dusky and warm and starlike, I put the book aside. . . .

I hesitate and add here one other confession. I want to tell this thing because it seems to me we are altogether too restrained and secretive about such matters. The cardinal thing in life sneaks in to us darkly and shamefully like a thief in the night.

One day during my Cambridge days – it must have been in my first year before I knew Hatherleigh – I saw in a print-shop window near the Strand an engraving of a girl that reminded me sharply of Penge and its dusky encounter. It was just a half length of a bare-shouldered, bare-breasted Oriental with arms akimbo, smiling faintly. I looked at it, went my way, then turned back and bought it. I felt I must have it. The odd thing is that I was more than a little shamefaced about it. I did not have it framed and hung in my room open to the criticism of my friends, but I kept it in the drawer of my writing-table. And I kept that drawer locked for a year. It speedily merged with and became identified with the dark girl of Penge. That engraving became in a way my mistress. Often when I had sported my oak and was supposed to be reading, I was sitting with it before me.

Obeying some instinct, I kept the thing very secret indeed. For a time nobody suspected what was locked in my drawer nor what was locked in me. I seemed as sexless as my world required.

5

These things stabbed through my life, intimations of things above and below and before me. They had an air of being no more than incidents, interruptions.

The broad substance of my existence at this time was the City Merchants School. Home was a place where I slept and read, and the mooning explorations of the south-eastern postal district which occupied the restless evenings and spare days of my vacations mere interstices, giving glimpses of enigmatical lights and distant spaces between the woven threads of a school-boy's career. School life began for me every morning at Herne Hill, for there I was joined by three or four other boys and the rest of the way we went together. Most of the streets and roads we traversed in our morning's walk from Victoria are still intact, the storms of rebuilding that have submerged so much of my boyhood's London have passed and left them, and I have revived the impression of them again and again in

58

recent years as I have clattered dinnerward in a hansom or hummed along in a motor cab to some engagement. The main gate still looks out with the same expression of ancient well-proportioned kindliness upon St. Margaret's Close. There are imposing new science laboratories in Chambers Street indeed, but the old playing fields are unaltered except for the big electric trams that go droning and spitting blue flashes along the western boundary. I know Ratten, the new Head, very well, but I have not been inside the school to see if it has changed at all since I went up to Cambridge.

I took all they put before us very readily as a boy, for I had a mind of vigorous appetite, but since I have grown mentally to man's estate and developed a more and more comprehensive view of our national process and our national needs, I am more and more struck by the oddity of the educational methods pursued, their aimless disconnectedness from the constructive forces in the community. I suppose if we are to view the public school as anything more than an institution that has just chanced to happen, we must treat it as having a definite function towards the general scheme of the nation, as being in a sense designed to take the crude young male of the more or less responsible class, to correct his harsh egotisms, broaden his outlook, give him a grasp of the contemporary developments he will presently be called upon to influence and control, and send him on to the university to be made a leading and ruling social man. It is easy enough to carp at schoolmasters and set up for an Educational Reformer, I know, but still it is impossible not to feel how infinitely more effectually—given certain impossibilities perhaps—the job might be done.

My memory of school has indeed no hint whatever of that quality of elucidation it seems reasonable to demand from it. Here all about me was London, a vast inexplicable being, a vortex of gigantic forces, that filled and overwhelmed me with impressions, that stirred my imagination to a perpetual vague inquiry ; and my school not only offered no key to it, but had practically no comment to make upon it at all. We were within three miles of Westminster and Charing Cross, the government offices of a fifth of mankind were all within an hour's stroll, great economic changes were going on under our eyes, now the hoardings flamed with election placards, now the Salvation

Army and now the unemployed came trailing in procession through the winter-grey streets, now the newspaper placards outside news-shops told of battles in strange places, now of amazing discoveries, now of sinister crimes, abject squalor and poverty, imperial splendour and luxury. Buckingham Palace, Rotten Row, Mayfair, the slums of Pimlico, garbage-littered streets of bawling costermongers, the inky silver of the barge-laden Thames—such was the background of our days. We went across St. Margaret's Close and through the school gate into a quiet puerile world apart from all these things. We joined in the earnest acquirement of all that was necessary for Greek epigrams and Latin verse, and for the rest played games. We dipped down into something clear and elegantly proportioned and time-worn and for all its high resolve of stalwart virility a little feeble, like our blackened and decayed portals by Inigo Jones.

Within, we were taught as the chief subjects of instruction Latin and Greek. We were taught very badly because the men who taught us did not habitually use either of these languages; nobody uses them any more now except perhaps for the Latin of a few Levantine monasteries. At the utmost our men read them. We were taught these languages because long ago Latin had been the language of civilization; the one way of escape from the narrow and localized life had lain in those days through Latin, and afterwards Greek had come in as the vehicle of a flood of new and amazing ideas. Once these two languages had been the sole means of initiation to the detached criticism and partial comprehension of the world. I can imagine the fierce zeal of our first Heads, Gardener and Roper, teaching Greek like passionate missionaries, as a progressive Chinaman might teach English to the boys of Pekin, clumsily, impatiently, with rod and harsh urgency, but sincerely, patriotically, because they felt that behind it lay revelations, the irresistible stimulus to a new phase of history. That was long ago. A new great world, a vaster Imperialism had arisen about the school, had assimilated all these amazing and incredible ideas, had gone on to new and yet more amazing developments of its own. But the City Merchants School still made the substance of its teaching Latin and Greek, still, with no thought of rotating crops, sowed in a dream amidst the harvesting.

There is no fierceness left in the teaching now. Just after I went up to Trinity, Gates, our Head, wrote a review article in defence of our curriculum. In this, among other indiscretions, he asserted that it was impossible to write good English without an illuminating knowledge of the classic tongues, and he split an infinitive and failed to button up a sentence in saying so. His main argument conceded every objection a reasonable person could make to the City Merchants' curriculum. He admitted that translation had now placed all the wisdom of the past at a common man's disposal, that scarcely a field of endeavour remained in which modern work had not long since passed beyond the ancient achievement. He disclaimed any utility. But there was, he said, a peculiar magic in these grammatical exercises no other subjects of instruction possessed. Nothing else provided the same strengthening and orderly discipline for the mind.

He said that, knowing the Senior Classics he did, himself a Senior Classic!

Yet in a dim confused way I think he was making out a case. In schools as he knew them, and with the sort of assistant available, the sort of assistant who has been trained entirely on the old lines, he could see no other teaching so effectual in developing attention, restraint, sustained constructive effort and various yet systematic adjustment. And that was as far as his imagination could go.

It is infinitely easier to begin organized human affairs than end them; the curriculum and the social organization of the English public school are the crowning instances of that. They go on because they have begun. Schools are not only immortal institutions but reproductive ones. Our founder, Jabez Arvon, knew nothing, I am sure, of Gates' pedagogic values and would, I feel certain, have dealt with them disrespectfully. But public schools and university colleges sprang into existence correlated, the scholars went on to the universities and came back to teach the schools, to teach as they themselves had been taught, before they had ever made any real use of the teaching; the crowd of boys herded together, a crowd perpetually renewed and unbrokenly the same, adjusted itself by means of spontaneously developed institutions. In a century, by its very success, this revolutionary innovation of Renascence public schools had become an immense tradition woven closely into the fabric of the national life. Intelligent and powerful people ceased to talk Latin or read Greek, they had got what was wanted, but that only left the schoolmaster the freer to elaborate his point. Since most men of any importance or influence in the country had been through the mill, it was naturally a little difficult to persuade them that it was not quite the best and most ennobling mill the wit of man could devise. And, moreover, they did not want their children made strange to them. There was all the machinery and all the men needed to teach the old subjects, and none to teach whatever new the critic might propose. Such science instruction as my father gave seemed indeed the uninviting alternative to the classical grind. It was certainly an altogether inferior instrument at that time.

So it was I occupied my mind with the exact study of dead languages for seven long years. It was the strangest of detachments. We would sit under the desk of such a master as Topham like creatures who had fallen into an enchanted pit, and he would do his considerable best to work us up to enthusiasm for, let us say, a Greek play. If we flagged he would lash himself to revive us. He would walk about the class-room mouthing great lines in a rich roar, and asking us with a flushed face and shining eyes if it was not 'glorious'. The very sight of Greek letters brings back to me the dingy, faded, ink-splashed quality of our class-room, the banging of books, Topham's disordered hair, the sheen of his alpaca gown, his deep unmusical intonations and the wide striding of his creaking boots. Glorious! And being plastic human beings we would consent that it was glorious, and some of us even achieved an answering reverberation and a sympathetic flush. I at times responded freely. We all accepted from him unquestioningly that these melodies, these strange sounds, exceeded any possibility of beauty that lay in the Gothic intricacy, the splash and glitter, the jar and recovery, the stabbing lights, the heights and broad distances of our English tongue. That indeed was the chief sin of him. It was not that he was for Greek and Latin, but that he was fiercely against every beauty that was neither classic nor deferred to classical canons.

And what exactly did we make of it, we seniors who

understood it best? We visualized dimly, through that dust and the grammatical difficulties, the spectacle of the chorus chanting grotesquely, helping out protagonist and antagonist, masked and buskined, with the telling of incomprehensible parricides, of inexplicable incest, of gods faded beyond symbolism, of that Relentless Law we did not believe in for a moment, that no modern western European can believe in. We thought of the characters in the unconvincing wigs and costumes of our school performance. No Gilbert Murray had come as yet to touch these things to life again. It was like the ghost of an antiquarian's toy theatre, a ghost that crumbled and condensed into a gritty dust of construing as one looked at it.

Marks, shindies, prayers and punishments, all flavoured with the leathery stuffiness of time-worn Big Hall. . . .

And then out one would come through our grey old gate into the evening light and the spectacle of London hurrying like a cataract, London in black and brown and blue and gleaming silver, roaring like the very loom of Time. We came out into the new world no teacher has yet had the power and courage to grasp and expound. Life and death sang all about one, joys and fears on such a scale, in such an intricacy as never Greek or Roman knew. The interminable procession of horse omnibuses went lumbering past, bearing countless people we knew not whence, we knew not whither. Hansoms clattered, foot passengers jostled one, a thousand appeals of shop and hoarding caught the eye. The multi-coloured lights of window and street mingled with the warm glow of the declining day under the softly flushing London skies; the ever-changing placards, the shouting news-vendors, told of a kaleidoscopic drama all about the globe. One did not realize what had happened to us, but the voice of Topham was suddenly drowned and lost, he and his minute, remote gesticulations. . . .

That submerged and isolated curriculum did not even join on to living interests where it might have done so. We were left absolutely to the hints of the newspapers, to casual political speeches, to the cartoons of the comic papers or a chance reading of some Socialist pamphlet for any general ideas whatever about the huge swirling world process in which we found ourselves. I always look back with particular exasperation to

**63**

the cessation of our modern history at the year 1815. There it pulled up abruptly, as though it had come upon something indelicate. . . .

But after all, what would Topham or Flack have made of the huge adjustments of the nineteenth century? Flack was the chief cricketer on the staff ; he belonged to that great cult which pretends that the place of this or that county in the struggle for the championship is a matter of supreme importance to boys. He obliged us to affect a passionate interest in the progress of county matches, to work up unnatural enthusiasms. What a fuss there would be when some well-trained boy, panting as if from Marathon, appeared with an evening paper! 'I say, you chaps, Middlesex all out for a hundred and five!'

Under Flack's pressure I became, I confess, a cricket humbug of the first class. I applied myself industriously year by year to mastering scores and averages ; I pretended that Lords and the Oval were the places nearest Paradise for me. (I never went to either.) Through a slight mistake about the county boundary I adopted Surrey for my loyalty, though as a matter of fact we were by some five hundred yards or so in Kent. It did quite as well for my purposes. I bowled rather straight and fast, and spent endless hours acquiring the skill to bowl Flack out. He was a bat in the Corinthian style, rich and voluminous, and succumbed very easily to a low shooter or an unexpected Yorker, but usually he was caught early by long leg. The difficulty was to bowl him before he got caught. He loved to lift a ball to leg. After one had clean bowled him at the practice nets one deliberately gave him a ball to leg just to make him feel nice again.

Flack went about a world of marvels dreaming of leg hits. He has been observed, going across the Park on his way to his highly respectable club in Piccadilly, to break from profound musings into a strange brief dance that ended with an imaginary swipe with his umbrella, a roofer, over the trees towards Buckingham Palace. The hit accomplished, Flack resumed his way.

Inadequately instructed foreigners would pass him in terror, needlessly alert.

64

## 6

These schoolmasters move through my memory as always a little distant and more than a little incomprehensible. Except when they wore flannels, I saw them almost always in old college caps and gowns, a uniform which greatly increased their detachment from the world of actual men. Gates, the Head, was a lean loose-limbed man, rather stupid I discovered when I reached the Sixth and came into contact with him, but honest, simple and very eager to be liberal-minded. He was bald, with an almost conical baldness, with a grizzled pointed beard, small featured and, under the stresses of a Zeitgeist that demanded liberality, with an expression of puzzled but resolute resistance to his own unalterable opinions. He made a tall dignified figure in his gown. In my junior days he spoke to me only three or four times, and then he annoyed me by giving me a wrong surname; it was a sore point because I was an outsider and not one of the old school families, the Shoesmiths, the Naylors, the Marklows, the Tophams, the Pevises and suchlike, who came generation after generation. I recall him most vividly against the background of faded brown book-backs in the old library in which we less destructive seniors were trusted to work, with the light from the stained-glass window falling in coloured patches on his face. It gave him the appearance of having no colour of his own. He had a habit of scratching the beard on his cheek as he talked, and he used to come and consult us about things and invariably do as we said. That, in his phraseology, was 'maintaining the traditions of the school.'

He had indeed an effect, not of a man directing a school, but of a man captured and directed by a school. Dead and gone Elizabethans had begotten a monster that could carry him about in its mouth.

Yet being a man, as I say, with his hair a little stirred by a Zeitgeist that made for change, Gates did at times display a disposition towards developments. City Merchants had no modern side, and utilitarian spirits were carping in the *Pall Mall Gazette* and elsewhere at the omissions from our curriculum, and particularly at our want of German. Moreover, four classes still worked together with much clashing and uproar in the old Big Hall that had once held in a common tumult the entire school. Gates used to come and talk to us older fellows about these things.

'I don't wish to innovate unduly,' he used to say. 'But we ought to get in some German, you know, – for those who like it. The army men will be wanting it some of these days.'

He referred to the organization of regular evening preparation for the lower boys in Big Hall as a 'revolutionary change,' but he achieved it, and he declared he began the replacement of the hacked wooden tables, at which the boys had worked since Tudor days, by sloping desks with safety inkpots and scientifically adjustable seats, 'with grave misgivings.' And though he never birched a boy in his life, and was, I am convinced, morally incapable of such a scuffle, he retained the block and birch in the school through all his term of office, and spoke at the Headmasters' Conference in temperate approval of corporal chastisement, comparing it, dear soul! to the power of the sword. . . .

I wish I could, in some measure and without tediousness, convey the effect of his discourses to General Assembly in Big Hall. But that is like trying to draw the obverse and reverse of a sixpence worn to complete illegibility. His tall fine figure stood high on the daïs, his thoughtful tenor filled the air as he steered his hazardous way through sentences that dragged inconclusive tails and dropped redundant prepositions. And he pleaded ever so urgently, ever so finely, that what we all knew for Sin was sinful, and on the whole best avoided altogether, and so went on with deepening notes and even with short arresting gestures of the right arm and hand, to stir and exhort us towards goodness, towards that modern, unsectarian goodness, goodness in general and nothing in particular, which the Zeitgeist seemed to indicate in those transitional years.

7

The school never quite got hold of me. Partly I think that was because I was a day-boy and so freer than most of the boys, partly because of a temperamental disposition to see things in my own way and have my private dreams, partly because I was a little antagonized by the family traditions that ran through the school. I was made to feel at first that I was a rank outsider, and I never quite forgot it. I suffered very little bullying, and I never had a fight – in all my time there were only three fights – but I followed my own curiosities. I was already a very keen theologian and politician before I was fifteen. I was also intensely interested in modern warfare. I read the morning papers in the Reading Room during the midday recess, never missed the illustrated weeklies, and often when I could afford it I bought a *Pall Mall Gazette* on my way home.

I do not think that I was very exceptional in that; most intelligent boys, I believe, want naturally to be men, and are keenly interested in men's affairs. There is not the universal passion for a magnified puerility among them it is customary to assume. I was indeed a voracious reader of everything but boys' books – which I detested – and fiction. I read histories, travel, popular science and controversy with particular zest, and I loved maps. School work and school games were quite subordinate affairs for me. I worked well and made a passable figure at games, and I do not think I was abnormally insensitive to the fine quality of our school, to the charm of its mediaeval nucleus, its Gothic cloisters, its scraps of Palladian and its dignified Georgian extensions; the contrast of the old quiet, that in spite of our presence pervaded it everywhere, with the rushing and impending London all about it, was indeed a continual pleasure to me. But these things were certainly not the living and central interests of my life.

I had to conceal my wider outlook to a certain extent – from the masters even more than from the boys. Indeed, I only let myself go freely with one boy, Britten, my especial chum, the son of the Agent-General for East Australia. We two discovered in a chance conversation *à propos* of a map in the library that we were both of us curious why there were Malays in Madagascar, and how the Mecca pilgrims came from the East Indies before steamships were available. Neither of us had suspected that there was any one at all in the school who knew or cared a rap about the Indian Ocean, except as water on the way to India. But Britten had come up through the Suez Canal, and his ship had spoken a pilgrim ship on the way. It gave him a startling quality of living knowledge. From these pilgrims we got to a comparative treatment of religions, and from that, by a sudden plunge, to entirely sceptical and disrespectful confessions concerning Gates' last outbreak of simple piety in School Assembly. We became congenial intimates from that hour.

The discovery of Britten happened to me when we were both in the Lower Fifth. Previously there had been a watertight compartment between the books I read and the thoughts they begot on the one hand and human intercourse on the other. Now I really began my higher education, and aired and examined and developed in conversation the doubts, the ideas, the interpretations that had been forming in my mind. As we were both dayboys with a good deal of control over our time, we organized walks and expeditions together, and my habit of solitary and rather vague prowling gave way to much more definite joint enterprises. I went several times to his house – he was the youngest of several brothers, one of whom was a medical student and let us assist at the dissection of a cat – and once or twice in vacation time he came to Penge, and we went with parcels of provisions to do a thorough day in the grounds and galleries of the Crystal Palace, ending with the fireworks at close quarters. We went in a river steamboat down to Greenwich, and fired by that made an excursion to Margate and back; we explored London docks and Bethnal Green Museum, Petticoat Lane and all sorts of out-of-the-way places together.

We confessed shyly to one another a common secret vice, 'Phantom warfare'. When we walked alone, especially in the country, we had both developed the same practice of fighting an imaginary battle about us as we walked. As we went along we were generals, and our attacks pushed along on either side, crouching and gathering behind hedges, cresting ridges, occupying copses, rushing open spaces, fighting from house to house. The hillsides about Penge were honeycombed in my imagination with the pits and trenches I had created to check a victorious invader coming out of Surrey. For him West Kensington was chiefly important as the scene of a desperate and successful last stand of insurrectionary troops (who had seized the Navy, the Bank and other advantages) against a royalist army – reinforced by Germans – advancing for reasons best known to themselves by way of Harrow and Ealing. It is a secret and solitary game, as we found when we tried to play it together. We made a success of that only once. All the way down to Margate we schemed defences and assailed and fought them as we came back against the sunset. Afterwards we recapitulated all that conflict by means of a large-scale map of the Thames and little paper ironclads in plan cut out of paper.

A subsequent revival of these imaginings was brought about by Britten's luck in getting, through a friend of his father's, admission for us both to the spectacle of volunteer officers fighting the war game in Caxton Hall. We developed a war game of our own at Britten's home with nearly a couple of hundred lead soldiers, some excellent spring cannons that shot hard and true at six yards, hills of books and a constantly elaborated set of rules. For some months that occupied an immense proportion of our leisure. Some of our battles lasted several days. We kept the game a profound secret from the other fellows. They would not have understood.

And we also began, it was certainly before we were sixteen, to write, for the sake of writing. We liked writing. We had discovered Lamb and the best of the middle articles in such weeklies as the *Saturday Gazette*, and we imitated them. Our minds were full of dim uncertain things we wanted to drag out into the light of expression. Britten had got hold of *In Memoriam*, and I had disinterred Pope's *Essay on Man* and *Rabbi Ben Ezra*, and these things had set our theological and cosmic solicitudes talking. I was somewhere between sixteen and eighteen, I know, when he and I walked along the Thames Embankment confessing shamefully to one another that we had never read Lucretius. We thought every one who mattered had read Lucretius.

When I was nearly sixteen my mother was taken ill very suddenly, and died of some perplexing complaint that involved a post-mortem examination; it was, I think, the trouble that has since those days been recognized as appendicitis. This led to a considerable change in my circumstances; the house at Penge was given up, and my Staffordshire uncle arranged for me to lodge during school terms with a needy solicitor and his wife in Vicars Street, sw, about a mile and a half from the school. So it was I came right into London; I had almost two years of London before I went to Cambridge.

Those were our great days together. Afterwards we were torn apart; Britten went to Oxford, and our circumstances never afterwards threw us continuously together until the days of the *Blue Weekly*.

As boys, we walked together, read and discussed the same books, pursued the same inquiries. We got a reputation as inseparables and the nickname of the Rose and the Lily, for Britten was short and thick-set with dark close curling hair and a ruddy Irish type of face; I was lean and fair-haired and some inches taller than he. Our talk ranged widely and yet had certain very definite limitations. We were amazingly free with politics and religion, we went to that little meeting-house of William Morris's at Hammersmith and worked out the principles of Socialism pretty thoroughly, and we got up the Darwinian theory with the help of Britten's medical-student brother and the galleries of the Natural History Museum in Cromwell Road. Those wonderful cases on the ground floor illustrating mimicry, dimorphism and so forth, were new in our times, and we went through them with earnest industry and tried over our Darwinism in the light of that. Such topics we did exhaustively. But on the other hand I do not remember any discussion whatever of human sex or sexual relationships. There, in spite of intense secret curiosities, our lips were sealed by a peculiar shyness. And I do not believe we ever had occasion either of us to use the word 'love'. It was not only that we were instinctively shy of the subject, but that we were mightily ashamed of the extent of our ignorance and uncertainty in these matters. We evaded them elaborately with an assumption of exhaustive knowledge.

We certainly had no shyness about theology. We marked the emancipation of our spirits from the frightful teachings that had oppressed our boyhood, by much indulgence in blasphemous wit. We had a secret literature of irreverent rhymes, and a secret art of theological caricature. Britten's father had delighted his family by reading aloud from Dr Richard Garnett's *Twilight of the Gods,* and Britten conveyed the precious volume to me. That and the *Bab Ballads* were the inspiration of some of our earliest lucubrations.

For an imaginative boy the first experience of writing is like a tiger's first taste of blood, and our literary flowerings led

70

very directly to the revival of the school magazine, which had been comatose for some years. But there we came upon a disappointment.

## 8

In that revival we associated certain other of the Sixth Form boys, and notably one for whom our enterprise was to lay the foundations of a career that has ended in the House of Lords, Arthur Cossington, now Lord Paddockhurst. Cossington was at that time a rather heavy, rather good-looking boy who was chiefly eminent in cricket, an outsider even as we were, and preoccupied no doubt, had we been sufficiently detached to observe him, with private imaginings very much of the same quality and spirit as our own. He was, we were inclined to think, rather a sentimentalist, rather a poseur, he affected a concise emphatic style, played chess very well, betrayed a belief in will-power, and earned Britten's secret hostility, Britten being a sloven, by the invariable neatness of his collars and ties. He came into our magazine with a vigour that we found extremely surprising and unwelcome.

Britten and I had wanted to write. We had indeed figured our project modestly as a manuscript magazine of satirical, liberal and brilliant literature by which in some rather inexplicable way the vague tumult of ideas that teemed within us was to find form and expression; Cossington, it was manifest from the outset, wanted neither to write nor writing, but a magazine. I remember the inaugural meeting in Shoesmith major's study – we had had great trouble in getting it together – and how effectually Cossington bolted with the proposal.

'I think we fellows ought to run a magazine,' said Cossington. 'The school used to have one. A school like this ought to have a magazine.'

'The last one died in '84,' said Shoesmith from the hearthrug. 'Called the *Observer*. Rot rather.'

'Bad title,' said Cossington.

'There was a *Tatler* before that,' said Britten, sitting on the writing-table at the window that was closed to deaden the cries of the Lower School at play, and clashing his boots together.

'We want something suggestive of City Merchants.'

71

'*City Merchandize*,' said Britten.

'Too fanciful. What of *Arvonian*? Richard Arvon was our founder, and it seems almost a duty –'

'They call them all -usians or -onians,' said Britten.

'I like *City Merchandize*,' I said. 'We could probably find a quotation to suggest – oh! mixed good things.'

Cossington regarded me abstractedly.

'Don't want to put the accent on the City, do we?' said Shoesmith, who had a feeling for county families, and Naylor supported him by a murmur of approval.

'We ought to call it the *Arvonian*,' decided Cossington, 'and we might very well have underneath, "With which is incorporated the *Observer*." That picks up the old traditions, makes an appeal to old boys and all that, and it gives us something to print under the title.'

I still held out for *City Merchandize*, which had taken my fancy. 'Some of the chaps' people won't like it,' said Naylor, 'certain not to. And it sounds Rum.'

'Sounds Weird,' said a boy who had not hitherto spoken.

'We aren't going to do anything Queer,' said Shoesmith, pointedly not looking at Britten.

The question of the title had manifestly gone against us. 'Oh! *have* it *Arvonian*,' I said.

'And next, what size shall we have?' said Cossington.

'Something like *Macmillan's Magazine – or Longmans*'; *Longmans*' is better because it has a whole page, not columns. It makes no end of difference to one's effects.'

'What effects?' asked Shoesmith abruptly.

'Oh! a pause or a white line or anything. You've got to write closer for a double column. It's nuggetty. You can't get a swing on your prose.' I had discussed this thoroughly with Britten.

'If the fellows are going to write –' began Britten.

'We ought to keep off fine writing,' said Shoesmith. 'It's cheek. I vote we don't have any.'

'We shan't get any,' said Cossington, and then as an olive branch to me, 'unless Remington does a bit. Or Britten. But it's no good making too much space for it.'

'We ought to be very careful about the writing,' said Shoesmith. 'We don't want to give ourselves away.'

'I vote we ask old Topham to see us through,' said Naylor.

Britten groaned aloud and every one regarded him. 'Greek epigrams on the fellows' names,' he said. 'Small beer in ancient bottles. Let's get a stuffed broody hen to *sit* on the magazine.'

'We might do worse than a Greek epigram,' said Cossington. 'One in each number. It – it impresses parents and keeps up our classical tradition. And the masters *can* help. We don't want to antagonize them. Of course we've got to departmentalize. Writing is only one section of the thing. The *Arvonian* has to stand for the school. There's questions of space and questions of expense. We can't turn out a great chunk of printed prose like – like wet cold toast and call it a magazine.'

Britten writhed, appreciating the image.

'There's to be a section of sports. *You* must do that.'

'I'm not going to do any fine writing,' said Shoesmith.

'What you've got to do is just to list all the chaps and put a note to their play: "Naylor minor must pass more. Football isn't the place for extreme Individualism," "Ammersham shapes well as half-back." Things like that.'

'I could do that all right,' said Shoesmith, brightening and manifestly becoming pregnant with judgements.

'One great thing about a magazine of this sort,' said Cossington, 'is to mention just as many names as you can in each number. It keeps the interest alive. Chaps will turn it over looking for their own little bit. Then it all lights up for them.'

'Do you want any reports of matches?' Shoesmith broke from his meditation.

'Rather. With comments.'

'Naylor surpassed himself and negotiated the lemon safely home,' said Shoesmith.

'Shut it,' said Naylor modestly.

'Exactly,' said Cossington. 'That gives us three features,' touching them off on his fingers, 'Epigram, Literary Section, Sports. Then we want a section to shove anything into, a joke, a notice of anything that's going on. So on. Our Note Book.'

'Oh, Hell!' said Britten, and clashed his boots, to the silent disapproval of every one.

'Then we want an editorial.'

'A *what*?' cried Britten, with a note of real terror in his voice.

'Well, don't we? Unless we have our Note Book to begin on

the front page. It gives a scrappy effect to do that. We want something manly and straightforward and a bit thoughtful, about Patriotism, say, or *Esprit de Corps,* or After-Life.'

I looked at Britten. Hitherto we had not considered Cossington mattered very much in the world.

He went over us as a motor-car goes over a dog. There was a sort of energy about him, a new sort of energy to us; we had never realized that anything of the sort existed in the world. We were hopelessly at a disadvantage. Almost instantly he had developed a clear and detailed vision of a magazine made up of everything that was most acceptable in the magazines that flourished in the adult world about us, and had determined to make it a success. He had by a kind of instinct, as it were, synthetically plagiarized every successful magazine and breathed into this dusty mixture the breath of life. He was elected at his own suggestion managing director, with the earnest support of Shoesmith and Naylor, and conducted the magazine so successfully and brilliantly that he even got a whole back page of advertisements from the big sports shop in Holborn, and made the printers pay at the same rate for a notice of certain books of their own which they said they had inserted by inadvertency to fill up space. The only literary contribution in the first number was a column by Topham in faultless stereotyped English in depreciation of some fancied evil called Utilitarian Studies and ending with that noble old quotation:

To the glory that was Greece and the grandeur that was Rome.

And Flack crowded us out of number two with a bright little paper on the 'Humours of Cricket', and the Head himself was profusely thoughtful all over the editorial under the heading of 'The School Chapel ; and How it Seems to an Old Boy'.

Britten and I found it difficult to express to each other with any grace or precision what we felt about that magazine.

# Chapter the Fourth

## Adolescence

### 1

I find it very difficult to trace how form was added to form and interpretation followed interpretation in my ever-spreading, ever-deepening, ever-multiplying and enriching vision of this world into which I had been born. Every day added its impressions, its hints, its subtle explications to the growing understanding. Day after day the living interlacing threads of a mind weave together. Every morning now for three weeks and more (for today is Thursday and I started on a Tuesday) I have been trying to convey some idea of the factors and early influences by which my particular scrap of subjective tapestry was shaped, to show the child playing on the nursery floor, the son perplexed by his mother, gazing aghast at his dead father, exploring interminable suburbs, touched by first intimations of the sexual mystery, coming in with a sort of confused avidity towards the centres of the life of London. It is only by such an effort to write it down that one realizes how marvellously crowded, how marvellously analytical and synthetic those years must be. One begins with the little child to whom the sky is a roof of blue, the world a screen of opaque and disconnected facts, the home a thing eternal, and 'being good' just simple obedience to unquestioned authority ; and one comes at last to the vast world of one's adult perception, pierced deep by flaring searchlights of partial understanding, here masked by mists, here refracted and distorted through half translucent veils, here showing broad prospects and limitless vistas, and here impenetrable dark.

I recall phases of deep speculation, doubts and even prayers by night, and strange occasions when by a sort of hypnotic contemplation of nothingness I sought to pierce the web of appearances about me. It is hard to measure these things in receding perspective, and now I cannot trace, so closely has mood succeeded and overlaid and obliterated mood, the phases by which an utter horror of death was replaced by the growing realization of its necessity and dignity. Difficulty of the imagination with infinite space, infinite time, entangled my mind; and moral distress for the pain and suffering of bygone ages that made all thought of reformation in the future seem but the grimmest irony upon now irreparable wrongs. Many an intricate perplexity of these broadening years did not so much get settled as cease to matter. Life crowded me away from it.

I have confessed myself a temerarious theologian, and in that passage from boyhood to manhood I ranged widely in my search for some permanently satisfying Truth. That, too, ceased after a time to be urgently interesting. I came at last into a phase that endures to this day, of absolute tranquillity, of absolute confidence in whatever that Incomprehensible Comprehensive which must needs be the substratum of all things may be. Feeling *of it,* feeling *by it,* I cannot feel afraid of it. I think I had got quite clearly and finally to that adjustment long before my Cambridge days were done. I am sure that the evil in life is transitory and finite like an accident or distress in the nursery; that God is my Father and that I may trust Him, even though life hurts so that one must needs cry out at it, even though it shows no consequence but failure, no promise but pain....

But while I was fearless of theology I must confess it was comparatively late before I faced and dared to probe the secrecies of sex. I was afraid of sex. I had an instinctive perception that it would be a large and difficult thing in my life, but my early training was all in the direction of regarding it as an irrelevant thing, as something disconnected from all the broad significances of life, as hostile and disgraceful in its quality. The world was never so emasculated in thought, I suppose, as it was in the Victorian time....

I was afraid to think either of sex or (what I have always found inseparable from a kind of sexual emotion) beauty. Even as a boy I knew the thing as a haunting and alluring mystery that I tried to keep away from. Its dim presence obsessed me none the less for all the extravagant decency, the stimulating silences of my upbringing....

The plaster Venuses and Apollos that used to adorn the vast aisle and huge grey terraces of the Crystal Palace were the first intimations of the beauty of the body that ever came into my life. As I write of it I feel again the shameful attraction of those gracious forms. I used to look at them not simply but curiously and askance. Once at least in my later days at Penge, I spent a shilling on admission chiefly for the sake of them. . . .

The strangest thing of all my odd and solitary upbringing seems to me now that swathing up of all the splendours of the flesh, that strange combination of fanatical terrorism and shyness that fenced me about with prohibitions. It caused me to grow up, I will not say blankly ignorant, but with an ignorance blurred and dishonoured by shame, by enigmatical warnings, by cultivated aversions, an ignorance in which a fascinated curiosity and desire struggled like a thing in a net. I knew so little and I felt so much. There was indeed no Aphrodite at all in my youthful Pantheon, but instead there was a mysterious and minatory gap. I have told how at last a new Venus was born in my imagination out of gas lamps and the twilight, a Venus with a cockney accent and dark eyes shining out of the dusk, a Venus who was a warm, passion-stirring atmosphere rather than incarnate in a body. And I have told, too, how I bought a picture.

All this was a thing apart from the rest of my life, a locked avoided chamber. . . .

It was not until my last year at Trinity that I really broke down the barriers of this unwholesome silence and brought my secret broodings to the light of day. Then a little set of us plunged suddenly into what we called at first sociological discussion. I can still recall even the physical feeling of those first tentative talks. I remember them mostly as occurring in the rooms of Ted Hatherleigh, who kept at the corner by the Trinity great gate, but we also used to talk a good deal at a man's in King's, a man named, if I remember rightly, Redmayne. The atmosphere of Hatherleigh's rooms was a haze of tobacco smoke against a background brown and deep. He professed himself a socialist with anarchistic leanings – he had suffered the martyrdom of ducking for it – and a huge French May-Day poster, displaying a splendid proletarian in red and black on a barricade against a flaring orange sky, dominated his decorations. Hatherleigh affected a fine untidiness, and all the place, even the floor, was littered with books, for the most part open and face downward ; deeper darknesses were supplied by a discarded gown and our caps, all conscientiously battered,

Hatherleigh's flopped like an elephant's ear, and inserted quill pens supported the corners of mine; the high lights of the picture came chiefly as reflections from his chequered blue mugs full of audit ale. We sat on oak chairs, except the four or five who crowded on a capacious settle, we drank a lot of beer and were often fuddled, and occasionally quite drunk, and we all smoked reckless-looking pipes, – there was a transient fashion among us for corncobs for which Mark Twain, I think, was responsible. Our little excesses with liquor were due far more to conscience than appetite, indicating chiefly a resolve to break away from restraints that we suspected were keeping us off the instructive knife-edges of life. Hatherleigh was a good Englishman of the premature type with a red face, a lot of hair, a deep voice and an explosive plunging manner, and it was he who said one evening – Heaven knows how we got to it – 'Look here, you know, it's all Rot, this Shutting Up about Women. We *ought* to talk about them. What are we going to do about them? It's got to come. We're all festering inside about it. Let's out with it. There's too much Decency altogether about this Infernal University!'

We rose to his challenge a little awkwardly and our first talk was clumsy, there were flushed faces and red ears, and I remember Hatherleigh broke out into a monologue on decency. 'Modesty and Decency,' said Hatherleigh, 'are Oriental vices. The Jews brought them to Europe. They're Semitic, just like our monasticism here and the seclusion of women and mutilating the dead on a battlefield. And all that sort of thing.'

Hatherleigh's mind progressed by huge leaps, leaps that were usually wildly inaccurate, and for a time we engaged hotly upon the topic of those alleged mutilations and the Semitic responsibility for decency. Hatherleigh tried hard to saddle the Semitic race with the less elegant war customs of the Soudan and the north-west frontier of India, and quoted Doughty, at that time a little-known author, and Cunninghame Graham to show that the Arab was worse than a county-town spinster in his regard for respectability. But his case was too preposterous, and Esmeer with his shrill penetrating voice and his way of pointing with all four fingers flat together, carried the point against him. He quoted Cato and Roman law and the monasteries of Tibet.

'Well, anyway,' said Hatherleigh, escaping from our hands like an intellectual frog, 'Semitic or not, I've got no use for decency.'

We argued points and Hatherleigh professed an unusually balanced and tolerating attitude. 'I don't mind a certain refinement and dignity,' he admitted generously. 'What I object to is this spreading out of decency until it darkens the whole sky, until it makes a man's father afraid to speak of the most important things, until it makes a man afraid to look a frank book in the face or think – even think! until it leads to our coming to – to the business at last with nothing but a few prohibitions, a few hints, a lot of dirty jokes and, and' – he waved a hand and seemed to seek and catch his image in the air – 'oh, a confounded buttered slide of sentiment, to guide us. I tell you I'm going to think about it and talk about it until I see a little more daylight than I do at present. I'm twenty-two. Things might happen to me anywhen. You men can go out into the world if you like, to sin like fools and marry like fools, not knowing what you are doing and ashamed to ask. You'll take the consequences, too, I expect, pretty meekly, sniggering a bit, sentimentalizing a bit, like – like Cambridge humorists. . . . *I* mean to know what I'm doing.'

He paused to drink, and I think I cut in with ideas of my own. But one is apt to forget one's own share in a talk, I find, more than one does the clear-cut objectivity of other people's, and I do not know how far I contributed to this discussion that followed. I am, however, pretty certain that it was then that ideal that we were pleased to call aristocracy and which soon became the common property of our set was developed. It was Esmeer, I know, who laid down and maintained the proposition that so far as minds went there were really only two sorts of man in the world, the aristocrat and the man who subdues his mind to other people's.

' "I couldn't *think* of it, Sir," ' said Esmeer in his elucidatory tones; 'that's what a servant says. His mind even is broken in to run between fences, and he admits it. *We've* got to be able to think of anything. And "such things aren't for the Likes of Us!" That's another servant's saying. Well, everything *is* for the Likes of Us. If we see fit, that is.'

A small fresh-coloured man in grey objected.

'Well,' exploded Hatherleigh, 'if that isn't so what the deuce are we up here for? Instead of working in mines? If some things aren't to be thought about ever! We've got the privilege of all these extra years for getting things straight in our heads, and then we won't use 'em. Good God! what do you think a university's for?' ...

Esmeer's idea came with an effect of real emancipation to several of us. We were not going to be afraid of ideas any longer, we were going to throw down every barrier of prohibition and take them in and see what came of it. We became for a time even intemperately experimental, and one of us, at the bare suggestion of an eminent psychic investigator, took hashish and very nearly died of it within a fortnight of our great elucidation.

The chief matter of our interchanges was of course the discussion of sex. Once the theme had been opened it became a sore place in our intercourse ; none of us seemed able to keep away from it. Our imaginations got astir with it. We made up for lost time and went round it and through it and over it exhaustively. I recall prolonged discussion of polygamy on the way to Royston, muddy November tramps to Madingley, when amidst much profanity from Hatherleigh at the serious treatment of so obsolete a matter, we weighed the reasons, if any, for the institution of marriage. The fine dim night-time spaces of the Great Court are bound up with the inconclusive finales of mighty hot-eared wrangles; the narrows of Trinity Street and Petty Cury and Market Hill have their particular associations for me with that spate of confession and free speech, that almost painful gaol delivery of long pent and crappled and sometimes crippled ideas.

And we went on a reading party that Easter to a place called Pulborough in Sussex, where there is a fishing inn and a river that goes under a bridge. It was a late Easter and a blazing one, and we boated and bathed and talked of being Hellenic and the beauty of the body until at moments it seemed to us that we were destined to restore the Golden Age, by the simple abolition of tailors and outfitters.

Those undergraduate talks! how rich and glorious they seemed, how splendidly new the ideas that grew and multiplied in our seething minds! We made long afternoon and evening raids over the Downs towards Arundel, and would come tramping back through the still keen moonlight singing and shouting. We formed romantic friendships with one another, and grieved more or less convincingly that there were no splendid women fit to be our companions in the world. But Hatherleigh, it seemed, had once known a girl whose hair was gloriously red. 'My God!' said Hatherleigh to convey the quality of her; just simply and with projectile violence: 'My God!'

Benton had heard of a woman who lived with a man refusing to be married to him – we thought that splendid beyond measure, – I cannot now imagine why. She was 'like a tender goddess,' Benton said. A sort of shame came upon us in the dark in spite of our liberal intentions when Benton committed himself to that. And after such talk we would fall upon great pauses of emotional dreaming, and if by chance we passed a girl in a governess cart, or some farmer's daughter walking to the station, we became alertly silent or obstreperously indifferent to her. For might she not be just that one exception to the banal decency, the sickly pointless conventionality, the sham modesty of the times in which we lived?

We felt we stood for a new movement, not realizing how perennially this same emancipation returns to those ancient courts beside the Cam. We were the anti-decency party, we discovered a catch phrase that we flourished about in the Union and made our watchword, namely, 'stark fact'. We hung nude pictures in our rooms much as if they had been flags, to the earnest concern of our bedders, and I disinterred my long-kept engraving and had it framed in fumed oak, and found for it a completer and less restrained companion, a companion I never cared for in the slightest degree. . . .

This efflorescence did not prevent, I think indeed it rather helped, our more formal university work, for most of us took Firsts, and three of us got Fellowships in one year or another. There was Benton who had a Research Fellowship and went to Tübingen, there was Esmeer and myself who both became Residential Fellows. I had taken the Mental and Moral Science Tripos (as it was then), and three years later I got a lectureship in political science. In those days it was disguised in the cloak of Political Economy.

## 2

It was our affectation to be a little detached from the main stream of undergraduate life. We worked pretty hard, but by virtue of our beer, our socialism and suchlike heterodoxy, held ourselves to be differentiated from the swatting reading man. None of us, except Baxter, who was a rowing blue, a rather abnormal blue with an appetite for ideas, took games seriously enough to train, and on the other hand we intimated contempt for the rather mediocre, deliberately humorous, consciously gentlemanly and consciously wild undergraduate men who made up the mass of Cambridge life. After the manner of youth we were altogether too hard on our contemporaries. We battered our caps and tore our gowns lest they should seem new, and we despised these others extremely for doing exactly the same things ; we had an idea of ourselves and resented beyond measure a similar weakness in these our brothers.

There was a type or at least there seemed to us to be a type – I'm a little doubtful at times now whether after all we didn't create it – for which Hatherleigh invented the nickname the 'Pinky Dinkys', intending thereby both contempt and abhorrence in almost equal measure. The Piny Dinky summarized all that we particularly did not want to be, and also, I now perceive, much of what we were and all that we secretly dreaded becoming.

But it is hard to convey the Pinky Dinky idea, for all that it meant so much to us. We spent one evening at least during that reading party upon the Pinky Dinky ; we sat about our one fire after a walk in the rain – it was our only wet day – smoked excessively virile pipes, and elaborated the natural history of the Pinky Dinky. We improvised a sort of Pinky Dinky litany, and Hatherleigh supplied deep notes for the responses.

'The Pinky Dinky extracts a good deal of amusement from life,' said someone.

'Damned prig!' said Hatherleigh.

'The Pinky Dinky arises in the Union and treats the question with a light gay touch. He makes the weird ones mad. But sometimes he cannot go on because of the amusement he extracts.'

'I want to shy books at the giggling swine,' said Hatherleigh.

'The Pinky Dinky says suddenly while he is making the tea, "We're all being frightfully funny. It's time for *you* to say something now." '

'The Pinky Dinky shakes his head and says: "I'm afraid I shall never be a responsible being." And he really *is* frivolous.'

'Frivolous but not vulgar,' said Esmeer.

'Pinky Dinkys are chaps who've had their buds nipped,' said Hatherleigh. 'They're Plebs and they know it. They haven't the Guts to get hold of things. And so they worry up all those silly little jokes of theirs to carry it off.' . . .

We tried bad ones for a time, viciously flavoured.

'Pinky Dinkys are due to over-production of the type that ought to keep outfitters' shops. Pinky Dinkys would like to keep outfitters' shops with whimsy 'scriptions on the boxes and make your bill out funny, and not be snobs to customers, no! – not even if they had titles.'

'Every Pinky Dinky's people are rather good people, and better than most Pinky Dinky's people. But he does not put on side.'

'Pinky Dinkys become playful at the sight of women.'

' "Croquet's my game," said the Pinky Dinky, and felt a man condescended.'

'But what the devil do they think they're up to, anyhow?' roared old Hatherleigh suddenly, dropping plump into bottomless despair.

We felt we had still failed to get at the core of the mystery of the Pinky Dinky.

We tried over things about his religion. 'The Pinky Dinky goes to King's Chapel, and sits and feels in the dusk. Solemn things! Oh *hush!* He wouldn't tell you –'

'He *couldn't* tell you.'

'Religion is so sacred to him he never talks about it, never reads about it, never thinks about it. Just feels!'

'But in his heart of hearts, oh! ever so deep, the Pinky Dinky has a doubt –'

Someone protested.

'Not a vulgar doubt,' Esmeer went on, 'but a kind of hesitation whether the Ancient of Days is really exactly what one would call good form. . . . There's a lot of horrid coarseness got into the world somehow. *Somebody* put it there. . . . And anyhow there's no particular reason why a man should be seen about with Him. He's jolly Awful of course and all that –'

'The Pinky Dinky for all his fun and levity has a clean mind.'

'A thoroughly clean mind. Not like Esmeer's – the Pig!'

'If once he began to think about sex, how could he be comfortable at croquet?'

'It's their Damned Modesty,' said Hatherleigh suddenly, 'that's what's the matter with the Pinky Dinky. It's Mental Cowardice dressed up as a virtue and taking the poor dears in. Cambridge is soaked with it; it's some confounded local bacillus. Like the thing that gives a flavour to Havana cigars. He comes up here to be made into a man and a ruler of the people, and he thinks it shows a nice disposition not to take on the job! How the Devil is a great Empire to be run with men like him?'

'All his little jokes and things,' said Esmeer, regarding his feet on the fender, 'it's just a nervous sniggering – because he's afraid. . . . Oxford's no better.'

'What's he afraid of?' said I.

'God knows!' exploded Hatherleigh and stared at the fire.

'*Life!*' said Esmeer. 'And so in a way are we,' he added, and made a thoughtful silence for a time.

'I say,' began Carter, who was doing the Natural Science Tripos, 'what is the adult form of the Pinky Dinky?'

But there we were checked by our ignorance of the world.

'What is the adult form of any of us?' asked Benton, voicing the thought that had arrested our flow.


3

I do not remember that we ever lifted our criticism to the dons and the organization of the University. I think we took them for granted. When I look back at my youth I am always astonished by the multitude of things that we took for granted. It seemed to us that Cambridge was in the order of things, for all the world like having eyebrows or a vermiform appendix. Now with the larger scepticism of middle age I can entertain very fundamental doubts about these old universities. Indeed I had a scheme –

I do not see what harm I can do now by laying bare the purpose of the political combinations I was trying to effect.

My educational scheme was indeed the starting-point of all the big project of conscious public reconstruction at which I aimed. I wanted to build up a new educational machine altogether for the governing class out of a consolidated system of special public service schools. I meant to get to work upon this whatever office I was given in the new government. I could have begun my plan from the Admiralty or the War Office quite as easily as from the Education Office. I am firmly convinced it is hopeless to think of reforming the old public schools and universities to meet the needs of a modern state, they send their roots too deep and far, the cost would exceed any good that could possibly be effected, and so I have sought a way round this invincible obstacle. I do think it would be quite practicable to side-track, as the Americans say, the whole system by creating hard-working, hard-living, modern and scientific boys' schools, first for the Royal Navy and then for the public service generally, and as they grew, opening them to the public without any absolute obligation to subsequent service. Simultaneously with this it would not be impossible to develop a new college system with strong faculties in modern philosophy, modern history, European literature and criticism, physical and biological science, education and sociology.

We could in fact create a new liberal education in this way, and cut the umbilicus of the classical languages for good and all. I should have set this going, and trusted it to correct or kill the old public schools and the Oxford and Cambridge tradition altogether. I had men in my mind to begin the work, and I should have found others. I should have aimed at making a hard-trained, capable, intellectually active, proud type of man. Everything else would have been made subservient to that. I should have kept my grip on the men through their vacation, and somehow or other I would have contrived a young woman to match them. I think I could have seen to it effectually enough that they didn't get at croquet and tennis with the vicarage daughters and discover sex in the Peeping Tom fashion I did, and that they realized quite early in life that it isn't really virile to reek of tobacco. I should have had military manoeuvres, training ships, aeroplane work, mountaineering and so forth, in

85

the place of the solemn trivialities of games, and I should have fed and housed my men clean and very hard – where there wasn't any audit ale, no credit tradesmen, and plenty of high-pressure douches. . . .

I have revisited Cambridge and Oxford time after time since I came down, and so far as the Empire goes, I want to get clear of those two places. . . .

Always I renew my old feelings, a physical oppression, a sense of lowness and dampness almost exactly like the feeling of an underground room where paper moulders and leaves the wall, a feeling of ineradicable contagion in the Gothic buildings, in the narrow ditch-like rivers, in those roads and roads of stuffy little villas. Those little villas have destroyed all the good of the old monastic system and none of its evil. . . .

Some of the most charming people in the world live in them, but their collective effect is below the quality of any individual among them. Cambridge is a world of subdued tones, of excessively subtle humours, of prim conduct and free thinking; it fears the Parent, but it has no fear of God; it offers amidst surroundings that vary between dinginess and antiquarian charm the inflammation of literature's purple draught; one hears there a peculiar thin scandal like no other scandal in the world – a covetous scandal – so that I am always reminded of Ibsen in Cambridge. In Cambridge and the plays of Ibsen alone does it seem appropriate for the heroine before the great crises of life to 'enter, take off her overshoes, and put her wet umbrella upon the writing desk.' . . .

We have to make a new Academic mind for modern needs, and the last thing to make it out of, I am convinced, is the old Academic mind. One might as soon try to fake the old *Victory* at Portsmouth into a line-of-battle-ship again. Besides which the old Academic mind, like those old bathless, damp Gothic colleges, is much too delightful in its peculiar and distinctive way to damage by futile patching.

My heart warms to a sense of affectionate absurdity as I recall dear old Codger, surely the most 'unleaderly' of men. No more than from the old Schoolmen, his kindred, could one get from him a School for Princes. Yet apart from his teaching he was as curious and adorable as a good Netsuké. Until quite recently he was a power in Cambridge, he could make and mar and destroy, and in a way he has become the quintessence of Cambridge in my thoughts.

I see him on his way to the morning's lecture, with his plump childish face, his round innocent eyes, his absurdly non-pre-hensile fat hand carrying his cap, his grey trousers braced up much too high, his feet a trifle inturned, and going across the great court with a queer tripping pace that seemed cultivated even to my naïve undergraduate eye. Or I see him lecturing. He lectured walking up and down between the desks, talking in a fluting rapid voice, and with the utmost lucidity. If he could not walk up and down he could not lecture. His mind and voice had precisely the fluid quality of some clear subtle liquid ; one felt it could flow round anything and overcome nothing. And its nimble eddies were wonderful! Or again I recall him drinking port with little muscular movements in his neck and cheek and chin and his brows knit – very judicial, very concentrated, pre-paring to say the apt just thing; it was the last thing he would have told a lie about.

When I think of Codger I am reminded of an inscription I saw on some occasion in Regent's Park above two eyes scarcely more limpidly innocent than his – 'Born in the Menagerie.' Never once since Codger began to display the early promise of scholarship at the age of eight or more, had he been outside the bars. His utmost travel had been to lecture here and lecture there. His student phase had culminated in papers of quite exceptional brilliance, and he had gone on to lecture with a cheerful combination of wit and mannerism that had made him a success from the beginning. He has lectured ever since. He lectures still. Year by year he has become plumper, more rubi-cund and more and more of an item for the intelligent visitor to see. Even in my time he was pointed out to people as part of our innumerable enrichments, and obviously he knew it. He has become now almost the leading Character in a little donnish world of much too intensely appreciated Characters.

He boasted he took no exercise, and also of his knowledge of port wine. Of other wines he confessed quite frankly he had no 'special knowledge.' Beyond these things he had little pride except that he claimed to have read every novel by a woman writer that had ever entered the Union Library. This, however, he held to be remarkable rather than ennobling, and such boasts as he made of it were tinged with playfulness. Certainly he had a scholar's knowledge of the works of Miss Marie Corelli, Miss Braddon, Miss Elinor Glyn and Madame Sarah Grand that would have astonished and flattered those ladies enormously, and he loved nothing so much in his hours of relaxation as to propound and answer difficult questions upon their books. Tusher of King's was his ineffectual rival in this field, their bouts were memorable and rarely other than glorious for Codger; but then Tusher spread himself too much, he also undertook to rehearse whole pages out of Bradshaw, and tell you with all the changes how to get from any station to any station in Great Britain by the nearest and cheapest routes. . . .

Codger lodged with a little deaf innocent old lady, Mrs Araminta Mergle, who was understood to be herself a very redoubtable Character in the Gyp-Bedder class; about her he related quietly absurd anecdotes. He displayed a marvellous invention in ascribing to her plausible expressions of opinion entirely identical in import with those of the Oxford and Harvard Pragmatists, against whom he waged a fierce obscure war. . . .

It was Codger's function to teach me philosophy, philosophy! the intimate wisdom of things. He dealt in a variety of Hegelian stuff like nothing else in the world, but marvellously consistent with itself. It was a wonderful web he spun out of that queer big active childish brain that had never lusted or hated or grieved or feared or passionately loved, – a web of iridescent threads. He had luminous final theories about Love and Death and Immortality, odd matters they seemed for him to think about! and all his woven thoughts lay across my perception of the realities of things, as flimsy and irrelevant and clever and beautiful, oh! – as a dew-wet spider's web slung in the morning sunshine across the black mouth of a gun. . . .


4

All through those years of development I perceive now there must have been growing in me, slowly, irregularly, assimilating to itself all the phrases and forms of patriotism, diverting my religious impulses; utilizing my aesthetic tendencies, my dominating idea, the statesman's idea, that idea of social service which is the protagonist of my story, that real though complex passion for Making, making widely and greatly, cities, national order, civilization, whose interplay with all those other factors in life I have set out to present. It was growing in me – as one's bones grow, no man intending it.

I have tried to show how, quite early in my life, the fact of disorderliness, the conception of social life as being a multitudinous confusion out of hand, came to me. One always of course simplifies these things in the telling, but I do not think I ever saw the world at large in any other terms. I never at any stage entertained the idea which sustained my mother, and which sustains so many people in the world, – the idea that the universe, whatever superficial discords it may present, is a matter of fact 'all right,' is being steered to definite ends by a serene and unquestionable God. My mother thought that Order prevailed, and that disorder was just incidental and foredoomed rebellion ; I feel and have always felt that order rebels against and struggles against disorder, that order has an up-hill job, in gardens, experiments, suburbs, everything alike ; from the very beginnings of my experience I discovered hostility to order, a constant escaping from control.

The current of living and contemporary ideas in which my mind was presently swimming made all in the same direction ; in place of my mother's attentive, meticulous but occasionally extremely irascible Providence, the talk was all of the Struggle for Existence and the survival not of the Best – that was nonsense, but of the fittest to survive.

The attempts to rehabilitate Faith in the form of the Individualist's *laissez faire* never won upon me. I disliked Herbert Spencer all my life until I read his autobiography, and then I laughed a little and loved him. I remember as early as the City Merchants days how Britten and I scoffed at that pompous question-begging word 'Evolution,' having, so to speak, found it out. Evolution, some illuminating talker had remarked at the Britten lunch table, had led not only to man but to the liverfluke and skunk, obviously it might lead anywhere; order came into things only through the struggling mind of man. That lit things wonderfully for us. When I went up to Cambridge I was perfectly clear that life was a various and splendid disorder of forces that the spirit of man sets itself to tame. I have never since fallen away from that persuasion.

I do not think I was exceptionally precocious in reaching these conclusions and a sort of religious finality for myself by eighteen or nineteen. I know men and women vary very much in these matters, just as children do in learning to talk. Some will chatter at eighteen months and some will hardly speak until three, and the thing has very little to do with their subsequent mental quality. So it is with young people ; some will begin their religious, their social, their sexual interest at fourteen, some not until far on in the twenties. Britten and I belonged to one of the precocious types, and Cossington very probably another. It wasn't that there was anything priggish about any of us; we should have been prigs to have concealed our spontaneous interest and ape the theoretical boy.

The world of man centred for my imagination in London, it still centres there ; the real and present world, that is to say, as distinguished from the wonderlands of atomic and microscopic science and the stars and future time. I had travelled scarcely at all, I had never crossed the Channel, but I had read copiously and I had formed a very good working idea of this round globe with its mountains and wildernesses and forests and all the sorts and conditions of human life that were scattered over its surface. It was all alive, I felt, and changing every day ; how it was changing, and the changes men might bring about, fascinated my mind beyond measure.

I used to find a charm in old maps that showed The World as Known to the Ancients, and I wish I could now without any suspicion of self-deception write down compactly the world as it was known to me at nineteen. So far as extension went it was, I fancy, very like the world I know now at forty-two ; I had practically all the mountains and seas, boundaries and races, products and possibilities that I have now. But its intention was very different. All the interval has been increasing and deepening my social knowledge, replacing crude and secondhand impressions by felt and realized distinctions.

In 1895 – that was my last year with Britten, for I went up to Cambridge in September – my vision of the world had much the same relation to the vision I have today that an ill-drawn daub of a mask has to the direct vision of a human face. Britten and I looked at our world and saw – what did we see? Forms and colours side by side that we had no suspicion were inter-dependent. We had no conception of the roots of things or of the reactions of things. It did not seem to us, for example, that business had anything to do with government, or that money and means affected the heroic issues of war. There were no waggons in our war game, and where there were guns, there it was assumed the ammunition was gathered together. Finance again was a sealed book to us; we did not so much connect it with the broad aspects of human affairs as regard it as a sort of intrusive nuisance to be earnestly ignored by all right-minded men. We had no conception of the quality of politics, or how 'interests' came into such affairs; we believed men were swayed by purely intellectual convictions and were either right or wrong, honest or dishonest (in which case they deserved to be shot), good or bad. We knew nothing of mental inertia, and could imagine the opinion of a whole nation changed by one lucid and convincing exposition. We were capable of the most incongruous transfers from the scroll of history to our own times, we could suppose Brixton ravaged and Hampstead burnt in civil wars for the succession to the throne, or Cheapside a lane of death and the front of the Mansion House set about with guillotines in the course of an accurately transposed French Revolution. We rebuilt London by Act of Parliament, and once in a mood of hygienic enterprise we transferred its population *en masse* to the North Downs by an order of the Local Government Board. We thought nothing of throwing religious organizations out of employment or superseding all the newspapers by freely distributed bulletins. We could con-template the possibility of laws abolishing whole classes; we were equal to such a dream as the peaceful and orderly procla-mation of Communism from the steps of St Paul's Cathedral, after the passing of a simply worded bill, – a close and not unnaturally an exciting division carrying the third reading. I remember quite distinctly evolving that vision. We were then fully fifteen and we were perfectly serious about it. We were not fools; it was simply that as yet we had gathered no experience at all of the limits and powers of legislation and conscious collective intention. . . .

I think this statement does my boyhood justice, and yet I

have my doubts. It is so hard now to say what one understood and what one did not understand. It isn't only that every day changed one's general outlook, but also that a boy fluctuates between phases of quite adult understanding and phases of tawdrily magnificent puerility. Sometimes I myself was in those tumbrils that went along Cheapside to the Mansion house, a Sydney Cartonesque figure, a white defeated Mirabeau; sometimes it was I who sat judging and condemning and ruling (sleeping in my clothes and feeding very simply) the soul and autocrat of the Provisional Government, which occupied, of all inconvenient places! the General Post Office at St Martin's-le-Grand! ...

I cannot trace the development of my ideas at Cambridge, but I believe the mere physical fact of going two hours' journey away from London gave that place for the first time an effect of unity in my imagination. I got outside London. It became tangible instead of being a frame almost as universal as sea and sky.

At Cambridge my ideas ceased to live in a duologue; in exchange for Britten, with whom, however, I corresponded lengthily, stylishly and self-consciously for some years, I had now a set of congenial friends. I got talking with some of the younger dons, I learnt to speak in the Union, and in my little set we were all pretty busily sharpening each other's wits and correcting each other's interpretations. Cambridge made politics personal and actual. At City Merchants we had had no sense of effective contact; we boasted, it is true, an under secretary and a colonial governor among our old boys, but they were never real to us; such distinguished sons as returned to visit the old school were allusive and pleasant in the best Pinky Dinky style, and pretended to be in earnest about nothing but our football and cricket, to mourn the abolition of 'water,' and find a shuddering personal interest in the ancient swishing block. At Cambridge I felt for the first time that I touched the thing that was going on. Real living statesmen came down to debate in the Union, the older dons had been their college intimates, their sons and nephews expounded them to us and made them real to us. They invited us to entertain ideas; I found myself for the first time in my life expected to read and think and discuss, my secret vice had become a virtue.

That combination-room world is at least larger and more

populous and various than the world of schoolmasters. The Shoesmiths and Naylors who had been the aristocracy of City Merchants fell into their place in my mind ; they became an undistinguished mass on the more athletic side of Pinky Dinkyism and their hostility to ideas and to the expression of ideas ceased to limit and trouble me. The brighter men of each generation stay up ; these others go down to propagate their tradition, as the fathers of families, as mediocre professional men, as assistant masters in schools. Cambridge which perfects them is by the nature of things least oppressed by them, – except when it comes to a vote in Convocation.

We were still in those days under the shadow of the great Victorians. I never saw Gladstone (as I never set eyes on the old Queen), but he had resigned office only a year before I went up to Trinity and the Combination Rooms were full of personal gossip about him and Disraeli and the other big figures of the gladiatorial stage of Parliamentary history, talk that leaked copiously into such sets as mine. The ceiling of our guest chamber at Trinity was glorious with the arms of Sir William Harcourt, whose Death Duties had seemed at first like a socialist dawn. Mr Evesham we asked to come to the Union every year, Masters, Chamberlain and the old Duke of Devonshire ; they did not come indeed, but their polite refusals brought us all, as it were, within personal touch of them. One heard of cabinet councils and meetings at country houses. Some of us, pursuing such interests, went so far as to read political memoirs and the novels of Disraeli and Mrs Humphry Ward. From gossip, example and the illustrated newspapers one learnt something of the way in which parties were split, coalitions formed, how permanent officials worked and controlled their ministers, how measures were brought forward and projects modified.

And while I was getting the great leading figures on the political stage, who had been presented to me in my schooldays not so much as men as the pantomimic monsters of political caricature, while I was getting them reduced in my imagination to the stature of humanity, and their motives to the quality of impulses like my own, I was also acquiring in my Tripos work a constantly developing and enriching conception of the world of men as a complex of economic, intellectual and moral processes. . . .

## 5

Socialism is an intellectual Proteus, but to the men of my generation it came as the revolt of the workers. Rodbertus we never heard of and the Fabian Society we did not understand ; Marx and Morris, the Chicago Anarchists, *Justice* and the Social Democratic Federation (as it was then) presented socialism to our minds. Hatherleigh was the leading exponent of the new doctrines in Trinity, and the figure upon his wall of a huge-muscled, black-haired toiler, swaggering sledgehammer in hand across a revolutionary barricade, seemed the quintessence of what he had to expound. Landlord and capitalist had robbed and enslaved the workers, and were driving them quite automatically to inevitable insurrection. They would arise and the capitalist system would flee and vanish like the mists before the morning, like the dews before the sunrise, giving place in the most simple and obvious manner to an era of Right and Justice and Virtue and Well-Being, and in short a Perfectly Splendid Time.

I had already discussed this sort of socialism under the guidance of Britten, before I went up to Cambridge. It was all mixed up with ideas about freedom and natural virtue and a great scorn for kings, titles, wealth and officials, and it was symbolized by the red ties we wore. Our simple verdict on existing arrangements was that they were 'all wrong'. The rich were robbers and knew it, kings and princes were usurpers and knew it, religious teachers were imposters in league with power, the economic system was an elaborate plot on the part of the few to expropriate the many. We went about feeling scornful of all the current forms of life, forms that esteemed themselves solid, that were, we knew, no more than shapes painted on a curtain that was presently to be torn aside. . . .

It was Hatherleigh's poster and his capacity for overstating things, I think, that first qualified my simple revolutionary enthusiasm. Perhaps also I had met with Fabian publications, but if I did I forget the circumstances. And no doubt my innate constructiveness, with its practical corollary of an analytical treatment of the material supplied, was bound to push me on beyond this melodramatic interpretation of human affairs.

I compared that Working Man of the poster with any sort of

working man I knew. I perceived that the latter was not going to change, and indeed could not under any stimulus whatever be expected to change, into the former. It crept into my mind as slowly and surely as the dawn creeps into a room that the former was not, as I had at first rather glibly assumed, an 'ideal', but a complete misrepresentation of the quality and possibilities of things.

I do not know whether it was during my school-days or at Cambridge that I first began not merely to see the world as a great contrast of rich and poor, but to feel the massive effect of that multitudinous majority of people who toil continually, who are for ever anxious about ways and means, who are restricted, ill clothed, ill fed and ill housed, who have limited outlooks and continually suffer misadventures, hardships and distresses through the want of money. My lot had fallen upon the fringe of the possessing minority; if I did not know the want of necessities I knew shabbiness, and the world that let me go on to a university education intimated very plainly that there was not a thing beyond the primary needs that my stimulated imagination might demand that it would not be an effort for me to secure. A certain aggressive radicalism against the ruling and propertied classes followed almost naturally from my circumstances. It did not at first connect itself at all with the perception of a planless disorder in human affairs that had been forced upon me by the atmosphere of my upbringing, nor did it link me in sympathy with any of the profounder realities of poverty. It was a personal independent thing. The dingier people one saw in the back streets and lower quarters of Bromstead and Penge, the drift of dirty children, ragged old women, street loafers, grimy workers that made the social background of London, the stories one heard of privation and sweating, only joined up very slowly with the general propositions I was making about life. We could become splendidly eloquent about the social revolution and the triumph of the Proletariat after the class war, and it was only by a sort of inspiration that it came to me that my bedder, a garrulous old thing with a dusty black bonnet over one eye and an ostentatiously clean apron outside the dark mysteries that clothed her, or the cheeky little ruffians who yelled papers about the streets, were really material to such questions.

Directly any of us young socialists of Trinity found ourselves in immediate contact with servants or cadgers or gyps or bedders or plumbers or navvies or cabmen or railway porters we became unconsciously and unthinkingly aristocrats. Our voices altered, our gestures altered. We behaved just as all the other men, rich or poor, swatters or sportsmen or Pinky Dinkys, behaved, and exactly as we were expected to behave. On the whole it is a population of poor quality round about Cambridge, rather stunted and spiritless and very difficult to idealize. That theoretical Working Man of ours! – if we felt the clash at all we explained it, I suppose, by assuming that he came from another part of the country; Esmeer, I remember, who lived somewhere in the Fens, was very eloquent about the Cornish fishermen, and Hatherleigh, who was a Hampshire man, assured us we ought to know the Scottish miner. My private fancy was for the Lancashire operative because of his co-operative societies, and because what Lancashire thinks today England thinks tomorrow. . . . And also I had never been in Lancashire.

By little increments of realization it was that the profounder verities of the problem of socialism came to me. It helped me very much that I had to go down to the Potteries several times to discuss my future with my uncle and guardian; I walked about and saw Bursley Wakes and much of the human aspects of organized industrialism at close quarters for the first time. The picture of a splendid Working Man cheated out of his innate glorious possibilities, and presently to arise and dash this scoundrelly and scandalous system of private ownership to fragments, began to give place to a limitless spectacle of inefficiency, to a conception of millions of people not organized as they should be, not educated as they should be, not simply prevented from but incapable of nearly every sort of beauty, mostly kindly and well-meaning, mostly incompetent, mostly obstinate, and easily humbugged and easily diverted. Even the tragic and inspiring idea of Marx, that the poor were nearing a limit of painful experience, and awakening to a sense of intolerable wrongs, began to develop into the more appalling conception that the poor were simply in a witless uncomfortable inconclusive way – 'muddling along'; that they wanted nothing very definitely or very urgently, that mean fears enslaved them and mean satisfactions decoyed them, that they took the very gift of life itself with a spiritless lassitude, hoarding it, being rather anxious not to lose it than to use it in any way whatever.

The complete development of that realization was the work of many years. I had only the first intimations at Cambridge. But I did have intimations. Most acutely do I remember the doubts that followed the visit of Chris Robinson. Chris Robinson was heralded by such heroic anticipations, and he was so entirely what he had not anticipated.

Hatherleigh got him to come, arranged a sort of meeting for him at Redmayne's rooms in King's, and was very proud and proprietorial. It failed to stir Cambridge at all profoundly. Beyond a futile attempt to screw up Hatherleigh made by some inexpert duffers who used nails instead of screws and gimlets, there was no attempt to rag. Next day Chris Robinson went and spoke at Bennett Hall in Newnham College, and left Cambridge in the evening amidst the cheers of twenty men or so. Socialism was at such a low ebb politically in those days that it didn't even rouse men to opposition.

And there sat Chris under that flamboyant and heroic Worker of the poster, a little wrinkled grey-bearded apologetic man in ready-made clothes, with watchful innocent brown eyes and a persistent and invincible air of being out of his element. He sat with his stout boots tucked up under his chair, and clung to a tea-cup and saucer and looked away from us into the fire, and we all sat about on tables and chair-arms and window-sills and boxes and anywhere except upon chairs, after the manner of young men. The only other chair whose seat was occupied was the one containing his knitted woollen comforter and his picturesque old beach-photographer's hat. We were all shy and didn't know how to take hold of him now we had got him, and, which was disconcertingly unanticipated, he was manifestly having the same difficulty with us. We had expected to be gripped.

'I'll not be knowing what to say to these Chaps,' he repeated with a north-country quality in his speech.

We made reassuring noises.

The Ambassador of the Workers stirred his tea earnestly through an uncomfortable pause.

'I'd best tell 'em something of how things are in Lancashire, what with the new machines and all that,' he speculated at last with red reflections in his thoughtful eyes.

We had an inexcusable dread that perhaps he would make a mess of the meeting.

But when he was no longer in the unaccustomed meshes of refined conversation, but speaking with an audience before him, he became a different man. He declared he would explain to us just exactly what socialism was, and went on at once to an impassioned contrast of social conditions. 'You young men,' he said, 'come from homes of luxury; every need you feel is supplied –'

We sat and stood and sprawled about him, occupying every inch of Redmayne's floor space except the hearthrug-platform, and we listened to him and thought him over. He was the voice of wrongs that made us indignant and eager. We forgot for a time that he had been shy and seemed not a little incompetent, his provincial accent became a beauty of his earnest speech, we were carried away by his indignations. We looked with shining eyes at one another and at the various dons who had dropped in and were striving to maintain a front of judicious severity. We felt more and more that social injustice must cease, and cease forthwith. We felt we could not sleep upon it. At the end we clapped and murmured our applause and wanted badly to cheer.

Then like a lancet stuck into a bladder came the heckling. Denson, the indolent liberal-minded sceptic, did most of the questioning. He lay contorted in a chair, with his ugly head very low, his legs crossed and his left boot very high, and he pointed his remarks with a long thin hand and occasionally adjusted the unstable glasses that hid his watery eyes. 'I don't want to carp,' he began. 'The present system, I admit, stands condemned. Every present system always *has* stood condemned in the minds of intelligent men. But where it seems to me you get thin, is just where everybody has been thin, and that's when you come to the remedy.'

'Socialism,' said Chris Robinson, as if it answered everything, and Hatherleigh said 'Hear! Hear!' very resolutely.

'I suppose I *ought* to take that as an answer,' said Denson, getting his shoulder-blades well down to the seat of his chair;

'but I don't. I don't, you know. It's rather a shame to cross-examine you after this fine address of yours' – Chris Robinson on the hearthrug made acquiescent and inviting noises – 'but the real question remains how exactly are you going to end all these wrongs? There are the administrative questions. If you abolish the private owner, I admit you abolish a very complex and clumsy way of getting businesses run, land controlled and things in general administered, but you don't get rid of the need of administration, you know.'

'Democracy,' said Chris Robinson.

'Organized somehow,' said Denson. 'And it's just the How perplexes me. I can quite easily imagine a socialist state administered in a sort of scrambling tumult that would be worse than anything we have got now.'

'Nothing could be worse than things are now,' said Chris Robinson. 'I have seen little children –'

'I submit life on an ill-provisioned raft, for example, could easily be worse – or life in a beleaguered town.' ·

Murmurs.

They wrangled for some time, and it had the effect upon me of coming out from the glow of a good matinée performance into the cold daylight of late afternoon. Chris Robinson did not shine in conflict with Denson ; he was an orator and not a dialectician, and he missed Denson's points and displayed a disposition to plunge into untimely pathos and indignation. And Denson hit me curiously hard with one of his shafts. 'Suppose,' he said, 'you found yourself prime minister –'

I looked at Chris Robinson, bright-eyed and his hair a little ruffled and his whole being rhetorical, and measured him against the huge machine of government muddled and mysterious. Oh! but I was perplexed.

And then we took him back to Hatherleigh's rooms and drank beer and smoked about him while he nursed his knee with hairy-wristed hands that protruded from his flannel shirt, and drank lemonade under the cartoon of that emancipated Worker, and we had a great discursive talk with him.

'Eh! you should see our big meetings up north!' he said.

Denson had ruffled him and worried him a good deal, and ever and again he came back to that discussion. 'It's all very easy for your learned men to sit and pick holes,' he said, 'while the children suffer and die. They don't pick holes up north. They mean business.'

He talked, and that was the most interesting part of it all, of his going to work in a factory when he was twelve – 'when you Chaps were all with your mammies' – and how he had educated himself of nights until he would fall asleep at his reading.

'It's made many of us keen for all our lives,' he remarked, 'all that clemming for education. Why! I longed all through one winter to read a bit of Darwin. I must know about this Darwin if I die for it, I said. And I couldno' get the book.'

Hatherleigh made an enthusiastic noise and drank beer at him with round eyes over the mug.

'Well, anyhow I wasted no time on Greek and Latin,' said Chris Robinson. 'And one learns to go straight at a thing without splitting straws. One gets hold of the Elementals.'

(Well, did they? That was the gist of my perplexity.)

'One doesn't quibble,' he said, returning to his rankling memory of Denson, 'while men decay and starve.'

'But suppose,' I said, suddenly dropping into opposition, 'the alternative is to risk a worse disaster – or do something patently futile.'

'I don't follow that,' said Chris Robinson. 'We don't propose anything futile, so far as I can see.'

6

The prevailing force in my undergraduate days was not Socialism but Kiplingism. Our set was quite exceptional in its socialistic professions. And we were all, you must understand, very distinctly Imperialists also, and professed a vivid sense of the 'White Man's Burden.'

It is a little difficult now to get back to the feelings of that period; Kipling has since been so mercilessly and exhaustively mocked, criticized and torn to shreds – never was a man so violently exalted and then, himself assisting, so relentlessly called down. But in the middle nineties this spectacled and moustached little figure with its heavy chin and its general effect of vehement gesticulation, its wild shouts of boyish enthusiasm for effective force, its lyric delight in the sounds and colours, in the very odours of empire, its wonderful discovery of machinery and cotton waste and the under officer and the engineer, and 'shop' as a poetic dialect became almost a national symbol. He got hold of us wonderfully, he filled us with tinkling and haunting quotations, he stirred Britten and myself to futile imitations, he coloured the very idiom of our conversation. He rose to his climax with his 'Recessional,' while I was still an undergraduate.

What did he give me exactly?

He helped to broaden my geographical sense immensely, and he provided phrases for just that desire for discipline and devotion and organized effort the Socialism of our time failed to express, that the current socialist movement still fails, I think, to express. The sort of thing that follows, for example, tore something out of my inmost nature and gave it a shape, and I took it back from him shaped and let much of the rest of him, the tumult and the bullying, the hysteria and the impatience, the incoherence and inconsistency, go uncriticized for the sake of it:

Keep ye the Law – be swift in all obedience –
Clear the land of evil, drive the road and bridge the ford,
Make ye sure to each his own
That he reap where he hath sown;
By the peace among Our peoples let men know we serve the Lord!

And then again, and for all our later criticism, this sticks in my mind, sticks there now as quintessential wisdom:

The 'eathen in 'is blindness bows down to wood an' stone;
'E don't obey no orders unless they is 'is own;
'E keeps 'is side-arms awful: 'e leaves 'em all about,
An' then comes up the regiment an' pokes the 'eathen out.
    All along o' dirtiness, all along o' mess,
    All along o' doin' things rather-more-or-less,
    All along of abby-nay, kul, an' hazar-ho,
    Mind you keep your rifle an' yourself jus' so!

It is after all a secondary matter that Kipling, not having been born and brought up in Bromstead and Penge, and the war in South Africa being yet in the womb of time, could quite honestly entertain the now remarkable delusion that England had her side arms at that time kept anything but 'awful.' He learnt better, and we all learnt with him in the dark years of

101

exasperating and humiliating struggle that followed, and I do not see that we fellow-learners are justified in turning resentfully upon him for a common ignorance and assumption. . . .

South Africa seems always painted on the back cloth of my Cambridge memories. How immense those disasters seemed at the time, disasters our facile English world has long since contrived in any edifying or profitable sense to forget! How we thrilled to the shouting newspaper sellers as the first false flush of victory gave place to the realization of defeat! Far away there our army showed itself human, mortal and human in the sight of all the world, the pleasant officers we had imagined would change to wonderful heroes at the first crackling of rifles remained the pleasant, rather incompetent men they had always been, failing to imagine, failing to plan and cooperate, failing to grip. And the common soldiers, too, they were just what our streets and country-side had made them, no sudden magic came out of the war bugles for them. Neither splendid nor disgraceful were they, – just ill-trained and fairly plucky and wonderfully good-tempered men – paying for it. And how it lowered our vitality all that first winter to hear of Nicholson's Nek, and then presently close upon one another, to realize the bloody waste of Magersfontein, the shattering retreat from Stormberg, Colenso – Colenso, that blundering battle, with White, as it seemed, in Ladysmith near the point of surrender! and so through the long unfolding catalogue of bleak disillusionments, of aching, unconcealed anxiety lest worse should follow. To advance upon your enemy singing about his lack of cleanliness and method went out of fashion altogether! The dirty retrogressive Boer vanished from our scheme of illusion.

All through my middle Cambridge period, the guns boomed and the rifles crackled away there on the veldt, and the horsemen rode and the tale of accidents and blundering went on. Men, mules, horses, stores and money poured into South Africa, and the convalescent wounded streamed home. I see it in my memory as if I had looked at it all through a window instead of through the pages of the illustrated papers ; I recall as if I had been there the wide open spaces, the ragged hillsides, the open-order attacks of helmeted men in khaki, the scarce visible smoke of the guns, the wrecked trains in great lonely

102

places, the burnt isolated farms, and at last the blockhouses and the fences of barbed wire uncoiling and spreading for endless miles across the desert, netting the elusive enemy until at last, though he broke the meshes again and again, we had him in the toils. If one's attention strayed in the lecture-room it wandered to those battle-fields.

And that imagined panorama of war unfolds to an accompaniment of yelling newsboys in the narrow old Cambridge streets, of the flicker of papers hastily bought and torn open in the twilight, of the doubtful reception of doubtful victories, and the insensate rejoicings at last that seemed to some of us more shameful than defeats. . . .

7

A book that stands out among these memories, that stimulated me immensely so that I forced it upon my companions, half in the spirit of propaganda and half to test it by their comments, was Meredith's *One of Our Conquerors*. It is one of the books that have made me. In that I got a supplement and corrective of Kipling. It was the first detached and adverse criticism of the Englishman I had ever encountered. It must have been published already nine or ten years when I read it. The country had paid no heed to it, had gone on to the expensive lessons of the War because of the dull aversion our people feel for all such intimations, and so I could read it as a book justified. The war endorsed its every word for me, underlined each warning indication of the gigantic dangers that gathered against our system across the narrow seas. It discovered Europe to me, as watching and critical.

But while I could respond to all its criticisms of my country's intellectual indolence, of my country's want of training and discipline and moral courage, I remember that the idea that on the continent there were other peoples going ahead of us, mentally alert while we fumbled, disciplined while we slouched, aggressive and preparing to bring our Imperial pride to a reckoning, was extremely novel and distasteful to me. It set me worrying of nights. It put all my projects for social and political reconstruction upon a new uncomfortable footing. It made them no longer merely desirable but urgent. Instead of pride and the love of making one might own to a baser motive. Under Kipling's sway I had a little forgotten the continent of Europe, treated it as a mere envious echo to our own world-wide display. I began now to have a disturbing sense as it were of busy searchlights over the horizon. . . .

One consequence of the patriotic chagrin Meredith produced in me was an attempt to belittle his merit. 'It isn't a good novel, anyhow,' I said.

The charge I brought against it was, I remember, a lack of unity. It professed to be a study of the English situation in the early nineties, but it was all deflected, I said, and all the interest was confused by the story of Victor Radnor's fight with society to vindicate the woman he had loved and never married. Now in the retrospect and with a mind full of bitter enlightenment, I can do Meredith justice, and admit the conflict was not only essential but cardinal in his picture, that the terrible inflexibility of the rich aunts and the still more terrible claim of Mrs Burman Radnor, the 'infernal punctilio,' and Dudley Sowerby's limitations, were the central substance of that inalertness the book set itself to assail. So many things have been brought together in my mind that were once remotely separated. A people that will not valiantly face and understand and admit love and passion can understand nothing whatever. But in those days what is now just obvious truth to me was altogether outside my range of comprehension. . . .

8

As I seek to recapitulate the interlacing growth of my apprehension of the world, as I flounder among the half-remembered developments that found me a crude schoolboy and left me a man, there comes out, as if it stood for all the rest, my first holiday abroad. That did not happen until I was twenty-two. I was a fellow of Trinity, and the Peace of Vereeniging had just been signed.

I went with a man named Willersley, a man some years senior to myself, who had just missed a fellowship and the higher division of the Civil Service, and who had become an enthusiastic member of the London School Board, upon which the cumulative vote and the support of the 'advanced' people

104

had placed him. He had, like myself, a small independent income that relieved him of any necessity to earn a living, and he had a kindred craving for social theorizing and some form of social service. He had sought my acquaintance after reading a paper of mine (begotten by the visit of Chris Robinson) on the limits of pure democracy. It had marched with some thoughts of his own.

We went by train to Spiez on the Lake of Thun, then up the Gemmi, and thence with one or two halts and digressions and a little modest climbing we crossed over by the Antrona pass (on which we were benighted) into Italy, and by way of Domo d'ossola and the Santa Maria Maggiore valley to Cannobio, and thence up the lake to Locarno (where, as I shall tell, we stayed some eventful days) and so up the Val Maggia and over to Airolo and home.

As I write of that long tramp of ours, something of its freshness and enlargement returns to me. I feel again the faint pleasant excitement of the boat train, the trampling procession of people with hand baggage and laden porters along the platform of the Folkestone pier, the scarcely perceptible swaying of the moored boat beneath our feet. Then, very obvious and simple, the little emotion of standing out from the homeland and seeing the long white Kentish cliffs recede. One walked about the boat doing one's best not to feel absurdly adventurous, and presently a movement of people directed one's attention to a white lighthouse on a cliff to the east of us, coming up suddenly; and then one turned to scan the little different French coast villages, and then, sliding by in a pale sunshine, came a long wooden pier with oddly dressed children upon it, and the clustering town of Boulogne.

One took it all with the outward calm that became a young man of nearly three and twenty, but one was alive to one's fingertips with pleasing little stimulations. The custom house examination excited one, the strangeness of babble in a foreign tongue; one found the French of City Merchants and Cambridge a shy and viscous flow, and then one was standing in the train as it went slowly through the rail-laid street to Boulogne Ville, and one looked out at the world in French, porters in blouses, workmen in enormous purple trousers, police officers in peaked caps instead of helmets and romantically cloaked, big carts, all on two wheels instead of four, green shuttered casements instead of sash windows, and great numbers of neatly dressed women in economical mourning.

'Oh! there's a priest!' one said, and was betrayed into such-like artless cries.

It was a real other world, with different government and different methods, and in the night one was roused from uneasy slumbers and sat blinking and surly, wrapped up in one's couverture and with one's oreiller all awry, to encounter a new social phenomenon, the German official, so different in manner from the British; and when one woke again after that one had come to Bâle, and out one tumbled to get coffee in Switzerland. . . .

I have been over that route dozens of times since, but it still revives a certain lingering youthfulness, a certain sense of cheerful release in me.

I remember that I and Willersley became very sociological as we ran on to Spiez, and made all sorts of generalizations from the steeply sloping fields on the hillsides, and from the people we saw on platforms and from little differences in the way things were done.

The clean prosperity of Bâle and Switzerland, the big clean stations, filled me with patriotic misgivings, as I thought of the vast dirtiness of London, the mean dirtiness of Cambridgeshire. It came to me that perhaps my scheme of international values was all wrong, that quite stupendous possibilities and challenges for us and our empire might be developing here – and I recalled Meredith's Skepsey in France with a new understanding.

Willersley had dressed himself in a world-worn Norfolk suit of greenish gray tweeds that ended unfamiliarly at his rather impending, spectacled, intellectual visage. I didn't, I remember, like the contrast of him with the drilled Swiss and Germans about us. Convict-coloured stockings and vast hobnailed boots finished him below, and all his luggage was a borrowed rucksack that he had tied askew. He did not want to shave in the train, but I made him at one of the Swiss stations – I dislike these Oxford slovenlinesses – and then, confound him! he cut himself and bled. . . .

Next morning we were breathing a thin exhilarating air that

106

seemed to have washed our very veins to an incredible cleanliness, and eating hard-boiled eggs in a vast clear space of rime-edged rocks, snow-mottled, above a blue-gashed glacier. All about us the monstrous rock surfaces rose towards the shining peaks above, and there were winding moraines from which the ice had receded, and then dark clustering fir trees far below.

I had an extraordinary feeling of having come out of things, of being outside.

'But this is the round world!' I said, with a sense of never having perceived it before ; 'this is the round world!'

9

That holiday was full of big comprehensive effects; the first view of the Rhône valley and the distant Valaisian Alps, for example, which we saw from the shoulder of the mountain above the Gemmi, and the early summer dawn breaking over Italy as we moved from our night's crouching and munched bread and chocolate and stretched our stiff limbs among the tumbled and precipitous rocks that hung over Lake Cingolo, and surveyed the winding tiring rocky track going down and down to Antronapiano.

And our thoughts were as comprehensive as our impressions. Willersley's mind abounded in historical matter ; he had an inaccurate abundant habit of topographical reference ; he made me see and trace and see again the Roman Empire sweep up these winding valleys, and the coming of the first great Peace among the warring tribes of men. . . .

In the retrospect each of us seems to have been talking about our outlook almost continually. Each of us, you see, was full of the same question, very near and altogether predominant to us, the question: 'What am I going to do with my life?' He saw it almost as importantly as I, but from a different angle, because his choice was largely made and mine still hung in the balance.

'I feel we might do so many things,' I said, 'and everything that calls one, calls one away from something else.'

Willersley agreed without any modest disavowals.

'We have got to think out,' he said, 'just what we are and what we are up to. We've got to do that now. And then – it's one of those questions it is inadvisable to reopen subsequently.'

He beamed at me through his glasses. The sententious use of long words was a playful habit with him, that and a slight deliberate humour, habits occasional Extension Lecturing was doing very much to intensify.

'You've made your decision?'

He nodded with a peculiar forward-movement of his head. 'How would you put it?'

'Social Service – education. Whatever else matters or doesn't matter, it seems to me there is one thing we *must* have and increase, and that is the number of people who can think a little – and have' – he beamed again – 'an adequate sense of causation.'

'You're sure it's worth while?'

'For me – certainly. I don't discuss that any more.'

'I don't limit myself too narrowly,' he added. 'After all, the work is all one. We who know, we who feel, are building the great modern state, joining wall to wall and way to way, the new great England rising out of the decaying old . . . we are the real statesmen – I like that use of "statesmen." . . .'

'Yes,' I said with many doubts. 'Yes, of course. . . .'

Willersley is middle-aged now, with silver in his hair and a deepening benevolence in his always amiable face, and he has very fairly kept his word. He has lived for social service and to do vast masses of useful, undistinguished, fertilizing work. Think of the days of arid administrative plodding and of contention still more arid and unrewarded, that he must have spent! His little affectations of gesture and manner, imitative affectations for the most part, have increased, and the humorous beam and the humorous intonations have become a thing he puts on every morning like an old coat. His devotion is mingled with a considerable whimsicality, and they say he is easily flattered by subordinates and easily offended into opposition by colleagues ; he has made mistakes at times and followed wrong courses, still there he is, a flat contradiction to all the ordinary doctrine of motives, a man who has foregone any chances of wealth and profit, foregone any easier paths to distinction, foregone marriage and parentage, in order to serve the community. He does it without any fee or reward except his personal self-satisfaction in doing this work, and he does it without any hope of future joys and punishments, for he is an implacable Rationalist. No doubt he idealizes himself a little, and dreams of recognition. No doubt he gets his pleasure from a sense of power, from the spending and husbanding of large sums of public money, and from the inevitable proprietorship he must feel in the fair, fine, well-ordered schools he has done so much to develop. 'But for me,' he can say 'there would have been a Job about those diagrams, and that subject or this would have been less ably taught.' ...

The fact remains that for him the rewards have been adequate, if not to content at any rate to keep him working. Of course he covets the notice of the world he has served, as a lover covets the notice of his mistress. Of course he thinks somewhere, somewhen, he will get credit. Only last year I heard some men talking of him, and they were noting, with little mean smiles, how he had shown himself self-conscious while there was talk of some honorary degree-giving or other; it would, I have no doubt, please him greatly if his work were to flower into a crimson gown in some Academic parterre. Why shouldn't it? But that is incidental vanity at the worst; he goes on anyhow. Most men don't.

But we had our walk twenty years and more ago now. He was oldish even then as a young man, just as he is oldish still in middle age. Long may his industrious elderliness flourish for the good of the world! He lectured a little in conversation then ; he lectures more now and listens less, toilsomely disentangling what you already understand, giving you in detail the data you know ; these are things like callosities that come from a man's work.

Our long three weeks' talk comes back to me as a memory of ideas and determinations slowly growing, all mixed up with a smell of wood smoke and pine woods and huge precipices and remote gleams of snow-fields and the sound of cascading torrents rushing through deep gorges far below. It is mixed, too, with gossips with waitresses and fellow-travellers, with my first essays in colloquial German and Italian, with disputes about the way to take, and other things that I will tell of in another section. But the white passion of human service was our dominant theme. Not simply perhaps nor altogether unselfishly, did we want to do fine and noble things, to help in their developing, to lessen misery, to broaden and exalt life. It

109

is very hard – perhaps it is impossible – to present in a page or two the substance and quality of nearly a month's conversation, conversation that is casual and discursive in form, that ranges carelessly from triviality to immensity, and yet is constantly resuming a constructive process, as workmen on a wall loiter and jest and go and come back, and all the while build.

We got it more and more definite that the core of our purpose beneath all its varied aspects must needs be order and discipline. 'Muddle,' said I, 'is the enemy.' That remains my belief to this day. Clearness and order, light and foresight, these things I know for Good. It was muddle had just given us all the still freshly painful disasters and humiliations of the war, muddle that gives us the visibly sprawling disorder of our cities and industrial country-side, muddle that gives us the waste of life, the limitations, wretchedness and unemployment of the poor. Muddle! I remember myself quoting Kipling –

> All along o' dirtiness, all along o' mess,
> All along o'doin' things rather-more-or-less.

'We build the state,' we said over and over again. 'That is what we are for – servants of the new reorganization!'

We planned, half in earnest and half Utopianizing, a League of Social Service.

We talked of the splendid world of men that might grow out of such unpaid and ill-paid work as we were setting our faces to do. We spoke of the intricate difficulties, the monstrous passive resistances, the hostilities to such a development as we conceived our work subserved, and we spoke with that underlying confidence in the invincibility of the causes we adopted that is natural to young and scarcely tried men.

We talked much of the detailed life of politics so far as it was known to us, and there Willersley was more experienced and far better informed than I; we discussed possible combinations and possible developments, and the chances of some great constructive movement coming from the heart-searchings the Boer war had occasioned. We would sink to gossip – even at the Suetonius level. Willersley would decline towards illuminating anecdotes that I capped more or less loosely from my private reading. We were particularly wise, I remember, upon

110

the management of newspapers, because about that we knew nothing whatever. We perceived that great things were to be done through newspapers. We talked of swaying opinion and moving great classes to massive action.

Men are egotistical even in devotion. All our splendid projects were thickest with the first personal pronoun. We both could write, and all that we said in general terms was reflected in the particular in our minds; it was ourselves we saw, and no others, writing and speaking that moving word. We had already produced manuscript and passed the initiations of proof reading; I had been a frequent speaker in the Union, and Willersley was an active man on the School Board. Our feet were already on the lower rungs that led up and up. He was six and twenty, and I twenty-two. We intimated our individual careers in terms of bold expectation. I had prophetic glimpses of walls and hoardings clamorous with 'Vote for Remington,' and Willersley no doubt saw himself chairman of this committee and that, saying a few slightly ironical words after the declaration of the poll, and then sitting friendly beside me on the government benches. There was nothing impossible in such dreams. Why not the Board of Education for him? My preference at that time wavered between the Local Government Board – I had great ideas about town-planning, about revisions of municipal areas and reorganized internal transit – and the War Office. I swayed strongly towards the latter as the journey progressed. My educational bias came later.

The swelling ambitions that have tramped over Alpine passes! How many of them, like mine, have come almost within sight of realization before they failed?

There were times when we posed like young gods (of unassuming exterior), and times when we were full of the absurdest little solicitudes about our prospects. There were times when one surveyed the whole world of men as if it was a little thing at one's feet, and by way of contrast I remember once lying in bed – it must have been during this holiday, though I cannot for the life of me fix where – and speculating whether perhaps some day I might not be a K.C.B., Sir Richard Remington, K.C.B., M.P.

But the big style prevailed. . . .

We could not tell from minute to minute whether we were

planning for a world of solid reality, or telling ourselves fairy tales about this prospect of life. So much seemed possible, and everything we could think of so improbable. There were lapses when it seemed to me I could never be anything but just the entirely unimportant and undistinguished young man I was for ever and ever. I couldn't even think of myself as five and thirty.

Once I remember Willersley going over a list of failures, and why they had failed – but young men in the twenties do not know much about failures.

## 10

Willersley and I professed ourselves Socialists, but by this time I knew my Rodbertus as well as my Marx, and there was much in our socialism that would have shocked Chris Robinson as much as anything in life could have shocked him. Socialism as a simple democratic cry we had done with for ever. We were socialists because Individualism for us meant muddle, meant a crowd of separated, undisciplined little people all obstinately and ignorantly doing things jarringly, each one in his own way. 'Each,' I said, quoting words of my father's that rose apt in my memory, 'snarling from his own little bit of property, like a dog tied to a cart's tail.'

'Essentially,' said Willersley, 'essentially we're for conscription, in peace and war alike. The man who owns property is a public official and has to behave as such. That's the gist of socialism as I understand it.'

'Or be dismissed from his post,' I said, 'and replaced by some better sort of official. A man's none the less an official because he's irresponsible. What he does with his property affects people just the same. Private! No one is really private but an outlaw. . . .'

Order and devotion were the very essence of our socialism, and a splendid collective vigour and happiness its end. We projected an ideal state, an organized state as confident and powerful as modern science, as balanced and beautiful as a body, as beneficent as sunshine, the organized state that should end muddle for ever; it ruled all our ideas and gave form to all our ambitions.

Every man was to be definitely related to that, to have his

112

predominant duty to that. Such was the England renewed we had in mind, and how to serve that end, to subdue undisciplined worker and undisciplined wealth to it, and make the Scientific Commonweal King, was the continuing substance of our intercourse.

## 11

Every day the wine of the mountains was stronger in our blood, and the flush of our youth deeper. We would go in the morning sunlight along some narrow Alpine mule-path shouting large suggestions for national reorganization, and weighing considerations as lightly as though the world was wax in our hands. 'Great England,' we said in effect, over and over again, 'and we will be among the makers! England renewed! The country has been warned; it has learnt its lesson. The disasters and anxieties of the war have sunk in. England has become serious. . . . Oh! there are big things before us to do; big enduring things!'

One evening we walked up to the loggia of a little pilgrimage church, I forget its name, that stands out on a conical hill at the head of a winding stair above the town of Locarno. Down below the houses clustered amidst a confusion of heat-bitten greenery. I had been sitting silently on the parapet, looking across to the purple mountain masses where Switzerland passes into Italy, and the drift of our talk seemed suddenly to gather to a head.

I broke into speech, giving form to the thoughts that had been accumulating. My words have long since passed out of my memory, the phrases of familiar expression have altered for me, but the substance remains as clear as ever. I said how we were in our measure emperors and kings, men undriven, free to do as we pleased with life; we classed among the happy ones, our bread and common necessities were given us for nothing, we had abilities, – it wasn't modesty but cowardice to behave as if we hadn't – and Fortune watched us to see what we might do with opportunity and the world.

'There are so many things to do, you see,' began Willersley, in his judicial lecturer's voice.

'So many things we may do,' I interrupted, 'with all these

113

years before us. . . . We're exceptional men. It's our place, our duty, to do things.

'Here anyhow,' I said, answering the faint amusement of his face, 'I've got no modesty. Everything conspires to set me up. Why should I run about like all those grubby little beasts down there, seeking nothing but mean little vanities and indulgences – and then take credit for modesty? I *know* I am capable. I *know* I have imagination. Modesty! I know if I don't attempt the very biggest things in life I am a damned shirk. The very biggest! Somebody has to attempt them. I feel like a loaded gun that is only a little perplexed because it has to find out just where to aim itself. . . .'

The lake and the frontier villages, a white puff of steam on the distant railway to Luino, the busy boats and steamers trailing triangular wakes of foam, the long vista eastward towards battlemented Bellinzona, the vast mountain distances, now tinged with sunset light, behind this nearer landscape, and the southward waters with remote coast towns shining dimly, waters that merged at last in a luminous golden haze, made a broad panoramic spectacle. It was as if one surveyed the world, – and it was like the games I used to set out upon my nursery floor. I was exalted by it ; I felt larger than men. So kings should feel.

That sense of largeness came to me then, and it has come to me since, again and again, a splendid intimation or a splendid vanity. Once, I remember, when I looked at Genoa from the mountain crest behind the town and saw that multitudinous place in all its beauty of width and abundance and clustering human effort, and once as I was steaming past the brown low hills of Staten Island towards the towering vigour and clamorous vitality of New York City, that mood rose to its quintessence. And once it came to me, as I shall tell, on Dover cliffs. And a hundred times when I have thought of England as our country might be, with no wretched poor, no wretched rich, a nation armed and ordered, trained and purposeful amidst its vales and rivers, that emotion of collective ends and collective purposes has returned to me. I felt as great as humanity. For a brief moment I was humanity, looking at the world I had made and had still to make. . . .

## 12

And mingled with these dreams of power and patriotic service there was another series of a different quality and a
different colour, like the antagonistic colour of a shot silk. The
white life and the red life, contrasted and interchanged, passing
swiftly at a turn from one to another, and refusing ever to
mingle peacefully one with the other. I was asking myself
openly and distinctly: what are you going to do for the world?
What are you going to do with yourself? and with an increasing strength and persistence Nature in spite of my averted attention was asking me in penetrating undertones: what are you
going to do about this other fundamental matter, the beauty of
girls and women and your desire for them?

I have told of my sisterless youth and the narrow circumstances of my upbringing. It made all womenkind mysterious
to me. If it had not been for my Staffordshire cousins I do not
think I should have known any girls at all until I was twenty.
Of Staffordshire I will tell a little later. But I can remember still
how through all those ripening years, the thought of women's
beauty, their magic presence in the world beside me and the
unknown, untried reactions of their intercourse, grew upon me
and grew, as a strange presence grows in a room when one is
occupied by other things. I busied myself and pretended to be
wholly occupied, and there the woman stood, full half of life
neglected, and it seemed to my averted mind sometimes that she
was there clad and dignified and divine, and sometimes Aphrodite shining and commanding, and sometimes that Venus who
stoops and allures.

This travel abroad seemed to have released a multitude of
things in my mind; the clear air, the beauty of the sunshine,
the very blue of the glaciers made me feel my body and quickened all those disregarded dreams. I saw the sheathed beauty
of women's forms all about me, in the cheerful waitresses at
the inns, in the pedestrians one encountered in the tracks, in
the chance fellow-travellers at the hotel tables. 'Confound it!'
said I, and talked all the more zealously of that greater England
that was calling us.

I remember that we passed two Germans, an old man and a
tall fair girl, father and daughter, who were walking down from

Saas. She came swinging and shining towards us, easy and strong. I worshipped her as she approached.

'Gut Tag!' said Willersley, removing his hat.

'Morgen!' said the old man, saluting.

I stared stockishly at the girl, who passed with an indifferent face.

That sticks in my mind as a picture remains in a room, it has kept there bright and fresh as a thing seen yesterday, for twenty years. . . .

I flirted hesitatingly once or twice with comely serving girls, and was a little ashamed lest Willersley should detect the keen interest I took in them, and then as we came over the pass from Santa Maria Maggiore to Cannobio, my secret preoccupation took me by surprise and flooded me and broke down my pretences.

The women in that valley are very beautiful – women vary from valley to valley in the Alps and are plain and squat here and divinities five miles away – and as we came down we passed a group of five or six of them resting by the wayside. Their burthens were beside them, and one like Ceres held a reaping-hook in her brown hand. She watched us approaching and smiled faintly, her eyes at mine.

There was some greeting, and two of them laughed together. We passed.

'Glorious girls they were,' said Willersley, and suddenly an immense sense of boredom enveloped me. I saw myself striding on down that winding road, talking of politics and parties and bills of parliament and all sorts of desiccated things. That road seemed to me to wind on for ever down to dust and infinite dreariness. I knew it for a way of death. Reality was behind us.

Willersley set himself to draw a sociological moral. 'I'm not so sure,' he said in a voice of intense discriminations, 'after all, that agricultural work isn't good for women.'

'Damn agricultural work!' I said, and broke out into a vigorous cursing of all I held dear. 'Fettered things we are!' I cried. 'I wonder why I stand it!'

'Stand what?'

'Why don't I go back and make love to those girls and let the world and you and everything go hang? Deep breasts and

116

rounded limbs – and we poor emasculated devils go tramping by with the blood of youth in us! . . .'

'I'm not quite sure, Remington,' said Willersley, looking at me with a deliberately quaint expression over his glasses, 'that picturesque scenery is altogether good for your morals.'

## 13

That fever was still in my blood when we came to Locarno.

Along the hot and dusty lower road between the Orrido of Traffiume and Cannobio Willersley had developed his first blister. And partly because of that and partly because there was a bag at the station that gave us the refreshment of clean linen and partly because of the lazy lower air into which we had come, we decided upon three or four days' sojourn in the Empress Hotel.

We dined that night at a table-d'hôte, and I found myself next to an Englishwoman who began a conversation that was resumed presently in the hotel lounge. She was a woman of perhaps thirty-three or thirty-four, slenderly built, with a warm reddish skin and very abundant fair golden hair, the wife of a petulant-looking heavy-faced man of perhaps fifty-three, who smoked a cigar and dozed over his coffee and presently went to bed. 'He always goes to bed like that,' she confided startlingly. 'He sleeps after all his meals. I never knew such a man to sleep.'

Then she returned to our talk, whatever it was.

We had begun at the dinner table with itineraries and the usual topographical talk, and she had envied our pedestrian travel. 'My husband doesn't walk,' she said. 'His heart is weak and he cannot manage the hills.'

There was something friendly and adventurous in her manner; she conveyed she liked me, and when presently Willersley drifted off to write letters our talk sank at once to easy confidential undertones. I felt enterprising, and indeed it is easy to be daring with people one has never seen before and may never see again. I said I loved beautiful scenery and all beautiful things, and the pointing note in my voice made her laugh. She told me I had bold eyes, and so far as I can remember I said she made them bold. 'Blue they are,' she remarked, smiling archly. 'I like blue eyes.' Then I think we compared ages, and she said she was the Woman of Thirty, 'George Moore's Woman of Thirty.'

I had not read George Moore at the time, but I pretended to understand.

That, I think, was our limit that evening. She went to bed, smiling good night quite prettily down the big staircase, and I and Willersley went out to smoke in the garden. My head was full of her, and I found it necessary to talk about her. So I made her a problem in sociology. 'Who the deuce are these people?' I said, 'and how do they get a living? They seem to have plenty of money. He strikes me as being – Willersley, what is a drysalter? I think he's a retired drysalter.'

Willersley theorized while I thought of the woman and that provocative quality of dash she had displayed. The next day at lunch she and I met like old friends. A huge mass of private thinking during the interval had been added to our effect upon one another. We talked for a time of insignificant things.

'What do you do,' she asked rather quickly, 'after lunch? Take a siesta?'

'Sometimes,' I said, and hung for a moment eye to eye.

We hadn't a doubt of each other, but my heart was beating like a steamer propeller when it lifts out of the water.

'Do you get a view from your room?' she asked after a pause.

'It's on the third floor, Number seventeen, near the staircase. My friend's next door.'

She began to talk of books. She was interested in Christian Science, she said, and spoke of a book. I forget altogether what that book was called, though I remember to this day with the utmost exactness the purplish magenta of its cover. She said she would lend it to me, and hesitated.

Willersley wanted to go for an expedition across the lake that afternoon, but I refused. He made some other proposals that I rejected abruptly. 'I shall write in my room,' I said.

'Why not write down here?'

'I shall write in my room.' I snarled like a thwarted animal, and he looked at me curiously. 'Very well,' he said ; 'then I'll make some notes and think about that order of ours out under the magnolias.'

I hovered about the lounge for a time buying postcards and feverishly restless, watching the movements of the other people.

118

Finally I went up to my room and sat down by the windows, staring out. There came a little tap at the unlocked door, and in an instant, like the go of a taut bowstring, I was up and had it open.

'Here is that book,' she said, and we hesitated.

'*Come in!*' I whispered, trembling from head to foot.

'You're just a boy,' she said in a low tone.

I did not feel a bit like a lover, I felt like a burglar with the safedoor nearly opened. 'Come in,' I said almost impatiently, for any one might .be in the passage, and I gripped her wrist and drew her towards me.

'What do you mean?' she answered with a faint smile on her lips, and awkward and yielding.

I shut the door behind her, still holding her with one hand, then turned upon her – she was laughing nervously – and without a word drew her to me and kissed her. And I remember that as I kissed her, her face, close to mine, became solemn and tender.

She was suddenly a different being from the discontented wife who had tapped a moment since on my door, a woman transfigured.

That evening I came down to dinner a monster of pride, for behold! I was a man. I felt myself the most wonderful and unprecedented of adventurers. It was hard to believe that any one in the world before had done as much. My mistress and I met smiling, we carried things off admirably, and it seemed to me that Willersley was the dullest old dog in the world. I wanted to give him advice. I wanted to give him derisive pokes. After dinner and coffee in the lounge I was too excited and hilarious to go to bed, I made him come with me down to the café under the arches by the pier, and there drank beer and talked extravagant nonsense about everything under the sun, in order not to talk about the happenings of the afternoon. All the time something shouted within me: 'I am a man! I am a man!' . . .

'What shall we do tomorrow?' said he.

'I'm for loafing,' I said. 'Let's row in the morning and spend tomorrow afternoon just as we did today.'

'They say the church behind the town is worth seeing.'

'We'll go up about sunset; that's the best time for it. We can start about five.'

119

We heard music, and went further along the arcade to discover a place where girls in operatic Swiss peasant costume were singing and dancing on a creaking, protesting little stage. I eyed their generous display of pink neck and arm with the seasoned eyes of a man who has lived in the world. Life was perfectly simple and easy, I felt, if one took it the right way.

Next day Willersley wanted to go on, but I delayed. Altogether I kept him back four days. Then abruptly my mood changed, and we decided to start early the following morning. I remember, though a little indistinctly, the feeling of my last talk with that woman whose surname, odd as it may seem, either I never learnt or have forgotten. (Her christian name was Milly.) She was tired and rather low-spirited, and disposed to be sentimental, and for the first time in our intercourse I found myself liking her for the sake of her own personality. There was something kindly and generous appearing behind the veil of naïve and uncontrolled sensuality she had worn. There was a curious quality of motherliness in her attitude to me that something in my nature answered and approved. She didn't pretend to keep it up that she had yielded to my initiative. 'I've done you no harm,' she said a little doubtfully, an odd note for a man's victim! And, 'we've had a good time. You have liked me, haven't you?'

She interested me in her lonely dissatisfied life; she was childless and had no hope of children, and her husband was the only son of a rich meat salesman, very mean, a mighty smoker – 'he reeks of it,' she said, 'always' – and interested in nothing but golf, billiards (which he played very badly), pigeon shooting, convivial Free Masonry and Stock Exchange punting. Mostly they drifted about the Riviera. Her mother had contrived her marriage when she was eighteen. They were the first samples I ever encountered of the great multitude of functionless property owners which encumbers modern civilization – but at the time I didn't think much of that aspect of them. . . .

I tell all this business as it happened without comment, because I have no comment to make. It was all strange to me, strange rather than wonderful, and, it may be, some dream of beauty died for ever in those furtive meetings; it happened to me, and I could scarcely have been more irresponsible in the

120

matter or controlled events less if I had been suddenly pushed over a cliff into water. I swam, of course – finding myself in it. Things tested me, and I reacted, as I have told. The bloom of my innocence, if ever there had been such a thing, was gone. And here is the remarkable thing about it ; at the time and for some days I was over-weeningly proud ; I have never been so proud before or since ; I felt I had been promoted to virility ; I was unable to conceal my exultation from Willersley. It was a mood of shining shameless ungracious self-approval. As he and I went along in the cool morning sunshine by the rice-fields in the throat of the Val Maggia a silence fell between us.

Willersley looked at me over the corner of his spectacles. 'I know,' he said abruptly.

'Know what?' I asked.

'I heard her. I heard her whispering. . . . The whispering and rustling and so on. I was in my room yesterday. . . . Any one might have heard you. . . .'

I went on with my head in the air. 'Well,' said I, 'since you know, I won't deny it. Why shouldn't I?'

'You might have been caught, and that would have meant endless trouble. You might have incurred all sorts of consequences. What did you know about her? . . . We have wasted four days in that hot close place. When we found that League of Social Service we were talking about,' he said with a determined eye upon me, 'chastity will be first among the virtues prescribed.'

'I shall form a rival league,' I said a little damped. 'I'm hanged if I give up a single desire in me until I know why.'

He lifted his chin and stared before him through his glasses at nothing. 'There are some things,' he said, 'that a man who means to work – to do great public services – *must* turn his back upon. I'm not discussing the rights or wrongs of this sort of thing. It happens to be the conditions we work under. It will probably always be so. If you want to experiment in that way, if you want even to discuss it, – out you go from political life. You must know that's so. . . . You're a strange man, Remington, with a kind of kink in you. You've a sort of force. You might happen to do immense things. . . . Only –'

He stopped. He had said all that he had forced himself to say.

'I mean to take myself as I am,' I said. 'I'm going to get

experience for humanity out of all my talents – and bury nothing.'

Willersley twisted his face to its humorous expression. 'I doubt if sexual proclivities,' he said drily, 'come within the scope of the parable.'

I let that go for a little while. Then I broke out. 'Sex!' said I, 'is a fundamental thing in life. We went through all this at Trinity. I'm going to look at it, experience it, think about it – and get it square with the rest of life. Career and Politics must take their chances of that. It's part of the general English slackness that they won't look this in the face. Gods! what a muffled time we're coming out of! Sex means breeding, and breeding is a necessary function in a nation. The Romans broke up upon that. The Americans fade out amidst their successes. Eugenics –'

'*That* wasn't Eugenics,' said Willersley.

'It was a woman,' I said after a little interval, feeling oddly that I had failed altogether to answer him and yet had a strong dumb case against him.

Book the Second

# Margaret

# Chapter the First

## Margaret in Staffordshire

### 1

I must go back a little way with my story. In the previous book I have described the kind of education that happens to a man of my class nowadays, and it has been convenient to leap a phase in my experience that I must now set out at length. I want to tell in this second book how I came to marry, and to do that I must give something of the atmosphere in which I first met my wife and some intimations of the forces that went to her making. I met her in Staffordshire while I was staying with that uncle of whom I have already spoken, the uncle who sold my father's houses and settled my mother in Penge. Margaret was twenty then and I was twenty-two.

It was just before the walking tour in Switzerland that opened up so much of the world to me. I saw her once, for an afternoon, and circumstances so threw her up in relief that I formed a very vivid memory of her. She was in the sharpest contrast with the industrial world about her ; she impressed me as a dainty blue flower might do, come upon suddenly on a clinker heap. She remained in my mind at once a perplexing interrogation and a symbol. . . .

But first I must tell of my Staffordshire cousins and the world that served as a foil for her.

### 2

I first went to stay with my cousins when I was an awkward youth of sixteen, wearing deep mourning for my mother. My uncle wanted to talk things over with me, he said, and if he could, to persuade me to go into business instead of going up to Cambridge.

I remember that visit on account of all sorts of novel things, but chiefly, I think, because it was the first time I encountered anything that deserves to be spoken of as wealth. For the first

125

time in my life I had to do with people who seemed to have endless supplies of money, unlimited good clothes, numerous servants; whose daily life was made up of things that I had hitherto considered to be treats or exceptional extravagances. My cousins of eighteen and nineteen took cabs, for instance, with the utmost freedom, and travelled first-class in the local trains that run up and down the district of the Five Towns, with an entire unconsciousness of the magnificence, as it seemed to me, of such a proceeding.

The family occupied a large villa in Newcastle, with big lawns before it and behind, a shrubbery with quite a lot of shrubs, a coach house and stable, and subordinate dwelling-places for the gardener and the coachman. Every bedroom contained a gas heater and a canopied brass bedstead, and had a little bath-room attached equipped with the porcelain baths and fittings my uncle manufactured, bright and sanitary and stamped with his name, and the house was furnished throughout with chairs and tables in bright shining wood, soft and pre-valently red Turkish carpets, cosy corners, curtained archways, gold-framed landscapes, overmantels, a dining-room sideboard like a palace, with a large Tantalus, and electric light fittings of a gay and expensive quality. There was a fine billiard-room on the ground floor with three comfortable sofas and a rotating bookcase containing an excellent collection of the English and American humorists from *Three Men in a Boat* to the penulti-mate Mark Twain. There was also a conservatory opening out of the dining-room, to which the gardener brought potted flow-ers in their season. ...

My aunt was a little woman with a scared look and a cap that would get over one eye, not very like my mother, and nearly eight years her junior; she was very much concerned with keeping everything nice, and unmercifully bullied by my two cousins, who took after their father and followed the imaginations of their own hearts. They were tall, dark, warmly flushed girls, handsome rather than pretty. Gertrude, the eldest and tallest, had eyes that were almost black; Sybil was of a stouter build, and her eyes, of which she was shamelessly proud, were dark blue. Sybil's hair waved, and Gertrude's was severely straight. They treated me on my first visit with all the contempt of the adolescent girl for a boy a little younger and infinitely less expert in the business of life than herself. They were very busy with the writings of notes and certain mysterious goings and comings of their own, and left me very much to my own devices. Their speech in my presence was full of unfathomable allusions. They were the sort of girls who will talk over and through an uninitiated stranger with the pleasantest sense of superiority.

I met them at breakfast and at lunch and at the half-past six o'clock high tea that formed the third chief meal of the day. I heard them rattling off the compositions of Chaminade and Moskowski, with great decision and effect, and hovered on the edge of tennis foursomes where it was manifest to the dullest intelligence that my presence was unnecessary. Then I went off to find some readable book in the place, but apart from miscellaneous popular novels, some veterinary works, a number of comic books, old bound volumes of *The Illustrated London News* and a large, popular illustrated History of England, there was very little to be found. My aunt talked to me in a casual feeble way, chiefly about my mother's last illness. The two had seen very little of each other for many years; she made no secret of it that the ineligible qualities of my father were the cause of the estrangement. The only other society in the house during the day was an old and rather decayed Skye terrier in constant conflict with what were no doubt imaginary fleas. I took myself off for a series of walks, and acquired a considerable knowledge of the scenery and topography of the Potteries.

It puzzled my aunt that I did not go westward, where it was country-side and often quite pretty, with hedgerows and fields and copses and flowers. But always I went eastward, where in a long valley industrialism smokes and sprawls. That was the stuff to which I turned by nature, to the human effort, and the accumulation and jar of men's activities. And in such a country as that valley social and economic relations were simple and manifest. Instead of the limitless confusion of London's population, in which no man can trace any but the most slender correlation between rich and poor, in which every one seems disconnected and adrift from every one, you can see here the works, the potbank or the ironworks or what not, and here close at hand the congested, meanly-housed workers, and at a little distance a small middle-class quarter, and again remoter, the big house of the employer. It was like a very simplified diagram – after the untraceable confusion of London.

I prowled alone, curious and interested, through shabby back streets of mean little homes; I followed canals, sometimes canals of mysteriously heated waters with ghostly wisps of steam rising against blackened walls or a distant prospect of dustbin-fed vegetable gardens, I saw the women pouring out from the potbanks, heard the hooters summoning the toilers to work, lost my way upon slag-heaps as big as the hills of the south country, dodged trains at manifestly dangerous level crossings, and surveyed across dark intervening spaces the flaming uproar, the gnome-like activities of iron foundries. I heard talk of strikes and rumours of strikes, and learnt, from the columns of some obscure labour paper I bought one day, of the horrors of the lead poisoning that was in those days one of the normal risks of certain sorts of pottery workers. Then back I came, by the ugly groaning and clanging steam tram of that period, to my uncle's house and lavish abundance of money and more or less furtive flirtations and the tinkle of Moskowski and Chaminade. It was, I say, diagrammatic. One saw the expropriator and the expropriated – as if Marx had arranged the picture. It was as jumbled and far more dingy and disastrous than any of the confusions of building and development that had surrounded my youth at Bromstead and Penge, but it had a novel quality of being explicable. I found great virtue in the word 'exploitation'.

There stuck in my mind as if it was symbolical of the whole thing the twisted figure of a man, whose face had been horribly scalded – I can't describe how, except that one eye was just expressionless white – and he ground at an organ bearing a card which told in weak and bitterly satirical phrasing that he had been scalded by the hot water from the tuyeres of the blast furnace of Lord Pandram's works. He had been scalded and quite inadequately compensated and dismissed. And Lord Pandram was worth half a million.

That upturned sightless white eye of his took possession of my imagination. I don't think that even then I was swayed by any crude melodramatic conception of injustice. I was quite prepared to believe the card wasn't a punctiliously accurate statement of fact, and that a case could be made out for Lord

Pandram. Still there in the muddy gutter, painfully and dreadfully, was the man, and he was smashed and scalded and wretched, and he ground his dismal hurdy-gurdy with a weary arm, calling upon Heaven and the passer-by for help, for help and some sort of righting – one could not imagine quite what. There he was as a fact, as a by-product of the system that heaped my cousins with trinkets and provided the comic novels and the abundant cigars and spacious billiard-room of my uncle's house. I couldn't disconnect him and them.

My uncle on his part did nothing to conceal the state of war that existed between himself and his workers, and the mingled contempt and animosity he felt from them.

### 3

Prosperity had overtaken my uncle. So quite naturally he believed that every man who was not as prosperous as he was had only himself to blame. He was rich and he had left school and gone into his father's business at fifteen, and that seemed to him the proper age at which every one's education should terminate. He was very anxious to dissuade me from going up to Cambridge, and we argued intermittently through all my visit.

I had remembered him as a big and buoyant man, striding destructively about the nursery floor of my childhood, and saluting my existence by slaps, loud laughter, and questions about half herrings and half eggs subtly framed to puzzle and confuse my mind. I didn't see him for some years until my father's death, and then he seemed rather smaller, though still a fair size, yellow instead of red and much less radiantly aggressive. This altered effect was due not so much to my own changed perspectives, I fancy, as to the facts that he was suffering for continuous cigar-smoking, and being taken in hand by his adolescent daughters who had just returned from school.

During my first visit there was a perpetual series of – the only word is rows, between them and him. Up to the age of fifteen or thereabouts, he had maintained his ascendancy over them by simple old-fashioned physical chastisement. Then after an interlude of a year it had dawned upon them that power had mysteriously departed from him. He had tried stopping their pocket money, but they found their mother financially amenable; besides which it was fundamental to my uncle's attitude that he should give them money freely. Not to do so would seem like admitting a difficulty in making it. So that after he had stopped their allowances for the fourth time Sybil and Gertrude were prepared to face beggary without a qualm. It had been his pride to give them the largest allowance of any girls at the school, not even excepting the grand-daughter of Fladden the Borax King, and his soul recoiled from this discipline as it had never recoiled from the ruder method of the earlier phase. Both girls had developed to a high pitch in their mutual recriminations a gift for damaging retort, and he found it an altogether deadlier thing than the power of the raised voice that had always cowed my aunt. Whenever he became heated with them, they frowned as if involuntarily, drew in their breath sharply, said: 'Daddy, you really must not say –' and corrected his pronunciation. Then, at a great advantage, they resumed the discussion. . . .

My uncle's views about Cambridge, however, were perfectly clear and definite. It was waste of time and money. It was all damned foolery. Did they make a man a better business man? Not a bit of it. He gave instances. It spoilt a man for business by giving him 'false ideas'. Some men said that at college a man formed useful friendships. What use were friendships to a business man? He might get to know lords, but, as my uncle pointed out, a lord's requirements in his line of faience were little greater than a common man's. If college introduced him to hotel proprietors there might be something in it. Perhaps it helped a man into Parliament, Parliament still being a confused retrogressive corner in the world where lawyers and suchlike sheltered themselves from the onslaughts of common-sense behind a fog of Latin and Greek and twaddle and tosh; but I wasn't the sort to go into Parliament, unless I meant to be a lawyer. Did I mean to be a lawyer? It cost no end of money and was full of uncertainties, and there were no judges or great solicitors among my relations. 'Young chaps think they get on by themselves,' said my uncle. 'It isn't so. Not unless they take their coats off. I took mine off before I was your age by nigh a year.'

We were at cross purposes from the outset, because I did not think men lived to make money; and I was obtuse to the hints

130

he was throwing out at the possibilities of his own potbank, not wilfully obtuse, but just failing to penetrate his meaning. Whatever City Merchants had or had not done for me, Flack, Topham and old Gates had certainly barred my mistaking the profitable production and sale of lavatory basins and bathroom fittings for the highest good. It was only upon reflection that it dawned upon me that the splendid chance for a young fellow with my uncle, 'me, having no son of my own,' was anything but an illustration for comparison with my own chosen career.

I still remember very distinctly my uncle's talk, – he loved to speak 'reet Staffordshire' – his rather flabby face with the mottled complexion that told of crude ill-regulated appetites, his clumsy gestures – he kept emphasizing his points by prodding at me with his finger – the ill-worn, costly, grey tweed clothes, the watch chain of plain solid gold, and soft felt hat thrust back from his head. He tackled me first in the garden after lunch, and then tried to raise me to enthusiasm by taking me to his potbank and showing me its organization, from the dusty grinding mills in which whitened men worked and coughed, through the highly ventilated glazing room in which strangely masked girls looked ashamed of themselves, – 'They'll risk death, the fools, to show their faces to a man,' said my uncle, quite audibly – to the firing kilns and the glazing kilns, and so round the whole place to the railway siding and the gratifying spectacle of three trucks laden with executed orders.

Then he went up a creaking outside staircase to his little office, and he showed off before me for a while, with one or two subordinates and the telephone.

'None of your Gas,' he said, 'all this. It's Real every bit of it. Hard cash and hard glaze.'

'Yes,' I said, with memories of a carelessly read pamphlet in my mind, and without any satirical intention, 'I suppose you *must* use lead in your glazes?'

Whereupon I found I had tapped the ruling grievance of my uncle's life. He hated leadless glazes more than he hated anything, except the benevolent people who had organized the agitation for their use. 'Leadless glazes ain't only fit for buns.' he said. 'Let me tell you, my boy –'

He began, in a voice of bland persuasiveness that presently warmed to anger, to explain the whole matter. I hadn't the

131

rights of the matter at all. Firstly, there was practically no such thing as lead poisoning. Secondly, not every one was liable to lead poisoning, and it would be quite easy to pick out the susceptible types – as soon as they had it – and put them to other work. Thirdly, the evil effects of lead poisoning were much exaggerated. Fourthly, and this was in a particularly confidential undertone, many of the people liked to get lead poisoning, especially the women, because it caused abortion. I might not believe it, but he knew it for a fact. Fifthly, the workpeople simply would not learn the gravity of the danger, and would eat with unwashed hands, and incur all sorts of risks, so that, as my uncle put it: 'the fools deserve what they get.' Sixthly, he and several associated firms had organized a simple and generous insurance scheme against lead-poisoning risks. Seventhly, he never wearied in rational (as distinguished from excessive, futile, and expensive) precautions against the disease. Eighthly, in the ill-equipped shops of his minor competitors lead poisoning was a frequent and virulent evil, and people had generalized from these exceptional cases. The small shops, he hazarded, looking out of the cracked and dirty window at distant chimneys, might be advantageously closed. . . .

'But what's the good of talking?' said my uncle, getting off the table on which he had been sitting. 'Seems to me there'll come a time when a master will get fined if he don't run round the works blowing his girls' noses for them. That's about what it'll come to.'

He walked to the black mantelpiece and stood on the threadbare rug, and urged me not to be misled by the stories of prejudiced and interested enemies of our national industries.

'They'll get a strike one of these days, of employers, and then we'll see a bit,' he said. 'They'll drive Capital abroad and then they'll whistle to get it back again.' . . .

He led the way down the shaky wooden steps and cheered up to tell me of his way of checking his coal consumption. He exchanged a ferocious greeting with one or two workpeople, and so we came out of the factory gates into the ugly narrow streets, paved with a peculiarly hard diapered brick of an unpleasing inky-blue colour, and bordered with the mean and squalid homes of his workers. Doors stood open and showed grimy interiors, and dirty ill-clad children played in the kennel.

132

We passed a sickly-looking girl with a sallow face, who dragged her limbs and peered at us dimly with painful eyes. She stood back, as partly blinded people will do, to allow us to pass, although there was plenty of room for us.

I glanced back at her.

'*That's* ploombism,' said my uncle casually.

'What?' said I.

'Ploombism. And the other day I saw a fool of a girl, and what d'you think? She'd got a basin that hadn't been fired, a cracked piece of biscuit it was, up on the shelf over her head, just all over glaze, killing glaze, man, and she was putting up her hand, if you please, and eating her dinner out of it. Got her dinner in it!

'Eating her dinner out of it,' he repeated in loud and bitter tones, and punched me hard in the ribs.

'And then they comes to *that* – and grumbles. And the fools up in Westminster want you to put in fans here and fans there – the Longton fools have. . . . And them eating their dinners out of it all the time!' . . .

At high tea that night – my uncle was still holding out against evening dinner – Sybil and Gertrude made what was evidently a concerted demand for a motor-car.

'You've got your mother's brougham,' he said, 'that's good enough for you.' But he seemed shaken by the fact that some Burslem rival was launching out with the new invention. 'He spoils his girls,' he remarked. 'He's a fool,' and became thoughtful.

Afterwards he asked me to come to him into his study; it was a room with a writing-desk and full of pieces of earthenware and suchlike litter, and we had our great row about Cambridge.

'Have you thought things over, Dick?' he said.

'I think I'll go to Trinity, Uncle,' I said firmly. 'I want to go to Trinity. It is a great college.'

He was manifestly chagrined. 'You're a fool,' he said.

I made no answer.

'You're a damned fool,' he said. 'But I suppose you've got to do it. You could have come here – That don't matter, though, now. . . . You'll have your time and spend your money, and be a poor half-starved clergyman, mucking about with the women all the day and afraid to have one of your own ever, or you'll be a schoolmaster or some such fool for the rest of your life. Or some newspaper chap. That's what you'll get from Cambridge. I've half a mind not to let you. Eh? More than half a mind. . . .

'You've got to do the thing you can,' he said, after a pause, 'and likely it's what you're fitted for.'

4

I paid several short visits to Staffordshire during my Cambridge days, and always these relations of mine produced the same effect of hardness. My uncle's thoughts had neither atmosphere nor mystery. He lived in a different universe from the dreams of scientific construction that filled my mind. He could as easily have understood Chinese poetry. His motives were made up of intense rivalries with other men of his class and kind, a few vindictive hates springing from real and fancied slights, a habit of acquisition that had become a second nature, a keen love both of efficiency and display in his own affairs. He seemed to me to have no sense of the state, no sense and much less any love of beauty, no charity and no sort of religious feeling whatever. He had strong bodily appetites, he ate and drank freely, smoked a great deal, and occasionally was carried off by his passions for a 'bit of a spree' to Birmingham or Liverpool or Manchester. The indulgences of these occasions were usually followed by a period of reaction, when he was urgent for the suppression of nudity in the local Art Gallery and a harsh and forcible elevation of the superficial morals of the valley. And he spoke of the ladies who ministered to the delights of his jolly-dog period, when he spoke of them at all, by the unprintable feminine equivalent. My aunt he treated with a kindly contempt and considerable financial generosity, but his daughters tore his heart ; he was so proud of them, so glad to find them money to spend, so resolved to own them, so instinctively jealous of every man who came near them.

My uncle has been the clue to a great number of men for me. He was an illuminating extreme. I have learnt what not to expect from them through him, and to comprehend resentments and dangerous sudden antagonisms I should have found incomprehensible in their more complex forms, if I had not first seen them in him in their feral state.

With his soft felt hat at the back of his head, his rather heavy, rather mottled face, his rationally thick boots and slouching tweed-clad form, a little round-shouldered and very obstinate looking, he strolls through all my speculations sucking his teeth audibly, and occasionally throwing out a shrewd aphorism, the intractable unavoidable ore of the new civilization.

Essentially he was simple. Generally speaking, he hated and despised in equal measure whatever seemed to suggest that he personally was not the most perfect human being conceivable. He hated all education after fifteen because he had had no education after fifteen, he hated all people who did not have high tea until he himself under duress gave up high tea, he hated every game except football, which he had played and could judge, he hated all people who spoke foreign languages because he knew no language but Staffordshire, he hated all foreigners because he was English, and all foreign ways because they were not his ways. Also he hated particularly, and in this order, Londoners, Yorkshiremen, Scotch, Welsh, and Irish, because they were not 'reet Staffordshire', and he hated all other Staffordshire men as insufficiently 'reet'. He wanted to have all his own women inviolate, and to fancy he had a call upon every other woman in the world. He wanted to have the best cigars and the best brandy in the world to consume or give away magnificently, and every one else to have inferior ones. (His billiard table was an extra large size, specially made and very inconvenient.) And he hated Trade Unions because they interfered with his autocratic direction of his works, and his workpeople because they were not obedient and untiring mechanisms to do his bidding. He was, in fact, a very naïve, vigorous human being. He was about as much civilized, about as much tamed to the ideas of collective action and mutual consideration as a Central African negro.

There are hordes of such men as he throughout all the modern industrial world. You will find the same type with the slightest modifications in the Pas de Calais or Rhenish Prussia or New Jersey or North Italy. No doubt you would find it in New Japan. Yet it is only in Arnold Bennett's novels that I

135

have ever found a picture of them. These men have raised themselves up from the general mass of untrained, uncultured, poorish people in a hard industrious selfish struggle. To drive others they have had first to drive themselves. They have never yet had occasion or leisure to think of the state or social life as a whole, and as for dreams of beauty, it was a condition of survival that they should ignore such cravings. All the distinctive qualities of my uncle can be thought of as dictated by his conditions; his success and harshness, the extravagances that expressed his pride in making money, the uncongenial luxury that sprang from rivalry, and his self-reliance, his contempt for broad views, his contempt for everything that he could not understand.

His daughters were the inevitable children of his life. Queer girls they were! Curiously 'spirited' as people phrase it, and curiously limited. During my Cambridge days I went down to Staffordshire several times. My uncle, though he still resented my refusal to go into his business, was also in his odd way proud of me. I was his nephew and poor relation, and yet there I was, a young gentleman learning all sorts of unremunerative things in the grandest manner, 'Latin and mook', while the sons of his neighbours, not nephews merely, but sons, stayed unpolished in their native town. Every time I went down I found extensive changes and altered relations, and before I had settled down to them off I went again. I don't think I was one person to them; I was a series of visitors. There is a gulf of ages between a gaunt schoolboy of sixteen in unbecoming mourning and two vividly self-conscious girls of eighteen and nineteen, but a Cambridge 'man' of two and twenty with a first and good tennis and a growing social experience, is a fair contemporary for two girls of twenty-three and twenty-four.

A motor-car appeared, I think in my second visit, a bottle-green affair that opened behind, had dark purple cushions, and was controlled mysteriously by a man in shiny black costume and a flat cap. The high tea had been shifted to seven and rechristened dinner, but my uncle would not dress or consent to have wine; and after one painful experiment, I gathered, and a scene, he put his foot down and prohibited any but high-necked dresses.

'Daddy's perfectly impossible,' Sybil told me.

136

The foot had descended vehemently. 'My own daughters!' he had said, 'dressed up like –' – and had arrested himself and fumbled and decided to say – 'actresses, and showin' their fat arms for every fool to stare at.' Nor would he have any people invited to dinner. He didn't, he had explained, want strangers poking about in his house when he came home tired. So such calling as occurred went on during his absence in the after-noon.

One of the peculiarities of the life of these ascendant families of the industrial class to which wealth has come is its tremen-dous insulations. There were no customs of intercourse in the Five Towns. All the isolated prosperities of the district sprang from economizing, hard-driven homes, in which there was neither time nor means for hospitality. Social intercourse centred very largely upon the church or chapel, and the chapels were better at bringing people together than the Establishment to which my cousins belonged. Their chief outlet to the wider world lay therefore through the acquaintances they had formed at school, and through two much less prosperous families of relations who lived at Longton and Hanley. A number of gos-siping friendships with old school mates were 'kept up', and my cousins would 'spend the afternoon' or even spend the day with these ; such occasions led to other encounters and inter-laced with the furtive correspondences and snatched meetings that formed the emotional thread of their lives. When the bil-liard table had been new, my uncle had taken to asking in a few approved friends for an occasional game, but mostly the billiard-room was for glory and the girls. Both of them played very well. They never, so far as I know, dined out, and when at last after bitter domestic conflicts they began to go to dances they went with the quavering connivance of my aunt, and changed into ball frocks at friends' houses on the way. There was a tennis club that formed a convenient afternoon rendez-vous, and I recall that in the period of my earlier visits the young bloods of the district found much satisfaction in taking girls for drives in dog-carts and suchlike high-wheeled vehicles, a disposition that died in tangled tandems at the apparition of motor-cars.

My aunt and uncle had conceived no plans in life for their daughters at all. In the undifferentiated industrial community

137

from which they had sprung, girls got married somehow, and it did not occur to them that the concentration of property that had made them wealthy had cut their children off from the general social sea in which their own awkward meeting had occurred, without necessarily opening any other world in exchange. My uncle was too much occupied with the works and his business affairs and his private vices to philosophize about his girls; he wanted them just to keep girls, preferably about sixteen, and to be a sort of animated flowers and make home bright, and be given things. He was irritated that they would not remain at this, and still more irritated that they failed to suppress altogether their natural interest in young men. The tandems would be steered by weird and devious routes to evade the bare chance of his blood-shot eye. My aunt seemed to have no ideas whatever about what was likely to happen to her children. She had indeed no ideas about anything; she took husband and the days as they came.

I can see now the pathetic difficulty of my cousins' position in life; the absence of any guidance or instruction or provision for their development. They supplemented the silences of home by the conversation of schoolfellows and the suggestions of popular fiction. They had to make what they could out of life with such hints as these. The church was far too modest to offer them any advice. It was obtruded upon my mind upon my first visit that they were both carrying on correspondences and having little furtive passings and seeings and meetings with the mysterious owners of certain initials, S. and L. K. and, if I remember rightly, 'the R.N.', brothers and cousins, I suppose, of their friends. The same thing was going on, with a certain intensification, at my next visit, excepting only that the initials were different. But when I came again their methods were maturer or I was no longer a negligible quantity, and the notes and the initials were no longer flaunted quite so openly in my face.

My cousins had worked it out from the indications of their universe that the end of life is to have a 'good time'. They used the phrase. That and the drives in dog-carts were only the first of endless points of resemblance between them and the commoner sort of American girl. When some years ago I paid my first and only visit to America I seemed to recover my cousins'

138

atmosphere as soon as I entered the train at Euston. There were three girls in my compartment supplied with huge decorated cases of sweets, and being seen off by a company of friends, noisily arch and eager about the 'steamer letters' they would get at Liverpool ; they were the very soul-sisters of my cousins. The chief elements of a good time, as my cousins judged it, as these countless thousands of rich young women judge it, are a petty eventfulness, laughter, and to feel that you are looking well and attracting attention. Shopping is one of its leading joys. You buy things, clothes and trinkets for yourself and presents for your friends. Presents always seemed to be flying about in that circle ; flowers and boxes of sweets were common currency. My cousins were always getting and giving, my uncle caressed them with parcels and cheques. They kissed him and he exuded sovereigns as a stroked *Aphis* exudes honey. It was like the new language of the Academy of Lagado to me, and I never learnt how to express myself in it, for nature and training make me feel encumbered to receive presents and embarrassed in giving them. But then, like my father, I hate and distrust possessions.

Of the quality of their private imagination I never learnt anything ; I suppose it followed the lines of the fiction they read and was romantic and sentimental. So far as marriage went, the married state seemed at once very attractive and dreadfully serious to them, composed in equal measure of becoming important and becoming old. I don't know what they thought about children. I doubt if they ever thought about them at all. It was very secret if they did.

As for the poor and dingy people all about them, my cousins were always ready to take part in a Charitable Bazaar. They were unaware of any economic correlation of their own prosperity and that circumambient poverty, and they knew of Trade Unions simply as disagreeable external things that upset my uncle's temper. They knew of nothing wrong in social life at all except that there were 'Agitators'. It surprised them a little, I think, that Agitators were not more drastically put down. But they had a sort of instinctive dread of social discussion as of something that might breach the happiness of their ignorance. . . .

## 5

My cousins did more than illustrate Marx for me; they also undertook a stage of my emotional education. Their method in that as in everything else was extremely simple, but it took my inexperience by surprise.

It must have been on my third visit that Sybil took me in hand. Hitherto I seemed to have seen her only in profile, but now she became almost completely full face, manifestly regarded me with those violet eyes of hers. She passed me things I needed at breakfast – it was the first morning of my visit – before I asked for them.

When young men are looked at by pretty cousins, they become intensely aware of those cousins. It seemed to me that I had always admired Sybil's eyes very greatly, and that there was something in her temperament congenial to mine. It was odd I had not noted it on my previous visits.

We walked round the garden somewhen that morning, and talked about Cambridge. She asked quite a lot of questions about my work and my ambitions. She said she had always felt sure I was clever.

The conversation languished a little, and we picked some flowers for the house. Then she asked if I could run. I conceded her various starts and we raced up and down the middle garden path. Then, a little breathless, we went into the new twenty-five-guinea summer-house at the end of the herbaceous border.

We sat side by side, pleasantly hidden from the house, and she became anxious about her hair, which was slightly and prettily disarranged, and asked me to help her with the adjustment of a hairpin. I had never in my life been so near the soft curly hair and the dainty eyebrow and eyelid and warm soft cheek of a girl, and I was stirred –

It stirs me now to recall it.

I became a battle ground of impulses and inhibitions.

'Thank you,' said my cousin, and moved a little away from me.

She began to talk about friendship, and lost her thread and forgot the little electric stress between us in a rather meandering analysis of her principal girl friends.

But afterwards she resumed her purpose.

I went to bed that night with one proposition overshadowing everything else in my mind, namely, that kissing my cousin Sybil was a difficult but not impossible achievement. I do not recall any shadow of a doubt whether on the whole it was worth doing. The thing had come into my existence, disturbing and interrupting its flow exactly as a fever does. Sybil had infected me with herself.

The next day matters came to a crisis in the little upstairs sitting-room which had been assigned me as a study during my visit. I was working up there, or rather trying to work in spite of the outrageous capering of some very primitive elements in my brain, when she came up to me, under a transparent pretext of looking for a book.

I turned round and then got up at the sight of her. I quite forget what our conversation was about, but I know she led me to believe I might kiss her. Then when I attempted to do so she averted her face.

'How *could* you?' she said; 'I didn't mean that!'

That remained the state of our relations for two days. I developed a growing irritation with and resentment against cousin Sybil, combined with an intense desire to get that kiss for which I hungered and thirsted. Cousin Sybil went about in the happy persuasion that I was madly in love with her, and her game, so far as she was concerned, was played and won. It wasn't until I had fretted for two days that I realized that I was being used for the commonest form of excitement possible to a commonplace girl; that dozens perhaps of young men had played the part of Tantalus at cousin Sybil's lips. I walked about my room at nights, damning her and calling her by terms which on the whole she rather deserved, while Sybil went to sleep pitying 'poor old Dick!'

'Damn it!' I said, 'I *will* be equal with you.'. . .

But I never did equalize the disadvantage, and perhaps it's as well, for I fancy that sort of revenge cuts both people too much for a rational man to seek it. . . .

'Why are men so silly?' said cousin Sybil next morning, wriggling back with down-bent head to release herself from what should have been a compelling embrace.

'Confound it!' I said, with a flash of clear vision. 'You *started* this game.'

'Oh!'

She stood back against a hedge of roses, a little flushed and excited and interested, and ready for the delightful defensive if I should renew my attack.

'Beastly hot for scuffling,' I said, white with anger. 'I don't know whether I'm so keen on kissing you, Sybil, after all. I just thought you wanted me to.'

I could have whipped her, and my voice stung more than my words.

Our eyes met; a real hatred in hers leaping up to meet mine.

'Let's play tennis,' I said, after a moment's pause.

'No,' she answered shortly, 'I'm going indoors.'

'Very well.'

And that ended the affair with Sybil.

I was still in the full glare of this disillusionment when Gertrude awoke from some preoccupation to an interest in my existence. She developed a disposition to touch my hand by accident, and let her fingers rest in contact with it for a moment, – she had pleasant soft hands; – she began to drift into summer-houses with me, to let her arm rest trustfully against mine, to ask questions about Cambridge. They were much the same questions that Sybil had asked. But I controlled myself and maintained a profile of intelligent and entirely civil indifference to her blandishments.

What Gertrude made of it came out one evening in some talk – I forget about what – with Sybil.

'Oh, Dick!' said Gertrude a little impatiently, 'Dick's Pi.'

And I never disillusioned her by any subsequent levity from this theory of my innate and virginal piety.


6

It was against this harsh and crude Staffordshire background that I think I must have seen Margaret for the first time. I say I think because it is quite possible that we had passed each other in the streets of Cambridge, no doubt with that affection of mutual disregard which was once customary between undergraduates and Newnham girls. But if that was so I had noted nothing of the slender graciousness that shone out so pleasingly against the bleaker midland surroundings.

She was a younger schoolfellow of my cousins', and the step-daughter of Seddon, a prominent solicitor of Burslem. She was not only not in my cousins' generation but not in their set, she was one of a small hard-working group who kept immaculate note-books, and did as much as is humanly possible of that insensate pile of written work that the Girls' Public School movement has inflicted upon schoolgirls. She really learnt French and German admirably and thoroughly, she got as far in mathematics as an unflinching industry can carry any one with no great natural aptitude, and she went up to Bennett Hall, Newnham, after the usual conflict with her family, to work for the History Tripos.

There in her third year she made herself thoroughly ill through overwork, so ill that she had to give up Newnham altogether and go abroad with her mother. She made herself ill, as so many girls do in those university colleges, through the badness of her home and school training. She thought study must needs be a hard straining of the mind. She worried her work, she gave herself no leisure to see it as a whole, she felt herself not making headway and she cut her games and exercise in order to increase her hours of toil, and worked into the night. She carried a knack of laborious thoroughness into the blind alleys and inessentials of her subject. It didn't need the badness of the food for which Bennett Hall is celebrated, and the remarkable dietary of nocturnal cocoa, cakes, and soft biscuits with which the girls have supplemented it, to ensure her collapse. Her mother brought her home, fretting and distressed, and then finding her hopelessly unhappy at home, took her and her half-brother, a rather ailing youngster of ten who died three years later, for a journey to Italy.

Italy did much to assuage Margaret's chagrin. I think all three of them had a very good time there. At home Mr Seddon, her step-father, played the part of a well-meaning blight by reason of the moods that arose from nervous dyspepsia. They went to Florence, equipped with various introductions and much sound advice from sympathetic Cambridge friends, and having acquired an ease in Italy there, went on to Siena, Orvieto, and at last Rome. They returned, if I remember rightly, by Pisa, Genoa, Milan, and Paris. Six months or more they had had abroad, and now Margaret was back in Burslem, in health again and consciously a very civilized person.

New ideas were abroad, it was Maytime and a spring of abundant flowers – daffodils were particularly good that year – and Mrs Seddon celebrated her return by giving an afternoon reception at short notice, with the clear intention of letting every one out into the garden if the weather held.

The Seddons had a big old farmhouse modified to modern ideas of comfort on the road out towards Misterton, with an orchard that had been rather pleasantly subdued from use to ornament. It had rich blossoming cherry and apple trees. Large patches of grass full of nodding yellow trumpets had been left amidst the not too precisely mown grass, which was as it were grass path with an occasional lapse into lawn or glade. And Margaret, hatless, with the fair hair above her thin, delicately pink face very simply done, came to meet our rather too consciously dressed party, – we had come in the motor four strong, with my aunt in grey silk. Margaret wore a soft flowing flowered blue dress of diaphanous material, all unconnected with the fashion and tied with pretty ribbons, like a slenderer, unbountiful Primavera.

It was one of those May days that ape the light and heat of summer, and I remember disconnectedly quite a number of brightly lit figures and groups walking about, and a white gate between orchard and garden and a large lawn with an oak tree and a red Georgian house with a verandah and open French windows, through which the tea drinking had come out upon the moss-edged flagstones, even as Mrs Seddon had planned.

The party was almost entirely feminine except for a little curate with a large head, a good voice and a radiant manner, who was obviously attracted by Margaret, and two or three young husbands still sufficiently addicted to their wives to accompany them. One of them I recall as a quite romantic figure with abundant blond curly hair on which was poised a grey felt hat encircled by a refined black band. He wore, moreover, a loose rich shot-silk tie of red and purple, a long frock coat, grey trousers and brown shoes, and presently he removed his hat and carried it in one hand. There were two tennis-playing youths besides myself. There was also one father with three daughters in anxious control, a father of the old school scarcely half broken in, reluctant, rebellious and consciously and conscientiously 'reet Staffordshire.' The daughters were all alert to suppress the possible plungings, the undesirable humorous impulses of this almost feral guest. They nipped his very gestures in the bud. The rest of the people were mainly mothers with daughters – daughters of all ages, and a scattering of aunts, and there was a tendency to clotting, parties kept together and regarded parties suspiciously. Mr Seddon was in hiding, I think, all the time, though not formally absent.

Matters centred upon the tea in the long room of the French windows, where four trim maids went to and fro busily between the house and the clumps of people seated or standing before it; and tennis and croquet were intermittently visible and audible beyond a bank of rockwork rich with the spikes and cups and bells of high spring.

Mrs Seddon presided at the tea urn, and Margaret partly assisted and partly talked to me and my cousin Sibyl – Gertrude had found a disused and faded initial and was partnering him at tennis in a state of gentle revival – while their mother exercised a divided chaperonage from a seat near Mrs Seddon. The little curate, stirring a partially empty cup of tea, mingled with our party, and preluded, I remember, every observation he made by a vigorous resumption of stirring.

We talked of Cambridge, and Margaret kept us to it. The curate was a Selwyn man and had taken a pass degree in theology, but Margaret had come to Gaylord's lectures in Trinity for a term before her breakdown, and understood these differences. She had the eagerness of an exile to hear the old familiar names of places and personalities. We capped familiar anecdotes and were enthusiastic about King's Chapel and the Backs, and the curate, addressing himself more particularly to Sibyl, told a long confused story illustrative of his disposition to reckless devilry (of a pure-minded kindly sort) about upsetting two canoes quite needlessly on the way to Grantchester.

I can still see Margaret as I saw her that afternoon, see her fresh fair face, with the little obliquity of the upper lip, and her brow always slightly knitted, and her manner as of one breathlessly shy but determined. She had rather open blue eyes, and she spoke in an even musical voice with the gentlest of stresses

145

and the ghost of a lisp. And it was true, she gathered, that Cambridge still existed. 'I went to Grantchester,' she said, 'last year, and had tea under the apple-blossom. I didn't think then I should have to come down.' (It was that started the curate upon his anecdote.)

'I've seen a lot of pictures, and learnt a lot about them – at the Pitti and the Brera, – the Brera is wonderful – wonderful places, – but it isn't like real study,' she was saying presently. ... 'We bought bales of photographs,' she said.

I thought the bales a little out of keeping.

But fair-haired and quite simply and yet graciously and fancifully dressed, talking of art and beautiful things and a beautiful land, and with so much manifest regret for learning denied, she seemed a different kind of being altogether from my smart, hard, high-coloured, black-haired, and resolutely hatted cousin; she seemed translucent beside Gertrude. Even the little twist and droop of her slender body was a grace to me.

I liked her from the moment I saw her, and set myself to interest and please her as well as I knew how.

We recalled a case of ragging that had rustled the shrubs of Newnham, and then Chris Robinson's visit – he had given a talk to Bennett Hall also – and our impression of him.

'He disappointed me too,' said Margaret.

I was moved to tell Margaret something of my own views in the matter of social progress, and she listened – oh! with a kind of urged attention, and her brow a little more knitted, very earnestly. The little curate desisted from the appendices and refuse heaps and general débris of his story, and made himself look very alert and intelligent.

'We did a lot of that when I was up in the eighties,' he said. 'I'm glad Imperialism hasn't swamped you fellows altogether.'

Gertrude, looking bright and confident, came to join our talk from the shrubbery; the initial, a little flushed and evidently in a state of refreshed relationship, came with her, and a cheerful lady in pink and more particularly distinguished by a pink bonnet joined our little group. Gertrude had been sipping admiration and was not disposed to play a passive part in the talk.

'Socialism!' she cried, catching the word. 'It's well Pa isn't here. He has Fits when people talk of socialism. Fits!'

The initial laughed in a general kind of way.

The curate said there was socialism *and* socialism, and looked at Margaret to gauge whether he had been too bold in this utterance. But she was all, he perceived, for broad-mindedness, and he stirred himself (and incidentally his tea) to still more liberality of expression. He said the state of the poor was appalling, simply appalling; that there were times when he wanted to shatter the whole system, 'only,' he said, turning to me appealingly, 'what have we got to put in its place?'

'The thing that exists is always the more evident alternative,' I said.

The little curate looked at it for a moment. 'Precisely,' he said explosively, and turned stirring and with his head a little on one side, to hear what Margaret was saying.

Margaret was saying, with a swift blush and an effect of daring, that she had no doubt she was a socialist.

'And wearing a gold chain!' said Gertrude, 'and drinking out of eggshell! I like that!'

I came to Margaret's rescue. 'It doesn't follow that because one is a socialist one ought to dress in sackcloth and ashes.'

The initial coloured deeply, and having secured my attention by prodding me slightly with the wrist of the hand that held his teacup, cleared his throat and suggested that 'one ought to be consistent.'

I perceived we were embarked upon a discussion of the elements. We began an interesting little wrangle, one of those crude discussions of general ideas that are dear to the heart of youth. I and Margaret supported one another as socialists, Gertrude and Sybil and the initial maintained an anti-socialist position, the curate attempted a cross-bench position with an air of intending to come down upon us presently with a casting vote. He reminded us of a number of useful principles too often overlooked in argument, that in a big question like this there was much to be said on both sides, that if every one did his or her duty to every one about them there would be no difficulty with social problems at all, that over and above all enactments we needed moral changes in people themselves. My cousin Gertrude was a difficult controversialist to manage, being unconscious of inconsistency in statement and absolutely impervious to reply. Her standpoint was essentially materialis-

147

tic ; she didn't see why she shouldn't have a good time because other people didn't ; they would have a good time, she was sure, if she didn't. She said that if we did give up everything we had to other people, they wouldn't very likely know what to do with it. She asked if we were so fond of work-people, why we didn't go and live among them, and expressed the inflexible persuasion that if we *had* socialism, everything would be just the same again in ten years' time. She also threw upon us the imputation of ingratitude for a beautiful world by saying that so far as she was concerned she didn't want to upset everything. She was contented with things as they were, thank you.

The discussion led in some way that I don't in the least recall now, and possibly by abrupt transitions, to a croquet foursome in which Margaret involved the curate without involving herself, and then stood beside me on the edge of the lawn while the others played. We watched silently for a moment.

'I *hate* that sort of view,' she said suddenly in a confidential undertone, with her delicate pink flush returning.

'It's want of imagination,' I said.

'To think we are just to enjoy ourselves,' she went on ; 'just to go on dressing and playing and having meals and spending money!' She seemed to be referring not simply to my cousins, but to the whole world of industry and property about us. 'But what is one to do?' she asked. 'I do wish I had not had to come down. It's all so pointless here. There seems to be nothing going forward, no ideas, no dreams. No one here seems to feel quite what I feel, the sort of need there is for *meaning* in things. I hate things without meaning.'

'Don't you do – local work?'

'I suppose I shall. I suppose I must find something. Do you think – if one were to attempt some sort of propaganda?'

'Could you –?' I began a little doubtfully.

'I suppose I couldn't,' she answered, after a thoughtful moment. 'I suppose it would come to nothing. And yet I feel there is so much to be done for the world, so much one ought to be doing. . . . I want to do something for the world.'

I can see her now as she stood there with her brows nearly frowning, her blue eyes looking before her, her mouth almost

148

petulant. 'One feels that there are so many things going on – out of one's reach,' she said.

I went back in the motor-car with my mind full of her, the quality of delicate discontent, the suggestion of exile. Even a kind of weakness in her was sympathetic. She told tremendously against her background. She was, I say, like a protesting blue flower upon a cinder heap. It is curious, too, how she connects and mingles with the furious quarrel I had with my uncle that very evening. That came absurdly. Indirectly Margaret was responsible. My mind was running on ideas she had revived and questions she had set clamouring, and quite inadvertently in my attempt to find solutions I talked so as to outrage his profoundest feelings. . . .

## 7

What a preposterous shindy that was!

I sat with him in the smoking-room, propounding what I considered to be the most indisputable and non-contentious propositions conceivable – until, to my infinite amazement, he exploded and called me a 'damned young puppy'.

It was seismic.

'Tremendously interesting time,' I said, 'just in the beginning of making a civilization.'

'Ah!' he said, with an averted face, and nodded, leaning forward over his cigar.

I had not the remotest thought of annoying him.

'Monstrous muddle of things we have got,' I said, 'jumbled streets, ugly population, ugly factories –'

'You'd do a sight better if you had to do with it,' said my uncle, regarding me askance.

'Not me. But a world that had a collective plan and knew where it meant to be going would do a sight better, anyhow. We're all swimming in a flood of ill-calculated chances –'

'You'll be making out I organized that business down there – by chance – next,' said my uncle, his voice thick with challenge.

I went on as though I was back in Trinity.

'There's a lot of chance in the making of all great businesses,' I said.

My uncle remarked that that showed how much I knew

149

about businesses. If chance made businesses, why was it that he always succeeded and grew while those fools Ackroyd and Sons always took second place? He showed a disposition to tell the glorious history of how once Ackroyd's overshadowed him, and how now he could buy up Ackroyd's three times over. But I wanted to get out what was in my mind.

'Oh!' I said, 'as between man and man and business and business, some of course get the pull by this quality or that – but it's forces quite outside the individual case that make the big part of any success under modern conditions. *You* never invented pottery, or any process in pottery that matters a rap in your works; it wasn't *your* foresight that joined all England up with railways and made it possible to organize production on an altogether different scale. You really at the utmost can't take credit for much more than being the sort of man who happened to fit what happened to be the requirements of the time, and who happened to be in a position to take advantage of them –'

It was then my uncle cried out and called me a damned young puppy, and became involved in some unexpected trouble of his own.

I woke up as it were from my analysis of the situation to discover him bent over a splendid spittoon, cursing incoherently, retching a little, and spitting out the end of his cigar which he had bitten off in his last attempt at self-control, and withal fully prepared as soon as he had cleared for action to give me just all that he considered to be the contents of his mind upon the condition of mine.

Well, why shouldn't I talk my mind to him? He'd never had an outside view of himself for years, and I resolved to stand up to him. We went at it hammer and tongs! It became clear that he supposed me to be a Socialist, a zealous, embittered hater of all ownership – and also an educated man of the vilest, most pretentiously superior description. His principal grievance was that I thought I knew everything; to that he recurred again and again. . . .

We had been maintaining an armed truce with each other since my resolve to go up to Cambridge, and now we had out all that had accumulated between us. There had been stupendous accumulations. . . .

150

The particular things we said and did in that bawling encounter matter nothing at all in this story. I can't now estimate how near we came to fisticuffs. It ended with my saying, after a pungent reminder of benefits conferred and remembered, that I didn't want to stay another hour in his house. I went upstairs, in a state of puerile fury, to pack and go off to the Railway Hotel, while he, with ironical civility, telephoned for a cab.

'Good riddance!' shouted my uncle, seeing me off into the night.

On the face of it our row was preposterous, but the underlying reality of our quarrel was the essential antagonism, it seemed to me, in all human affairs, the antagonism between ideas and the established method, that is to say, between ideas and the rule of thumb. The world I hate is the rule-of-thumb world, the thing I and my kind of people exist for primarily is battle with that, to annoy it, disarrange it, reconstruct it. We question everything, disturb anything that cannot give a clear justification to our questioning, because we believe inherently that our sense of disorder implies the possibility of a better order. Of course we are detestable. My uncle was of that other vaster mass who accept everything for the thing it seems to be, hate inquiry and analysis as a tramp hates washing, dread and resist change, oppose experiment, despise science. The world is our battleground; and all history, all literature that matters, all science, deals with this conflict of the thing that is and the speculative 'if' that will destroy it.

But that is why I did not see Margaret again for five years.

# Margaret in London

## 1

I was twenty-seven when I met Margaret again, and the intervening five years had been years of vigorous activity for me, if not of very remarkable growth. When I saw her again, I could count myself a grown man. I think, indeed, I counted myself more completely grown than I was. At any rate, by all ordinary standards, I had 'got on' very well, and my ideas, if they had not changed very greatly, had become much more definite and my ambitions clearer and bolder.

I had long since abandoned my fellowship and come to London. I had published two books that had been talked about, written several articles, and established a regular relationship with the *Weekly Review* and the *Evening Gazette*. I was a member of the Eighty Club and learning to adapt the style of the Cambridge Union to larger uses. The London world had opened out to me very readily. I had developed a pleasant variety of social connexions. I had made the acquaintance of Mr Evesham, who had been attracted by my *New Ruler*, and who talked about it and me, and so did a very great deal to make a way for me into the company of prominent and amusing people. I dined out quite frequently. The glitter and interest of good London dinner parties became a common experience. I liked the sort of conversation one got at them extremely, the little glow of duologues burning up into more general discussions, the closing-in of the men after the going of the women, the sage, substantial masculine gossiping, the later resumption of effective talk with some pleasant woman, graciously at her best. I had a wide range of houses; Cambridge had linked me to one or two correlated sets of artistic and literary people, and my books and Mr Evesham had opened to me the big vague world of 'society'. I wasn't aggressive or particularly snobbish or troublesome, sometimes I talked well, and if I had nothing interesting to say I said as little as possible, and I had a youthful gravity of manner that was liked by hostesses. And the other side of my nature that first flared through the cover of restraints at Locarno, that too had had opportunity to develop along the line London renders practicable. I had had my experiences and secrets and adventures among that fringe of ill-mated or erratic or discredited women the London world possesses. The thing had long ago ceased to be a matter of magic or mystery, and had become a question of appetites and excitement, and among other things the excitement of not being found out.

I write rather doubtfully of my growing during this period. Indeed I find it hard to judge whether I can say that I grew at all in any real sense of the word, between three and twenty and twenty-seven. It seems to me now to have been rather a phase of realization and clarification. All the broad lines of my thought were laid down, I am sure, by the date of my Locarno adventure, but in those five years I discussed things over and over again with myself and others, filled out with concrete fact forms I had at first apprehended sketchily and conversationally, measured my powers against my ideals and the forces in the world about me. It was evident that many men no better than myself and with no greater advantages than mine had raised themselves to influential and even decisive positions in the worlds of politics and thought. I was gathering the confidence and knowledge necessary to attack the world in the large manner; I found I could write, and that people would let me write if I chose, as one having authority and not as the scribes. Socially and politically and intellectually I knew myself for an honest man, and that quite without any deliberation on my part this showed and made things easy for me. People trusted my good faith from the beginning – for all that I came from nowhere and had no better position than any adventurer.

But the growth process was arrested, I was nothing bigger at twenty-seven than at twenty-two, however much saner and stronger, and any one looking closely into my mind during that period might well have imagined growth finished altogether. It is particularly evident to me now that I came no nearer to any understanding of women during that time. That Locarno affair was infinitely more to me than I had supposed. It ended something – nipped something in the bud perhaps –

took me at a stride from a vague, fine, ignorant, closed world
of emotion to intrigue and a perfectly definite and limited
sensuality. It ended my youth, and for a time it prevented my
manhood. I had never yet even peeped at the sweetest, profoundest thing in the world, the heart and meaning of a girl,
or dreamt with any quality of reality of a wife or any such
thing as a friend among womankind. My vague anticipation
of such things in life had vanished altogether. I turned away
from their possibility. It seemed to me I knew what had to be
known about womankind. I wanted to work hard, to get on to
a position in which I could develop and forward my constructive projects. Women, I thought, had nothing to do with that.
It seemed clear I could not marry for some years ; I was attractive to certain types of women, I had vanity enough to give me
an agreeable confidence in love-making, and I went about
seeking a convenient mistress quite deliberately, some one who
should serve my purpose and say in the end, like that kindly
first mistress of mine, 'I've done you no harm', and so release
me. It seemed the only wise way of disposing of urgencies that
might otherwise entangle and wreck the career I was intent
upon.

I don't apologize for, or defend, my mental and moral
phases. So it was I appraised life and prepared to take it, and
so it is a thousand ambitious men see it today. . . .

For the rest these five years were a period of definition. My
political conceptions were perfectly plain and honest. I had
one constant desire ruling my thoughts. I meant to leave England and the empire better ordered than I found it, to organize
and discipline, to build up a constructive and controlling State
out of my world's confusions. We had, I saw, to suffuse education with public intention, to develop a new better-living
generation, with a collectivist habit of thought, to link now
chaotic activities in every human affair, and particularly to
catch that escaped, world-making, world-ruining, dangerous
thing, industrial and financial enterprise, and bring it back to
the service of the general good. I had then the precise image
that still serves me as a symbol for all I wish to bring about,
the image of an engineer building a lock in a swelling torrent –
with water-pressure as his only source of power. My thoughts
and acts were habitually turned to that enterprise ; it gave

shape and direction to all my life. The problem that most engaged my mind during those years was the practical and personal problem of just where to apply myself to serve this almost innate purpose. How was I, a child of this confusion, struggling upward through the confusion, to take hold of things? Somewhere between politics and literature my grip must needs be found, but where? Always I seem to have been looking for that in those opening years, and disregarding everything else to discover it.

2

The Baileys, under whose auspices I met Margaret again, were in the sharpest contrast with the narrow industrialism of the Staffordshire world. They were indeed at the other extreme of the scale, two active self-centred people, excessively devoted to the public service. It was natural I should gravitate to them, for they seemed to stand for the maturer, more disciplined, better informed expression of all I was then urgent to attempt and do. The bulk of their friends were politicians or public officials, they described themselves as publicists – a vague yet sufficiently significant term. They lived and worked in a hard little house in Chambers Street, Westminster, and made a centre for quite an astonishing amount of political and social activity.

Willersley took me there one evening. The place was almost pretentiously matter-of-fact and unassuming. The narrow passage-hall, papered with some ancient yellowish paper, grained to imitate wood, was choked with hats and cloaks and an occasional feminine wrap. Motioned on rather than announced by a tall Scotch servant woman, the only domestic I ever remember seeing there, we made our way up a narrow staircase past the open door of a small study packed with blue-books, to discover Altiora Bailey receiving before the fireplace in her drawing-room. She was a tall commanding figure, splendid but a little untidy in black silk and red beads, with dark eyes that had no depths, with a clear hard voice that had an almost visible prominence, aquiline features and straight black hair that was apt to get astray, that was now astray like the head feathers of an eagle in a gale. She stood with her hands behind

155

her back, and talked in a high tenor of a projected Town Planning Bill with Blupp, who was practically in those days the secretary of the Local Government Board. A very short broad man with thick ears, and fat white hands writhing intertwined behind him, stood with his back to us, eager to bark interruptions into Altiora's discourse. A slender girl in pale blue, manifestly a young political wife, stood with one foot on the fender listening with an expression of entirely puzzled propitiation. A tall sandy-bearded bishop with the expression of a man in a trance completed this central group.

The room was one of those long apartments once divided by folding doors, and reaching from back to front, that are common upon the first floors of London houses. Its walls were hung with two or three indifferent water colours, there was scarcely any furniture but a sofa or so and a chair, and the floor, severely carpeted with matting, was crowded with a curious medley of people, men predominating. Several were in evening dress, but most had the morning garb of the politician; the women were either severely rational or radiantly magnificent. Willersley pointed out to me the wife of the Secretary of State for War, and I recognized the Duchess of Clynes, who at that time cultivated intellectuality. I looked round, identifying a face here or there, and stepping back trod on some one's toe, and turned to find it belonged to the Right Hon. G. B. Mottisham, dear to the *Punch* caricaturists. He received my apology with that intentional charm that is one of his most delightful traits, and resumed his discussion. Beside him was Esmeer of Trinity, whom I had not seen since my Cambridge days. . . .

Willersley found an ex-member of the School Board for whom he had affinities, and left me to exchange experiences and comments upon the company with Esmeer. Esmeer was still a don; but he was nibbling, he said, at certain negotiations with *The Times* that might bring him down to London. He wanted to come to London. 'We peep at things from Cambridge,' he said.

'This sort of thing,' I said, 'makes London necessary. It's the oddest gathering.'

'Every one comes here,' said Esmeer. 'Mostly we hate them like poison – jealousy – and little irritations – Altiora can be a horror at times – but we *have* to come.'

'Things are being done?'

'Oh! – no doubt of it. It's one of the parts of the British machinery – that doesn't show. . . . But nobody else could do it.

'Two people,' said Esmeer, 'who've planned to be a power – in an original way. And by Jove! they've done it!'

I did not for some time pick out Oscar Bailey, and then Esmeer showed him to me in elaborately confidential talk in a corner with a distinguished-looking stranger wearing a ribbon. Oscar had none of the fine appearance of his wife; he was a short sturdy figure with a rounded protruding abdomen and a curious broad, flattened, clean-shaven face that seemed nearly all forehead. He was of Anglo-Hungarian extraction, and I have always fancied something Mongolian in his type. He peered up with reddish swollen-looking eyes over gilt-edged glasses that were divided horizontally into portions of different refractive power, and he talked in an ingratiating undertone, with busy thin lips, and eager lisp and nervous movements of the hand.

People say that thirty years before at Oxford he was almost exactly the same eager, clever little man he was when first I met him. He had come up to Balliol bristling with extraordinary degrees and prizes captured in provincial and Irish and Scotch universities – and had made a name for himself as the most formidable dealer in exact fact the rhetoricians of the Union had ever had to encounter. From Oxford he had gone on to a position in the Higher Division of the Civil Service, I think in the War Office, and had speedily made a place for himself as a political journalist. He was a particularly neat controversialist, and very full of political and sociological ideas. He had a quite astounding memory for facts and a mastery of detailed analysis, and the time afforded scope for these gifts. The later eighties were full of politico-social discussion, and he became a prominent name upon the contents list of the *Nineteenth Century*, the *Fortnightly* and *Contemporary* chiefly as a half sympathetic but frequently very damaging critic of the socialism of that period. He won the immense respect of every one specially interested in social and political questions, he soon achieved the limited distinction that is awarded such capacity, and at that I think he would have

157

remained for the rest of his life if he had not encountered Altiora.

But Altiora Macvitie was an altogether exceptional woman, an extraordinary mixture of qualities, the one woman in the world who could make something more out of Bailey than that. She had much of the vigour and handsomeness of a slender impudent young man, and an unscrupulousness altogether feminine. She was one of those women who are wanting in – what is the word? – muliebrity. She had courage and initiative and a philosophical way of handling questions, and she could be bored by regular work like a man. She was entirely unfitted for her sex's sphere. She was neither uncertain, coy nor hard to please, and altogether too stimulating and aggressive for any gentleman's hours of ease. Her cookery would have been about as sketchy as her hand-writing, which was generally quite illegible, and she would have made, I feel sure, a shocking bad nurse. Yet you mustn't imagine she was an inelegant or unbeautiful woman, and she is inconceivable to me in high collars or any sort of masculine garment. But her soul was bony, and at the base of her was a vanity gaunt and greedy! When she wasn't in a state of personal untidiness that was partly a protest against the waste of hours exacted by the toilet and partly a natural disinclination, she had a gypsy splendour of black and red and silver all her own. And somewhen in the early nineties she met and married Bailey.

I know very little about her early years. She was the only daughter of Sir Deighton Macvitie, who applied the iodoform process to cotton, and only his subsequent unfortunate attempts to become a Cotton King prevented her being a very rich woman. As it was she had a tolerable independence. She came into prominence as one of the more able of the little shoal of young women who were led into politico-philanthropic activities by the influence of the earlier novels of Mrs Humphry Ward – the Marcella crop. She went 'slumming' with distinguished vigour, which was quite usual in those days – and returned from her experiences as an amateur flower girl with clear and original views about the problem – which is and always had been unusual. She had not married, I suppose because her standards were high, and men are cowards and with an instinctive appetite for muliebrity. She had kept house for her father by speaking occasionally to the housekeeper, butler and cook her mother had left her, and gathering the most interesting dinner parties she could, and had married off four orphan nieces in a harsh and successful manner. After her father's smash and death she came out as a writer upon social questions and a scathing critic of the Charity Organization Society, and she was three and thirty and a little at loose ends when she met Oscar Bailey, so to speak, in the *Contemporary Review*. The lurking woman in her nature was fascinated by the ease and precision with which the little man rolled over all sorts of important and authoritative people, she was the first to discover a sort of imaginative bigness in his still growing mind, the forehead perhaps carried him off physically, and she took occasion to meet and subjugate him, and, so soon as he had sufficiently recovered from his abject humility and a certain panic at her attentions, marry him.

This had opened a new phase in the lives of Bailey and herself. The two supplemented each other to an extraordinary extent. Their subsequent career was, I think, almost entirely her invention. She was aggressive, imaginative, and had a great capacity for ideas, while he was almost destitute of initiative, and could do nothing with ideas except remember and discuss them. She was, if not inexact, at least indolent, with a strong disposition to save energy by sketching – even her handwriting showed that – while he was inexhaustibly industrious with a relentless invariable caligraphy that grew larger and clearer as the years passed by. She had a considerable power of charming ; she could be just as nice to people – and incidentally just as nasty – as she wanted to be. He was always just the same, a little confidential and *sotto voce*, artlessly rude and egoistic in an undignified way. She had considerable social experience, good social connexions, and considerable social ambition, while he had none of these things. She saw in a flash her opportunity to redeem his defects, use his powers, and do large, novel, rather startling things. She ran him. Her marriage, which shocked her friends and relations beyond measure – for a time they would only speak of Bailey as 'that gnome' – was a stroke of genius, and forthwith they proceeded to make themselves the most formidable and distinguished couple conceivable.

159

P.B.P., she boasted, was engraved inside their wedding rings, Pro Bono Publico, and she meant it to be no idle threat. She had discovered very early that the last thing influential people will do is to work. Everything in their lives tends to make them dependent upon a supply of confidently administered detail. Their business is with the window and not the stock behind, and in the end they are dependent upon the stock behind for what goes into the window. She linked with that the fact that Bailey had a mind as orderly as a museum, and an invincible power over detail. She saw that if two people took the necessary pains to know the facts of government and administration with precision, to gather together knowledge that was dispersed and confused, to be able to say precisely what had to be done and what avoided in this eventuality or that, they would necessarily become a centre of reference for all sorts of legislative proposals and political expedients, and she went unhesitatingly upon that.

Bailey, under her vigorous direction, threw up his post in the Civil Service and abandoned sporadic controversies, and they devoted themselves to the elaboration and realization of this centre of public information she had conceived as their rôle. They set out to study the methods and organization and realities of government in the most elaborate manner. They did the work as no one had ever hitherto dreamt of doing it. They planned the research on a thoroughly satisfying scale, and arranged their lives almost entirely for it. They took that house in Chambers Street and furnished it with severe economy, they discovered that Scotch domestic who is destined to be the guardian and tyrant of their declining years, and they set to work. Their first book, 'The Permanent Official', fills three plump volumes, and took them and their two secretaries upwards of four years to do. It is an amazingly good book, an enduring achievement. In a hundred directions the history and the administrative treatment of the public service was clarified for all time. . . .

They worked regularly every morning from nine to twelve, they lunched lightly but severely, in the afternoon they 'took exercise' or Bailey attended meetings of the London School Board, on which he served, he said, for the purposes of study – he also became a railway director for the same end. In the late

160

afternoon Altiora was at home to various callers, and in the evening came dinner or a reception or both.

Her dinners and gatherings were a very important feature in their scheme. She got together all sorts of interesting people in or about the public service, she mixed the obscurely efficient with the ill-instructed famous and the rudderless rich, got together in one room more of the factors in our strange jumble of a public life than had ever met easily before. She fed them with a shameless austerity that kept the conversation brilliant, on a soup, a plain fish, and mutton or boiled fowl and milk pudding, with nothing to drink but whisky and soda, and hot and cold water, and milk and lemonade. Everybody was soon very glad indeed to come to that. She boasted how little her housekeeping cost her, and sought constantly for fresh economies that would enable her, she said, to sustain an additional private secretary. Secretaries were the Baileys' one extravagance; they loved to think of searches going on in the British Museum, and letters being cleared up and précis made overhead, while they sat in the little study and worked together, Bailey with a clockwork industry, and Altiora in splendid flashes between intervals of cigarettes and meditation. 'All efficient public careers,' said Altiora, 'consist in the proper direction of secretaries.'

'If everything goes well I shall have another secretary next year,' Altiora told me. 'I wish I could refuse people dinner napkins. Imagine what it means in washing! I dare most things. . . . But as it is, they stand a lot of hardship here.'

'There's something of the miser in both these people,' said Esmeer, and the thing was perfectly true. For, after all, the miser is nothing more than a man who either through want of imagination or want of suggestion misapplies to a base use a natural power of concentration upon one end. The concentration itself is neither good nor evil, but a power that can be used in either way. And the Baileys gathered and reinvested usuriously not money, but knowledge of the utmost value in human affairs. They produced an effect of having found themselves – completely. One envied them at times extraordinarily. I was attracted, I was dazzled – and at the same time there was something about Bailey's big wrinkled forehead, his lisping broad mouth, the gestures of his hands and an uncivil preoccupation I could not endure. . . .


3

Their effect upon me was from the outset very considerable.

Both of them found occasion on that first visit of mine to talk to me about my published writings and particularly about my then just published book *The New Ruler*, which had interested them very much. It fell in indeed so closely with their own way of thinking that I doubt if they ever understood how independently I had arrived at my conclusions. It was their weakness to claim excessively. That irritation, however, came later. We discovered each other immensely ; for a time it produced a tremendous sense of kindred and co-operation.

Altiora, I remember, maintained that there existed a great army of such constructive-minded people as ourselves – as yet undiscovered by one another.

'It's like boring a tunnel through a mountain,' said Oscar, 'and presently hearing the tapping of the workers from the other end.'

'If you didn't know of them beforehand,' I said, 'it might be a rather badly joined tunnel.'

'Exactly,' said Altiora with a high note, 'and that's why we all want to find out each other. . . .'

They didn't talk like that on our first encounter, but they urged me to lunch with them next day, and then it was we went into things. A woman Factory Inspector and the Educational Minister for New Banksland and his wife were also there, but I don't remember they made any contribution to the conversation. The Baileys saw to that. They kept on at me in an urgent litigious way.

'We have read your book,' each began – as though it had been a joint function. 'And we consider –'

'Yes,' I protested, '*I* think –'

That was a secondary matter.

They did not consider, said Altiora, raising her voice and going right over me, that I had allowed sufficiently for the inevitable development of an official administrative class in the modern state.

'Nor of its importance,' echoed Oscar.

That, they explained in a sort of chorus, was the cardinal idea of their lives, what they were up to, what they stood for. 'We want to suggest to you,' they said – and I found this was a stock opening of theirs – 'that from the mere necessities of convenience elected bodies *must* avail themselves more and more of the services of expert officials. We have that very much in mind. The more complicated and technical affairs become, the less confidence will the elected official have in himself. We want to suggest that these expert officials must necessarily develop into a new class and a very powerful class in the community. We want to organize that. It may be *the* power of the future. They will necessarily have to have very much of a common training. We consider ourselves as amateur unpaid precursors of such a class.' . . .

The vision they displayed for my consideration as the aim of public-spirited endeavour seemed like a harder, narrower, more specialized version of the idea of a trained and disciplined state that Willersley and I had worked out in the Alps. They wanted things more organized, more correlated with government and a collective purpose, just as we did, but they saw it not in terms of a growing collective understanding, but in terms of functionaries, legislative change, and methods of administration. . . .

It wasn't clear at first how we differed. The Baileys were very anxious to win me to co-operation, and I was quite prepared at first to identify their distinctive expressions with phrases of my own, and so we came very readily into an alliance that was to last some years, and break at last very painfully. Altiora manifestly liked me, I was soon discussing with her the perplexity I found in placing myself efficiently in the world, the problem of how to take hold of things that occupied my thoughts, and she was sketching out careers for my consideration, very much as an architect on his first visit sketches houses, considers requirements, and puts before you this example and that of the more or less similar thing already done. . . .

It is easy to see how much in common there was between the Baileys and me, and how natural it was that I should become a constant visitor at their house and an ally of theirs in many enterprises. It is not nearly so easy to define the profound antagonism of spirit that also held between us. There was a difference in texture, a difference in quality. How can I express it? The shapes of our thoughts were the same, but the substance quite different. It was as if they made in china or cast iron what I had made in transparent living matter. (The comparison is manifestly from my point of view.) Certain things never seemed to show through their ideas that were visible, refracted perhaps and distorted, but visible always through mine.

I thought for a time the essential difference lay in our relation to beauty. With me beauty is quite primary in life; I like truth, order and goodness, wholly because they are beautiful or lead straight to beautiful consequences. The Baileys either hadn't got that or they didn't see it. They seemed at times to prefer things harsh and ugly. That puzzled me extremely. The aesthetic quality of many of their proposals, the 'manner' of their work, so to speak, were at times as dreadful as – well, War Office barrack architecture. A caricature by its exaggerated statements will sometimes serve to point a truth by antagonizing falsity and falsity. I remember talking to a prominent museum official in need of more public funds for the work he had in hand. I mentioned the possibility of enlisting Bailey's influence.

'Oh, we don't want Philistines like that infernal Bottle-Imprunning us,' he said hastily, and would hear of no concerted action for the end he had in view. 'I'd rather not have the extension.'

'You see,' he went on to explain, 'Bailey's wanting in the essentials.'

'What essentials?' said I.

'Oh! he'd be like a nasty oily efficient little machine for some merely subordinate necessity among all my delicate stuff. He'd do all we wanted no doubt in the way of money and powers – and he'd do it wrong and mess the place for ever. Hands all black, you know. He's just a means. Just a very aggressive and unmanageable means. This isn't a plumber's job. . . .'

I stuck to my argument.

'I don't *like* him,' said the official conclusively, and it seemed to me at the time he was just blind prejudice speaking. . . .

I came nearer the truth of the matter as I came to realize that our philosophies differed profoundly. That isn't a very curable difference, – once people have grown up. Theirs was a philosophy devoid of *finesse*. Temperamentally the Baileys were specialized, concentrated, accurate, while I am urged, either by some inner force or some entirely assimilated influence in my training, always to round off and shadow my outlines. I hate them hard. I would sacrifice detail to modelling always, and the Baileys, it seemed to me, loved a world as flat and metallic as Sidney Cooper's cows. If they had the universe in hand, I know they would take down all the trees and put up stamped tin green shades and sunlight accumulators. Altiora thought trees hopelessly irregular and sea cliffs a great mistake. . . . I got things clearer as time went on. Though it was a Hegelian mess of which I had partaken at Codger's table by way of a philosophical training, my sympathies have always been Pragmatist. I belong almost by nature to that school of Pragmatism that, following the mediaeval Nominalists, bases itself upon a denial of the reality of classes and of the validity of general laws. The Baileys classified everything. They were in the scholastic sense – which so oddly contradicts the modern use of the word – 'Realists.' They believed classes were *real* and independent of their individuals. This is the common habit of all so-called educated people who have no metaphysical aptitude and no metaphysical training. It leads them to a progressive misunderstanding of the world. It was a favourite trick of Altiora's to speak of everybody as a 'type'; she saw men as samples moving; her dining-room became a chamber of representatives. It gave a tremendously scientific air to many of their generalizations, using 'scientific' in its nineteenth-century uncritical Herbert Spencer sense, an air that only began to disappear when one thought them over again in terms of actuality and the people one knew. . . .

At the Baileys' one always seemed to be getting one's hands on the very strings that guided the world. You heard legislation projected to affect this 'type' and that; statistics marched by you with sin and shame and injustice and misery reduced to

165

quite manageable percentages, you found men who were to frame or amend bills in grave and intimate exchange with Bailey's omniscience, you heard Altiora canvassing approaching resignations and possible appointments that might make or mar a revolution in administrative methods, and doing it with a vigorous directness that manifestly swayed the decision; and you felt you were in a sort of signal-box with levers all about you, and the world outside there, albeit a little dark and mysterious beyond the window, running on its lines in ready obedience to these unhesitating lights, true and steady to trim termini.

And then with all this administrative fizzle, this pseudoscientific administrative chatter, dying away in your head, out you went into the limitless grimy chaos of London streets and squares, roads and avenues lined with teeming houses, each larger than the Chambers Street house and at least equally alive, you saw the chaotic clamour of hoardings, the jumble of traffic, the coming and going of mysterious myriads, you heard the rumble of traffic like the noise of a torrent; a vague incessant murmur of cries and voices, wanton crimes and accidents bawled at you from the placards; imperative unaccountable fashions swaggered triumphant in the dazzling windows of the shops; and you found yourself swaying back to the opposite conviction that the huge formless spirit of the world it was that held the strings and danced the puppets on the Bailey stage. . . .

Under the lamps you were jostled by people like my Staffordshire uncle out for a spree, you saw shy youths conversing with prostitutes, you passed young lovers pairing with an entire disregard of the social suitability of the 'types' they might blend or create, you saw men leaning drunken against lamp-posts whom you knew for the 'type' that will charge with fixed bayonets into the face of death, and you found yourself unable to imagine little Bailey achieving either drunkenness or the careless defiance of annihilation. You realized that quite a lot of types were under-represented in Chambers Street, that feral and obscure and altogether monstrous forces must be at work, as yet altogether unassimilated by those neat administrative reorganizations.

# 5

Altiora, I remember, preluded Margaret's reappearance by announcing her as a 'new type.'

I was accustomed to go early to the Baileys' dinners in those days, for a preliminary gossip with Altiora in front of her drawing-room fire. One got her alone, and that early arrival was a little sign of appreciation she valued. She had every woman's need of followers and servants.

'I'm going to send you down tonight,' she said, 'with a very interesting type indeed – one of the new generation of serious gals. Middle-class origin – and quite well off. Rich in fact. Her step-father was a solicitor and something of an *entrepreneur* towards the end, I fancy – in the Black Country. There was a little brother died, and she's lost her mother quite recently. Quite on her own, so to speak. She's never been out into society very much, and doesn't seem really very anxious to go. . . . Not exactly an intellectual person, you know, but quiet, and great force of character. Came up to London on her own and came to us – some one had told her we were the sort of people to advise her – to ask what to do. I'm sure she'll interest you. . . .'

'What *can* people of that sort do?' I asked. 'Is she capable of investigation?'

Altiora compressed her lips and shook her head. She always did shake her head when you asked that of any one.

'Of course what she ought to do,' said Altiora, with her silk dress pulled back from her knee before the fire, and with a lift of her voice towards a chuckle at her daring way of putting things, 'is to marry a member of Parliament and see he does his work . . . Perhaps she will. It's a very exceptional gal who can do anything by herself – quite exceptional. The more serious they are – without being exceptional – the more we want them to marry.'

Her exposition was truncated by the entry of the type in question.

'Well!' cried Altiora, turning, and with a high note of welcome, 'Here you are!'

Margaret had gained in dignity and prettiness by the lapse of five years, and she was now very beautiful and richly and

167

simply dressed. Her fair hair had been done in some way that made it seem softer and more abundant than it was in my memory, and a gleam of purple velvet-set diamonds showed amidst its mist of little golden and brown lines. Her dress was of white and violet, the last trace of mourning for her mother, and confessed the gracious droop of her tall and slender body. She did not suggest Staffordshire at all, and I was puzzled for a moment to think where I had met her. Her sweetly shaped mouth with the slightly obliquity of the lip and the little kink in her brow were extraordinarily familiar to me. But she had either been prepared by Altiora or she remembered my name. 'We met,' she said, 'while my step-father was alive – at Misterton. You came to see us'; and instantly I recalled the sunshine between the apple blossom and a slender pale blue girlish shape among the daffodils, like something that had sprung from a bulb itself. I recalled at once that I had found her very interesting, though I did not clearly remember how it was she had interested me.

Other guests arrived – it was one of Altiora's boldly blended mixtures of people with ideas and people with influence or money who might perhaps be expected to resonate to them. Bailey came down late with an air of hurry, and was introduced to Margaret and said absolutely nothing to her – there being no information either to receive or impart and nothing to do – but stood snatching his left cheek until I rescued him and her, and left him free to congratulate the new Lady Snape on her husband's K.C.B.

I took Margaret down. We achieved no feats of mutual expression, except that it was abundantly clear we were both very pleased and interested to meet again, and that we had both kept memories of each other. We made that Misterton tea-party and the subsequent marriages of my cousins, and the world of Burslem generally, matter for quite an agreeable conversation until at last Altiora, following her inevitable custom, called me by name imperatively out of our duologue. 'Mr Remington,' she said, 'we want your opinion –' in her entirely characteristic effort to get all the threads of conversation into her own hands for the climax that always wound up her dinners. How the other women used to hate those concluding raids of hers! I forget most of the other women at that dinner, nor can I re-

168

call what the crowning rally was about. It didn't in any way join on to my impression of Margaret.

In the drawing-room of the matting floor I rejoined her, with Altiora's manifest connivance, and in the interval I had been thinking of our former meeting.

'Do you find London,' I asked, 'gives you more opportunity for doing things and learning things than Burslem?'

She showed at once she appreciated my allusion to her former confidences. 'I was very discontented then,' she said, and paused. 'I've really only been in London for a few months. It's so different. In Burslem, life seems all business and getting – without any reason. One went on and it didn't seem to mean anything. At least anything that mattered. . . . London seems to be so full of meanings – all mixed up together.'

She knitted her brows over her words and smiled appealingly at the end as if for consideration for her inadequate expression, appealingly and almost humorously.

I looked understandingly at her. 'We have all,' I agreed, 'to come to London.'

'One sees so much distress,' she added, as if she felt she had completely omitted something, and needed a codicil.

'What are you doing in London?'

'I'm thinking of studying. Some social question. I thought perhaps I might go and study social conditions as Mrs Bailey did, go perhaps as a work-girl or see the reality of living in, but Mrs Bailey thought perhaps it wasn't quite my work.'

'Are you studying?'

'I'm going to a good many lectures, and perhaps I shall take up a regular course at the Westminster School of Politics and Sociology. But Mrs Bailey doesn't seem to believe very much in that either.'

Her faintly whimsical smile returned. 'I seem rather indefinite,' she apologized, 'but one does not want to get entangled in things one can't do. One – one has so many advantages, one's life seems to be such a trust and such a responsibility –'

She stopped.

'A man gets driven into work,' I said.

'It must be splendid to be Mrs Bailey,' she replied with a glance of envious admiration across the room.

'*She* has no doubts, anyhow,' I remarked.

'She *had*,' said Margaret with the pride of one who has received great confidences.

6

'You've met before?' said Altiora, a day or so later.
I explained when.
'You find her interesting?'
I saw in a flash that Altiora meant to marry me to Margaret.
Her intention became much clearer as the year developed.
Altiora was systematic even in matters that evaded system. I
was to marry Margaret, and freed from the need of making an
income I was to come into politics – as an exponent of Baileyism. She put it down with the other excellent and advantageous
things that should occupy her summer holiday. It was her pride
and glory to put things down and plan them out in detail beforehand, and I'm not quite sure that she did not even mark off
the day upon which the engagement was to be declared. If she
did, I disappointed her. We didn't come to an engagement, in
spite of the broadest hints and the glaring obviousness of
everything, that summer.

Every summer the Baileys went out of London to some
house they hired or borrowed, leaving their secretaries toiling
behind, and they went on working hard in the mornings and
evenings and taking exercise in the open air in the afternoon.
They cycled assiduously and went for long walks at a trot, and
raided and studied (and incidentally explained themselves to)
any social 'types' that lived in the neighbourhood. One invaded type, resentful under research, described them with a
dreadful aptness as Donna Quixote and Sancho Panza – and
himself as a harmless windmill, hurting no one and signifying
nothing. She did rather tilt at things. This particular summer
they were at a pleasant farmhouse in level country near Pangbourne, belonging to the Hon Wilfred Winchester, and they
asked me to come down to rooms in the neighbourhood –
Altiora took them for a month for me in August – and board
with them upon extremely reasonable terms ; and when I got
there I found Margaret sitting in a hammock at Altiora's feet.
Lots of people, I gathered, were coming and going in the
neighbourhood, the Ponts were in a villa on the river, and the

Rickhams' houseboat was to moor for some days; but these irruptions did not impede a great deal of duologue between Margaret and myself.

Altiora was efficient rather than artistic in her match-making. She sent us off for long walks together – Margaret was a fairly good walker – she exhumed some defective croquet things and incited us to croquet, not understanding that detestable game is the worst stimulant for lovers in the world. And Margaret and I were always getting left about, and finding ourselves for odd half-hours in the kitchen garden with nothing to do except talk, or we were told with a wave of the hand to run away and amuse each other.

Altiora even tried a picnic in canoes, knowing from fiction rather than imagination or experience the conclusive nature of such excursions. But there she fumbled at the last moment, and elected at the river's bank to share a canoe with me. Bailey showed so much zeal and so little skill – his hat fell off and he became miraculously nothing but paddle-clutching hands and a vast wrinkled brow – that at last he had to be paddled ignominiously by Margaret, while Altiora, after a phase of rigid discretion, as nearly as possible drowned herself – and me no doubt into the bargain – with a sudden lateral gesture of the arm to emphasize the high note with which she dismissed the efficiency of the Charity Organization Society. We shipped about an inch of water and sat in it for the rest of the time, an inconvenience she disregarded heroically. We had difficulties in landing Oscar from his frail craft upon the ait of our feasting – he didn't balance sideways and was much alarmed – and afterwards, as Margaret had a pain in her back, I took him in my canoe, let him hide his shame with an ineffectual but not positively harmful paddle, and towed the other by means of the joined painters. Still it was the fault of the inadequate information supplied in the books and not of Altiora that that was not the date of my betrothal.

I find it not a little difficult to state what kept me back from proposing marriage to Margaret that summer, and what urged me forward at last to marry her. It is so much easier to remember one's resolutions than to remember the moods and suggestions that produced them.

Marrying and getting married was, I think, a pretty simple

171

affair to Altiora ; it was something that happened to the adolescent and unmarried when you threw them together under the circumstances of health, warmth and leisure. It happened with the kindly and approving smiles of the more experienced elders who had organized these proximities. The young people married, settled down, children ensued, and father and mother turned their minds, now decently and properly disillusioned, to other things. That to Altiora was the normal sexual life, and she believed it to be the quality of the great bulk of the life about her.

One of the great barriers to human understanding is the wide temperamental difference one finds in the values of things relating to sex. It is the issue upon which people most need training in charity and imaginative sympathy. Here are no universal standards at all, and indeed for no single man or woman does there seem to be fixed any standard, so much do the accidents of circumstance and one's physical phases affect one's interpretations. There is nothing in the whole range of sexual fact that may not seem supremely beautiful or humanly jolly or magnificently wicked or disgusting or trivial or utterly insignificant, according to the eye that sees or the mood that colours. Here is something that may fill the skies and every waking hour or be almost completely banished from a life. It may be everything on Monday and less than nothing on Saturday. And we make our laws and rules as though in these matters all men and women were commensurable one with another, with an equal steadfast passion and an equal constant duty. . . .

I don't know what dreams Altiora may have had in her schoolroom days, I always suspected her of suppressed and forgotten phases, but certainly her general effect now was of an entirely passionless worldliness in these matters. Indeed, so far as I could get at her, she regarded sexual passion as being hardly more legitimate in a civilized person than – let us say – homicidal mania. She must have forgotten – and Bailey too. I suspect she forgot before she married him. I don't suppose either of them had the slightest intimation of the dimensions sexual love can take in the thoughts of the great majority of people with whom they came in contact. They loved in their way – an intellectual way it was and a fond way – but it had

172

no relation to beauty and physical sensation – except that there seemed a decree of exile against these things. They got their glow in high moments of altruistic ambition – and in moments of vivid worldly success. They sat at opposite ends of their dinner table with so and so 'captured', and so and so, flushed with a mutual approval. They saw people in love forgetful and distraught about them, and just put it down to forgetfulness and distraction. At any rate, Altiora manifestly viewed my situation and Margaret's with an abnormal and entirely misleading simplicity. There was the girl, rich, with an acceptable claim to be beautiful, shiningly virtuous, quite capable of political interests, and there was I, talented, ambitious and full of political and social passion, in need of just the money, devotion and regularization Margaret could provide. We were both unmarried – white sheets of uninscribed paper. Was there ever a simpler situation? What more could we possibly want?

She was even a little offended at the inconclusiveness that did not settle things at Pangbourne. I seemed to her, I suspect, to reflect upon her judgement and good intentions.


7

I didn't see things with Altiora's simplicity.

I admired Margaret very much, I was fully aware of all that she and I might give each other ; indeed, so far as Altiora went we were quite in agreement. But what seemed solid ground to Altiora and the ultimate footing of her emasculated world, was to me just the superficial covering of a gulf – oh! abysses of vague and dim, and yet stupendously significant things.

I couldn't dismiss the interests and the passion of sex as Altiora did. Work, I agreed, was important ; career and success ; but deep unanalyzable instincts told me this preoccupation was a thing quite as important ; dangerous, interfering, destructive indeed, but none the less a dominating interest in life. I have told how flittingly and uninvited it came like a moth from the outer twilight into my life, how it grew in me with my manhood, how it found its way to speech and grew daring, and led me at last to experience. After that adventure at Locarno sex and the interests and desires of sex never left me for long at peace. I went on with my work and my career, and all the time

173

it was like – like some one talking ever and again in a room while one tries to write.

There were times when I could have wished the world a world all of men, so greatly did this unassimilated series of motives and curiosities hamper me; and times when I could have wished the world all of women. I seemed always to be seeking something in women, in girls, and I was never clear what it was I was seeking. But never – even at my coarsest – was I moved by physical desire alone. Was I seeking help and fellowship? Was I seeking some intimacy with beauty? It was a thing too formless to state, that I seemed always desiring to attain and never attaining. Waves of gross sensuousness arose out of this preoccupation, carried me to a crisis of gratification or disappointment that was clearly not the needed thing; they passed and left my mind free again for a time to get on with the permanent pursuits of my life. And then presently this solicitude would have me again, an irrelevance as it seemed, and yet a constantly recurring demand.

I don't want particularly to dwell upon things that are disagreeable for others to read, but I cannot leave them out of my story and get the right proportions of the forces I am balancing. I was no abnormal man, and that world of order we desire to make must be built of such stuff as I was and am and can beget. You cannot have a world of Baileys; it would end in one orderly generation. Humanity is begotten in Desire, lives by Desire.

> Love which is lust, is the Lamp in the Tomb;
> Love which is lust, is the Call from the Gloom.

I echo Henley.

I suppose the life of celibacy which the active, well-fed, well-exercised and imaginatively stirred young man of the educated classes is supposed to lead from the age of nineteen or twenty, when Nature certainly meant him to marry, to thirty or more, when civilization permits him to do so, is the most impossible thing in the world. We deal here with facts that are kept secret and obscure, but I doubt for my own part if more than one man out of five in our class satisfies that ideal demand. The rest are even as I was, and Hatherleigh and Esmeer and all the men I knew. I draw no lessons and offer no panacea; I have to tell the quality of life, and this is how it is. This is how it will remain until men and women have the courage to face the facts of life.

I was no systematic libertine, you must understand ; things happened to me and desire drove me. Any young man would have served for that Locarno adventure, and after that what had been a mystic and wonderful thing passed rapidly into a gross, manifestly misdirected and complicating one. I can count a meagre tale of five illicit loves in the days of my youth, to include that first experience, and of them all only two were sustained relationships. Besides these five 'affairs', on one or two occasions I dipped so low as the inky dismal sensuality of the streets, and made one of those pairs of correlated figures, the woman in her squalid finery sailing homeward, the man modestly aloof and behind, that every night in the London year flit by the score of thousands across the sight of the observant. . . .

How ugly it is to recall ; ugly and shameful now without qualification! Yet at the time there was surely something not altogether ugly in it – something that has vanished, some fine thing mortally ailing.

One such occasion I recall as if it were a vision deep down in a pit, as if it had happened in another state of existence to some one else. And yet it is the sort of thing that has happened, once or twice at least, to half the men in London who have been in a position to make it possible. Let me try and give you its peculiar effect. Man or women, you ought to know of it.

Figure to yourself a dingy room, somewhere in that network of streets that lies about Tottenham Court Road, a dingy bedroom lit by a solitary candle and carpeted with scraps and patches, with curtains of cretonne closing the window, and a tawdry ornament of paper in the grate. I sit on a bed beside a weary-eyed, fair-haired, sturdy young woman, half undressed, who is telling me in broken German something that my knowledge of German is at first inadequate to understand. . . .

I thought she was boasting about her family, and then slowly the meaning came to me. She was a Lett from near Libau in Courland, and she was telling me – just as one tells something too strange for comment or emotion – how her father had been shot and her sister outraged and murdered before her eyes.

It was as if one had dipped into something primordial and stupendous beneath the smooth and trivial surfaces of life. There was I, you know, the promising young don from Cambridge, who wrote quite brilliantly about politics and might presently get into Parliament, with my collar and tie in my hand, and a certain sense of shameful adventure fading out of my mind.

'Ach Gott!' she sighed by way of comment, and mused deeply for a moment before she turned her face to me, as to something forgotten and remembered, and assumed the half-hearted meretricious smile.

'Bin ich eine hubsche?' she asked like one who repeats a lesson.

I was moved to crave her pardon and come away.

'Bin ich eine hubsche?' she asked a little anxiously, laying a detaining hand upon me and evidently not understanding a word of what I was striving to say.


8

I find it extraordinarily difficult to recall the phases by which I passed from my first admiration of Margaret's earnestness and unconscious daintiness to an intimate acquaintance. The earlier encounters stand out clear and hard, but then the impressions become crowded and mingle not only with each other but with all the subsequent developments of relationship, the enormous evolutions of interpretation and comprehension between husband and wife. Dipping into my memories is like dipping into a ragbag, one brings out this memory or that, with no intimation of how they came in time or what led to them and joined them together. And they are all mixed up with subsequent associations, with sympathies and discords, habits of intercourse, surprises and disappointments and discovered misunderstandings. I know only that always my feelings for Margaret were complicated feelings, woven of many and varied strands.

It is one of the curious neglected aspects of life how at the same time and in relation to the same reality we can have in our mind streams of thought at quite different levels. We can be at the same time idealizing a person and seeing and criticizing that person quite coldly and clearly, and we slip unconsciously from level to level and produce all sorts of inconsistent acts. In a sense I had no illusions about Margaret; in a sense my conception of Margaret was entirely poetic illusion. I don't think I was ever blind to certain defects of hers, and quite as certainly they didn't seem to matter in the slightest degree. Her mind had a curious want of vigour, 'flatness' is the only word; she never seemed to escape from her phrase; her way of thinking, her way of doing was indecisive; she remained in her attitude, it did not flow out to easy, confirmatory action.

I saw this quite clearly, and when we walked and talked together I seemed always trying for animation in her and never finding it. I would state my ideas. 'I know,' she would say, 'I know.'

I talked about myself and she listened wonderfully, but she made no answering revelations. I talked politics, and she remarked with her blue eyes wide and earnest: 'Every *word* you say seems so just.'

I admired her appearance tremendously but – I can only express it by saying I didn't want to touch her. Her fair hair was always delectably done. It flowed beautifully over her pretty small ears, and she would tie its fair coilings with fillets of black or blue velvet that carried pretty buckles of silver and paste. The light, the faint down on her brow and cheek, was delightful. And it was clear to me that I made her happy.

My sense of her deficiencies didn't stand in the way of my falling at last very deeply in love with her. Her very shortcomings seemed to offer me something. . . .

She stood in my mind for goodness – and for things from which it seemed to me my hold was slipping.

She seemed to promise a way of escape from the deepening opposition in me between physical passions and the constructive career, the career of wide aims and human service, upon which I had embarked. All the time that I was seeing her as a beautiful fragile, rather ineffective girl, I was also seeing her just as consciously as a shining slender figure, a radiant reconciliation, coming into my darkling disorders of lust and impulse. I could understand clearly that she was incapable of the most necessary subtleties of political thought, and yet I could contemplate praying to her and putting all the intricate troubles of my life at her feet.

177

Before the reappearance of Margaret in my world at all an unwonted disgust with the consequences and quality of my passions had arisen in my mind. Among other things that moment with the Lettish girl haunted me persistently. I would see myself again and again sitting amidst those sluttish surroundings, collar and tie in hand, while her heavy German words grouped themselves to a slowly apprehending meaning. I would feel again with a fresh stab of remorse that this was not a flash of adventure, this was not seeing life in any permissible sense, but a dip into tragedy, dishonour, hideous degradation, and the pitiless cruelty of a world as yet uncontrolled by any ordered will.

'Good God!' I put it to myself, 'that I should finish the work those Cossacks had begun! I who want order and justice before everything! There's no way out of it, no decent excuse! If I didn't think, I ought to have thought!' ...

'How did I get to it?' ... I would ransack the phases of my development from the first shy unveiling of a hidden wonder to that last extremity as a man will go through muddled account books to find some disorganizing error....

I was also involved at that time – I find it hard to place these things in the exact order of their dates because they were so disconnected with the regular progress of my work and life – in an intrigue, a clumsy, sensuous, pretentious, artificially stimulated intrigue, with a Mrs Larrimer, a woman living separated from her husband. I will not go into particulars of that episode, nor how we quarrelled and chafed one another. She was at once unfaithful and jealous and full of whims about our meetings; she was careless of our secret, and vulgarized our relationship by intolerable interpretations; except for some growing moments of gratification, except for the recurrent and essentially vicious desire that drew us back to each other again, we both fretted at a vexatious and unexpectedly binding intimacy. The interim was full of the quality of work delayed, of time and energy wasted, of insecure precautions against scandal and exposure. Disappointment is almost inherent in illicit love. I had, and perhaps it was part of her recurrent irritation also, a feeling as though one had followed something fine and beautiful into a net – into bird lime! These furtive scuffles, this sneaking into shabby houses of assignation, was what we had made out of the suggestion of pagan beauty; this was the reality of our vision of nymphs and satyrs dancing for the joy of life amidst incessant sunshine. We had laid hands upon the wonder and glory of bodily love and wasted them. . . .

It was the sense of waste, of finely beautiful possibilities getting entangled and marred for ever that oppressed me. I had missed, I had lost. I did not turn from these things after the fashion of the Baileys, as one turns from something low and embarrassing. I felt that these great organic forces were still to be wrought into a harmony with my constructive passion. I felt too that I was not doing it. I had not understood the forces in this struggle or its nature, and as I learnt I failed. I had been started wrong, I had gone on wrong, in a world that was muddled and confused, full of false counsel and erratic shames and twisted temptations. I learnt to see it so by failures that were perhaps destroying any chance of profit in my lessons. Moods of clear keen industry alternated with moods of relapse and indulgence and moods of dubiety and remorse. I was not going on as the Baileys thought I was going on. There were times when the blindness of the Baileys irritated me intensely. Beneath the ostensible success of those years, between twenty-three and twenty-eight, this rottenness, known to scarcely any one but myself, grew and spread. My sense of the probability of a collapse intensified. I knew indeed now, even as Willersley had prophesied five years before, that I was entangling myself in something that might smother all my uses in the world. Down there among those incommunicable difficulties, I was puzzled and blundering. I was losing my hold upon things ; the chaotic and adventurous element in life was spreading upward and getting the better of me, over-mastering me and all my will to rule and make. . . . And the strength, the drugging urgency of the passion! . . .

Margaret shone at times in my imagination like a radiant angel in a world of mire and disorder, in a world of cravings, hot and dull red like scars inflamed. . . .

I suppose it was because I had so great a need of such help as her whiteness proffered, that I could ascribe impossible perfections to her, a power of intellect, a moral power and patience to which she, poor fellow mortal, had indeed no claim. If only a few of us *were* angels and freed from the tangle of effort, how easy life might be! I wanted her so badly, so very badly, to be what I needed. I wanted a woman to save me. I forced myself to see her as I wished to see her. Her tepidities became infinite delicacies, her mental vagueness an atmospheric realism. The harsh precisions of the Baileys and Altiora's blunt directness threw up her fineness into relief and made a grace of every weakness.

Mixed up with the memory of times when I talked with Margaret as one talks politely to those who are hopelessly inferior in mental quality, explaining with a false lucidity, welcoming and encouraging the feeblest response, when possible moulding and directing, are times when I did indeed, as the old phrase goes, worship the ground she trod on. I was equally honest and unconscious of inconsistency at each extreme. But in neither phase could I find it easy to make love to Margaret. For in the first I did not want to, though I talked abundantly to her of marriage and so forth, and was a little puzzled at myself for not going on to some personal application; and in the second she seemed inaccessible – I felt I must make confessions and put things before her that would be the grossest outrage upon the noble purity I attributed to her.

9

I went to Margaret at last to ask her to marry me, wrought up to the mood of one who stakes his life on a cast. Separated from her, and with the resonance of an evening of angry recriminations with Mrs Larrimer echoing in my mind, I discovered myself to be quite passionately in love with Margaret. Last shreds of doubt vanished. It has always been a feature of our relationship that Margaret absent means more to me than Margaret present; her memory distils from its dross and purifies in me. All my criticisms and qualifications of her vanished into some dark corner of my mind. She was the lady of my salvation ; I must win my way to her or perish.

I went to her at last, for all that I knew she loved me, in passionate self-abasement, white and a-tremble. She was staying with the Rockleys at Woking, for Shena Rockley had been at Bennett Hall with her and they had resumed a close intimacy; and I went down to her on an impulse, unheralded. I was kept

180

waiting for some minutes, I remember, in a little room upon which a conservatory opened, a conservatory full of pots of large mauve-edged, white cyclamens in flower. And there was a big lacquer cabinet, a Chinese thing, I suppose, of black and gold against the red-toned wall. To this day the thought of Margaret is inseparably bound up with the sight of a cyclamen's back-turned petals.

She came in, looking pale and drooping rather more than usual. I suddenly realized that Altiora's hint of a disappointment leading to positive illness was something more than a vindictive comment. She closed the door and came across to me and took and dropped my hand and stood still. 'What is it you want with me?' she asked.

The speech I had been turning over and over in my mind on the way vanished at the sight of her.

'I want to talk to you,' I answered lamely.

For some seconds neither of us said a word.

'I want to tell you things about my life,' I began.

She answered with a scarcely audible 'yes.'

'I almost asked you to marry me at Pangbourne,' I plunged. 'I didn't. I didn't because – because you had too much to give me.'

'Too much!' she echoed, 'to give you!' She had lifted her eyes to my face and the colour was coming into her cheeks.

'Don't misunderstand me,' I said hastily. 'I want to tell you things, things you don't know. Don't answer me. I want to tell you.'

She stood before the fireplace with her ultimate answer shining through the quiet of her face. 'Go on,' she said, very softly. It was so pitilessly manifest she was resolved to idealize the situation whatever I might say. I began walking up and down the room between those cyclamens and the cabinet. There were little gold fishermen on the cabinet fishing from little islands that each had a pagoda and a tree, and there were also men in boats or something, I couldn't determine what, and some obscure sub-office in my mind concerned itself with that quite intently. Yet I seem to have been striving with all my being to get words for the truth of things. 'You see,' I emerged, 'you make everything possible to me. You can give me help and sympathy, support, understanding. You know my political

181

ambitions. You know all that I might do in the world. I do so intensely want to do constructive things, big things perhaps, in this wild jumble. ... Only you don't know a bit what I am. I want to tell you what I am. I'm complex. ... I'm streaked.'

I glanced at her, and she was regarding me with an expression of blissful disregard for any meaning I was seeking to convey.

'You see,' I said, 'I'm a bad man.'

She sounded a note of valiant incredulity.

Everything seemed to be slipping away from me. I pushed on to the ugly facts that remained over from the wreck of my interpretation. 'What has held me back,' I said, 'is the thought that you could not possibly understand certain things in my life. Men are not as pure as women are. I have had love affairs. I mean I have had affairs. Passion – desire. You see, I have had a mistress, I have been entangled –'

She seemed about to speak, but I interrupted. 'I'm not telling you,' I said, 'what I meant to tell you. I want you to know clearly that there is another side to my life, a dirty side. Deliberately I say, dirty. It didn't seem so at first –'

I stopped blankly. 'Dirty', I thought, was the most idiotic choice of words to have made.

I had never in any tolerable sense of the word been dirty.

'I drifted into this – as men do,' I said after a little pause and stopped again.

She was looking at me with her wide blue eyes.

'Did you imagine,' she began, 'that I thought you – that I expected –'

'But how can you know?'

'I know. I do know.'

'But –' I began.

'I know,' she persisted, dropping her eyelids. 'Of course I know,' and nothing could have convinced me more completely that she did not know.

'All men –' she generalized. 'A woman does not understand these temptations.'

I was astonished beyond measure at her way of taking my confession. ...

'Of course,' she said, hesitating a little over a transparent difficulty, 'it's all over and past.'

182

'It's all over and past,' I answered.

There was a little pause.

'I don't want to know,' she said. 'None of that seems to matter now in the slightest degree.'

She looked up and smiled as though we had exchanged some acceptable commonplaces. 'Poor dear!' she said, dismissing everything, and put out her arms, and it seemed to me that I could hear the Lettish girl in the background – doomed safety-valve of purity in this intolerable world! – telling something in indistinguishable German – I knew not what nor why. . . .

I took Margaret in my arms and kissed her. Her eyes were wet with tears. She clung to me and was near, I felt, to sobbing.

'I have loved you,' she whispered presently, 'oh! ever since we met in Misterton – six years and more ago.'

# Margaret in Venice

## 1

There comes into my mind a confused memory of conversations with Margaret; we must have had dozens altogether, and they mix in now for the most part inextricably not only with one another, but with later talks and with things we discussed at Pangbourne. We had the immensest anticipations of the years and opportunities that lay before us. I was now very deeply in love with her indeed. I felt not that I had cleaned up my life, but that she had. We called each other 'confederate', I remember, and made during our brief engagement a series of visits to the various legislative bodies in London, the County Council, the House of Commons, where we dined with Villiers, and the St Pancras Vestry, where we heard Shaw speaking. I was full of plans and so was she of the way in which we were to live and work. We were to pay back in public service whatever excess of wealth beyond his merits old Seddon's economic advantage had won for him from the toiling people in the potteries. The end of the Boer War was so recent that that blessed word 'efficiency' echoed still in people's minds and thoughts. Lord Rosebery in a memorable oration had put it into the heads of the big outer public, but the Baileys with a certain show of justice claimed to have set it going in the channels that took it to him – if as a matter of fact it was taken to him. But then it was their habit to make claims of that sort. They certainly did their share to keep 'efficient' going. Altiora's highest praise was 'thoroughly efficient'. We were to be a 'thoroughly efficient' political couple of the 'new type'. She explained us to herself and Oscar, she explained us to ourselves, she explained us to the people who came to her dinners and afternoons until the world was highly charged with explanation and expectation, and the proposal that I should be the Liberal candidate for the Kinghamstead Division seemed the most natural development in the world.

I was full of the ideal of hard restrained living and relentless activity, and throughout a beautiful November at Venice, where chiefly we spent our honeymoon, we turned over and over again and discussed in every aspect our conception of a life tremendously focussed upon the ideal of social service.

Most clearly there stands out a picture of ourselves talking in a gondola on our way to Torcello. Far away behind us the smoke of Murano forms a black stain upon an immense shining prospect of smooth water, water as unruffled and luminous as the sky above, a mirror on which rows of posts and distant black high-stemmed swan-necked boats with their minutely clear swinging gondoliers, float aerially. Remote and low before us rises the little tower of our destination. Our men swing together and their oars swirl leisurely through the water, bump back in the rowlocks, splash sharply and go swishing back again. Margaret lies back on cushions, with her face shaded by a holland parasol, and I sit up beside her.

'You see,' I say, and in spite of Margaret's note of perfect acquiescence I feel myself reasoning against an indefinable antagonism, 'it is so easy to fall into a slack way with life. There may seem to be something priggish in a meticulous discipline, but otherwise it is so easy to slip into indolent habits – and to be distracted from one's purpose. The country, the world, wants men to serve its constructive needs, to work out and carry out plans. For a man who has to make a living the enemy is immediate necessity; for people like ourselves it's – it's the constant small opportunity of agreeable things.'

'Frittering away,' she says, 'time and strength.'

'That is what I feel. It's so pleasant to pretend one is simply modest, it looks so foolish at times to take one's self too seriously. We've *got* to take ourselves seriously.'

She endorses my words with her eyes.

'I feel I can do great things with life.'

'I *know* you can.'

'But that's only to be done by concentrating one's life upon one main end. We have to plan our days, to make everything subserve our scheme.'

'I feel,' she answers softly, 'we ought to give – every hour.'

Her face becomes dreamy. 'I *want* to give every hour,' she adds.

## 2

That holiday in Venice is set in my memory like a little artificial lake in uneven confused country, as something very bright and skylike, and discontinuous with all about it. The faded quality of the very sunshine of that season, the mellow discoloured palaces and places, the huge, time-ripened paintings of departed splendours, the whispering, nearly noiseless passage of hearse-black gondolas, for the horrible steam launch had not yet ruined Venice, the stilled magnificences of the depopulated lagoons, the universal autumn, made me feel altogether in recess from the teeming uproars of reality. There were not a dozen people all told, no Americans and scarcely any English, to dine in the big cavern of a dining-room, with its vistas of separate tables, its distempered walls and its swathed chandeliers. We went about seeing beautiful things, accepting beauty on every hand, and taking it for granted that all was well with ourselves and the world. It was ten days or a fortnight before I became fretful and anxious for action; a long tranquillity for such a temperament as mine.

Our pleasures were curiously impersonal, a succession of shared aesthetic appreciation threads all that time. Our honeymoon was no exultant coming together, no mutual shout of '*you!*' We were almost shy with one another, and felt the relief of even a picture to help us out. It was entirely in my conception of things that I should be very watchful not to shock or distress Margaret or press the sensuous note. Our love-making had much of the tepid smoothness of the lagoons. We talked in delicate innuendo of what should be glorious freedoms. Margaret had missed Verona and Venice in her precious Italian journey – fear of the mosquito had driven her mother across Italy to the westward route – and now she could fill up her gaps and see the Titians and Paul Veroneses she already knew in colourless photographs, the Carpaccios, (the St George series delighted her beyond measure,) the Basaitis and that great statue of Bartolomeo Colleoni that Ruskin praised.

But since I am not a man to look at pictures and architectural effects day after day, I did watch Margaret very closely and store a thousand memories of her. I can see her now, her long body drooping a little forward, her sweet face upraised to

186

some discovered familiar masterpiece and shining with a delicate enthusiasm. I can hear again the soft cadences of her voice murmuring commonplace comments, for she had no gift of expressing the shapeless satisfactions these things gave her.

Margaret, I perceived, was a cultivated person, the first cultivated person with whom I had ever come into close contact. She was cultivated and moral, and I, I now realize, was never either of these things. She was passive, and I am active. She did not simply and naturally look for beauty, but she had been incited to look for it at school, and took perhaps a keener interest in books and lectures and all the organization of beautiful things than she did in beauty itself; she found much of her delight in being guided to it. Now a thing ceases to be beautiful to me when some finger points me out its merits. Beauty is the salt of life, but I take my beauty as a wild beast gets its salt, as a constituent of the meal. . . .

And besides, there was that between us that should have seemed more beautiful than any picture. . . .

So we went about Venice tracking down pictures and spiral staircases and such-like things, and my brains were busy all the time with such things as a comparison of Venice and its nearest modern equivalent, New York, with the elaboration of schemes of action when we returned to London, with the development of a theory of Margaret.

Our marriage had done this much at least – that it had fused and destroyed those two independent ways of thinking about her that had gone on in my mind hitherto. Suddenly she had become very near to me, and a very big thing, a sort of comprehensive generalization behind a thousand questions, like the sky or England. The judgements and understandings that had worked when she was, so to speak, miles away from my life had now to be altogether revised. Trifling things began to matter enormously, that she had a weak and easily fatigued back, for example, or that when she knitted her brows and stammered a little in talking, it didn't really mean that an exquisite significance struggled for utterance.

We visited pictures in the mornings chiefly. In the afternoon, unless we were making a day-long excursion in a gondola, Margaret would rest for an hour while I prowled about in search of English newspapers, and then we would go to tea in

187

the Piazza San Marco and watch the drift of people feeding the pigeons and going into the little doors beneath the sunlit arches and domes of Saint Mark's. Then perhaps we would stroll on the Piazzetta, or go out into the sunset in a gondola. Margaret became very interested in the shops that abound under the colonnades, and decided at last to make an extensive purchase of table glass. 'These things,' she said, 'are quite beautiful, and far cheaper than anything but the most ordinary-looking English ware.' I was interested in her idea, and a good deal charmed by the delightful qualities of tinted shape, slender handle and twisted stem. I suggested we should get not simply tumblers and wineglasses, but bedroom water-bottles, fruit- and sweet-dishes, water-jugs, and in the end we made quite a business-like afternoon of it.

I was beginning now to long quite definitely for events. Energy was accumulating in me and worrying me for an outlet. I found *The Times* and the *Daily Telegraph*, and the other papers I managed to get hold of, more and more stimulating. I nearly wrote to the former paper one day in answer to a letter by Lord Grimthorpe – I forget now upon what point. I chafed secretly against this life of tranquil appreciations more and more. I found my attitudes of restrained and delicate affection for Margaret increasingly difficult to sustain. I surprised myself and her by little gusts of irritability, gusts like the cat's-paws before a gale. I was alarmed at these symptoms.

One night when Margaret had gone up to her room, I put on a light overcoat, went out into the night and prowled for a long time through the narrow streets, smoking and thinking. I returned and went and sat on the edge of her bed to talk to her.

'Look here, Margaret,' I said ; 'this is all very well, but I'm restless.'

'Restless!' she said with a faint surprise in her voice.

'Yes. I think I want exercise. I've got a sort of feeling – I've never had it before – as though I was getting fat.'

'My dear!' she cried.

'I want to do things ; – ride horses, climb mountains, take the devil out of myself.'

She watched me thoughtfully.

'Couldn't we *do* something?' she said.

'Do what?'

'I don't know. Couldn't we perhaps go away from here soon – and walk in the mountains – on our way home.'

I thought. 'There seems to be no exercise at all in this place.'

'Isn't there some walk?'

'I wonder,' I answered. 'We might walk to Chioggia, perhaps, along the Lido.' And we tried that, but the long stretch of beach fatigued Margaret's back, and gave her blisters, and we never got beyond Malamocco. . . .

A day or so after we went out to those pleasant black-robed, bearded Armenians in their monastery at San Lazzaro, and returned towards sundown. We fell into a silence. '*Piu lento*,' said Margaret to the gondolier, and released my accumulated resolution.

'Let us go back to London,' I said abruptly.

Margaret looked at me with surprised blue eyes.

'This is beautiful beyond measure, you know,' I said, sticking to my point, 'but I have work to do.'

She was silent for some seconds. 'I had forgotten,' she said.

'So had I,' I sympathized, and took her hand. 'Suddenly I have remembered.'

She remained quite still. 'There is so much to be done,' I said, almost apologetically.

She looked long away from me across the lagoon, and at last sighed, like one who has drunk deeply, and turned to me.

'I suppose one ought not to be so happy,' she said. 'Everything has been so beautiful and so simple and splendid. And clean. It has been just With You – the time of my life. It's a pity such things must end. But the world is calling you, dear. . . . I ought not to have forgotten it. I thought you were resting – and thinking. But if you are rested – Would you like us to start tomorrow?'

She looked at once so fragile and so devoted that on the spur of the moment I relented, and we stayed in Venice four more days.

# Chapter the Fourth
## The House in Westminster

1

Margaret had already taken a little house in Radnor Square, Westminster, before our marriage, a house that seemed particularly adaptable to our needs as public-spirited efficients; it had been very pleasantly painted and papered under Margaret's instructions, white paint and clean open purples and green predominating, and now we set to work at once upon the interesting business of arranging and – with our Venetian glass as a beginning – furnishing it. We had been fairly fortunate with our wedding presents, and for the most part it was open to us to choose just exactly what we would have and just precisely where we would put it.

Margaret had a sense of form and colour altogether superior to mine, and so, quite apart from the fact that it was her money equipped us, I stood aside from all these matters or obeyed her summons to a consultation only to endorse her judgement very readily. Until everything was settled I went every day to my old rooms in Vincent Square and worked at a series of papers that were originally intended for the *Fortnightly Review*, the papers that afterwards became my fourth book, 'New Aspects of Liberalism'.

I still remember as delightful most of the circumstances of getting into 79 Radnor Square. The thin flavour of indecision about Margaret disappeared altogether in a shop; she had the precisest ideas of what she wanted, and the devices of the salesman did not sway her. It was very pleasant to find her taking things out of my hands with a certain masterfulness, and showing the distinctest determination to make a house in which I should be able to work in that great project of 'doing something for the world'.

'And I do want to make things pretty about us,' she said. 'You don't think it wrong to have things pretty?'

'I want them so.'

'Altiora has things hard.'

'Altiora,' I answered, 'takes a pride in standing ugly and uncomfortable things. But I don't see that they help her. Anyhow, they won't help me.'

So Margaret went to the best shops and got everything very simple and very good. She bought some pictures very well indeed ; there was a little Sussex landscape, full of wind and sunshine, by Nicholson, for my study, that hit my taste far better than if I had gone out to get some such expression for myself.

'We will buy a picture just now and then,' she said, 'sometimes – when we see one.'

I would come back through the January mire or fog from Vincent Square to the door of 79, and reach it at last with a quite childish appreciation of the fact that its solid Georgian proportions and its fine brass furnishings belonged to *my* home ; I would use my latchkey and discover Margaret in the warm-lit, spacious hall with a partially opened packing-case, fatigued but happy, or go to have tea with her out of the right tea-things, 'come at last', or be told to notice what was fresh there. It wasn't simply that I had never had a house before, but I had really never been, except in the most transitory way, in any house that was nearly so delightful as mine promised to be. Everything was fresh and bright, and softly and harmoniously toned. Downstairs we had a green dining-room with gleaming silver, dark oak, and English colour-prints ; above was a large drawing-room that could be made still larger by throwing open folding doors, and it was all carefully done in greys and blues, for the most part with real Sheraton supplemented by Sheraton so skilfully imitated by an expert Margaret had discovered as to be indistinguishable except to a minute scrutiny. And for me, above this and next to my bedroom, there was a roomy study, with specially thick stair-carpet outside and thick carpets in the bedroom overhead and a big old desk for me to sit at and work between fire and window, and another desk specially made for me by that expert if I chose to stand and write, and open bookshelves and bookcases and every sort of convenient fitting. There were electric heaters beside the open fire, and everything was put for me to make tea at any time – electric kettle, infuser, biscuits and fresh butter, so that I could get up and work at any hour of the day or night. I could do no work in this apartment for a long time, I was so interested in the perfection of the arrangements. And when I brought in my books and papers from Vincent Square, Margaret seized upon all the really shabby volumes and had them re-bound in a fine official-looking leather.

I can remember sitting down at that desk and looking round me and feeling with a queer effect of surprise that after all even a place in the Cabinet, though infinitely remote, was nevertheless in the same large world with these fine and quietly expensive things.

On the same floor Margaret had a 'den', a very neat and pretty den with good colour-prints of Botticellis and Carpaccios, and there was a third apartment for secretarial purposes should the necessity for them arise, with a severe-looking desk equipped with patent files. And Margaret would come flitting into the room to me, or appear noiselessly standing, a tall gracefully drooping form, in the wide open doorway. 'Is everything right, dear?' she would ask.

'Come in,' I would say ; 'I'm sorting out papers.'

She would come to the hearthrug.

'I mustn't disturb you,' she would remark.

'I'm not busy yet.'

'Things are getting into order. Then we must make out a time-table as the Baileys do, and *begin!*'

Altiora came in to see us once or twice, and a number of serious young wives known to Altiora called and were shown over the house, and discussed its arrangements with Margaret. They were all tremendously keen on efficient arrangements.

'A little pretty,' said Altiora, with the faintest disapproval, 'still –'

It was clear she thought we should grow out of that.

From the day of our return we found other people's houses open to us and eager for us. We went out of London for weekends and dined out, and began discussing our projects for reciprocating these hospitalities. As a single man unattached, I had had a wide and miscellaneous social range, but now I found myself falling into place in a set. For a time I acquiesced in this. I went very little to my clubs, the Climax and the National Liberal, and participated in no bachelor dinners at all. For a time, too, I dropped out of the garrulous literary and journalistic circles I had frequented. I put up for the Reform, not so much for the use of the club as a sign of serious and substantial political standing. I didn't go up to Cambridge, I remember, for nearly a year, so occupied was I with my new adjustments.

The people we found ourselves among at this time were people, to put it roughly, of the Parliamentary candidate class, or people already actually placed in the political world. They ranged between very considerable wealth and such a hard bare independence as old Willersley and the sister who kept house for him possessed. There were quite a number of young couples like ourselves, a little younger and more artless, or a little older and more established. Among the younger men I had a sort of distinction because of my Cambridge reputation and my writing, and because, unlike them, I was an adventurer and had won and married my way into their circles instead of being naturally there. They couldn't quite reckon upon what I should do ; they felt I had reserves of experience and incalculable traditions. Close to us were the Cramptons, Willie Crampton, who has since been Postmaster-General, rich and very important in Rockshire, and his younger brother Edward, who has specialized in history and become one of those unimaginative men of letters who are the glory of latter-day England. Then there was Lewis, further towards Kensington, where his cousins the Solomons and the Hartsteins lived, a brilliant representative of his race, able, industrious and invariably uninspired, with a wife a little in revolt against the racial tradition of feminine servitude and inclined to the suffragette point of view ; and Bunting Harblow, an old blue, and with an erratic disposition well under the control of the able little cousin he had married. I had known all these men, but now (with Altiora floating angelically in benediction) they opened their hearts to me and took me into their order. They were all, like myself, prospective Liberal candidates, with a feeling that the period of wandering in the wilderness of opposition was drawing near its close. They were all tremendously keen upon social and political service, and all greatly under the sway of the ideal of a simple strenuous life, a life finding its satisfactions in political achievements and distinctions. The young wives were as keen about it as the young husbands, Margaret most of all, and I – whatever elements in me didn't march with the attitudes and

193

habits of this set were very much in the background during that time.

We would give little dinners and have evening gatherings at which everything was very simple and very good, with a slight but perceptible austerity, and there was more good fruit and flowers and less perhaps in the way of savouries, patties, and entrées than was customary. Sherry we banished, and Marsala and liqueurs, and there was always good home-made lemonade available. No men waited, but very expert parlourmaids. Our meat was usually Welsh mutton – I don't know why, unless that mountains have ever been the last refuge of the severer virtues. And we talked politics and books and ideas and Bernard Shaw (who was a department by himself and supposed in those days to be ethically sound at bottom), and mingled with the intellectuals – I myself was, as it were, a promoted intellectual.

The Cramptons had a tendency to read good things aloud on their less frequented receptions, but I have never been able to participate submissively in this hyper-digestion of written matter, and generally managed to provoke a disruptive debate. We were all very earnest to make the most of ourselves and to be and do, and I wonder still at times, with an unassuaged perplexity, how it is that in that phase of utmost earnestness I have always seemed to myself to be most remote from reality.

## 2

I look back now across the detaching intervention of sixteen crowded years, critically and I fancy, almost impartially, to those beginnings of my married life. I try to recall in something near to their proper order the developing phases of relationship. I am struck most of all by the immense unpremeditated, generous-spirited insincerities upon which Margaret and I were building.

It seems to me that here I have to tell perhaps the commonest experience of all among married educated people, the deliberate, shy, complex effort to fill the yawning gaps in temperament as they appear, the sustained, failing attempt to bridge abysses, level barriers, evade violent pressures. I have come in these latter years of my life to believe that it is possible for a man and a woman to be absolutely real with one another, to stand

194

naked souled to each other, unashamed and unafraid, because of the natural all-glorifying love between them. It is possible to love and be loved untroubling, as a bird flies through the air. But it is a rare and intricate chance that brings two people within sight of that essential union, and for the majority marriage must adjust itself on other terms. Most coupled people never really look at one another. They look a little away to preconceived ideas. And each from the first days of love-making *hides* from the other, is afraid of disappointing, afraid of offending, afraid of discoveries in either sense. They build not solidly upon the rock of truth, but upon arches and pillars and queer provisional supports that are needed to make a common foundation, and below in the imprisoned darknesses, below the fine fabric they sustain together begins for each of them a cavernous hidden life. Down there things may be prowling that scarce ever peep out to consciousness except in the grey halflight of sleepless nights, passions that flash out for an instant in an angry glance and are seen no more, starved victims and beautiful dreams bricked up to die. For the most of us there is no jail delivery of those inner depths, and the life above goes on to its honourable end.

I have told how I loved Margaret and how I came to marry her. Perhaps already unintentionally I have indicated the quality of the injustice our marriage did us both. There was no kindred between us and no understanding. We were drawn to one another by the unlikeness of our quality, by the things we misunderstood in each other. I know a score of couples who had married in that fashion.

Modern conditions and modern ideas, and in particular the intenser and subtler perceptions of modern life, press more and more heavily upon a marriage tie whose fashion comes from an earlier and less discriminating time. When the wife was her husband's subordinate, meeting him simply and uncritically for simple ends, when marriage was a purely domestic relationship, leaving thought and the vivid things of life almost entirely to the unencumbered man, mental and temperamental incompatibilities mattered comparatively little. But now the wife, and particularly the loving childless wife, unpremeditatedly makes a relentless demand for a complete association, and the husband exacts unthought-of delicacies of understanding and cooperation. These are stupendous demands. People not only think more fully and elaborately about life than they ever did before, but marriage obliges us to make that evermore accidented progress a three-legged race of carelessly assorted couples. . . .

Our very mental texture was different. I was rough-minded, to use the phrase of William James, primary and intuitive and illogical; she was tender-minded, logical, refined and secondary. She was loyal to pledges and persons, sentimental and faithful; I am loyal to ideas and instincts, emotional and scheming. My imagination moves in broad gestures; hers was delicate with a real dread of extravagance. My quality is sensuous and ruled by warm impulses; hers was discriminating and essentially inhibitory. I like the facts of the case and to mention everything; I like naked bodies and the jolly smells of things. She abounded in reservations, in circumlocutions and evasions, in keenly appreciated secondary points. Perhaps the reader knows that Tintoretto in the National Gallery, the Origin of the Milky Way. It is an admirable test of temperamental quality. In spite of my early training I have come to regard that picture as altogether delightful; to Margaret it has always been 'needlessly offensive'. In that you have our fundamental breach. She had a habit, by no means rare, of damning what she did not like or find sympathetic in me on the score that it was not my 'true self', and she did not so much accept the universe as select from it and do her best to ignore the rest. And also I had far more initiative than had she. This is no catalogue of rights and wrongs, or superiorities and inferiorities; it is a catalogue of differences between two people linked in a relationship that constantly becomes more intolerant of differences.

This is how we stood to each other, and none of it was clear to either of us at the outset. To begin with, I found myself reserving myself from her, then slowly apprehending a jarring between our minds and what seemed to me at first a queer little habit of misunderstanding in her. . . .

It did not hinder my being very fond of her. . . .

Where our system of reservation became at once most usual and most astounding was in our personal relations. It is not too much to say that in that regard we never for a moment achieved sincerity with one another during the first six years of

196

our life together. It goes even deeper than that, for in my effort to realize the ideal of my marriage I ceased even to attempt to be sincere with myself. I would not admit my own perceptions and interpretations. I tried to fit myself to her thinner and finer determinations. There are people who will say with a note of approval that I was learning to conquer myself. I record that much without any note of approval. . . .

For some years I never deceived Margaret about any concrete fact nor, except for the silence about my earlier life that she had almost forced upon me, did I hide any concrete fact that seemed to affect her, but from the outset I was guilty of immense spiritual concealments, my very marriage was based, I see now, on a spiritual subterfuge ; I hid moods from her, pretended feelings. . . .


3

The interest and excitement of setting-up house, of walking about it from room to room and from floor to floor, of sitting at one's own dinner-table and watching one's wife control conversation with a pretty, timid resolution, of taking a place among the secure and free people of our world, passed almost insensibly into the interest and excitement of my Parliamentary candidature for the Kinghamstead Division, that shapeless chunk of agricultural midland between the Great Western and the North Western railways. I was going to 'take hold' at last, the Kinghamstead Division was my appointed handle. I was to find my place in the rather indistinctly sketched constructions that were implicit in the minds of all our circle. The precise place I had to fill and the precise functions I had to discharge were not as yet very clear, but all that, we felt sure, would become plain as things developed.

A few brief months of the vague activities of 'nursing' gave place to the excitements of the contest that followed the return of Mr Campbell-Bannerman to power in 1905. So far as the Kinghamstead Division was concerned, it was a depressed and tepid battle. I went about the constituency making three speeches that were soon threadbare, and an odd little collection of people worked for me ; two solicitors, a cheap photographer, a democratic parson, a number of dissenting ministers, the

Mayor of Kinghamstead, a Mrs Bulger, the widow of an old Chartist who had grown rich through electric traction patents, Sir Roderick Newton, a Jew who had bought Calersham Castle, and old Sir Graham Rivers, that sturdy old soldier, were among my chief supporters. We had headquarters in each town and village, mostly they were empty shops we leased temporarily, and there at least a sort of fuss and a coming and going were maintained. The rest of the population stared in a state of suspended judgement as we went about the business. The country was supposed to be in a state of intellectual conflict and deliberate decision, in history it will no doubt figure as a momentous conflict. Yet except for an occasional flare of bill-sticking or a bill in a window or a placard-plastered motor-car or an argumentative group of people outside a public-house or a sluggish movement towards the schoolroom or village hall, there was scarcely a sign that a great empire was revising its destinies. Now and then one saw a canvasser on a doorstep. For the most part people went about their business with an entirely irresponsible confidence in the stability of the universe. At times one felt a little absurd with one's flutter of colours and one's air of saving the country.

My opponent was a quite undistinguished Major-General who relied upon his advocacy of Protection, and was particularly anxious we should avoid 'personalities' and fight the constituency in a gentlemanly spirit. He was always writing me notes, apologizing for excesses on the part of his supporters, or pointing out the undesirability of some course taken by mine.

My speeches had been planned upon broad lines, but they lost touch with these as the polling approached. To begin with I made a real attempt to put what was in my mind before the people I was to supply with a political voice. I spoke of the greatness of our empire and its destinies, of the splendid projects and possibilities of life and order that lay before the world, of all that a resolute and constructive effort might do at the present time. 'We are building a state,' I said, 'secure and splendid, we are in the dawn of the great age of mankind.' Sometimes that would get a solitary ' 'Ear! 'ear!' Then having created, as I imagined, a fine atmosphere, I turned upon the history of the last Conservative administration and brought it

198

into contrast with the wide occasions of the age ; discussed its failure to control the grasping financiers in South Africa, its failure to release public education from sectarian squabbles, its misconduct of the Boer War, its waste of the world's resources. . . .

It soon became manifest that my opening and my general spaciousness of method bored my audiences a good deal. The richer and wider my phrases the thinner sounded my voice in these non-resonating gatherings. Even the platform supporters grew restive unconsciously, and stirred and coughed. They did not recognize themselves as mankind. Building an empire, preparing a fresh stage in the history of humanity, had no appeal for them. They were mostly everyday, toiling people, full of small personal solicitudes, and they came to my meetings, I think, very largely as a relaxation. This stuff was not relaxing. They did not think politics was a great constructive process, they thought it was a kind of dog-fight. They wanted fun, they wanted spice, they wanted hits, they wanted also a chance to say ' 'Ear! 'ear!' in an intelligent and honourable manner and clap their hands and drum with their feet. The great constructive process in history gives so little scope for clapping and drumming and saying ' 'Ear, 'ear!' One might as well think of hounding on the solar system.

So after one or two attempts to lift my audiences to the level of the issues involved, I began to adapt myself to them. I cut down my review of our imperial outlook and destinies more and more, and developed a series of hits and anecdotes and – what shall I call them? – 'crudifications' of the issue. My helpers congratulated me on the rapid improvement of my platform style. I ceased to speak of the late Prime Minister with the respect I bore him, and began to fall in with the popular caricature of him as an artful rabbit-witted person intent only on keeping his leadership, in spite of the vigorous attempts of Mr Joseph Chamberlain to oust him therefrom. I ceased to qualify my statement that Protection would make food dearer for the agricultural labourer. I began to speak of Mr Alfred Lyttelton as an influence at once insane and diabolical, as a man inspired by a passionate desire to substitute manacled but still criminal Chinese for honest British labourers throughout the world. And when it came to the mention of our own kindly

199

leader, of Mr John Burns or any one else of any prominence at all on our side, I fell more and more into the intonation of one who mentions the high gods. And I had my reward in brighter meetings and readier and readier applause.

One goes on from phase to phase in these things.

'After all,' I told myself, 'if one wants to get to Westminster one must follow the road that leads there,' but I found the road, nevertheless, rather unexpectedly distasteful. 'When one gets there,' I said, 'then it is one begins.'

But I would lie awake at nights with that sore throat and headache and fatigue which come from speaking in ill-ventilated rooms, and wondering how far it was possible to educate a whole people to great political ideals. Why should political work always rot down to personalities and personal appeals in this way? Life is, I suppose, to begin with and end with a matter of personalities, from personalities all our broader interests arise and to personalities they return. All our social and political effort, all of it, is like trying to make a crowd of people fall into formation. The broader lines appear, but then come a rush and excitement and irrelevancy, and forthwith the incipient order has vanished and the marshals must begin the work over again!

My memory of all that time is essentially confusion. There was a frightful lot of tiresome locomotion in it; for the King-hamstead Division is extensive, abounding in ill-graded and badly metalled cross-roads and vicious little hills, and singularly unpleasing to the eye in a muddy winter. It is sufficiently near to London to have undergone the same process of ill-regulated expansion that made Bromstead the place it is. Several of its overgrown villages have developed strings of factories and sidings along the railway lines, and there is an abundance of petty villas. There seemed to be no place at which one could take hold of more than this or that element of the population. Now we met in a meeting-house, now in a Masonic Hall or Drill Hall; I also did a certain amount of open-air speaking in the dinner hour outside gas-works and groups of factories. Some special sort of people was, as it were, secreted in response to each special appeal. One said things carefully adjusted to the distinctive limitations of each gathering. Jokes of an incredible silliness and shallowness drifted about us. Our advisers made us declare that if we were elected we would live in the district, and one hasty agent had bills printed, 'If Mr Remington is elected he will live here.' The enemy obtained a number of these bills and stuck them on outhouses, pigstyes, dog-kennels; you cannot imagine how irksome the repetition of the jest became. The vast drifting indifference in between my meetings impressed me more and more. I realized the vagueness of my own plans as I had never done before I brought them to the test of this experience. I was perplexed by the riddle of just how far I was, in any sense of the word, taking hold at all, how far I wasn't myself flowing into an accepted groove.

Margaret was troubled by no such doubts. She was clear I had to go into Parliament on the side of Liberalism and the light, as against the late Government and darkness. Essential to the memory of my first contest, is the memory of her clear bright face, very resolute and grave, helping me consciously, steadfastly, with all her strength. Her quiet confidence, while I was so dissatisfied, worked curiously towards the alienation of my sympathies. I felt she had no business to be so sure of me. I had moments of vivid resentment at being thus marched to-wards Parliament.

I seemed now always to be discovering alien forces of character in her. Her way of taking life diverged from me more and more. She sounded amazing, independent notes. She bought some particularly costly furs for the campaign that roused enthusiasm whenever she appeared. She also made me a birthday present in November of a heavily fur-trimmed coat, and this she would make me remove as I went on to the plat-form, and hold over her arm until I was ready to resume it. It was fearfully heavy for her and she liked it to be heavy for her. That act of servitude was in essence a towering self-assertion. I would glance sideways while some chairman floundered through his introduction and see the clear blue eye with which she regarded the audience, which existed so far as she was con-cerned merely to return me to Parliament. It was a friendly eye, provided they were not silly or troublesome. But it kindled a little at the hint of a hostile question. After we had come so far and taken so much trouble!

She constituted herself the dragoman of our political travels.

In hotels she was serenely resolute for the quietest and the best, she rejected all their proposals for meals and substituted a severely nourishing dietary of her own, and even in private houses she astonished me by her tranquil insistence upon special comforts and sustenance. I can see her face now as it would confront a hostess, a little intent, but sweetly resolute and assured.

Since our marriage she had read a number of political memoirs, and she had been particularly impressed by the career of Mrs Gladstone. I don't think it occurred to her to compare and contrast my quality with that of Mrs Gladstone's husband. I suspect her of a deliberate intention of achieving parallel results by parallel methods. I was to be Gladstonized. Gladstone, it appeared, used to lubricate his speeches with a mixture — if my memory serves me right — of egg beaten up in sherry, and Margaret was very anxious I should take a leaf from that celebrated book. She wanted, I know, to hold the glass in her hand while I was speaking.

But here I was firm. 'No,' I said, very decisively, 'simply I won't stand that. It's a matter of conscience. I shouldn't feel — democratic. I'll take my chance of the common water in the carafe on the chairman's table.'

'I *do* wish you wouldn't,' she said, distressed. . . .

It was absurd to feel irritated; it was so admirable of her, a little childish, infinitely womanly and devoted and fine — and I see now how pathetic. But I could not afford to succumb to her. I wanted to follow my own leading, to see things clearly, and this reassuring pose of a high destiny, of an almost terribly efficient pursuit of a fixed end when as a matter of fact I had a very doubtful end and an aim as yet by no means fixed, was all too seductive for dalliance. . . .


4

And into all these things with the manner of a trifling and casual incident comes the figure of Isabel Rivers. My first impressions of her were of a rather ugly and ungainly, extraordinarily interesting schoolgirl with a beautiful quick flush under her warm brown skin, who said and did amusing and surprising things. When first I saw her she was riding a very old bicycle downhill with her feet on the fork of the frame – it seemed to me to the public danger, but afterwards I came to understand the quality of her nerve better – and on the third occasion she was for her own private satisfaction climbing a tree. On the intervening occasion we had what seems now to have been a long sustained conversation about the political situation and the books and papers I had written.

I wonder if it was.

What a delightful mixture of child and grave woman she was at that time, and how little I reckoned on the part she would play in my life! And since she has played that part, how impossible it is to tell now of those early days! Since I wrote that opening paragraph to this section my idle pen has been, as it were, playing by itself and sketching faces on the blotting pad – one impish wizened visage is oddly like little Bailey – and I have been thinking cheek on fist amidst a limitless wealth of memories. She sits below me on the low wall under the olive trees with our little child in her arms. She is now the central fact in my life. It still seems a little incredible that that should be so. She has destroyed me as a politician, brought me to this belated rebeginning of life. When I sit down and try to make her a girl again, I feel like the Arabian fisherman who tried to put the genie back into the pot from which it had spread gigantic across the skies. . . .

I have a very clear vision of her rush downhill past our labouring ascendant car – my colours fluttered from handle-bar and shoulder-knot – and her waving hand and the sharp note of her voice. She cried out something. I don't know what, some greeting.

'What a pretty girl!' said Margaret.

Parvill, the cheap photographer, that industrious organizer for whom by way of repayment I got those magic letters, that knighthood of the underlings, 'J.P.,' was in the car with us and explained her to us. 'One of the best workers you have,' he said. . . .

And then after a toilsome troubled morning we came, rather cross from the strain of sustained amiability, to Sir Graham Rivers' house. It seemed all softness and quiet – I recall dead white panelling and oval mirrors horizontally set and a marble fireplace between white marble-blind Homer and marble-blind

Virgil, very grave and fine – and how Isabel came in to lunch in a shapeless thing like a blue smock that made her bright quick-changing face seem yellow under her cloud of black hair. Her step-sister was there, Miss Gamer, to whom the house was to descend, a well-dressed lady of thirty, amiably disavowing responsibility for Isabel in every phrase and gesture. And there was a very pleasant doctor, an Oxford man, who seemed on excellent terms with every one. It was manifest that he was in the habit of sparring with the girl, but on this occasion she wasn't sparring and refused to be teased into a display in spite of the taunts of either him or her father. She was, they discovered with rising eyebrows, shy. It seemed an opportunity too rare for them to miss. They proclaimed her enthusiasm for me in a way that brought a flush to her cheek and a look into her eye between appeal and defiance. They declared she had read my books, which I thought at the time was exaggeration, their dry political quality was so distinctly not what one was accustomed to regard as schoolgirl reading. Miss Gamer protested to protect her, 'When once in a blue moon Isabel is well-behaved . . . !'

Except for these attacks I do not remember much of the conversation at table; it was, I know, discursive and concerned with the sort of topographical and social and electioneering fact natural to such a visit. Old Rivers struck me as a delightful person, modestly unconscious of his doubly-earned V.C. and the plucky defence of Kardin-Bergat that won his baronetcy. He was that excellent type, the soldier radical, and we began that day a friendship that was only ended by his death in the hunting-field three years later. He interested Margaret into a disregard of my plate and the fact that I had secured the illegal indulgence of Moselle. After lunch we went for coffee into another low room, this time brown-panelled and looking through French windows on a red-walled garden, graceful even in its winter desolation. And there the conversation suddenly picked up and became good. It had fallen to a pause, and the doctor, with an air of definitely throwing off a mask and wrecking an established tranquillity, remarked: 'Very probably you Liberals will come in, though I'm not sure you'll come in so mightily as you think, but what you'll do when you do come in passes my comprehension.'

'There's good work sometimes,' said Sir Graham, 'in undoing.'

'You can't govern a great empire by amending and repealing the Acts of your predecessors,' said the doctor.

There came that kind of pause that happens when a subject is broached too big and difficult for the gathering. Margaret's blue eyes regarded the speaker with quiet disapproval for a moment, and then came to me in the not too confident hope that I would snub him out of existence with some prompt rhetorical stroke. A voice spoke out of the big armchair.

'We'll do things,' said Isabel.

The doctor's eye lit with the joy of the fisherman who strikes his fish at last. 'What will you do?' he asked her.

'Everyone knows we're a mixed lot,' said Isabel.

'Poor old chaps like me!' interjected the general.

'But that's not a programme,' said the doctor.

'But Mr Remington has published a programme,' said Isabel.

The doctor cocked half an eye at me.

'In some review,' the girl went on. 'After all, we're not going to elect the whole Liberal party in the Kinghamstead Division. I'm a Remington-ite!'

'But the programme,' said the doctor, 'the programme –'

'In front of Mr Remington!'

'Scandal always comes home at last,' said the doctor. 'Let him hear the worst.'

'I'd like to hear,' I said. 'Electioneering shatters convictions and enfeebles the mind.'

'Not mine,' said Isabel stoutly. 'I mean – Well, anyhow I take it Mr Remington stands for constructing a civilized state out of this muddle.'

'*This* muddle,' protested the doctor with an appeal of the eye to the beautiful long room and the ordered garden outside the bright clean windows.

'Well, *that* muddle, if you like! There's a slum within a mile of us already. The dust and blacks get worse and worse, Sissie?'

'They do,' agreed Miss Gamer.

'Mr Remington stands for construction, order, education, discipline.'

'And you?' said the doctor.

'I'm a good Remington-ite.'

'Discipline!' said the doctor.

'Oh!' said Isabel. 'At times one has to be – Napoleonic. They want to libel me, Mr Remington. A political worker can't always be in time for meals, can she? At times one has to make – splendid cuts.'

Miss Gamer said something indistinctly.

'Order, education, discipline,' said Sir Graham. 'Excellent things! But I've a sort of memory – in my young days – we talked about something called liberty.'

'Liberty under the law,' I said, with an unexpected approving murmur from Margaret, and took up the defence. 'The old Liberal definition of liberty was a trifle uncritical. Privilege and legal restrictions are not the only enemies of liberty. An uneducated, underbred, and underfed propertyless man is a man who has lost the possibility of liberty. There's no liberty worth a rap for him. A man who is swimming hopelessly for life wants nothing but the liberty to get out of the water; he'll give every other liberty for it – until he gets out.'

Sir Graham took me up, and we fell into a discussion of the changing qualities of Liberalism. It was a good give-and-take talk, extraordinarily refreshing after the nonsense and crowding secondary issues of the electioneering outside. We all contributed more or less except Miss Gamer ; Margaret followed with knitted brows and occasional interjections. 'People won't *see* that,' for example, and 'It all seems so plain to me.' The doctor showed himself clever but unsubstantial and inconsistent. Isabel sat back with her black mop of hair buried deep in the chair, looking quickly from face to face. Her colour came and went with her vivid intellectual excitement ; occasionally she would dart a word, usually a very apt word, like a lizard's tongue into the discussion. I remember chiefly that a chance illustration betrayed that she had read Bishop Burnet. . . .

After that it was not surprising that Isabel should ask for a lift in our car as far as the Lurky Committee Room, and that she should offer me quite sound advice *en route* upon the intellectual temperament of the Lurky gasworkers. . . .

On the third occasion that I saw Isabel she was, as I have said, climbing a tree – and a very creditable tree – for her own private satisfaction. It was a lapse from the high seriousness of politics, and I perceived she felt that I might regard it as such

206

and attach too much importance to it. I had some difficulty in reassuring her. And it's odd to note now – it has never occurred to me before – that from that day to this I do not think I have ever reminded Isabel of that encounter.

And after that memory she seems to be flickering about always in the election, an inextinguishable flame; now she flew by on her bicycle, now she dashed into committee rooms, now she appeared on doorsteps in animated conversation with dubious voters; I took every chance I could to talk to her – I had never met anything like her before in the world, and she interested me immensely – and before the polling day she and I had become, in the frankest simplicity, fast friends. . . .

That, I think, sets out very fairly the facts of our early relationship. But it is hard to get it true, either in form or texture, because of the bright, translucent, coloured, and refracting memories that come between. One forgets not only the tint and quality of thoughts and impressions through that intervening haze, one forgets them altogether. I don't remember now that I ever thought in those days of passionate love or the possibility of such love between us. I may have done so again and again. But I doubt it very strongly. I don't think I ever thought of such aspects. I had no more sense of any danger between us, seeing the years and things that separated us, than I could have had if she had been an intelligent bright-eyed bird. Isabel came into my life as a new sort of thing; she didn't join on at all to my previous experiences of womanhood. They were not, as I have laboured to explain, either very wide or very penetrating experiences, on the whole 'strangled dinginess' expresses them, but I do not believe they were narrower or shallower than those of many other men of my class. I thought of women as pretty things and beautiful things, pretty rather than beautiful, attractive and at times disconcertingly attractive, often bright and witty, but, because of the vast reservations that hid them from me, wanting, subtly and inevitably wanting, in understanding. My idealization of Margaret had evaporated insensibly after our marriage. The shrine I had made for her in my private thoughts stood at last undisguisedly empty. But Isabel did not for a moment admit of either idealization or interested contempt. She opened a new sphere of womanhood to me. With her steady amber-brown eyes, her unaffected interest in

207

impersonal things, her upstanding waistless blue body, her energy, decision and courage, she seemed rather some new and infinitely finer form of boyhood than a feminine creature, as I had come to measure femininity. She was my perfect friend. Could I have foreseen, had my world been more wisely planned, to this day we might have been such friends.

She seemed at that time unconscious of sex, though she has told me since how full she was of protesting curiosities and restrained emotions. She spoke, as indeed she has always spoken, simply, clearly, and vividly; schoolgirl slang mingled with words that marked ample voracious reading, and she moved quickly with the free directness of some graceful young animal. She took many of the easy freedoms a man or a sister might have done with me. She would touch my arm, lay a hand on my shoulder as I sat, adjust the lapel of a breast-pocket as she talked to me. She says now she loved me always from the beginning. I doubt if there was a suspicion of that in her mind in those days. I used to find her regarding me with the clearest, steadiest gaze in the world, exactly like the gaze of some nice healthy innocent animal in a forest, interested, inquiring, speculative, but singularly untroubled. . . .

5

Polling day came after a last hoarse and dingy crescendo. The excitement was not of the sort that makes one forget one is tired out. The waiting for the end of the count has left a long blank mark on my memory, and then every one was shaking my hand and repeating, 'Nine hundred and seventy-six.'

My success had been a foregone conclusion since the afternoon, but we all behaved as though we had not been anticipating this result for hours, as though any other figures but nine hundred and seventy-six would have meant something entirely different. 'Nine hundred and seventy-six!' said Margaret. 'They didn't expect three hundred.'

'Nine hundred and seventy-six,' said a little short man with a paper. 'It means a big turnover. Two dozen short of a thousand, you know.'

A tremendous hullaboo began outside, and a lot of fresh people came into the room.

Isabel, flushed but not out of breath, Heaven knows where she had sprung from at that time of night! was running her hand down my sleeve almost caressingly, with the innocent bold affection of a girl. 'Got you in!' she said. 'It's been no end of a lark.'

'And now,' said I, 'I must go and be constructive.'

'Now you must go and be constructive,' she said.

'You've got to live here,' she added.

'By Jove! yes,' I said. 'We'll have to house-hunt.'

'I shall read all your speeches.'

She hesitated.

'I wish I was you,' she said, and said it as though it was not exactly the thing she was meaning to say.

'They want you to speak,' said Margaret, with something unsaid in her face.

'You must come out with me,' I answered, putting my arm through hers, and felt some one urging me to the French windows that gave on the balcony.

'If you think –' she said, yielding gladly.

'Oh, *rather*!' said I.

The Mayor of Kinghamstead, a managing little man with no great belief in my oratorical powers, was sticking his face up to mine.

'It's all over,' he said, 'and you've won. Say all the nice things you can and say them plainly.'

I turned and handed Margaret out through the window and stood looking over the Market-place, which was more than half filled with swaying people. The crowd set up a roar of approval at the sight of us, tempered by a little booing. Down in one corner of the square a fight was going on for a flag, a fight that even the prospect of a speech could not instantly check. 'Speech!' cried voices, 'Speech!' and then a brief 'boo-oo-oo' that was drowned in a cascade of shouts and cheers. The conflict round the flag culminated in the smashing of a pane of glass in the chemist's window and instantly sank to peace.

'Gentlemen voters of the Kinghamstead Division,' I began.

'Votes for Women!' yelled a voice, amidst laughter – the first time I remember hearing that memorable war-cry.

'Three cheers for Mrs Remington!'

'Mrs Remington asks me to thank you,' I said, amidst further uproar and reiterated cries of 'Speech!'

Then silence came with a startling swiftness.

Isabel was still in my mind, I suppose. 'I shall go to Westminster,' I began. I sought for some compelling phrase and could not find one. 'To do my share,' I went on, 'in building up a great and splendid civilization.'

I paused and there was a weak gust of cheering, and then a renewal of booing.

'This election,' I said, 'has been the end and the beginning of much. New ideas are abroad –'

'Chinese labour,' yelled a voice, and across the square swept a wildfire of hooting and bawling.

It is one of the few occasions when I quite lost my hold on a speech. I glanced sideways and saw the Mayor of Kinghamstead speaking behind his hand to Parvill. By a happy chance Parvill caught my eye.

'What do they want?' I asked.

'Eh?'

'What do they want?'

'Say something about general fairness – the other side,' prompted Parvill, flattered but a little surprised by my appeal. I pulled myself hastily into a more popular strain with a gross eulogy of my opponent's good taste.

'Chinese labour!' cried the voice again.

'You've given that notice to quit,' I answered.

The Market-place roared delight, but whether that delight expressed hostility to Chinamen or hostility to their practical enslavement no student of the General Election of 1906 has ever been able to determine. Certainly one of the most effective posters on our side displayed a hideous yellow face, just that and nothing more. There was not even a legend to it. How it impressed the electorate we did not know, but that it impressed the electorate profoundly there can be no disputing.


6

Kinghamstead was one of the earliest constituencies fought, and we came back – it must have been Saturday – triumphant but very tired, to our house in Radnor Square. In the train we read the first intimations that the victory of our party was likely to be a sweeping one.

Then came a period when one was going about receiving and giving congratulations and watching the other men arrive, very like a boy who has returned to school with the first batch after the holidays. The London world reeked with the General Election ; it had invaded the nurseries. All the children of one's friends had got big maps of England cut up into squares to represent constituencies and were busy sticking gummed blue labels over the conquered red of Unionism that had hitherto submerged the country. And there were also orange labels, if I remember rightly, to represent the new Labour party, and green for the Irish. I engaged myself to speak at one or two London meetings, and lunched at the Reform, which was fairly tepid, and dined and spent one or two tumultuous evenings at the National Liberal Club, which was in active eruption. The National Liberal became feverishly congested towards midnight as the results of the counting came dropping in. A big green-baize screen had been fixed up at one end of the large smoking-room with the names of the constituencies that were voting that day, and directly the figures came to hand, up they went, amidst cheers that at last lost their energy through sheer repetition, whenever there was record of a Liberal gain. I don't remember what happened when there was a Liberal loss ; I don't think that any were announced while I was there.

How packed and noisy the place was, and what a reek of tobacco and whisky fumes we made! Everybody was excited and talking, making waves of harsh confused sound that beat upon one's ears, and every now and then hoarse voices would shout for some one to speak. Our little set was much in evidence. Both the Cramptons were in, Lewis, Bunting Harblow. We gave brief addresses attuned to this excitement and the late hour, amidst much enthusiasm.

'Now we can do things!' I said amidst a rapture of applause. Men I did not know from Adam held up glasses and nodded to me in solemn fuddled approval as I came down past them into the crowd again.

Men were betting whether the Unionists would lose more or less than two hundred seats.

'I wonder just what we shall do with it all,' I heard one sceptic speculating. . . .

After these orgies I would get home very tired and excited, and find it difficult to get to sleep. I would lie and speculate about what it was we *were* going to do. One hadn't anticipated quite such a tremendous accession to power for one's party. Liberalism was swirling in like a flood. . . .

I found the next few weeks very unsatisfactory and distressing. I don't clearly remember what it was I had expected; I suppose the fuss and strain of the General Election had built up a feeling that my return would in some way put power into my hands, and instead I found myself a mere undistinguished unit in a vast but rather vague majority. There were moments when I felt very distinctly that a majority could be too big a crowd altogether. I had all my work still before me, I had achieved nothing as yet but opportunity, and a very crowded opportunity it was at that. Every one about me was chatting Parliament and appointments; one breathed distracting and irritating speculations as to what would be done and who would be asked to do it. I was chiefly impressed by what was unlikely to be done and by the absence of any general plan of legislation to hold us all together. I found the talk about Parliamentary procedure and etiquette particularly trying. We dined with the elder Cramptons one evening, and old Sir Edward was lengthily sage about what the House liked, what it didn't like, what made a good impression and what a bad one. 'A man shouldn't speak more than twice in his first session, and not at first on too contentious a topic,' said Sir Edward.

'No.'

'Very much depends on manner. The House hates a lecturer. There's a sort of airy earnestness –'

He waved his cigar to eke out his words.

'Little peculiarities of costume count for a great deal. I could name one man who spent three years living down a pair of spatterdashers. On the other hand – a thing like that – if it catches the eye of the *Punch* man, for example, may be your making.'

He went off into a lengthy speculation of why the House had come to like an originally unpopular Irishman named Biggar. . . .

The opening of Parliament gave me some peculiar moods. I began to feel more and more like a branded sheep. We were sworn in in batches, dozens and scores of fresh men, trying not to look too fresh under the inspection of policemen and messengers, all of us carrying new silk hats and wearing magisterial coats. It is one of my vivid memories from this period, the sudden outbreak of silk hats in the smoking-room of the National Liberal Club. At first I thought there must have been a funeral. Familiar faces that one had grown to know under soft felt hats, under bowlers, under liberal-minded wide brims, and above artistic ties and tweed jackets, suddenly met one, staring with the stern gaze of self-consciousness, from under silk hats of incredible glossiness. There was a disposition to wear the hat too forward, I thought, for a good Parliamentary style.

There was much play with the hats all through; a tremendous competition to get in first and put hats on coveted seats. A memory hangs about me of the House in the early afternoon, an inhumane desolation inhabited almost entirely by silk hats. The current use of cards to secure seats came later. There were yards and yards of empty green benches with hats and hats and hats distributed along them, resolute-looking top hats, lax top hats with a kind of shadowy grin under them, sensible top hats brim upward, and one scandalous incontinent that had rolled from a back Opposition bench right to the middle of the floor. A headless hat is surely the most soulless thing in the world, far worse even than a skull. . . .

At last, in a leisurely muddled manner we got to the Address; and I found myself packed in a dense elbowing crowd to the right of the Speaker's chair ; while the attenuated Opposition, nearly leaderless after the massacre, tilted its brim to its nose and sprawled at its ease amidst its empty benches.

There was a tremendous hullaboo about something, and I craned to see over the shoulder of the man in front. 'Order, order, order !'

'What's it about?' I asked.

The man in front of me was clearly no better informed, and then I gathered from a slightly contemptuous Scotchman beside me that it was Chris Robinson who had walked between the honourable member in possession of the house and the

Speaker. I caught a glimpse of him blushingly whispering about his misadventure to a colleague. He was just that same little figure I had once assisted to entertain at Cambridge, but grey-haired now, and still it seemed with the same knitted muffler he had discarded for a reckless half-hour while he talked to us in Hatherleigh's rooms.

It dawned upon me that I wasn't particularly wanted in the House, and that I should get all I needed of the opening speeches next day from *The Times*.

I made my way out, and was presently walking rather aimlessly through the outer lobby.

I caught myself regarding the shadow that spread itself out before me, multiplied itself in blue tints of various intensity, shuffled itself like a pack of cards under the many lights, the square shoulders, the silk hat, already worn with a parliamentary tilt backward ; I found I was surveying this statesmanlike outline with a weak approval. 'A *member*!' I felt the little cluster of people that were scattered about the lobby must be saying.

'Good God!' I said in hot reaction, 'what am I doing here?'

It was one of those moments, infinitely trivial in themselves, that yet are cardinal in a man's life. It came to me with extreme vividness that it wasn't so much that I had got hold of something as that something had got hold of me. I distinctly recall the rebound of my mind. Whatever happened in this Parliament, I at least would attempt something. 'By God!' I said, 'I won't be overwhelmed. I am here to do something, and do something I will!'

But I felt that for the moment I could not remain in the House.

I went out by myself with my thoughts into the night. It was a chilling night, and rare spots of rain were falling. I glanced over my shoulder at the lit windows of the Lords. I walked, I remember, westward, and presently came to the Grosvenor Embankment and followed it, watching the glittering black rush of the river and the dark, dimly lit barges round which the water swirled. Across the river was the hunched skyline of Doulton's potteries, and a kiln flared redly. Dimly luminous trams were gliding amidst a dotted line of lamps, and two little trains crawled into Waterloo station. Mysterious black figures

214

came by me and were suddenly changed to the commonplace at the touch of the nearer lamps. It was a big confused world, I felt, for a man to lay his hands upon.

I remember I crossed Vauxhall Bridge and stood for a time watching the huge black shapes in the darkness under the gas-works. A shoal of coal barges lay indistinctly on the darkly shining mud and water below, and a colossal crane was perpetually hauling up coal into mysterious blacknesses above, and dropping the empty clutch back to the barges. Just one or two minute black featureless figures of men toiled amidst these monster shapes. They did not seem to be controlling them, but only moving about among them. These gas-works have a big chimney that belches a lurid flame into the night, a livid shivering bluish flame, shot with strange crimson streaks. . . .

On the other side of Lambeth Bridge broad stairs go down to the lapping water of the river; the lower steps are luminous under the lamps, and one treads unwarned into thick soft Thames mud. They seem to be purely architectural steps, they lead nowhere, they have an air of absolute indifference to mortal ends.

Those shapes and large inhuman places – for all of mankind that one sees at night about Lambeth is minute and pitiful beside the industrial monsters that snort and toil there – mix up inextricably with my memories of my first days as a legislator. Black figures drift by me, heavy vans clatter, a newspaper rough tears by on a motor bicycle, and presently, on the Albert Embankment, every seat has its one or two outcasts huddled together and slumbering.

'These things come, these things go,' a whispering voice urged upon me, 'as once those vast unmeaning Saurians whose bones encumber museums came and went, rejoicing noisily in fruitless lives.' . . .

Fruitless lives! – was that the truth of it all? . . .

Later I stood within sight of the Houses of Parliament in front of the colonnades of St Thomas's Hospital. I leant on the parapet close by a lamp-stand of twisted dolphins – and I prayed!

I remember the swirl of the tide upon the water, and how a string of barges presently came swinging and bumping round as high water turned to ebb. That sudden change of position and my brief perplexity at it, sticks like a paper pin through the substance of my thoughts. It was then I was moved to prayer. I prayed that night that life might not be in vain, that in particular I might not live in vain. I prayed for strength and faith, that the monstrous blundering forces in life might not overwhelm me, might not beat me back to futility and a meaningless acquiescence in existent things. I knew myself for the weakling I was, I knew that nevertheless it was set for me to make such order as I could out of these disorders, and my task cowed me, gave me at the thought of it a sense of yielding feebleness.

'Break me, O God,' I prayed at last, 'disgrace me, torment me, destroy me as you will, but save me from self-complacency and little interests and little successes and the life that passes like the shadow of a dream.'

Book the Third

The Heart of Politics

# Chapter the First

## The Riddle for the Statesman

### 1

I have been planning and replanning, writing and rewriting, this next portion of my book for many days. I perceive I must leave it raw-edged and ill joined. I have learnt something of the impossibility of History. For all I have had to tell is the story of one man's convictions and aims and how they reacted upon his life; and I find it too subtle and involved and intricate for the doing. I find it taxes all my powers to convey even the main forms and forces in that development. It is like looking through moving media of changing hue and variable refraction at something vitally unstable. Broad theories and generalizations are mingled with personal influences, with prevalent prejudices; and not only coloured but altered by phases of hopefulness and moods of depression. The web is made up of the most diverse elements, beyond treatment multitudinous. . . . For a week or so I desisted altogether, and walked over the mountains and returned to sit through the warm soft mornings among the shaded rocks above this little perched-up house of ours, discussing my difficulties with Isabel, and I think on the whole complicating them further in the effort to simplify them to manageable and stateable elements.

Let me, nevertheless, attempt a rough preliminary analysis of this confused process. A main strand is quite easily traceable. This main strand is the story of my obvious life, my life as it must have looked to most of my acquaintances. It presents you with a young couple, bright, hopeful, and energetic, starting out under Altiora's auspices to make a career. You figure us well dressed and active, running about in motor-cars, visiting in great people's houses, dining amidst brilliant companies, going to the theatre, meeting in the lobby. Margaret wore hundreds of beautiful dresses. We must have had an air of succeeding meritoriously during that time.

We did very continually and faithfully serve our joint career.

I thought about it a great deal, and did and refrained from doing ten thousand things for the sake of it. I kept up a solicitude for it, as it were by inertia, long after things had happened and changes occurred in me that rendered its completion impossible. Under certain very artless pretences, we wanted steadfastly to make a handsome position in the world, achieve respect, *succeed*. Enormous unseen changes had been in progress for years in my mind and the realities of my life, before our general circle could have had any inkling of their existence, or suspected the appearances of our life. Then suddenly our proceedings began to be deflected, our outward unanimity visibly strained and marred by the insurgence of these so long-hidden developments.

That career had its own hidden side, of course ; but when I write of these unseen factors I do not mean that but something altogether broader. I do not mean the everyday pettiness which gave the cynical observer scope and told of a narrower, baser aspect of the fair but limited ambitions of my ostensible self. This 'sub-careerist' element noted little things that affected the career, made me suspicious of the rivalry of so-and-so, propitiatory to so-and-so, whom, as a matter of fact, I didn't respect or feel in the least sympathetic towards ; guarded with that man, who for all his charm and interest wasn't helpful, and a little touchy at the appearance of neglect from that. No, I mean something greater and not something smaller when I write of a hidden life.

In the ostensible self who glowed under the approbation of Altiora Bailey, and was envied and discussed, praised and depreciated, in the House and in smoking-room gossip, you really have as much of a man as usually figures in a novel or an obituary notice. But I am tremendously impressed now in the retrospect by the realization of how little that frontage represented me, and just how little such frontages do represent the complexities of the intelligent contemporary. Behind it, yet struggling to disorganize and alter it altogether, was a far more essential reality, a selfless personal, less individualized, and broader in its references. Its aims were never simply to get on ; it had an altogether different system of demands and satisfactions. It was critical, curious, more than a little unfeeling – and relentlessly illuminating.

It is just the existence and development of this more generalized self-behind-the-frontage that is making modern life so
much more subtle and intricate to render, and so much more
hopeful in its relations to the perplexities of the universe. I see
this mental and spiritual hinterland vary enormously in the
people about me, between a type which seems to keep, as
people say, all its goods in the window, to others who, like myself, come to regard the ostensible existence more and more as
a mere experimental feeder and agent for that greater personality behind. And this back-self has its history and phases, its
crises and happy accidents and irrevocable conclusions, more
or less distinct from the adventures and achievements of the
ostensible self. It meets persons and phrases, it assimilates the
spirit of a book, it is startled into new realizations by some
accident that seems altogether irrelevant to the general tenor of
one's life. Its increasing independence of the ostensible career
makes it the organ of corrective criticism ; it accumulates disturbing energy. Then it breaks our overt promises and repu-
diates our pledges, coming down at last like an overbearing
mentor upon the small engagements of the pupil.

In the life of the individual it takes the role that the growth
of philosophy, science, and creative literature may play in the
development of mankind.


2

It is curious to recall how Britten helped to shatter that obvious, lucidly explicable presentation of myself upon which I
had embarked with Margaret. He returned to revive a memory
of adolescent dreams and a habit of adolescent frankness ; he
reached through my shallow frontage as no one else seemed
capable of doing, and dragged that back-self into relation with
it.

I remember very distinctly a dinner and a subsequent walk
with him which presents itself now as altogether typical of the
quality of his influence.

I had come upon him one day while lunching with Somers
and Sutton at the Playwrights' Club, and had asked him to
dinner on the spur of the moment. He was oddly the same
curly-headed, red-faced ventriloquist, and oddly different,

rather seedy as well as untidy, and at first a little inclined to make comparisons with my sleek successfulness. But that disposition presently evaporated, and his talk was good and fresh and provocative. And something that had long been straining at its checks in my mind flapped over, and he and I found ourselves of one accord.

Altiora wasn't at this dinner. When she came matters were apt to become confusedly strenuous. There was always a slight and ineffectual struggle at the end on the part of Margaret to anticipate Altiora's overpowering tendency to a rally and the establishment of some entirely unjustifiable conclusion by a *coup-de-main*. When, however, Altiora was absent, the quieter influence of the Cramptons prevailed ; temperance and information for its own sake prevailed excessively over dinner and the play of thought. . . . Good Lord! what bores the Cramptons were! I wonder I endured them as I did. They had all of them the trick of lying in wait conversationally ; they had no sense of the self-exposures, the gallant experiments in statement that are necessary for good conversation. They would watch one talking with an expression exactly like peeping through bushes. Then they would, as it were, dash out, dissent succinctly, contradict some secondary fact, and back to cover. They gave one twilight nerves. Their wives were easier but still difficult at a stretch ; they talked a good deal about children and servants, but with an air caught from Altiora of making observations upon sociological types. Lewis gossiped about the House in an entirely finite manner. He never raised a discussion ; nobody ever raised a discussion. He would ask what we thought of Evesham's question that afternoon, and Edward would say it was good, and Mrs Willie, who had been behind the grille, would think it was very good, and then Willie, parting the branches, would say rather conclusively that he didn't think it was very much good, and I would deny hearing the question in order to evade a profitless statement of views in that vacuum, and then we would cast about in our minds for some other topic of equal interest. . . .

On this occasion Altiora was absent, and to qualify our Young Liberal bleakness we had Mrs Millingham, with her white hair and her fresh mind and complexion, and Esmeer. Willie Crampton was with us, but not his wife, who was having

222

her third baby on principle; his brother Edward was present, and the Lewises, and of course the Bunting Harblows. There was also some other lady. I remember her as pale blue, but for the life of me I cannot remember her name.

Quite early there was a little breeze between Edward Crampton and Esmeer, who had ventured an opinion about the partition of Poland. Edward was at work then upon the seventh volume of his monumental Life of Kosciusko, and a little impatient with views perhaps not altogether false but betraying a lamentable ignorance of accessible literature. At any rate, his correction of Esmeer was magisterial. After that there was a distinct and not altogether delightful pause, and then some one, it may have been the pale-blue lady, asked Mrs Lewis whether her aunt Lady Carmixter had returned from her rest-and-sun-cure in Italy. That led to a rather anxiously sustained talk about regimen, and Willie told us how he had profited by the no-breakfast system. It had increased his power of work enormously. He could get through ten hours a day now without inconvenience.

'What do you do?' said Esmeer abruptly.

'Oh! no end of work. There's all the estate and looking after things.'

'But publicly?'

'I asked three questions yesterday. And for one of them I had to consult nine books!'

We were drifting, I could see, towards Doctor Haig's system of dietary, and whether the exclusion or inclusion of fish and chicken were most conducive to high efficiency, when Britten, who had refused lemonade and claret and demanded Burgundy, broke out, and was discovered to be demanding in his throat just what we Young Liberals thought we were up to.

'I want,' said Britten, repeating his challenge a little louder, 'to hear just exactly what you think you are doing in Parliament.'

Lewis laughed nervously, and thought we were 'Seeking the Good of the Community.'

'*How?*'

'Beneficent Legislation,' said Lewis.

'Beneficent in what direction?' insisted Britten. 'I want to know where you think you are going.'

'Amelioration of Social Conditions,' said Lewis.

'That's only a phrase!'

'You wouldn't have me sketch bills at dinner?'

'I'd like you to indicate directions,' said Britten, and waited.

'Upward and On,' said Lewis with conscious neatness, and turned to ask Mrs Bunting Harblow about her little boy's French.

For a time talk frothed over Britten's head, but the natural mischief in Mrs Millingham had been stirred, and she was presently echoing his demand in lisping, quasi-confidential undertones. 'What *are* we Liberals doing?' Then Esmeer fell in with the revolutionaries.

To begin with, I was a little shocked by this clamour for fundamentals – and a little disconcerted. I had the experience that I suppose comes to every one at times of discovering oneself together with two different sets of people with whom one has maintained two different sets of attitudes. It had always been, I perceived, an instinctive suppression in our circle that we shouldn't be more than vague about our political ideals. It had almost become part of my morality to respect this convention. It was understood we were all working hard, and keeping ourselves fit, tremendously fit, under Altiora's inspiration, Pro Bono Publico. Bunting Harblow had his under-secretaryship, and Lewis was on the verge of the Cabinet, and these things we considered to be in the nature of confirmations. . . . It added to the discomfort of the situation that these plunging enquiries were being made in the presence of our wives.

The rebel section of our party forced the talk.

Edward Crampton was presently declaring – I forget in what relation: 'The country is with us.'

My long-controlled hatred of the Cramptons' stereotyped phrases about the Country and the House got the better of me. I showed my cloven hoof to my friends for the first time.

'We don't respect the Country as we used to do,' I said. 'We haven't the same belief we used to have in the will of the people. It's no good, Crampton, trying to keep that up. We Liberals know as a matter of fact – nowadays every one knows – that the monster that brought us into power has, among other deficiencies, no head. We've got to give it one – if possible with brains and a will. That lies in the future. For the present if the country is with us, it means merely that we happen to have hold of its tether.'

Lewis was shocked. A 'mandate' from the Country was sacred to his system of pretences.

Britten wasn't subdued by his first rebuff; presently he was at us again. There were several attempts to check his outbreak of interrogation; I remember the Cramptons asked questions about the welfare of various cousins of Lewis who were unknown to the rest of us, and Margaret tried to engage Britten in a sympathetic discussion of the Arts and Crafts exhibition. But Britten and Esmeer were persistent, Mrs Millingham was mischievous, and in the end our rising hopes of Young Liberalism took to their thickets for good, while we talked all over them of the prevalent vacuity of political intentions. Margaret was perplexed by me. It is only now I perceive just how perplexing I must have been. 'Of course,' she said with that faint stress of apprehension in her eyes, 'one must have aims.' And, 'it isn't always easy to put everything into phrases.' 'Don't be long,' said Mrs Edward Crampton to her husband as the wives trooped out. And afterwards when we went upstairs I had an indefinable persuasion that the ladies had been criticizing Britten's share in our talk in an altogether unfavourable spirit. Mrs Edward evidently thought him aggressive and impertinent, and Margaret, with a quiet firmness that brooked no resistance, took him at once into a corner and showed him Italian photographs by Coburn. We dispersed early.

I walked with Britten along the Chelsea back streets towards Battersea Bridge – he lodged on the south side.

'Mrs Millingham's a dear,' he began.

'She's a dear.'

'I liked her demand for a hansom because a four-wheeler was too safe.'

'She was worked up,' I said. 'She's a woman of faultless character, but her instincts, as Altiora would say, are anarchistic – when she gives them a chance.'

'So she takes it out in hansom cabs.'

'Hansom cabs.'

'She's wise,' said Britten. . . .

'I hope, Remington,' he went on after a pause, 'I didn't rag your other guests too much. I've a sort of feeling at moments –

Remington, those chaps are so infernally not – not bloody. It's part of a man's duty sometimes at least to eat red beef and get drunk. How is he to understand government if he doesn't? It scares me to think of your lot – by a sort of misapprehension – being in power. A kind of neuralgia in the head, by way of government. I don't understand where *you* come in. Those others – they've no lusts. Their ideal is anaemia. You and I, we had at least a lust to take hold of life and make something of it. They – they want to take hold of life and make nothing of it. They want to cut out all the stimulants. Just as though life was anything else but a reaction to stimulation!' . . .

He began to talk of his own life. He had had ill-fortune through most of it. He was poor and unsuccessful, and a girl he had been very fond of had been attacked and killed by a horse in a field in a very horrible manner. These things had wounded and tortured him, but they hadn't broken him. They had, it seemed to me, made a kind of crippled and ugly demigod of him. He was, I began to perceive, so much better than I had any right to expect. At first I had been rather struck by his unkempt look, and it made my reaction all the stronger. There was about him something, a kind of raw and bleeding faith in the deep things of life, that stirred me as he showed it. My set of people had irritated him and disappointed him. I discovered at his touch how they irritated me. He reproached me boldly. He made me feel ashamed of my easy acquiescences as I walked in my sleek tall neatness beside his rather old coat, his rather battered hat, his sturdier shorter shape, and listened to his denunciations of our self-satisfied New Liberalism and Progressivism.

'It has the same relation to progress – the reality of progress – that the things they paint on door panels in the suburbs have to art and beauty. There's a sort of filiation. . . . Your Altiora's just the political equivalent of the ladies who sell traced cloth for embroidery ; she's a dealer in Refined Social Reform for the Parlour. The real progress, Remington, is a graver thing and a painfuller thing and a slower thing altogether. Look! *that*' – and he pointed to where under a hoarding in the light of a gas lamp a dingy prostitute stood lurking – 'was in Babylon and Nineveh. Your little lot make believe there won't be anything of the sort after this Parliament! They're going to vanish at a few top notes from Altiora Bailey! Remington! – It's foolery. It's prigs at play. It's make-believe, make-believe! Your people there haven't got hold of things, aren't beginning to get hold of things, don't know anything of life at all, shirk life, avoid life, get in little bright clean rooms and talk big over your bumpers of lemonade while the Night goes by outside – untouched. Those Crampton fools slink by all this' – he waved at the woman again – 'pretend it doesn't exist, or is going to be vanished root and branch by an Act to keep children in the wet outside public-houses. Do you think they really care, Remington? *I* don't. It's make-believe. What they want to do, what Lewis wants to do, what Mrs Bunting Harblow wants her husband to do, is to sit and feel very grave and necessary and respected on the Government benches. They think of putting their feet out like statesmen, and tilting shining hats with becoming brims down over their successful noses. Presentation portrait to a club at fifty. That's their Reality. That's their scope. They don't, it's manifest, *want* to think beyond that. The things there *are*, Remington, they'll never face! the wonder and the depth of life, – lust, and the night-sky, – pain.'

'But the good intention,' I pleaded, 'the Good Will!'

'Sentimentality,' said Britten. 'No Good Will is anything but dishonesty unless it frets and burns and hurts and destroys a man. That lot of yours have nothing but a good will to think they have good will. Do you think they lie awake of nights searching their hearts as we do? Lewis? Crampton? Or those neat, admiring, satisfied little wives? See how they shrank from the probe!'

'We all,' I said, 'shrink from the probe.'

'God help us!' said Britten. . . .

'We are but vermin at the best, Remington,' he broke out, 'and the greatest saint only a worm that has lifted its head for a moment from the dust. We are damned, we are meant to be damned, coral animalculae building upward, upward in a sea of damnation. But of all the damned things that ever were damned, your damned shirking, temperate, sham-efficient, self-satisfied, respectable, make-believe, Fabian-spirited Young Liberal is the utterly damnedest.' He paused for a moment, and resumed in an entirely different note: 'Which is why I was so surprised, Remington, to find *you* in this set!'

'You're just the old plunger you used to be, Britten,' I said. 'You're going too far with all your might for the sake of the damns. Like a donkey that drags its cart up a bank to get thistles. There's depths in Liberalism —'

'We were talking about Liberals.'

'Liberty!'

'Liberty! What do *your* little lot know of liberty?'

'What does any little lot know of liberty?'

'It waits outside, too big for our understanding. Like the night and the stars. And lust, Remington! lust and bitterness! Don't I know them? with all the sweetness and hope of life bitten and trampled, the dear eyes and the brain that loved and understood — and my poor mumble of a life going on! I'm within sight of being a drunkard. Remington! I'm a failure by most standards! Life has cut me to the bone. But I'm not afraid of it any more. I've paid something of the price, I've seen something of the meaning.'

He flew off at a tangent. 'I'd rather die in Delirium Tremens,' he cried, 'than be a Crampton or a Lewis. . . .'

'Make-believe. Make-believe.' The phrase and Britten's squat gestures haunted me as I walked homeward alone. I went to my room and stood before my desk and surveyed papers and files and Margaret's admirable equipment of me.

I perceived in the lurid light of Britten's suggestions that so it was Mr George Alexander would have mounted a states-man's private room. . . .

3

I was never at any stage a loyal party man. I doubt if party will ever again be the force it was during the eighteenth and nine-teenth centuries. Men are becoming increasingly constructive and selective, less patient under tradition and the bondage of initial circumstances. As education becomes more universal and liberating, men will sort themselves more and more by their intellectual temperaments and less and less by their acci-dental associations. The past will rule them less; the future more. It is not simply party but school and college and county and country that lose their glamour. One does not hear nearly as much as our forefathers did of the 'old Harrovian', 'old

Arvonian', 'old Etonian' claim to this or that unfair advantage or unearnt sympathy. Even the Scotch and the Devonians weaken a little in their clannishness. A widening sense of fair play destroys such things. They follow freemasonry down – freemasonry of which one is chiefly reminded nowadays in England by propitiatory symbols outside shady public-houses. . . .

There is, of course, a type of man which clings very obstinately to party ties. These are the men with strong reproductive imaginations and no imaginative initiative, such men as Cladingbowl, for example, or Dayton. They are the scholars-at-large in life. For them the fact that the party system has been essential in the history of England for two hundred years gives it an overwhelming glamour. They have read histories and memoirs, they see the great pile of Westminster not so much for what it is as for what it was, rich with dramatic memories, populous with glorious ghosts, phrasing itself inevitably in anecdotes and quotations. It seems almost scandalous that new things should continue to happen, swamping with strange qualities the savour of these old associations.

That Mr Ramsay MacDonald should walk through Westminster Hall, thrust himself, it may be, through the very piece of space that once held Charles the Martyr pleading for his life, seems horrible profanation to Dayton, a last posthumous outrage ; and he would, I think, like to have the front benches left empty now for ever, or at most adorned with laureated ivory tablets, 'Here Dizzy sat', and 'On this Spot William Ewart Gladstone made his First Budget Speech.' Failing this, he demands, if only as signs of modesty and respect on the part of the survivors, meticulous imitation. 'Mr G.,' he murmurs, 'would not have done that,' and laments a vanished subtlety even while Mr Evesham is speaking. He is always gloomily disposed to lapse into wonderings about what things are coming to, wonderings that have no grain of curiosity. His conception of perfect conduct is industrious persistence along the worn-down, well-marked grooves of the great recorded days. So infinitely more important to him is the documented, respected thing than the elusive present.

Cladingbowl and Dayton do not shine in the House, though Cladingbowl is a sound man on a committee, and Dayton keeps the *Old Country Gazette,* the most gentlemanly paper in

London. They prevail, however, in their clubs at lunch-time. There, with the pleasant consciousness of a morning's work free from either zeal or shirking, they mingle with permanent officials, prominent lawyers, even a few of the soberer type of business men, and relax their minds in the discussion of the morning paper, of the architecture of the West End, of the latest public appointments, of golf, of holiday resorts, of the last judicial witticisms and forensic 'crushers'. The New Year and Birthday honours lists are always very sagely and exhaustively considered, and anecdotes are popular and keenly judged. They do not talk of the things that are really active in their minds, but in the formal and habitual manner they suppose to be proper to intelligent but still honourable men. Socialism, individual money matters, and religion are forbidden topics, and sex and women only in so far as they appear in the law courts. It is to me the strangest of conventions, this assumption of unreal loyalties and traditional respects, this repudiation and concealment of passionate interests. It is like wearing gloves in summer fields, or bathing in a gown, or falling in love with the heroine of a novel, or writing under a pseudonym, or becoming a masked Tuareg. . . .

It is not, I think, that men of my species are insensitive to the great past that is embodied in Westminster and its traditions; we are not so much wanting in the historical sense as alive to the greatest of our present opportunities and the still vaster future that is possible to us. London is the most interesting, beautiful, and wonderful city in the world to me, delicate in her incidental and multitudinous littleness, and stupendous in her pregnant totality: I cannot bring myself to use her as a museum or an old bookshop. When I think of Whitehall that little affair on the scaffold outside the Banqueting Hall seems trivial and remote in comparison with the possibilities that offer themselves to my imagination within the great grey Government buildings close at hand.

It gives me a qualm of nostalgia even to name those places now. I think of St Stephen's tower streaming upwards into the misty London night and the great wet quadrangle of New Palace Yard, from which the hansom cabs of my first experiences were ousted more and more by taxicabs as the second Parliament of King Edward the Seventh aged; I think of the

Admiralty and War Office with their tall Marconi masts send-
ing out invisible threads of direction to the armies in the camps,
to great fleets about the world. The crowded, darkly shining
river goes flooding through my memory once again, on to those
narrow seas that part us from our rival nations; I see quad-
rangles and corridors of spacious grey-toned offices in which
undistinguished little men and little files of papers link us to
islands in the tropics, to frozen wildernesses gashed for gold, to
vast temple-studded plains, to forest worlds and mountain
worlds, to ports and fortresses and lighthouses and watch-
towers and grazing lands and corn lands all about the globe.
Once more I traverse Victoria Street, grimy and dark, where
the Agents of the Empire jostle one another, pass the big
embassies in the West End with their flags and scutcheons,
follow the broad avenue that leads to Buckingham Palace,
witness the coming and going of troops and officials and guests
along it from every land on earth. . . . Interwoven in the texture
of it all, mocking, perplexing, stimulating beyond measure, is
the gleaming consciousness, the challenging knowledge: 'You
and your kind might still, if you could but grasp it here, mould
all the destiny of Man!'

## 4

My first three years in Parliament were years of active discontent. The little group of younger Liberals to which I belonged
was very ignorant of the traditions and qualities of our older
leaders, and quite out of touch with the mass of the party. For
a time Parliament was enormously taken up with moribund
issues and old quarrels. The early Educational legislation was
sectarian and unenterprising, and the Licensing Bill went little
further than the attempted rectification of a Conservative mistake. I was altogether for the nationalization of the public-
house, and of this end the Bill gave no intimations. It was just
beer-baiting. I was recalcitrant almost from the beginning, and
spoke against the Government so early as the second reading of
the first Education Bill, the one the Lords rejected in 1906. I
went a little beyond my intention in the heat of speaking, – it
is a way with inexperienced men. I called the Bill timid, narrow, a mere sop to the jealousies of sects and little-minded

people. I contrasted its aim and methods with the manifest needs of the time.

I am not a particularly good speaker ; after the manner of a writer, I worry to fine my meaning too much ; but this was one of my successes. I spoke after dinner and to a fairly full House, for people were already a little curious about me because of my writings. Several of the Conservative leaders were present and stayed, and Mr Evesham, I remember, came ostentatiously to hear me, with that engaging friendliness of his, and gave me at the first chance an approving 'Hear, Hear!' I can still recall quite distinctly my two futile attempts to catch the Speaker's eye before I was able to begin, the nervous quiver of my rather too prepared opening, the effect of hearing my own voice and my subconscious wonder as to what I could possibly be talking about, the realization that I was getting on fairly well, the immense satisfaction afterwards of having on the whole brought it off, and the absurd gratitude I felt for that encouraging cheer.

Addressing the House of Commons is like no other public speaking in the world. Its semi-colloquial methods give it an air of being easy, but its shifting audience, the comings and goings and hesitations of members behind the chair – not mere audience units, but men who matter – the desolating emptiness that spreads itself round the man who fails to interest, the little compact, disciplined crowd in the strangers' gallery, the light, elusive, flickering movements high up behind the grille, the wigged, attentive, weary Speaker, the table and the mace and the chapel-like Gothic background with its sombre shadows, conspire together, produce a confused, uncertain feeling in me, as though I was walking upon a pavement full of trapdoors and patches of uncovered morass. A misplaced, well-meant 'Hear, Hear!' is apt to be extraordinarily disconcerting, and under no other circumstances have I had to speak with quite the same sideways twist that the arrangement of the House imposes. One does not recognize one's own voice threading out into the stirring brown. Unless I was excited or speaking to the mind of some particular person in the House, I was apt to lose my feeling of an auditor. I had no sense of whither my sentences were going, such as one has with a public meeting well under one's eye. And to lose one's sense of an auditor is for a man of my temperament to lose one's sense of the immediate, and to become prolix and vague with qualifications.

5

My discontents with the Liberal party and my mental exploration of the quality of party generally are curiously mixed up with certain impressions of things and people in the National Liberal Club. The National Liberal Club is Liberalism made visible in the flesh – and Doultonware. It is an extraordinarily big club done in a bold, wholesale, shiny, marbled style, richly furnished with numerous paintings, steel engravings, busts, and full-length statues of the late Mr Gladstone ; and its spacious dining-rooms, its long, hazy, crowded smoking-room with innumerable little tables and groups of men in armchairs, its magazine room and library upstairs, have just that undistinguished and unconcentrated diversity which is for me the Liberal note. The pensive member sits and hears perplexing dialects and even fragments of foreign speech, and among the clustering masses of less insistent whites his roving eye catches profiles and complexions that send his mind afield to Calcutta or Rangoon or the West Indies or Sierra Leone or the Cape. . . .

I was not infrequently that pensive member. I used to go to the Club to doubt about Liberalism.

About two o'clock in the day the great smoking-room is crowded with countless little groups. They sit about small round tables, or in circles of chairs, and the haze of tobacco seems to prolong the great narrow place, with its pillars and bays, to infinity. Some of the groups are big, as many as a dozen men talk in loud tones ; some are duologues, and there is always a sprinkling of lonely, dissociated men. At first one gets an impression of men going from group to group and as it were linking them, but as one watches closely one finds that these men just visit three or four groups at the outside, and know nothing of the others. One begins to perceive more and more distinctly that one is dealing with a sort of human mosaic ; that each patch in that great place is of a different quality and colour from the next and never to be mixed with it. Most clubs have a common link, a lowest common denominator in the Club Bore, who spares no one, but even the National Liberal bores are specialized and sectional. As one looks round one sees here a clump of men from the North Country or the Potteries, here an island of South London politicians, here a couple of young Jews ascendant from Whitechapel, here a circle of journalists and writers, here a group of Irish politicians, here two East Indians, here a priest or so, here a clump of old-fashioned Protestants, here a little knot of eminent Rationalists indulging in a blasphemous story *sotto voce*. Next to them are a group of anglicized Germans and highly specialized chess-players, and then two of the oddest-looking persons – bulging with documents and intent upon extraordinary business transactions over long cigars. . . .

I would listen to a stormy sea of babblement, and try to extract some constructive intimations. Every now and then I got a whiff of politics. It was clear they were against the Lords – against plutocrats – against Cossington's newspapers – against the brewers. . . . It was tremendously clear what they were against. The trouble was to find out what on earth they were *for!* . . .

As I sat and thought, the streaked and mottled pillars and walls, the various views, aspects, and portraits of Mr and Mrs Gladstone, the partitions of polished mahogany, the yellow-vested waiters, would dissolve and vanish, and I would have a vision of this sample of miscellaneous men of limited, diverse interests and a universal littleness of imagination enlarged, unlimited, no longer a sample but a community, spreading, stretching out to infinity – all in little groups and duologues and circles, all with their special and narrow concerns, all with their backs to most of the others.

What but a common antagonism would ever keep these multitudes together? I understood why modern electioneering is more than half of it denunciation. Let us condemn, if possible, let us obstruct and deprive, but not let us do. There is no real appeal to the commonplace mind in 'Let us do'. That calls for the creative imagination, and few have been accustomed to respond to that call. The other merely needs jealousy and hate, of which there are great and easily accessible reservoirs in every human heart. . . .

I remember that vision of endless, narrow, jealous individuality very vividly. A seething limitlessness it became at last, like a waste place covered by crawling locusts that men sweep up by the sackload and drown by the million in ditches. . . .

Grotesquely against it came the lean features, the sidelong shy movements of Edward Crampton, seated in a circle of talkers close at hand. I had a whiff of his strained, unmusical voice, and behold! he was saying something about the 'Will of the People. . . .'

The immense and wonderful disconnectednesses of human life! I forgot the smoke and jabber of the club altogether ; I became a lonely spirit flung aloft by some queer accident, a stone upon a ledge in some high and rocky wilderness, and below as far as the eye could reach stretched the swarming infinitesimals of humanity, like grass upon the field, like pebbles upon unbounded beaches. Was there ever to be in human life more than that endless struggling individualism? Was there indeed some giantry, some immense valiant synthesis, still to come – or present it might be and still unseen by me, or was this the beginning and withal the last phase of mankind? . . .

I glimpsed for a while the stupendous impudence of our ambitions, the tremendous enterprise to which the modern statesman is implicitly addressed. I was as it were one of a little swarm of would-be reef builders looking back at the teeming slime upon the ocean floor. All the history of mankind, all the history of life, has been and will be the story of something struggling out of the indiscriminated abyss, struggling to exist and prevail over and comprehend individual lives – an effort of insidious attraction, an idea of invincible appeal. That something greater than ourselves, which does not so much exist as seek existence, palpitating between being and not-being, how marvellous it is! It has worn the form and visage of ten thousand different Gods, sought a shape for itself in stone and ivory and music and wonderful words, spoken more and more clearly of a mystery of love, a mystery of unity, dabbling meanwhile in blood and cruelty beyond the common impulses of men. It is something that comes and goes, like a light that shines and is withdrawn; withdrawn so completely that one doubts if it has ever been. . . .

I would mark with a curious interest the stray country member of the club up in town for a night or so. My mind would be busy with speculations about him, about his home, his family, his reading, his horizons, his innumerable fellows who didn't belong and never came up. I would fill in the outline of him with memories of my uncle and his Staffordshire neighbours. He was perhaps Alderman This or Councillor That down there, a great man in his ward, J.P. within seven miles of the boundary of the borough, and a God in his home. Here he was nobody, and very shy, and either a little too arrogant or a little too meek towards our very democratic-mannered but still liveried waiters. Was he perhaps the backbone of England? He over-rated himself lest he should appear mean, went through our Special Dinner conscientiously, drank, unless he was teetotal, of unfamiliar wines, and did his best, in spite of the rules, to tip. Afterwards, in a state of flushed repletion, he would have old brandy, black coffee, and a banded cigar, or in the name of temperance omit the brandy and have rather more coffee, in the smoking-room. I would sit and watch that stiff dignity of self-indulgence, and wonder, wonder. . . .

An infernal clairvoyance would come to me. I would have visions of him in relation to his wife, checking always, some-times bullying, sometimes being ostentatiously 'kind' ; I would see him glance furtively at his domestic servants upon his stair-case, or stiffen his upper lip against the reluctant, protesting business employee. We imaginative people are base enough, heaven knows, but it is only in rare moods of bitter penetration that we pierce down to the baser lusts, the viler shames, the ever-lasting lying and muddle-headed self-justification of the dull.

I would turn my eyes down the crowded room and see others of him and others. What did he think he was up to? Did he for a moment realize that his presence under that ceramic glory of a ceiling with me meant, if it had any rational meaning at all, that we were jointly doing something with the nation and the empire and mankind? . . . How on earth could any one get hold of him, make any noble use of him? He didn't read be-yond his newspaper. He never thought, but only followed

imaginings in his heart. He never discussed. At the first hint of
discussion his temper gave way. He was, I knew, a deep, thinly-
covered tank of resentments and quite irrational moral rages.
Yet withal I would have to resist an impulse to go over to him
and nudge him and say to him, 'Look here! What indeed do
you think we are doing with the nation and the empire and
mankind? You know – *Mankind!*'

I wonder what reply I should have got?

So far as any average could be struck and so far as any backbone could be located, it seemed to me that this silent, shy,
replete, sub-angry, middle-class sentimentalist was in his endless
species and varieties and dialects the backbone of our party.
So far as I could be considered as representing anything in the
House, I pretended to sit for the elements of *him*. . . .


7

For a time I turned towards the Socialists. They at least had
an air of coherent intentions. At that time Socialism had come
into politics again after a period of depression and obscurity,
with a tremendous *éclat*. There was visibly a following of
Socialist members to Chris Robinson ; mysteriously uncom-
municative gentlemen in soft felt hats and short coats and
squared-toed boots who replied to casual advances a little sur-
prisingly in rich North Country dialects. Members became
aware of a 'seagreen incorruptible', as Colonel Marlow put it
to me, speaking on the Address, a slender twisted figure supporting itself on a stick and speaking with a fire that was altogether revolutionary. This was Philip Snowden, the member for
Blackburn. They had come in nearly forty strong altogether,
and with an air of presently meaning to come in much stronger.
They were only one aspect of what seemed at that time a big
national movement. Socialist societies, we gathered, were
springing up all over the country, and every one was inquiring
about Socialism and discussing Socialism. It had taken the
Universities with particular force, and any youngster with the
slightest intellectual pretension was either actively for or brilliantly against. For a time our Young Liberal group was ostentatiously sympathetic. . . .

When I think of the Socialists there comes a vivid memory of certain evening gatherings at our house. . . .

These gatherings had been organized by Margaret as the outcome of a discussion at the Baileys'. Altiora had been very emphatic and uncharitable upon the futility of the Socialist movement. It seemed that even the leaders fought shy of dinner-parties.

'They never meet each other,' said Altiora, 'much less people on the other side. How can they begin to understand politics until they do that?'

'Most of them have totally unpresentable wives,' said Altiora, 'totally!' and quoted instances, 'and they *will* bring them. Or they won't come! Some of the poor creatures have scarcely learnt their table manners. They just make holes in the talk. . . .'

I thought there was a great deal of truth beneath Altiora's outburst. The presentation of the Socialist case seemed very greatly crippled by the want of a common intimacy in its leaders ; the want of intimacy didn't at first appear to be more than an accident, and our talk led to Margaret's attempt to get acquaintance and easy intercourse afoot among them and between them and the Young Liberals of our group. She gave a series of weekly dinners, planned, I think, a little too accurately upon Altiora's model, and after each we had as catholic a reception as we could contrive.

Our receptions were indeed, I should think, about as catholic as receptions could be. Margaret found herself with a weekly houseful of insoluble problems in intercourse. One did one's best, but one got a nightmare feeling as the evening wore on.

It was one of the few unanimities of these parties that every one should be a little odd in appearance, funny about the hair or the tie or the shoes or more generally, and that bursts of violent aggression should alternate with an attitude entirely defensive. A number of our guests had an air of waiting for a clue that never came, and stood and sat about silently, mildly amused but not a bit surprised that we did not discover their distinctive Open-Sesames. There was a sprinkling of manifest seers and prophetesses in shapeless garments, far too many, I thought, for really easy social intercourse, and any conversation at any moment was liable to become oracular. One was in a state of tension from first to last ; the most innocent remark

238

seemed capable of exploding resentment, and replies came out at the most unexpected angles. We Young Liberals went about puzzled but polite to the gathering we had evoked. The Young Liberals' tradition is on the whole wonderfully discreet, superfluous steam is let out far away from the home in the Balkans or Africa, and the neat stiff figures of the Cramptons, Bunting Harblow, and Lewis, either in extremely well-cut morning coats indicative of the House, or in what is sometimes written of as 'faultless evening dress', stood about on those evenings, they and their very quietly and simply and expensively dressed little wives, like a datum line amidst lakes and mountains.

I didn't at first see the connexion between systematic social reorganization and arbitrary novelties in dietary and costume, just as I didn't realize why the most comprehensive constructive projects should appear to be supported solely by odd and exceptional personalities. On one of these evenings a little group of rather jolly-looking pretty young people seated themselves for no particular reason in a large circle on the floor of my study, and engaged, so far as I could judge, in the game of Hunt the Meaning, the intellectual equivalent of Hunt the Slipper. It must have been that same evening I came upon an unbleached young gentleman before the oval mirror on the landing engaged in removing the remains of an anchovy sandwich from his protruded tongue – visible ends of cress having misled him into the belief that he was dealing with doctrinally permissible food. It was not unusual to be given hand-bills and printed matter by our guests, but there I had the advantage over Lewis, who was too tactful to refuse the stuff, too neatly dressed to pocket it, and had no writing-desk available upon which he could relieve himself in a manner flattering to the giver. So that his hands got fuller and fuller. A relentless, compact little woman in what Margaret declared to be an extremely expensive black dress has also printed herself on my memory ; she had set her heart upon my contributing to a weekly periodical in the lentil interest with which she was associated, and I spent much time and care in evading her.

Mingling with the more hygienic types were a number of Anti-Puritan Socialists, bulging with bias against temperance, and breaking out against austere methods of living all over their faces. Their manner was packed with heartiness. They were apt to choke the approaches to the little buffet Margaret had set up downstairs, and there engage in discussions of Determinism – it always seemed to be Determinism – which became heartier and noisier, but never acrimonious even in the small hours. It seemed impossible to settle about this Determinism of theirs – ever. And there were worldly Socialists also. I particularly recall a large, active, buoyant, lady-killing individual with an eye-glass borne upon a broad black ribbon, who swam about us one evening. He might have been a slightly frayed actor, in his large frock-coat, his white waistcoat, and the sort of black-and-white check trousers that twinkle. He had a high-pitched voice with aristocratic intonations, and he seemed to be in a perpetual state of interrogation. 'What are we all he-a for?' he would ask only too audibly. 'What are we doing he-a? What's the connexion?'

What *was* the connexion?

We made a special effort with our last assembly in June, 1907. We tried to get something like a representative collection of the parliamentary leaders of Socialism, the various exponents of Socialist thought and a number of Young Liberal thinkers into one room. Dorvil came, and Horatio Bulch; Featherstonehaugh appeared for ten minutes and talked charmingly to Margaret and then vanished again; there was Wilkins the novelist and Toomer and Dr Tumpany. Chris Robinson stood about for a time in a new comforter, and Magdeberg and Will Pipes and five or six Labour members. And on our side we had our particular little group, Bunting Harblow, Crampton, Lewis, all looking as broadminded and open to conviction as they possibly could, and even occasionally talking out from their bushes almost boldly. But the gathering as a whole refused either to mingle or dispute, and as an experiment in intercourse the evening was a failure. Unexpected dissociations appeared between Socialists one had supposed friendly. I could not have imagined it was possible for half so many people to turn their backs on everybody else in such small rooms as ours. But the unsaid things those backs expressed broke out, I remarked, with refreshed virulence in the various organs of the various sections of the party next week.

I talked, I remember, with Dr Tumpany, a large young man in a still larger professional frock-coat, and with a great shock of very fair hair, who was candidate for some North Country constituency. We discussed the political outlook, and, like so many Socialists at that time, he was full of vague threatenings against the Liberal party. I was struck by a thing in him that I had already observed less vividly in many others of these Socialist leaders, and which gave me at last a clue to the whole business. He behaved exactly like a man in possession of valuable patent rights, who wants to be dealt with. He had an air of having a corner in ideas. Then it flashed into my head that the whole Socialist movement was an attempted corner in ideas. . . .

8

Late that night I found myself alone with Margaret amid the débris of the gathering.

I sat before the fire, hands in pockets, and Margaret, looking white and weary, came and leant upon the mantel.

'Oh Lord!' said Margaret.

I agreed. Then I resumed my meditation.

'Ideas,' I said, 'count for more than I thought in the world.'

Margaret regarded me with that neutral expression behind which she was accustomed to wait for clues.

'When you think of the height and depth and importance and wisdom of the Socialist ideas, and see the men who are running them,' I explained. . . . 'A big system of ideas like Socialism grows up out of the obvious common sense of our present conditions. It's as impersonal as science. All these men – They've given nothing to it. They're just people who have pegged out claims upon a big intellectual No-Man's-Land – and don't feel quite sure of the law. There's a sort of quarrelsome uneasiness. . . . If we professed Socialism do you think they'd welcome us? Not a man of them! They'd feel it was burglary. . . .'

'Yes,' said Margaret, looking into the fire. 'That is just what *I* felt about them all the evening. . . . Particularly Dr Tumpany.'

'We mustn't confuse Socialism with the Socialists,' I said; 'that's the moral of it. I suppose if God were to find He had made a mistake in dates or something, and went back and annihilated everybody from Owen onwards who was in any way known as a Socialist leader or teacher, Socialism would be exactly where it is and what it is today – a growing realization of constructive needs in every man's mind, and a little corner in party politics. So, I suppose, it will always be. . . . But they *were* a damned lot, Margaret!'

I looked up at the little noise she made. '*Twice!*' she said, smiling indulgently, 'today!' (Even the smile was Altiora's.)

I returned to my thoughts. They *were* a damned human lot. It was an excellent world in that connexion. . . .

But the ideas marched on, the ideas marched on, just as though men's brains were no more than stepping-stones, just as though some great brain in which we are all little cells and corpuscles was thinking them! . . .

'I don't think there is a man among them who makes me feel he is trustworthy,' said Margaret; 'unless it is Featherstone-haugh.'

I sat taking in this proposition.

'They'll never help us, I feel,' said Margaret.

'Us?'

'The Liberals.'

'Oh, damn the Liberals!' I said. 'They'll never even help themselves.'

'I don't think I could possibly get on with any of those people,' said Margaret, after a pause.

She remained for a time looking down at me and, I could feel, perplexed by me, but I wanted to go on with my thinking, and so I did not look up, and presently she stooped to my forehead and kissed me and went rustling softly to her room.

I remained in my study for a long time with my thoughts crystallizing out. . . .

It was then, I think, that I first apprehended clearly how that opposition to which I have already alluded of the immediate life and the mental hinterland of a man can be applied to public and social affairs. The ideas go on – and no person or party succeeds in embodying them. The reality of human progress never comes to the surface; it is a power in the deeps, an under-tow. It goes on in silence while men think, in studies where they write self-forgetfully, in laboratories under the urgency of an impersonal curiosity, in the rare illumination of honest talk, in moments of emotional insight, in thoughtful reading, but not in everyday affairs. Everyday affairs and whatever is made an everyday affair are transactions of the ostensible self, the being of habits, interests, usage. Temper, vanity, hasty reaction to imitation, personal feeling, are their substance. No man can abolish his immediate self and specialize in the depths; if he attempts that, he simply turns himself into something a little less than the common man. He may have an immense hinterland, but that does not absolve him from a frontage. That is the essential error of the specialist philosopher, the specialist teacher, the specialist publicist. They repudiate frontage; claim to be pure hinterland. That is what bothered me about Codger, about those various schoolmasters who had prepared me for life, about the Baileys and their dream of an official ruling class. A human being who is a philosopher in the first place, a teacher in the first place, or a statesman in the first place, is thereby and inevitably, though he bring God-like gifts to the pretence – a quack. These are attempts to live deep-side shallow, inside out. They produce merely a new pettiness. To understand Socialism, again, is to gain a new breadth of outlook; to join a Socialist organization is to join a narrow cult which is not even tolerably serviceable in presenting or spreading the ideas for which it stands. . . .

I perceived I had got something quite fundamental here. It had taken me some years to realize the true relation of the great constructive ideas that swayed me not only to political parties, but to myself. I had been disposed to identify the formulæ of some one party with social construction, and to regard the other as necessarily anti-constructive, just as I had been inclined to follow the Baileys in the self-righteousness of supposing myself to be wholly constructive. But I saw now that every man of intellectual freedom and vigour is necessarily constructive-minded nowadays, and that no man is disinterestedly so. Each of us repeats in himself the conflict of the race between the splendour of its possibilities and its immediate associations. We may be shaping immortal things, but we must sleep and answer the dinner gong, and have our salt of flattery and self-approval. In politics a man counts not for what he is in moments of imaginative expansion, but for his common, workaday, selfish self; and political parties are held together not by a community of ultimate aims, but by the stabler bond of an accustomed life. Everybody almost is for progress in

243

general, and nearly everybody is opposed to any change, except in so far as gross increments are change, in his particular method of living and behaviour. Every party stands essentially for the interests and mental usages of some definite class or group of classes in the existing community, and every party has its scientific-minded and constructive leading section, with well-defined hinterlands formulating its social functions in a public-spirited form, and its superficial-minded following confessing its meannesses and vanities and prejudices. No class will abolish itself, materially alter its way of life, or drastically reconstruct itself, albeit no class is indisposed to co-operate in the unlimited socialization of any other class. In that capacity for aggression upon other classes lies the essential driving force of modern affairs. The instincts, the persons, the parties, and vanities sway and struggle. The ideas and understandings march on and achieve themselves for all – in spite of everyone. . . .

The methods and traditions of British politics maintain the form of two great parties, with rider groups seeking to gain specific ends in the event of a small Government majority. These two main parties are more or less heterogeneous in composition. Each, however, has certain necessary characteristics. The Conservative Party has always stood quite definitely for the established propertied interests. The landowner, the big lawyer, the Established Church, and latterly the huge private monopoly of the liquor trade which has been created by temperance legislation, are the essential Conservatives. Interwoven now with the native wealthy are the families of the great international usurers, and a vast miscellaneous mass of financial enterprise. Outside the range of resistance implied by these interests, the Conservative Party has always shown itself just as constructive and collectivist as any other party. The great landowners have been as well-disposed towards the endowment of higher education, and as willing to co-operate with the Church in protective and mildly educational legislation for children and the working class, as any political section. The financiers, too, are adventurous-spirited and eager for mechanical progress and technical efficiency. They are prepared to spend public money upon research, upon ports and harbours and public communications, upon sanitation and hygienic

244

organization. A certain rude benevolence of public intention is equally characteristic of the liquor trade. Provided his comfort leads to no excesses of temperance, the liquor trade is quite eager to see the common man prosperous, happy, and with money to spend in a bar. All sections of the party are aggressively patriotic and favourably inclined to the idea of an upstanding well-fed, and well-exercised population in uniform. Of course there are reactionary landowners and old-fashioned country clergy, full of localized self-importance, jealous even of the cottager who can read, but they have neither the power nor the ability to retard the constructive forces in the party as a whole. On the other hand, when matters point to any definitely confiscatory proposal, to the public ownership and collective control of land, for example, or state mining and manufactures, or the nationalization of the so-called public-house or extended municipal enterprise, or even to an increase of the taxation of property, then the Conservative Party presents a nearly adamantine bar. It does not stand for, it *is*, the existing arrangement in these affairs.

Even more definitely a class party is the Labour Party, whose immediate interest is to raise wages, shorten hours of labour, increase employment, and make better terms for the working-man tenant and working-man purchaser. Its leaders are no doubt constructive minded, but the mass of the following is naturally suspicious of education and discipline, hostile to the higher education, and – except for an obvious antagonism to employers and property owners – almost destitute of ideas. What else can it be? It stands for the expropriated multitude, whose whole situation and difficulty arise from its individual lack of initiative and organizing power. It favours the nationalization of land and capital with no sense of the difficulties involved in the process; but, on the other hand, the equally reasonable socialization of individuals which is implied by military service is steadily and quite naturally and quite illogically opposed by it. It is only in recent years that Labour has emerged as a separate party from the huge hospitable caravanserai of Liberalism, and there is still a very marked tendency to step back again into that multitudinous assemblage.

For multitudinousness has always been the Liberal characteristic. Liberalism never has been nor ever can be anything but a diversified crowd. Liberalism has to voice everything that is left out by these other parties. It is the party against the predominating interests. It is at once the party of the failing and of the untried ; it is the party of decadence and hope. From its nature it must be a vague and planless association in comparison with its antagonist, neither so constructive on the one hand, nor on the other so competent to hinder the inevitable constructions of the civilized state. Essentially it is the party of criticism, the 'Anti' party. It is a system of hostilities and objections that somehow achieves at times an elusive common soul. It is a gathering together of all the smaller interests which find themselves at a disadvantage against the big established classes, the leasehold tenant as against the landowner, the retail tradesman as against the merchant and moneylender, the Nonconformist as against the Churchman, the small employer as against the demoralizing hospitable publican, the man without introductions and broad connexions against the man who has these things. It is the party of the many small men against the fewer prevailing men. It has no more essential reason for loving the Collectivist state than the Conservatives ; the small dealer is doomed to absorption in that just as much as the large owner ; but it resorts to the state against its antagonists as in the middle ages common men pitted themselves against the barons by siding with the king. The Liberal Party is the party against 'class privilege' because it represents no class advantages, but it is also the party that is on the whole most set against Collective control because it represents no established responsibility. It is constructive only so far as its antagonism to the great owner is more powerful than its jealousy of the state. It organizes only because organization is forced upon it by the organization of its adversaries. It lapses in and out of alliance with Labour as it sways between hostility to wealth and hostility to public expenditure. . . .

Every modern European state will have in some form or other these three parties: the resistant, militant, authoritative, dull, and unsympathetic party of establishment and success, the rich party; the confused, sentimental, spasmodic, numerous party of the small, struggling, various, undisciplined men, the poor man's party; and a third party sometimes detaching itself from the second and sometimes reuniting with it, the party of the altogether expropriated masses, the proletarians, Labour. Change Conservative and Liberal to Republican and Democrat, for example, and you have the conditions in the United States. The Crown or a dethroned dynasty, the Established Church or a dispossessed church, nationalist secessions, the personalities of party leaders, may break up, complicate, and confuse the self-expression of these three necessary divisions in the modern social drama, the analyst will make them out none the less for that. . . .

And then I came back as if I came back to a refrain ; – the ideas go on – as though we are all no more than little cells and corpuscles in some great brain beyond our understanding. . . .

So it was I sat and thought my problem out. . . . I still remember my satisfaction at seeing things plainly at last. It was like clouds dispersing to show the sky. Constructive ideas, of course, couldn't hold a party together alone, 'interests and habits, not ideas', I had that now, and so the great constructive scheme of Socialism, invading and inspiring all parties, was necessarily claimed only by this collection of odds and ends, this residuum of disconnected and exceptional people. This was true not only of the Socialist idea, but of the scientific idea, the idea of veracity – of human confidence in humanity – of all that mattered in human life outside the life of individuals. . . . The only real party that would ever profess Socialism was the Labour Party, and that in the entirely one-sided form of an irresponsible and non-constructive attack on property. Socialism in that mutilated form, the teeth and claws without the eyes and brain, I wanted as little as I wanted anything in the world.

Perfectly clear it was, perfectly clear, and why hadn't I seen it before? . . . I looked at my watch, and it was half-past two.

I yawned, stretched, got up and went to bed.

9

My ideas about statecraft have passed through three main phases to the final convictions that remain. There was the first immediacy of my dream of ports and harbours and cities, railways, roads, and administered territories – the vision I had seen in the haze from that little church above Locarno. Slowly that had passed into a more elaborate legislative constructiveness, which had led to my uneasy association with the Baileys and the professedly constructive Young Liberals. To get that ordered life I had realized the need of organization, knowledge, expertness, a wide movement of co-ordinated methods. On the individual side I thought that a life of urgent industry, temperance, and close attention was indicated by my perception of these ends. I married Margaret and set to work. But something in my mind refused from the outset to accept these determinations as final. There was always a doubt lurking below, always a faint resentment, a protesting criticism, a feeling of vitally important omissions.

I arrived at last at the clear realization that my political associates, and I in my association with them, were oddly narrow, priggish, and unreal, that the Socialists with whom we were attempting co-operation were preposterously irrelevant to their own theories, that my political life didn't in some way comprehend more than itself, that rather perplexingly I was missing the thing I was seeking. Britten's footnotes to Altiora's self-assertions, her fits of energetic planning, her quarrels and rallies and vanities, his illuminating attacks on Cramptonism and the heavy-spirited triviality of such Liberalism as the Children's Charter, served to point my way to my present conclusions. I had been trying to deal all along with human progress as something immediate in life, something to be immediately attacked by political parties and groups primarily to that end. I now began to see that just as in my own being there was the rather shallow, rather vulgar, self-seeking careerist, who wore an admirable silk hat and bustled self-consciously through the lobby, and a much greater and indefinitely growing unpublished personality behind him – my hinterland, I have called it – so in human affairs generally the permanent reality is also a hinterland, which is never really immediate, which draws continually upon human experience and influences human action more and more, but which is itself never the actual player upon the stage. It is the unseen dramatist who never takes a call. Now it was just through the fact that our group about the Baileys didn't understand this, that with a sort of frantic energy they were trying to develop that sham expert officialdom of theirs to plan, regulate, and direct the affairs of humanity, that the perplexing note of silliness and shallowness that I had always felt, and felt now most acutely under Britten's gibes, came in. They were neglecting human life altogether in social organization.

In the development of intellectual modesty lies the growth of statesmanship. It has been the chronic mistake of statecraft and all organizing spirits to attempt immediately to scheme and arrange and achieve. Priests, schools of thought, political schemers, leaders of men, have always slipped into the error of assuming that they can think out the whole – or at any rate completely think out definite parts – of the purpose and future of man, clearly and finally; they have set themselves to legislate and construct on that assumption, and, experiencing the perplexing obduracy and evasions of reality, they have taken to dogma, persecution, training, pruning, secretive education, and all the stupidities of self-sufficient energy. In the passion of their good intentions they have not hesitated to conceal fact, suppress thought, crush disturbing initiatives and apparently detrimental desires. And so it is blunderingly and wastefully, destroying with the making, that any extension of social organization is at present achieved.

Directly, however, this idea of an emancipation from immediacy is grasped, directly the dominating importance of this critical, less personal, mental hinterland in the individual and of the collective mind in the race is understood, the whole problem of the statesman and his attitude towards politics gain a new significance, and become accessible to a new series of solutions. He wants no longer to 'fix up', as people say, human affairs, but to devote his forces to the development of that needed intellectual life without which all his shallow attempts at fixing up are futile. He ceases to build on the sands, and sets himself to gather foundations.

You see, I began in my teens by wanting to plan and build cities and harbours for mankind; I ended in the middle thirties by desiring only to serve and increase a general process of thought, a process fearless, critical, real-spirited, that would in its own time give cities, harbours, air, happiness, everything at a scale and quality and in a light altogether beyond the match-striking imaginations of a contemporary mind. I wanted freedom of speech and suggestion, vigour of thought, and the cultivation of that impulse of veracity that lurks more or less discouraged in every man. With that I felt there must go an

249

emotion. I hit upon a phrase that became at last something of a refrain in my speech and writings, to convey the spirit that I felt was at the very heart of real human progress – love and fine thinking.

(I suppose that nowadays no newspaper in England gets through a week without the repetition of that phrase.)

My convictions crystallized more and more definitely upon this. The more of love and fine thinking the better for men, I said ; the less, the worse. And upon this fresh basis I set myself to examine what I as a politician might do. I perceived I was at last finding an adequate expression for all that was in me, for those forces that had rebelled at the crude presentations of Bromstead, at the secrecies and suppressions of my youth, at the dull unrealities of City Merchants, at the conventions and timidities of the Pinky Dinkys, at the philosophical recluse of Trinity and the phrases and tradition-worship of my political associates. None of these things were half alive, and I wanted life to be intensely alive and awake. I wanted thought like an edge of steel and desire like a flame. The real work before mankind now, I realized once and for all, is the enlargement of human expression, the release and intensification of human thought, the vivider utilization of experience and the invigoration of research – and whatever one does in human affairs has or lacks value as it helps or hinders that.

With that I had got my problem clear, and the solution, so far as I was concerned, lay in finding out the point in the ostensible life of politics at which I could most subverse these ends. I was still against the muddles of Bromstead, but I had hunted them down now to their essential form. The jerry-built slums, the roads that went nowhere, the tarred fences, litigious notice-boards and barbed wire fencing, the litter and the heaps of dump, were only the outward appearances whose ultimate realities were jerry-built conclusions, hasty purposes, aimless habits of thoughts, and imbecile bars and prohibitions in the thoughts and souls of men. How are we through politics to get at that confusion?

We want to invigorate and reinvigorate education. We want to create a sustained counter-effort to the perpetual tendency of all educational organizations towards classicalism, secondary issues, and the evasion of life.

250

We want to stimulate the expression of life through art and literature, and its exploration through research.

We want to make the best and finest thought accessible to everyone, and more particularly to create and sustain an enormous free criticism, without which art, literature, and research alike degenerate into tradition or imposture.

Then all the other problems which are now so insoluble, destitution, disease, the difficulty of maintaining international peace, the scarcely faced possibility of making life generally and continually beautiful, become – *easy*. . . .

It was clear to me that the most vital activities in which I could engage would be those which most directly affected the Church, public habits of thought, education, organized research, literature, and the channels of general discussion. I had to ask myself how my position as Liberal member for Kinghamstead squared with and conduced to this essential work.

# Seeking Associates

## 1

I have told of my gradual abandonment of the pretensions and habits of party Liberalism. In a sense I was moving towards aristocracy. Regarding the development of the social and individual mental hinterland as the essential thing in human progress, I passed on very naturally to the practical assumption that we wanted what I may call 'hinterlanders'. Of course I do not mean by aristocracy the changing unorganized medley of rich people and privileged people who dominate the civilized world today, but as opposed to this, a possibility of co-ordinating the will of the finer individuals, by habit and literature, into a broad common aim. We must have an aristocracy – not of privilege, but of understanding and purpose – or mankind will fail. I find this dawning more and more clearly when I look through my various writings of the years between 1903 and 1910. I was already emerging to plain statements in 1908.

I reasoned after this fashion. The line of human improvement and the expansion of human life lies in the direction of education and fine initiatives. If humanity cannot develop an education far beyond anything that is now provided, if it cannot collectively invent devices and solve problems on a much richer, broader scale than it does at the present time, it cannot hope to achieve any very much finer order or any more general happiness than it now enjoys. We must believe, therefore, that it *can* develop such a training and education, or we must abandon secular constructive hope. And here my peculiar difficulty as against crude democracy comes in. If humanity at large is capable of that high education and those creative freedoms our hope demands, much more must its better and more vigorous types be so capable. And if those who have power and leisure now, and freedom to respond to imaginative appeals, cannot be won to the idea of collective self-development, then the whole of humanity cannot be won to that. From that one passes to what has become my general conception in politics, the conception of the constructive imagination working upon the vast complex of powerful people, clever people, enterprising people, influential people, amidst whom power is diffused today, to produce that self-conscious, highly selective, open-minded, devoted aristocratic culture which seems to me to be the necessary next phase in the development of human affairs. I see human progress, not as the spontaneous product of crowds of raw minds swayed by elementary needs, but as a natural but elaborate result of intricate human inter-dependencies, of human energy and curiosity liberated and acting at leisure, of human passions and motives, modified and re-directed by literature and art. . . .

But now the reader will understand how it came about that, disappointed by the essential littleness of Liberalism, and disillusioned about the representative quality of the professed Socialists, I turned my mind more and more to a scrutiny of the big people, the wealthy and influential people, against whom Liberalism pits its forces. I was asking myself definitely whether, after all, it was not my particular job to work through them and not against them. Was I not altogether out of my element as an Anti? Weren't there big bold qualities about these people that common men lack, and the possibility of far more splendid dreams? Were they really obstacles, might they not be rather the vehicles of the possible new braveries of life?

2

The faults of the Imperialist movement were obvious enough. The conception of the Boer War had been clumsy and puerile, the costly errors of that struggle appalling, and the subsequent campaign of Mr Chamberlain for Tariff Reform seemed calculated to combine the financial adventurers of the Empire in one vast conspiracy against the consumer. The cant of Imperialism was easy to learn and use ; it was speedily adopted by all sorts of base enterprises and turned to all sorts of base ends. But a big child is permitted big mischief, and my mind was now continually returning to the persuasion that after all in some development of the idea of Imperial patriotism might be found that wide, rough, politically acceptable expression of a constructive dream capable of sustaining a great educational and philosophical movement such as no formula of Liberalism supplied. The fact that it readily took vulgar forms only witnessed to its strong popular appeal. Mixed in with the noisiness and humbug of the movement there appeared a real regard for social efficiency, a real spirit of animation and enterprise. There suddenly appeared in my world – I saw them first, I think, in 1908 – a new sort of little boy, a most agreeable development of the slouching, cunning, cigarette-smoking, town-bred youngster, a small boy in a khaki hat, and with bare knees and athletic bearing, earnestly engaged in wholesome and invigorating games up to and occasionally a little beyond his strength – the Boy Scout. I liked the Boy Scout, and I find it difficult to express how much it mattered to me, with my growing bias in favour of deliberate national training, that Liberalism hadn't been able to produce, and had indeed never attempted to produce, anything of this kind.

3

In those days there existed a dining club called – there was some lost allusion to the exorcism of party feeling in its title – the Pentagram Circle. It included Bailey and Dayton and myself, Sir Herbert Thorns, Lord Charles Kindling, Minns the poet, Gerbault the big railway man, Lord Gane, fresh from the settlement of Framboya, and Rumbold, who later became Home Secretary and left us. We were men of all parties and very various experiences, and our object was to discuss the welfare of the Empire in a disinterested spirit. We dined monthly at the Mermaid in Westminster, and for a couple of years we kept up an average attendance of ten out of fourteen. The dinner-time was given up to desultory conversation, and it is odd how warm and good the social atmosphere of that little gathering became as time went on; then over the dessert, so soon as the waiters had swept away the crumbs and ceased to fret us, one of us would open with perhaps fifteen or twenty minutes' exposition of some specially prepared question, and after him we would deliver ourselves in turn, each for three or four minutes. When everyone present had spoken once talk became general again, and it was rare we emerged upon Hendon

Street before midnight. Sometimes, as my house was conveniently near, a knot of men would come home with me and go on talking and smoking in my dining-room until two or three. We had Fred Neal, that wild Irish journalist, among us towards the end, and his stupendous flow of words materially prolonged our closing discussions and made our continuance impossible.

I learned very much and very many things at those dinners, but more particularly did I become familiarized with the habits of mind of such men as Neal, Crupp, Gane, and the one or two other New Imperialists who belonged to us. They were nearly all, like Bailey, Oxford men, though mostly of a younger generation, and they were all mysteriously and inexplicably advocates of Tariff Reform, as if it were the principal instead of at best a secondary aspect of constructive policy. They seemed obsessed by the idea that streams of trade could be diverted violently so as to link the parts of the Empire by common interests, and they were persuaded, I still think mistakenly, that Tariff Reform would have an immense popular appeal. They were also very keen on military organization, and with a curious little martinet twist in their minds that boded ill for that side of public liberty. So much against them. But they were disposed to spend money much more generously on education and research of all sorts than our formless host of Liberals seemed likely to do ; and they were altogether more accessible than the Young Liberals to bold, constructive ideas affecting the universities and upper classes. The Liberals are abjectly afraid of the universities. I found myself constantly falling into line with these men in our discussions, and more and more hostile to Dayton's sentimentalizing evasions of definite schemes and Minns' trust in such things as the 'Spirit of our People' and the 'General Trend of Progress'. It wasn't that I thought them very much righter than their opponents; I believe all definite party 'sides' at any time are bound to be about equally right and equally lop-sided ; but that I thought I could get more out of them and, what was more important to me, more out of myself if I co-operated with them. By 1908 I had already arrived at a point where I could be definitely considering a transfer of my political allegiance.

These abstract questions are inseparably interwoven with

255

my memory of a shining long white table, and our hock bottles and burgundy bottles, and bottles of Perrier and St Galmier and the disturbed central trophy of dessert, and scattered glasses and nutshells and cigarette-ends and menu-cards used for memoranda. I see old Dayton sitting back and cocking his eye to the ceiling in a way he had while he threw warmth into the ancient platitudes of Liberalism, and Minns leaning forward, and a little like a cockatoo with a taste for confidences, telling us in a hushed voice of his faith in the Destiny of Mankind. Thorns lounges, rolling his round face and round eyes from speaker to speaker and sounding the visible depths of misery whenever Neal begins. Gerbault and Gane were given to conversation in undertones, and Bailey pursued mysterious purposes in lisping whispers. It was Crupp attracted me most. He had, as people say, his eye on me from the beginning. He used to speak at me, and drifted into a custom of coming home with me very regularly for an after-talk.

He opened his heart to me.

'Neither of us,' he said, 'are dukes, and neither of us are horny-handed sons of toil. We want to get hold of the handles, and to do that one must go where the power is, and give it just as constructive a twist as we can. That's *my* Toryism.'

'Is it Kindling's – or Gerbault's?'

'No. But theirs is soft, and mine's hard. Mine will wear theirs out. You and I and Bailey are all after the same thing, and why aren't we working together?'

'Are you a Confederate?' I asked suddenly.

'That's a secret nobody tells,' he said.

'What are the Confederates after?'

'Making aristocracy work, I suppose. Just as, I gather, you want to do.' . . .

The Confederates were being heard of at that time. They were at once attractive and repellent to me, an odd secret society whose membership nobody knew, pledged, it was said, to impose Tariff Reform and an ample constructive policy upon the Conservatives. In the press, at any rate, they had an air of deliberately organized power. I have no doubt the rumour of them greatly influenced my ideas. . . .

In the end I made some very rapid decisions, but for nearly two years I was hesitating. Hesitations were inevitable in such

256

a matter. I was not dealing with any simple question of principle, but with elusive and fluctuating estimates of the trend of diverse forces and of the nature of my own powers. All through that period I was asking over and over again: how far are these Confederates mere dreamers? How far – and this was more vital – are they rendering lip-service to social organization? Is it true they desire war because it confirms the ascendancy of their class? How far can Conservatism be induced to plan and construct before it resists the thrust towards change? Is it really in bulk anything more than a mass of prejudice and conceit, cynical indulgence, and a hard suspicion of and hostility to the expropriated classes in the community?

That is a research which yields no statistics, an inquiry like asking what is the ruling colour of a chameleon. The shadowy answer varied with my health, varied with my mood and the conduct of the people I was watching. How fine can people be? How generous? – not incidentally, but all round? How far can you educate sons beyond the outlook of their fathers, and how far lift a rich, proud, self-indulgent class above the protests of its business agents and solicitors and its own habits and vanity? Is chivalry in a class possible? – was it ever, indeed, or will it ever indeed be possible? Is the progress that seems attainable in certain directions worth the retrogression that may be its price?


4

It was to the Pentagram Circle that I first broached the new conceptions that were developing in my mind. I count the evening of my paper the beginning of the movement that created the *Blue Weekly* and our wing of the present New Tory party. I do that without any excessive egotism, because my essay was no solitary man's production; it was my reaction to forces that had come to me very largely through my fellow-members; its quick reception by them showed that I was, so to speak, merely the first of the chestnuts to pop. The atmospheric quality of the evening stands out very vividly in my memory. The night, I remember, was warmly foggy when after midnight we went to finish our talk at my house.

We had recently changed the rules of the club to admit visitors, and so it happened that I had brought Britten, and Crupp introduced Arnold Shoesmith, my former schoolfellow at City Merchants, and now the wealthy successor of his father and elder brother. I remember his heavy, inexpressively handsome face lighting to his rare smile at the sight of me, and how little I dreamt of the tragic entanglement that was destined to involve us both. Gane was present, and Esmeer, a newly-added member, but I think Bailey was absent. Either he was absent, or he said something so entirely characteristic and undistinguished that it has left no impression on my mind.

I had broken a little from the traditions of the club even in my title, which was deliberately a challenge to the liberal idea: it was, 'The World Exists for Exceptional People.' It is not the title I should choose now – for since that time I have got my phrase of 'mental hinterland' into journalistic use. I should say now, 'The World Exists for Mental Hinterland.'

The notes I made of that opening have long since vanished with a thousand other papers, but some odd chance has preserved and brought with me to Italy the menu for the evening; its back black with the scrawled notes I made of the discussion for my reply. I found it the other day among some letters from Margaret and a copy of the 1909 Report of the Poor Law Commission, also rich with pencilled marginalia.

My opening was a criticism of the democratic idea and method, upon lines such as I have already sufficiently indicated in the preceding sections. I remember how old Dayton fretted in his chair, and tushed and pished at that, even as I gave it, and afterwards we were treated to one of his platitudinous harangues, he sitting back in his chair with that small obstinate eye of his fixed on the ceiling, and a sort of cadaverous glow upon his face, repeating – quite regardless of all my reasoning and all that had been said by others in the debate – the sacred empty phrases that were his soul's refuge from reality. 'You may think it very clever,' he said, with a nod of his head to mark his sense of his point, 'not to Trust the People. I do.' And so on. Nothing in his life or work had ever shown that he did trust in the people, but that was beside the mark. He was the party Liberal, and these were the party incantations.

After my preliminary attack on vague democracy I went on to show that all human life was virtually aristocratic; people must either recognize aristocracy in general or else fol-

258

low leaders, which is aristocracy in particular, and so I came to my point that the reality of human progress lay necessarily through the establishment of freedoms for the human best and a collective receptivity and understanding. There was a disgusted grunt from Dayton, 'Superman rubbish – Nietzsche. Shaw! Ugh!' I sailed on over him to my next propositions. The prime essential in a progressive civilization was the establishment of a more effective selective process for the privilege of higher education, and the very highest educational opportunity for the educable. We were too apt to patronize scholarship winners, as though a scholarship was toffee given as a reward for virtue. It wasn't any reward at all ; it was an invitation to capacity. We had no more right to drag in virtue, or any merit but quality, than we had to involve it in a search for the tallest man. We didn't want a mere process for the selection of good as distinguished from gifted and able boys – 'No, you *don't*,' from Dayton – we wanted all the brilliant stuff in the world concentrated upon the development of the world. Just to exasperate Dayton further I put in a plea for gifts as against character in educational, artistic, and legislative work. 'Good teaching,' I said, 'is better than good conduct. We are becoming idiotic about character.'

Dayton was too moved to speak. He slewed round upon me an eye of agonized aversion.

I expatiated on the small proportion of the available ability that is really serving humanity today. 'I suppose today all the thought, all the art, all the increments of knowledge that matter, are supplied so far as the English-speaking community is concerned by – how many? – by three or four thousand individuals. ('Less,' said Thorns.) By, to be more precise, the mental hinterlands of three or four thousand individuals. We who know some of the band entertain no illusions as to their innate rarity. We know that they are just the few out of many, the few who got, in our world of chance and confusion, the timely stimulus, the apt suggestion at the fortunate moment, the needed training, the leisure. The rest are lost in the crowd, fail through the defects of their qualities, become commonplace workmen and second-rate professional men, marry commonplace wives, are as much waste as the driftage of superfluous pollen in a pine forest is waste.'

'Decent honest lives!' said Dayton to his breadcrumbs, with his chin in his necktie. *'Waste!'*

'And the people who do get what we call opportunity get it usually in extremely limited and cramping forms. No man lives a life of intellectual productivity alone; he needs not only material and opportunity, but helpers, resonators. Round and about what I might call the *real* men, you want the sympathetic co-operators, who help by understanding. It isn't that our – *salt* of three or four thousand is needlessly rare; it is sustained by far too small and undifferentiated a public. Most of the good men we know are not really doing the very best work of their gifts; nearly all are a little adapted, most are shockingly adapted, to some second-best use. Now, I take it, this is the very centre and origin of the muddle, futility, and unhappiness that distress us; it's the cardinal problem of the state – to discover, develop, and use the exceptional gifts of men. And I see that best done – I drift more and more away from the common stuff of legislative and administrative activity – by a quite revolutionary development of the educational machinery, but by a still more unprecedented attempt to keep science going, to keep literature going, and to keep what is the necessary spur of all science and literature, an intelligent and appreciative criticism going. You know none of these things have ever been kept going hitherto; they've come unexpectedly and inexplicably.'

'Hear, hear!' from Dayton, cough, nodding of the head, and an expression of mystical profundity.

'They've lit up a civilization and vanished, to give place to darkness again. Now the modern state doesn't mean to go back to darkness again – and so it's got to keep its light burning.' I went on to attack the present organization of our schools and universities, which seemed elaborately designed to turn the well-behaved, uncritical, and uncreative men of each generation into the authoritative leaders of the next, and I suggested remedies upon lines that I have already indicated in the earlier chapters of this story. . . .

So far I had the substance of the club with me, but I opened new ground and set Crupp agog by confessing my doubts from which party or combination of groups these developments of science and literature and educational organization could most reasonably be expected. I looked up to find Crupp's dark little eye intent upon me.

There I left it to them.

We had an astonishingly good discussion ; Neal burst once, but we emerged from his flood after a time, and Dayton had his interlude. The rest was all close, keen examination of my problem.

I see Crupp now with his arm bent before him on the table in a way he had, as though it was jointed throughout its length like a lobster's antenna, his plump, short-fingered hand crushing up a walnut shell into smaller and smaller fragments. 'Remington,' he said, 'has given us the data for a movement, a really possible movement. It's not only possible, but necessary – urgently necessary, I think, if the Empire is to go on.'

'We're working altogether too much at the social basement in education and training,' said Gane. 'Remington is right about our neglect of the higher levels.'

Britten made a good contribution with an analysis of what he called the spirit of a country and what made it. 'The modern community needs its serious men to be artistic and its artists to be taken seriously,' I remember his saying. 'The day has gone by for either dull responsibility or merely witty art.'

I remember very vividly how Shoesmith harped on an idea I had thrown out of using some sort of review or weekly to express and elaborate these conceptions of a new, severer, aristocratic culture.

'It would have to be done amazingly well,' said Britten, and my mind went back to my schooldays and that ancient enterprise of ours, and how Cossington had rushed it. Well, Cossington had too many papers nowadays to interfere with us, and we perhaps had learnt some defensive devices.

'But this thing has to be linked to some political party,' said Crupp, with his eye on me. 'You can't get away from that. The Liberals,' he added, 'have never done anything for research or literature.'

'They had a Royal Commission on the Dramatic Censorship,' said Thorns, with a note of minute fairness. 'It shows what they were made of,' he added.

'It's what I've told Remington again and again,' said Crupp, 'we've got to pick up the tradition of aristocracy, reorganize it, and make it work. But he's certainly suggested a method.'

'There won't be much aristocracy to pick up,' said Dayton, darkly to the ceiling, 'if the House of Lords throws out the Budget.'

'All the more reason for picking it up,' said Neal. 'For we can't do without it.'

'Will they go to the bad, or will they rise from the ashes, aristocrats indeed – if the Liberals come in overwhelmingly?' said Britten.

'It's we who might decide that,' said Crupp, insidiously.

'I agree,' said Gane.

'No one can tell,' said Thorns. 'I doubt if they will get beaten.'

It was an odd, fragmentary discussion that night. We were all with ideas in our minds at once fine and imperfect. We threw out suggestions that showed themselves at once for inadequate, and we tried to qualify them by minor self-contradictions. Britten, I think, got more said than any one. 'You all seem to think you want to organize people, particular groups and classes of individuals.' he insisted. 'It isn't that. That's the standing error of politicians. You want to organize a culture. Civilization isn't a matter of concrete groupings ; it's a matter of prevailing ideas. The problem is how to make bold, clear ideas prevail. The question for Remington and us is just what groups of people will most help this culture forward.'

'Yes, but how are the Lords going to behave?' said Crupp. 'You yourself were asking that a little while ago.'

'If they win or if they lose,' Gane maintained, 'there will be a movement to reorganize aristocracy – Reform the House of Lords, they'll call the political form of it.'

'Bailey thinks that,' said some one.

'The labour people want abolition,' said some one.

'Let 'em,' said Thorns.

He became audible, sketching a possible line of action.

'Suppose all of us were able to work together. It's just one of those indeterminate, confused, eventful times ahead when a steady jets of ideas might produce enormous results.'

'Leave me out of it,' said Drayton, 'if you please.'

'We should,' said Thorns under his breath.

I took up Crupp's initiative, I remember, and expanded it.

'I believe we could do – extensive things,' I insisted.

'Revivals and revisions of Toryism have been tried so often,' said Thorns, 'from the Young England movement onward.'

'Not one but has produced its enduring effects,' I said. 'It's the peculiarity of English conservatism that it's persistently progressive and rejuvenescent.'

I think it must have been about that point that Dayton fled our presence, after some clumsy sentence that I decided upon reflection was intended to remind me of my duty to my party.

Then I remember Thorns firing doubts at me obliquely across the table. 'You can't run a country through its spoilt children,' he said. 'What you call aristocrats are really spoilt children. They've had too much of everything, except bracing experience.'

'Children can always be educated,' said Crupp.

'I said *spoilt* children,' said Thorns.

'Look here, Thorns!' said I. 'If this Budget row leads to a storm, and these big people get their power clipped, what's going to happen? Have you thought of that? When they go out, lock, stock, and barrel, who comes in?'

'Nature abhors a Vacuum,' said Crupp, supporting me.

'Bailey's trained officials,' suggested Gane.

'Quacks with a certificate of approval from Altiora,' said Thorns. 'I admit the horrors of the alternative. There'd be a massacre in three years.'

'One may go on trying possibilities for ever,' I said. 'One thing emerges. Whatever accidents happen, our civilization needs, and almost consciously needs, a culture of fine creative minds, and all the necessary tolerances, opennesses, considerations, that march with that. For my own part, I think that is the Most Vital Thing. Build your ship of state as you will; get your men as you will; I concentrate on what is clearly the affair of my sort of man, – I want to ensure the quality of the quarter-deck.'

'Hear, hear!' said Shoesmith, suddenly – his first remark for a long time. 'A first-rate figure,' said Shoesmith, gripping it.

'Our danger is in missing that,' I went on. 'Muddle isn't ended by transferring power from the muddle-headed few to the muddle-headed many, and then cheating the many out of it again in the interests of a bureaucracy of sham experts. But that seems the limit of the liberal imagination. There is no real progress in a country, except a rise in the level of its free intellectual activity. Other progress is secondary and dependent. If you take on Bailey's dreams of efficient machinery and a sort of fanatical discipline with no free-moving brains behind it, confused ugliness becomes rigid ugliness, – that's all. No doubt things are moving from looseness to discipline, and from irresponsible controls to organized controls – and also and rather contrariwise everything is becoming, as people say, democratized ; but all the more need in that, for an ark in which the living element may be saved.'

'Hear, hear!' said Shoesmith, faint but pursuing.

It must have been in my house afterwards that Shoesmith became noticeable. He seemed trying to say something vague and difficult that he didn't get said at all on that occasion. 'We could do immense things with a weekly,' he repeated, echoing Neal, I think. And there he left off and became a mute expressiveness, and it was only afterwards, when I was in bed, that I saw we had our capitalist in our hands. . . .

We parted that night on my doorstep in a tremendous glow – but in that sort of glow one doesn't act upon without much reconsideration, and it was some months before I made my decision to follow up the indications of that opening talk.


5

I find my thoughts lingering about the Pentagram Circle. In my development it played a large part, not so much by starting new trains of thought as by confirming the practicability of things I had already hesitatingly entertained. Discussion with these other men so prominently involved in current affairs endorsed views that otherwise would have seemed only a little less remote from actuality than the guardians of Plato or the labour laws of More. Among other questions that were never very distant from our discussions, that came apt to every topic, was the true significance of democracy, Tariff Reform as a method of international hostility, and the imminence of war. On the first issue I can still recall little Bailey, glib and winking, explaining that democracy was really just a dodge for getting assent to the ordinances of the expert official by means of the polling booth. 'If they don't like things,' said he, 'they can vote for the opposition candidate and see what happens then – and that, you see, is why we don't want proportional representation to let in the wild men.' I opened my eyes – the lids had dropped for a moment under the caress of those smooth sounds – to see if Bailey's artful forefinger wasn't at the side of his predominant nose.

The international situation exercised us greatly. Our meetings were pervaded by the feeling that all things moved towards a day of reckoning with Germany, and I was largely instrumental in keeping up the suggestion that India was in a state of unstable equilibrium, that sooner or later something must happen there – something very serious to our Empire. Dayton frankly detested these topics. He was full of that old Middle Victorian persuasion that whatever is inconvenient or disagreeable to the English mind could be annihilated by not thinking about it. He used to sit low in his chair and look mulish. 'Militarism,' he would declare in a tone of the utmost moral fervour, 'is a curse. It's an unmitigated curse.' Then he would cough shortly and twitch his head back and frown, and seem astonished beyond measure that after this conclusive statement we could still go on talking of war.

All our Imperialists were obsessed by the thought of international conflict, and their influence revived for a time those uneasinesses that had been aroused in me for the first time by my continental journey with Willersley and by Meredith's 'One of Our Conquerors.' That quite justifiable dread of a punishment for all the slackness, mental dishonesty, presumption, mercenary respectability, and sentimentalized commercialism of the Victorian period, at the hands of the better organized, more vigorous, and now far more highly civilized peoples of Central Europe, seemed to me to have both a good and bad series of consequences. It seemed the only thing capable of bracing English minds to education, sustained constructive effort, and research; but on the other hand it produced the quality of panic, hasty preparation, impatience of thought, a wasteful and sometimes quite futile immediacy. In 1909, for example, there was a vast clamour for eight additional Dreadnoughts –

> We want eight
> And we won't wait,

but no clamour at all about our national waste of inventive talent, our mean standard of intellectual attainment, our disingenuous criticism, and the consequent failure to distinguish men of the quality needed to carry on the modern type of war. Almost universally we have the wrong men in our places of responsibility and the right men in no place at all, almost universally we have poorly qualified, hesitating, and resentful subordinates, because our criticism is worthless and, so habitually as to be now almost unconsciously, dishonest. Germany is beating England in every matter upon which competition is possible, because she attended sedulously to her collective mind for sixty pregnant years, because in spite of tremendous defects she is still far more anxious for quality in achievement than we are. I remember saying that in my paper. From that, I remember, I went on to an image that had flashed into my mind. 'The British Empire.' I said, 'is like some of those early vertebrated monsters, the Brontosaurus and the Atlantosaurus and suchlike; it sacrifices intellect to character; its backbone, that is to say, – especially in the visceral region – is bigger than its cranium. It's no accident that things are so. We've worked for backbone. We brag about backbone, and if the joints are anchylosed so much the better. We're still but only half awake to our error. You can't change that suddenly.'

'Turn it round and make it go backwards,' interjected Thorns.

'It's trying to do that,' I said, 'in places.'

And afterwards Crupp declared I had begotten a nightmare which haunted him of nights; he was trying desperately and belatedly to blow a brain as one blows soap-bubbles or such a Mesozoic saurian as I had conjured up, while the clumsy monster's fate, all teeth and brains, crept nearer and nearer. . . .

I've grown, I think, since those days out of the urgency of that apprehension. I still think a European war, and conceivably a very humiliating war for England, may occur at no very distant date, but I do not think there is any such heroic quality in our governing class as will make that war catastrophic. The prevailing spirit in English life – it is one of the essential secrets of our imperial endurance – is one of underbred aggression in prosperity and diplomatic compromise in moments of danger ; we bully haughtily where we can and assimilate where

266

we must. It is not for nothing that our upper- and middle-class youth is educated by teachers of the highest character, scholars and gentlemen, men who can pretend quite honestly that Darwinism hasn't upset the historical fall of man, that cricket is moral training, and that Socialism is an outrage upon the teachings of Christ. A sort of dignified dexterity of evasion is the national reward. Germany, with a larger population, a vigorous and irreconcilable proletariat, a bolder intellectual training, a harsher spirit, can scarcely fail to drive us at last to a realization of intolerable strain. So we may never fight at all. The war of preparations that has been going on for thirty years may end like a sham-fight at last in an umpire's decision. We shall proudly but very firmly take the second place. For my own part, since I love England as much as I detest her present lethargy of soul, I pray for a chastening war – I wouldn't mind her flag in the dirt if only her spirit would come out of it. So I was able to shake off that earlier fear of some final and irrevocable destruction truncating all my schemes. At the most, a European war would be a dramatic episode in the reconstruction I had in view.

In India, too, I no longer foresee, as once I was inclined to see, disaster. The English rule in India is surely one of the most extraordinary accidents that has ever happened in history. We are there like a man who has fallen off a ladder on to the neck of an elephant, and doesn't know what to do or how to get down. Until something happens he remains. Our functions in India are absurd. We English do not own that country, do not even rule it. We make nothing happen ; at the most we prevent things happening. We suppress our own literature there. Most English people cannot even go to this land they possess; the authorities would prevent it. If Messrs Perowne or Cook organized a cheap tour of Manchester operatives, it would be stopped. No one dare bring the average English voter face to face with the reality of India, or let the Indian native have a glimpse of the English voter. In my time I have talked to English statesmen, Indian officials and ex-officials, viceroys, soldiers, everyone who might be supposed to know what India signifies, and I have prayed them to tell me what they thought we were up to there. I am not writing without my book in these matters. And beyond a phrase or so about 'even-handed

267

justice' – and look at our sedition trials! – they told me nothing. Time after time I have heard of that apocryphal native ruler in the north-west, who, when asked what would happen if we left India, replied that in a week his men would be in the saddle, and in six months not a rupee or a virgin would be left in Lower Bengal. That is always given as our conclusive justification. But is it our business to preserve the rupees and virgins of Lower Bengal in a sort of magic inconclusiveness? Better plunder than paralysis, better fire and sword than futility. Our flag is spread over the peninsula, without plans, without intentions – a vast preventive. The sum total of our policy is to arrest any discussion, any conferences that would enable the Indians to work out a tolerable scheme of the future for themselves. But that does not arrest the resentment of men held back from life. Consider what it must be for the educated Indian sitting at the feast of contemporary possibilities with his mouth gagged and his hands bound behind him! The spirit of insurrection breaks out in spite of espionage and seizures. Our conflict for inaction develops stupendous absurdities. The other day the British Empire was taking off and examining printed cotton stomach wraps for seditious emblems and inscriptions. . . .

In some manner we shall have to come out of India. We have had our chance, and we have demonstrated nothing but the appalling dullness of our national imagination. We are not good enough to do anything with India. Codger and Flack, and Gates and Dayton, Cladingbowl in the club, and the *Home Churchman* in the home, cant about 'character', worship of strenuous force and contempt of truth ; for the sake of such men and things as these, we must abandon in fact, if not in appearance, that empty domination. Had we great schools and a powerful teaching, could we boast great men, had we the spirit of truth and creation in our lives, then indeed it might be different. But a race that bears a sceptre must carry gifts to justify it.

It does not follow that we shall be driven catastrophically from India. That was my earlier mistake. We are not proud enough in our bones to be ruined by India as Spain was by her empire. We may be able to abandon India with an air of still remaining there. It is our new method. We train our future

268

rulers in the public schools to have a very wholesome respect for strength, and as soon as a power arises in India in spite of us, be it a man or a culture, or a native state, we shall be willing to deal with it. We may or may not have a war, but our governing class will be quick to learn when we are beaten. Then they will repeat our South African diplomacy, and arrange for some settlement that will abandon the reality, such as it is, and preserve the semblance of power. The conqueror *de facto* will become the new 'loyal Briton', and the democracy at home will be invited to celebrate our recession – triumphantly. I am no believer in the imminent dissolution of our Empire ; I am less and less inclined to see in either India or Germany the probability of an abrupt truncation of those slow intellectual constructions which are the essentials of statecraft.

## 6

I sit writing in this little loggia to the sound of dripping water – this morning we had rain, and the roof of our little casa is still not dry, there are pools in the rocks under the sweet chestnuts, and the torrent that crosses the salita is full and boastful, – and I try to recall the order of my impressions during that watching, dubious time, before I went over to the Conservative Party. I was trying – chaotic task! – to gauge the possibilities inherent in the quality of the British aristocracy. There comes a broad spectacular effect of wide parks, diversified by woods and bracken valleys, and dappled with deer ; of great smooth lawns shaded by ancient trees ; of big façades of sunlit building dominating the countryside ; of large fine rooms full of handsome, easy-mannered people. As a sort of representative picture to set off against those other pictures of Liberals and of Socialists I have given, I recall one of those huge assemblies the Duchess of Clynes inaugurated at Stamford House. The place itself is one of the vastest private houses in London, a huge clustering mass of white-and-gold saloons with polished floors and wonderful pictures, and staircases and galleries on a Gargantuan scale. And there she sought to gather all that was most representative of English activities, and did, in fact, in those brilliant nocturnal crowds, get samples of nearly every section of our social and intellectual life, with a marked predominance upon the political and social side.

I remember sitting in one of the recesses at the end of the big saloon with Mrs Redmondson, one of those sharp-minded, beautiful rich women one meets so often in London, who seem to have done nothing and to be capable of everything, and we watched the crowd – uniforms and splendours were streaming in from a State ball – and exchanged information. I told her about the politicians and intellectuals, and she told me about the aristocrats, and we sharpened our wit on them and counted the percentage of beautiful people among the latter, and wondered if the general effect of tallness was or was not an illusion.

They were, we agreed, for the most part bigger than the average of people in London, and a handsome lot, even when they were not subtly individualized. 'They look so well nurtured,' I said, 'well cared for. I like their quiet, well-trained movements, their pleasant consideration for each other.'

'Kindly, good tempered, and at bottom utterly selfish,' she said, 'like big, rather carefully trained, rather pampered children. What else can you expect from them?'

'They are good tempered, anyhow,' I witnessed, 'and that's an achievement. I don't think I could ever be content under a bad-tempered, sentimentalizing, strenuous Government. That's why I couldn't stand the Roosevelt *régime* in America. One's chief surprise when one comes across these big people for the first time is their admirable easiness and a real personal modesty. I confess I admire them. Oh! I like them. I wouldn't at all mind, I believe, giving over the country to this aristocracy – given *something*—'

'Which they haven't got.'

'Which they haven't got – or they'd be the finest sort of people in the world.'

'That something?' she inquired.

'I don't know. I've been puzzling my wits to know. They've done all sorts of things—'

'That's Lord Wrassleton,' she interrupted, 'whose leg was broken – you remember? – at Spion Kop.'

'It's healed very well. I like the gold lace and the white glove resting, with quite a nice awkwardness, on the sword. When I was a little boy I wanted to wear clothes like that. And the stars! He's got the V.C. Most of these people here have at any rate shown pluck, you know – brought something off.'

'Not quite enough,' she suggested.

'I think that's it,' I said. 'Not quite enough – not quite hard enough,' I added.

She laughed and looked at me. 'You'd like to make us,' she said.

'What?'

'Hard.'

'I don't think you'll go on if you don't get hard.'

'We shan't be so pleasant if we do.'

'Well, there my puzzled wits come in again. I don't see why an aristocracy shouldn't be rather hard trained, and yet kindly. I'm not convinced that the resources of education are exhausted. I want to better this, because it already looks so good.'

'How are we to do it?' asked Mrs Redmondson.

'Oh, there you have me! I've been spending my time lately in trying to answer that! It makes me quarrel with' – I held up my fingers and ticked the items off – 'the public schools, the private tutors, the army exams, the Universities, the Church, the general attitude of the country towards science and literature—'

'We all do,' said Mrs Redmondson. 'We can't begin again at the beginning,' she added.

'Couldn't one,' I nodded at the assembly in general, 'start a movement?'

'There's the Confederates,' she said, with a faint smile that masked a gleam of curiosity. . . . 'You want,' she said, 'to say to the aristocracy, "Be aristocrats. *Noblesse oblige.*" Do you remember what happened to the monarch who was told to "Be a King"?'

'Well,' I said, 'I want an aristocracy.'

'This,' she said, smiling, 'is the pick of them. The backwoodsmen are off the stage. These are the brilliant ones – the smart and the blues. . . . They cost a lot of money, you know.'

So far Mrs Redmondson, but the picture remained full of things not stated in our speech. They were on the whole handsome people, charitable minded, happy, and easy. They led spacious lives, and there was something free and fearless about

271

their bearing that I liked extremely. The women particularly were wide-reading, fine-thinking. Mrs Redmondson talked as fully and widely and boldly as a man, and with those flashes of intuition, those startling, sudden delicacies of perception few men display. I liked, too, the relations that held between women and men, their general tolerance, their antagonism to the harsh jealousies that are the essence of the middle-class order. . . .

After all, if one's game resolved itself into the development of a type and culture of men, why shouldn't one begin at this end?


## 7

It is very easy indeed to generalize about a class of human beings, but much harder to produce a sample. Was old Lady Forthundred, for instance, fairly a sample? I remember her as a smiling, magnificent presence, a towering accumulation of figure and wonderful shimmering blue silk and black lace and black hair, and small fine features and chins and chins and chins, disposed in a big cane chair with wraps and cushions upon the great terrace of Champneys. Her eye was blue and hard, and her accent and intonation were exactly what you would expect from a rather commonplace dressmaker pretending to be aristocratic. I was, I am afraid, posing a little as the intelligent but respectful inquirer from below investigating the great world, and she was certainly posing as my informant. She affected a cynical coarseness. She developed a theory on the governance of England, beautifully frank and simple. 'Give 'um all a peerage when they get twenty thousand a year,' she maintained. 'That's my remedy.'

In my new role of theoretical aristocrat I felt a little abashed.

'Twenty thousand,' she repeated with conviction.

It occurred to me that I was in the presence of the aristocratic theory currently working as distinguished from my as yet unformulated intentions.

'You'll get a lot of loafers and scamps among 'um,' said Lady Forthundred. 'You get loafers and scamps everywhere, but you'll get a lot of men who'll work hard to keep things together, and that's what we're all after, isn't ut?'

272

'It's not an ideal arrangement.'

'Tell me anything better,' said Lady Forthundred.

On the whole, and because she refused emphatically to believe in education, Lady Forthundred scored.

We had been discussing Cossington's recent peerage, for Cossington, my old schoolfellow at City Merchants, and my victor in the affair of the magazine, had clambered to an amazing wealth up a piled heap of energetically pushed penny and halfpenny magazines, and a group of daily newspapers. I had expected to find the great lady hostile to the newcomer, but she accepted him, she gloried in him.

'We're a peerage,' she said, 'but none of us have ever had any nonsense about nobility.'

She turned and smiled down on me. 'We English,' she said, 'are a practical people. We assimilate 'um.'

'Then, I suppose, they don't give trouble?'

'Then they don't give trouble.'

'They learn to shoot?'

'And all that,' said Lady Forthundred. 'Yes. And things go on. Sometimes better than others, but they go on – somehow. It depends very much on the sort of butler who pokes 'um about.'

I suggested that it might be possible to get a secure twenty thousand a year by at least detrimental methods – socially speaking.

'We must take the bad and the good of 'um,' said Lady Forthundred, courageously. . . .

Now, was she a sample? It happened she talked. What was there in the brains of the multitude of her first, second, third, fourth, and fifth cousins, who didn't talk, who shone tall, and bearing themselves finely, against a background of deft, attentive maids and valets, on every spacious social scene? How did things look to them?


8


Side by side with Lady Forthundred, it is curious to put Evesham with his tall, bent body, his little-featured almost elvish face, his unequal mild brown eyes, his gentle manner, his sweet, amazing oratory. He led all these people wonderfully.

He was always curious and interested about life, wary beneath a pleasing frankness – and I tormented my brain to get to the bottom of him. For a long time he was the most powerful man in England under the throne ; he had the Lords in his hand, and a great majority in the Commons, and the discontents and intrigues that are the concomitants of an overwhelming party advantage broke against him as waves break against a cliff. He foresaw so far in these matters that it seemed he scarcely troubled to foresee. He brought political art to the last triumph of naturalness. Always for me he has been the typical aristocrat, so typical and above the mere forms of aristocracy, that he remained a commoner to the end of his days.

I had met him at the beginning of my career ; he read some early papers of mine, and asked to see me, and I conceived a flattered liking for him that strengthened to a very strong feeling indeed. He seemed to me to stand alone without an equal, the greatest man in British political life. Some men one sees through and understands, some one cannot see into or round because they are of opaque clay, but about Evesham I had a sense of things hidden as it were by depth and mists, because he was so big and atmospheric a personality. No other contemporary has had that effect upon me. I've sat beside him at dinners, stayed in houses with him – he was in the big house party at Champneys – talked to him, sounded him, watching him as I sat beside him. I could talk to him with extraordinary freedom and a rare sense of being understood. Other men have to be treated in a special manner ; approached through their own mental dialect, flattered by a minute regard for what they have said and done. Evesham was as widely and charitably receptive as any man I have ever met. The common politicians beside him seemed like rows of stuffy little rooms looking out upon the sea.

And what was he up to? What did *he* think we were doing with Mankind? That I thought worth knowing.

I remember his talking on one occasion at the Hartsteins', at a dinner so tremendously floriferous and equipped that we were almost forced into duologues, about the possible common constructive purpose in politics.

'I feel so much,' he said, 'that the best people in every party converge. We don't differ at Westminster as they do in the

274

county towns. There's a sort of extending common policy that goes on under every government, because on the whole it's the right thing to do, and people know it. Things that used to be matters of opinion become matters of science – and cease to be party questions.'

He instanced education.

'Apart,' said I, 'from the religious question.'

'Apart from the religious question.'

He dropped that aspect with an easy grace, and went on with his general theme that political conflict was the outcome of uncertainty. 'Directly you get a thing established, so that people can say, "Now this is Right," with the same conviction that people can say that water is a combination of oxygen and hydrogen, there's no more to be said. The thing has to be done. . . .'

And to put against this effect of Evesham, broad and humanely tolerant, posing as the minister of a steadily developing constructive conviction, there are other memories.

Have I not seen him in the House, persistent, persuasive, indefatigable, and by all my standards wickedly perverse, leaning over the table with those insistent movements of his hand upon it, or swaying forward with a grip upon his coat lapel, fighting with a diabolical skill to preserve what are in effect religious tests, tests he must have known would outrage and humiliate and injure the consciences of a quarter – and that perhaps the best quarter – of the youngsters who come to the work of elementary education?

In playing for points in the game of party advantage Evesham displayed at times a quite wicked unscrupulousness in the use of his subtle mind. I would sit on the Liberal benches and watch him, and listen to his urbane voice, fascinated by him. Did he really care? Did anything matter to him? And if it really mattered nothing, why did he trouble to serve the narrowness and passion of his side? Or did he see far beyond my scope, so that this petty iniquity was justified by greater, remoter ends of which I had no intimation?

They accused him of nepotism. His friends and family were certainly well cared for. In private life he was full of an affectionate intimacy; he pleased by being charmed and pleased. One might think at times there was no more of him than a clever man happily circumstanced, and finding an interest and occupation in politics. And then came a glimpse of thought, of imagination, like the sight of a soaring eagle through a stair-case skylight. Oh, beyond question he was great! No other contemporary politician had his quality. In no man have I perceived so sympathetically the great contrast between warm, personal things and the white dream of statecraft. Except that he had it seemed no hot passions, but only interests and fine affections and indolences, he paralleled the conflict of my life. He saw and thought widely and deeply; but at times it seemed to me his greatness stood over and behind the reality of his life, like some splendid servant, thinking his own thoughts, who waits behind a lesser master's chair. . . .

## 9

Of course, when Evesham talked of this ideal of the organized state becoming so finely true to practicability and so clearly stated as to have the compelling conviction of physical science, he spoke quite after my heart. Had he really embodied the attempt to realize that, I could have done no more than follow him blindly. But neither he nor I embodied that, and there lies the gist of my story. And when it came to a study of others among the leading Tories and Imperialists the doubt increased, until with some at last it was possible to question whether they had any imaginative conception of constructive statecraft at all; whether they didn't opaquely accept the world for what it was, and set themselves single-mindedly to make a place for themselves and cut a figure in it.

There were some very fine personalities among them: there were the great peers who had administered Egypt, India, South Africa, Framboya – Cromer, Kitchener, Curzon, Milner, Gane, for example. So far as that easier task of holding sword and scales had gone, they had shown the finest qualities, but they had returned to the perplexing and exacting problem of the home country, a little glorious, a little too simply bold. They wanted to arm and they wanted to educate, but the habit of immediate necessity made them far more eager to arm than to educate, and their experience of heterogeneous controls made them overrate the need for obedience in a homogeneous

276

country. They didn't understand raw men, ill-trained men, uncertain minds, and intelligent women; and these are the things that matter in England. . . . There were also the great business adventurers, from Cranber to Cossington (who was now Lord Paddockhurst). My mind remained unsettled, and went up and down the scale between a belief in their far-sighted purpose and the perception of crude vanities, coarse ambitions, vulgar competitiveness, and a mere habitual persistence in the pursuit of gain. For a time I saw a good deal of Cossington – I wish I had kept a diary of his talk and gestures, to mark how he could vary from day to day between a *poseur*, a smart tradesman, and a very bold and wide-thinking political schemer. He had a vanity of sweeping actions, motor-car pounces, Napoleonic rushes, that led to violent ineffectual changes in the policy of his papers, and a haunting pursuit by parallel columns in the liberal press that never abashed him in the slightest degree. By an accident I plumbed the folly in him – but I feel I never plumbed his wisdom. I remember him one day after a lunch at the Barhams' saying suddenly, out of a profound meditation over the end of a cigar, one of those sentences that seem to light the whole interior being of a man. 'Some day,' he said softly, rather to himself than to me, and *à propos* of nothing – 'some day I will raise the country.'

'Why not?' I said, after a pause, and leant across him for the little silver spirit-lamp, to light my cigarette. . . .

Then the Tories had for another section the ancient creations, and again there were the financial peers, men accustomed to reserve, and their big lawyers, accustomed to – well, qualified statement. And below the giant personalities of the party were the young bloods, young, adventurous men of the type of Lord Tarvrille, who had seen service in South Africa, who had travelled and hunted; explorers, keen motorists, interested in aviation, active in army organization. Good, brown-faced stuff they were, but impervious to ideas outside the range of their activities, more ignorant of science than their chauffeurs, and of the quality of English people than welt-politicians; contemptuous of school and university by reason of the Gateses and Flacks and Codgers who had come their way, witty, light-hearted, patriotic at the Kipling level, with a certain aptitude for bullying. They varied in insensible gradations between the noble sportsmen on the one hand, and men like Gane and the Tories of our Pentagram club on the other. You perceive how a man might exercise his mind in the attempt to strike an average of public serviceability in this miscellany! And mixed up with these, mixed up sometimes in the same man, was the pure reactionary, whose predominant idea was that the village schools should confine themselves to teaching the catechism, hat-touching and curtsying, and be given a holiday whenever beaters were in request. . . .

I find now in my mind as a sort of counterpoise to Evesham the figure of old Lord Wardingham, asleep in the largest arm-chair in the library of Stamford Court after lunch. One foot rested on one of those things – I think they are called gout stools. He had been playing golf all the morning and wearied a weak instep; at lunch he had sat at my table and talked in the overbearing manner permitted to irascible important men whose insteps are painful. Among other things he had flouted the idea that women would ever understand statecraft or be more than a nuisance in politics, denied flatly that Hindus were capable of anything whatever except excesses in population, regretted he could not censor picture galleries and circulating libraries, and declared that dissenters were people who pretended to take theology seriously with the express purpose of upsetting the entirely satisfactory compromise of the Established Church. 'No sensible people, with anything to gain or lose, argue about religion,' he said. 'They mean mischief.' Having delivered his soul upon these points, and silenced the little conversation to the left of him from which they had arisen, he became, after an appreciative encounter with a sanguinary woodcock, more amiable, responded to some respectful initiatives of Crupp's, and related a number of classical anecdotes of those blighting snubs, vindictive retorts and scandalous miscarriages of justice that are so dear to the forensic mind. Now he reposed. He was breathing heavily with his mouth a little open and his head on one side. One whisker was turned back against the comfortable padding. His plump strong hands gripped the arms of his chair, and his frown was a little assuaged. How tremendously fed up he looked! Honours, wealth, influence, respect, he had them all. How scornful and hard it had made his unguarded expression!

I note without comment that it didn't even occur to me then to wake him up and ask him what *he* was up to with mankind.

## 10

One countervailing influence to my drift to Toryism in those days was Margaret's quite religious faith in the Liberals. I realized that slowly and with a mild astonishment. It set me, indeed, even then questioning my own change of opinion. We came at last incidentally, as our way was, to an exchange of views. It was as nearly a quarrel as we had before I came over to the Conservative side. It was at Champneys, and I think during the same visit that witnessed my exploration of Lady Forthundred. It arose indirectly, I think, out of some comments of mine upon our fellow-guests, but it is one of those memories of which the scene and quality remain more vivid than the things said, a memory without any very definite beginning or end. It was afternoon, in the pause between tea and the dressing bell, and we were in Margaret's big silver-adorned, chintz-bright room, looking out on the trim Italian garden. . . . Yes, the beginning of it has escaped me altogether, but I remember it as an odd, exceptional little wrangle.

At first we seem to have split upon the moral quality of the aristocracy, and I had an odd sense that in some way too feminine for me to understand our hostess had aggrieved her. She said, I know, that Champneys distressed her ; made her 'eager for work and reality again'.

'But aren't these people real?'

'They're so superficial, so extravagant!'

I said I was not shocked by their unreality. They seemed the least affected people I had ever met. 'And are they really so extravagant?' I asked, and put it to her that her dresses cost quite as much as any other woman's in the house.

'It's not only their dresses,' Margaret parried. 'It's the scale and spirit of things.'

I questioned that. 'They're cynical,' said Margaret, staring before her out of the window.

I challenged her, and she quoted the Brabants, about whom there had been an ancient scandal. She'd heard of it from Altiora, and it was also Altiora who'd given her a horror of

279

Lord Carnaby, who was also with us. 'You know his reputation,' said Margaret. 'That Normandy girl. Every one knows
about it. I shiver when I look at him. He seems – oh! like
something not of *our* civilization. He *will* come and say little
things to me.'

'Offensive things?'

'No, politenesses and things. Of course his manners are –
quite right. That only makes it worse, I think. It shows he
might have helped – all that happened. I do all I can to make
him see I don't like him. But none of the others make the
slightest objection to him.'

'Perhaps these people imagine something might be said for
him.'

'That's just it,' said Margaret.

'Charity,' I suggested.

'I don't like that sort of toleration.'

I was oddly annoyed. 'Like eating with publicans and sinners,' I said. 'No! . . .'

But scandals, and the contempt for rigid standards their con-
donation displayed, weren't more than the sharp edge of the
trouble. 'It's their whole position, their selfish predominance,
their class conspiracy against the mass of people,' said Margaret. 'When I sit at dinner in that splendid room, with its
glitter and white reflections and candlelight, and its flowers and
its wonderful service and its candelabra of solid gold, I seem
to feel the slums and the mines and the over-crowded cottages
stuffed away under the table.'

I reminded Margaret that she was not altogether innocent of
unearned increment.

'But aren't we doing our best to give it back?' she said.

I was moved to question her. 'Do you really think,' I asked,
'that the Tories and peers and rich people are to blame for
social injustice as we have it today? Do you really see politics
as a struggle of light on the Liberal side against darkness on
the Tory?'

'They *must* know,' said Margaret.

I found myself questioning that. I see now that to Margaret
it must have seemed the perversest carping against manifest
things, but at the time I was concentrated simply upon the
elucidation of her view and my own; I wanted to get her con-

ception in the sharpest, hardest lines that were possible. It was perfectly clear that she saw Toryism as the diabolical element in affairs. The thing showed in its hopeless untruth all the clearer for the fine, clean emotion with which she gave it out to me. My sleeping peer in the library at Stamford Court and Evesham talking luminously behind the Harstein flowers embodied the devil, and my replete citizen sucking at his cigar in the National Liberal Club, Willie Crampton discussing the care and management of the stomach over a specially hygienic lemonade, and Dr Tumpany in his aggressive frock-coat pegging out a sort of copyright in Socialism, were the centre and wings of the angelic side. It was nonsense. But how was I to put the truth to her?

'I don't see things at all as you do,' I said. 'I don't see things in the same way.'

'Think of the poor,' said Margaret, going off at a tangent.

'Think of every one,' I said. 'We Liberals have done more mischief through well-intentioned benevolence than all the selfishness in the world could have done. We built up the liquor interest.'

'*We!*' cried Margaret. 'How can you say that? It's against us.'

'Naturally. But we made it a monopoly in our clumsy efforts to prevent people drinking what they liked, because it interfered with industrial regularity –'

'Oh!' cried Margaret, stung ; and I could see she thought I was talking mere wickedness.

'That's it,' I said.

'But would you have people drink whatever they pleased?'

'Certainly. What right have I to dictate to other men and women?'

'But think of the children!'

'Ah! there you have the folly of modern Liberalism, its half-cunning, half-silly way of getting at everything in a roundabout fashion. If neglecting children is an offence, and it *is* an offence, then deal with it as such, but don't go badgering and restricting people who sell something that may possibly in some cases lead to a neglect of children. If drunkenness is an offence, punish it, but don't punish a man for selling honest drink that perhaps after all won't make any one drunk at all.

281

Don't intensify the viciousness of the public-house by assuming the place isn't fit for women and children. That's either spite or folly. Make the public-house *fit* for women and children. Make it a real public-house. If we Liberals go on as we are going, we shall presently want to stop the sale of ink and paper because those things tempt men to forgery. We do already threaten the privacy of the post because of betting touts' letters. The drift of all that kind of thing is narrow, unimaginative, mischievous, stupid. . . .'

I stopped short and walked to the window and surveyed a pretty fountain, facsimile of one in Verona, amidst trim-cut borderings of yew. Beyond, and seen between the stems of ilex trees, was a great blaze of yellow flowers. . . .

'But prevention,' I heard Margaret behind me, 'is the essence of our work!'

I turned. 'There's no prevention but education. There's no antiseptics in life but love and fine thinking. Make people fine, make fine people. Don't be afraid. These Tory leaders are better people individually than the average ; why cast them for the villains of the piece? The real villain in the piece – in the whole human drama – is the muddle-headedness, and it matters very little if it's virtuous-minded or wicked. I want to get at muddle-headedness. If I could do that I could let all that you call wickedness in the world run about and do what it jolly well pleased. It would matter about as much as a slightly neglected dog – in an otherwise well-managed home.'

My thoughts had run away with me.

'I can't understand you,' said Margaret, in the profoundest distress. 'I can't understand how it is you are coming to see things like this.'


11

The moods of a thinking man in politics are curiously evasive and difficult to describe. Neither the public nor the historian will permit the statesman moods. He has from the first to assume he has an Aim, a definite Aim, and to pretend to an absolute consistency with that. Those subtle questionings about the very fundamentals of life which plague us all so relentlessly nowadays are supposed to be silenced. He lifts his chin and pursues his Aim explicitly in the sight of all men. Those who have no real political experience can scarcely imagine the immense mental and moral strain there is between one's everyday acts and utterances on the one hand and the 'thinking-out' process on the other. It is perplexingly difficult to keep in your mind, fixed and firm, a scheme essentially complex, to keep balancing a swaying possibility while at the same time under jealous, hostile, and stupid observation you tread your part in the platitudinous, quarrelsome, ill-presented march of affairs. . . .

The most impossible of all autobiographies is an intellectual autobiography. I have thrown together in the crudest way the elements of the problem I struggled with, but I can give no record of the subtle details; I can tell nothing of the long vacillations between Protean values, the talks and re-talks, the meditation, the bleak lucidities of sleepless nights. . . .

And yet these things I have struggled with must be thought out, and, to begin with, they must be thought out in this muddled, experimenting way. To go into a study to think about statecraft is to turn your back on the realities you are constantly needing to feel and test and sound if your thinking is to remain vital; to choose an aim and pursue it in despite of all subsequent questionings is to bury the talent of your mind. It is no use dealing with the intricate as though it were simple, to leap haphazard at the first course of action that presents itself; the whole world of politicians is far too like a man who snatches a poker to a failing watch. It is easy to say he wants to 'get something done,' but the only sane thing to do for the moment is to put aside that poker and take thought and get a better implement. . . .

One of the results of these fundamental preoccupations of mine was a curious irritability towards Margaret that I found difficult to conceal. It was one of the incidental cruelties of our position that this should happen. I was in such doubt myself, that I had no power to phrase things for her in a form she could use. Hitherto I had stage-managed our 'serious' conversations. Now I was too much in earnest and too uncertain to go on doing this. I avoided talk with her. Her serene, sustained confidence in vague formulae and sentimental aspirations exasperated me; her want of sympathetic apprehension made my few efforts to indicate my changing attitudes distressing and futile. It wasn't that I was always thinking right, and that she was always saying wrong. It was that I was struggling to get hold of a difficult thing that was, at any rate, half true, I could not gauge how true, and that Margaret's habitual phrasing ignored these elusive elements of truth, and without premeditation fitted into the weaknesses of my new intimations, as though they had nothing but weaknesses. It was, for example, obvious that these big people, who were the back-bone of Imperialism and Conservatism, were temperamentally lax, much more indolent, much more sensuous, than our deliberately virtuous Young Liberals. I didn't want to be reminded of that, just when I was in full effort to realize the finer elements in their composition. Margaret classed them and disposed of them. It was our incurable differences in habits and gestures of thought coming between us again.

The desert of misunderstanding widened. I was forced back upon myself and my own secret counsels. For a time I went my way alone; an unmixed evil for both of us. Except for that Pentagram evening, a series of talks with Isabel Rivers, who was now becoming more and more important in my intellectual life, and the arguments I maintained with Crupp, I never really opened my mind at all during that period of indecisions, slow abandonments, and slow acquisitions.

# Chapter the Third

# Secession

## 1

At last, out of a vast accumulation of impressions, decision distilled quite suddenly. I succumbed to Evesham and that dream of the right thing triumphant through expression. I determined I would go over to the Conservatives, and use my every gift and power on the side of such forces on that side as made for educational reorganization, scientific research, literature, criticism, and intellectual development. That was in 1909. I judged the Tories were driving straight at a conflict with the country, and I thought them bound to incur an electoral defeat. I under-estimated their strength in the counties. There would follow, I calculated, a period of profound reconstruction in method and policy alike. I was entirely at one with Crupp in perceiving in this an immense opportunity for the things we desired. An aristocracy quickened by conflict and on the defensive, and full of the idea of justification by reconstruction, might prove altogether more apt for thought and high professions than Mrs Redmondson's spoilt children. Behind the now inevitable struggle for a reform of the House of Lords, there would be great heart-searchings and educational endeavour. On that we reckoned. . . .

At last we talked it out to the practical pitch, and Crupp and Shoesmith, and I and Gane, made our definite agreement together. . . .

I emerged from enormous silences upon Margaret one evening.

She was just back from the display of some new musicians at the Hartsteins'. I remember she wore a dress of gold satin, very rich-looking and splendid. About her slender neck there was a rope of gold-set amber beads. Her hair caught up and echoed and returned these golden notes. I, too, was in evening dress, but where I had been escapes me, – some forgotten dinner, I suppose. I went into her room. I remember I didn't

speak for some moments. I went across to the window and
pulled the blind aside, and looked out upon the railed garden
of the square, with its shrubs and shadowed turf gleaming
pallidly and irregularly in the light of the big electric standard
in the corner.

'Margaret,' I said, 'I think I shall break with the party.'

She made no answer. I turned presently, a movement of
inquiry.

'I was afraid you meant to do that,' she said.

'I'm out of touch,' I explained. 'Altogether.'

'Oh! I know.'

'It places me in a difficult position,' I said.

Margaret stood at her dressing-table, looking steadfastly at
herself in the glass, and with her fingers playing with a litter of
stoppered bottles of tinted glass. 'I was afraid it was coming to
this,' she said.

'In a way,' I said, 'we've been allies. I owe my seat to you.
I couldn't have gone into parliament . . .'

'I don't want considerations like that to affect us,' she interrupted.

There was a pause. She sat down in a chair by her dressing-
table, lifted an ivory hand-glass, and put it down again.

'I wish,' she said, with something like a sob in her voice, 'it
were possible that you shouldn't do this.' She stopped abruptly,
and I did not look at her, because I could feel the effort she
was making to control herself.

'I thought,' she began again, 'when you came into parliament –'

There came another silence. 'It's all gone so differently,' she
said. 'Everything has gone so differently.'

I had a sudden memory of her, shining triumphant after the
Kinghamstead election, and for the first time I realized just
how perplexing and disappointing my subsequent career must
have been to her.

'I'm not doing this without consideration,' I said.

'I know,' she said, in a voice of despair, 'I've seen it
coming.

'But – I still don't understand it. I don't understand how you
can go over.'

'My ideas have changed and developed,' I said.

I walked across to her bearskin hearthrug, and stood by the mantel.

'To think that you,' she said; 'you who might have been leader –' She could not finish it. 'All the forces of reaction,' she threw out.

'I don't think they are the forces of reaction,' I said. 'I think I can find work to do – better work on that side.'

'Against us!' she said. 'As if progress wasn't hard enough! As if it didn't call upon every able man!'

'I don't think Liberalism has a monopoly of progress.'

She did not answer that. She sat quite still, looking in front of her. *'Why* have you gone over?' she asked abruptly as though I had said nothing.

There came a silence that I was impelled to end. I began a stiff dissertation from the hearthrug. 'I am going over, because I think I may join in an intellectual renascence on the Conservative side. I think that in the coming struggle there will be a partial and altogether confused and demoralizing victory for democracy, that will stir the classes which now dominate the Conservative party into an energetic revival. They will set out to win back, and win back. Even if my estimate of contemporary forces is wrong and they win, they will still be forced to reconstruct their outlook. A war abroad will supply the chastening if home politics fail. The effort at renascence is bound to come by either alternative. I believe I can do more in relation to that effort than in any other connexion in the world of politics at the present time. That's my case, Margaret.'

She certainly did not grasp what I said. 'And so you will throw aside all the beginnings, all the beliefs and pledges –' Again her sentence remained incomplete. 'I doubt if even, once you have gone over, they will welcome you.'

'That hardly matters.'

I made an effort to resume my speech.

'I came into parliament, Margaret,' I said, 'a little prematurely. Still – I suppose it was only by coming into parliament that I could see things as I do now in terms of personality and imaginative range. . . .' I stopped. Her stiff, unhappy, unlistening silence broke up my disquisition.

'After all,' I remarked, 'most of this has been implicit in my writings.'

She made no sign of admission.

'What are you going to do?' she asked.

'Keep my seat for a time and make the reasons of my breach clear. Then either I must resign or – probably this new Budget will lead to a General Election. It's evidently meant to strain the Lords and provoke a quarrel.'

'You might, I think, have stayed to fight the Budget.'

'I'm not,' I said, 'so keen against the Lords.'

On that we halted.

'But what are you going to do?' she asked.

'I shall make my quarrel over some points in the Budget. I can't quite tell you yet where my chance will come. Then I shall either resign my seat – or if things drift to a dissolution I shan't stand again.'

'It's political suicide.'

'Not altogether.'

'I can't imagine you out of parliament again. It's just like – like undoing all we have done. What will you do?'

'Write. Make a new, more definite place for myself. You know, of course, there's already a sort of group about Crupp and Gane.'

Margaret seemed lost for a time in painful thought.

'For me,' she said at last, 'our political work has been a religion – it has been more than a religion.'

I heard in silence. I had no form of protest available against the implications of that.

'And then I find you turning against all we aimed to do – talking of going over, almost lightly – to those others.' . . .

She was white-lipped as she spoke. In the most curious way she had captured the moral values of the situation. I found myself protesting ineffectually against her fixed conviction. 'It's because I think my duty lies in this change that I make it,' I said.

'I don't see how you can say that,' she replied quietly.

There was another pause between us.

'Oh!' she said, and clenched her hand upon the table. 'That it should have come to this!'

She was extraordinarily dignified and extraordinarily absurd. She was hurt and thwarted beyond measure. She had no place in her ideas, I thought, for me. I could see how it appeared to

288

her, but I could not make her see anything of the intricate process that had brought me to this divergence. The opposition of our intellectual temperaments was like a gag in my mouth. What was there for me to say? A flash of intuition told me that behind the white dignity was a passionate disappointment, a shattering of dreams that needed before everything else the relief of weeping.

'I've told you,' I said awkwardly, 'as soon as I could.'

There was another long silence. 'So that is how we stand,' I said, with an air of having things defined. I walked slowly to the door.

She had risen, and stood now staring in front of her.

'Good night,' I said, making no movement towards our habitual kiss.

'Good night,' she answered in a tragic note. . . .

I closed the door softly. I remained for a moment or so on the big landing, hesitating between my bedroom and my study. As I did so I heard the soft rustle of her movement and the click of the key in her bedroom door. Then everything was still. . . .

She hid her tears from me. Something gripped my heart at the thought.

'Damnation!' I said, wincing. 'Why the devil can't people at least *think* in the same manner?'


2

And that insufficient colloquy was the beginning of a prolonged estrangement between us. It was characteristic of our relations that we never reopened the discussion. The thing had been in the air for some time; we had recognized it now; the widening breach between us was confessed. My own feelings were curiously divided. It is remarkable that my very real affection for Margaret only became evident to me with this quarrel. The changes of the heart are very subtle changes. I am quite unaware how or when my early romantic love for her purity and beauty and high-principled devotion evaporated from my life; but I do know that quite early in my parliamentary days there had come a vague, unconfessed resentment at the tie that seemed to hold me in servitude to her standards of private living and public act. I felt I was caught, and none the less so because it had been my own act to rivet on my shackles. So long as I still held myself bound to her that resentment grew. Now, since I had broken my bonds and taken my line it withered again, and I could think of Margaret with a returning kindliness.

But I still felt embarrassments with her. I felt myself dependent upon her for house room and food and social support, as it were under false pretences. I would have liked to have separated our financial affairs altogether. But I knew that to raise the issue would have seemed a last brutal indelicacy. So I tried almost furtively to keep my personal expenditure within the scope of the private income I made by writing, and we went out together in her motor brougham, dined and made appearances, met politely at breakfast – parted at night with a kiss upon her cheek. The locking of her door upon me, which at that time I quite understood, which I understand now, became for a time in my mind, through some obscure process of the soul, an offence. I never crossed the landing to her room again.

In all this matter, and, indeed, in all my relations with Margaret, I perceive now I behaved badly and foolishly. My manifest blunder is that I, who was several years older than she, much subtler and in many ways wiser, never in any measure sought to guide and control her. After our marriage I treated her always as an equal, and let her go her way ; held her responsible for all the weak and ineffective and unfortunate things she said and did to me. She wasn't clever enough to justify that. It wasn't fair to expect her to sympathize, anticipate, and understand. I ought to have taken care of her, roped her to me when it came to crossing the difficult places. If I had loved her more, and wiselier and more tenderly, if there had not been the consciousness of my financial dependence on her always stiffening my pride, I think she would have moved with me from the outset, and left the Liberals with me. But she did not get any inkling of the ends I sought in my change of sides. It must have seemed to her inexplicable perversity. She had, I knew – for surely I knew it then! – an immense capacity for loyalty and devotion. There she was with these treasures untouched, neglected and perplexed. A woman who loves wants to give. It is the duty and business of the man she has married

290

for love to help her to help and give. But I was stupid. My eyes had never been opened. I was stiff with her and difficult to her, because even on my wedding morning there had been, deep down in my soul, voiceless though present, something weakly protesting, a faint perception of wrong-doing, the infinitesimally small, slow-multiplying germs of shame.

3

I made my breach with the party on the Budget.

In many ways I was disposed to regard the 1909 Budget as a fine piece of statecraft. Its production was certainly a very unexpected display of vigour on the Liberal side. But, on the whole, this movement towards collectivist organization on the part of the Liberals rather strengthened than weakened my resolve to cross the floor of the house. It made it more necessary, I thought, to leaven the purely obstructive and reactionary elements that were at once manifest in the opposition. I assailed the land taxation proposals in one main speech and a series of minor speeches in committee. The line of attack I chose was that the land was a great public service that needed to be controlled on broad and far-sighted lines. I had no objection to its nationalization, but I did object most strenuously to the idea of leaving it in private hands, and attempting to produce beneficial social results through the pressure of taxation upon the landowning class. That might break it up in an utterly disastrous way. The drift of the government proposals was all in the direction of sweating the landowner to get immediate values from his property, and such a course of action was bound to give us an irritated and vindictive landowning class, the class upon which we had hitherto relied – not unjustifiably – for certain broad, patriotic services and an influence upon our collective judgements that no other class seemed prepared to exercise. Abolish landlordism if you will, I said, buy it out, but do not drive it to a defensive fight, and leave it still sufficiently strong and wealthy to become a malcontent element in your state. You have taxed and controlled the brewer and the publican until the outraged Liquor Interest has become a national danger. You now propose to do the same thing on a larger scale. You turn a class which has many fine and truly aristocratic traditions towards revolt, and there is nothing in these or any other of your proposals that shows any sense of the need for leadership to replace these traditional leaders you are ousting. This was the substance of my case, and I hammered at it not only in the House, but in the press. . . .

The Kinghamstead division remained for some time insensitive to my defection.

Then it woke up suddenly, and began, in the columns of the *Kinghamstead Guardian*, an indignant, confused outcry. I was treated to an open letter, signed 'Junius Secundus', and I replied in provocative terms. There were two thinly attended public meetings at different ends of the constituency, and then I had a correspondence with my old friend Parvill, the photographer, which ended in my seeing a deputation.

My impression is that it consisted of about eighteen or twenty people. They had had to come upstairs to me, and they were manifestly full of indignation and a little short of breath. There was Parvill himself, J.P., dressed wholly in black – I think to mark his sense of the occasion – and curiously suggestive in his respect for my character and his concern for the honourableness of the *Kinghamstead Guardian* editor, of Mark Antony at the funeral of Caesar. There was Mrs Bulger, also in mourning ; she had never abandoned the widow's streamers since the death of her husband ten years ago, and her loyalty to Liberalism of the severest type was part as it were of her weeds. There was a nephew of Sir Roderick Newton, a bright young Hebrew of the graver type, and a couple of dissenting ministers in high collars and hats that stopped halfway between the bowler of this world and the shovel-hat of heaven. There was also a young solicitor from Lurky done in the horsey style, and there was a very little nervous man with a high brow and a face contracting below as though the jawbones and teeth had been taken out and the features compressed. The rest of the deputation, which included two other public-spirited ladies and several ministers of religion, might have been raked out of any omnibus going Strandward during the May meetings. They thrust Parvill forward as spokesman, and manifested a strong disposition to say 'Hear, hear!' to his more strenuous protests provided my eye wasn't upon them at the time.

I regarded this appalling deputation as Parvill's apologetic but quite definite utterances drew to an end. I had a moment of vision. Behind them I saw the wonderful array of skeleton forces that stand for public opinion, that are as much public opinion as exists indeed at the present time. The whole process of politics which bulks so solidly in history seemed for that clairvoyant instant but a froth of petty motives above abysms of indifference. . . .

Some one had finished. I perceived I had to speak.

'Very well,' I said, 'I won't keep you long in replying. I'll resign if there isn't a dissolution before next February, and if there is I shan't stand again. You don't want the bother and expense of a bye-election' (approving murmurs) 'if it can be avoided. But I may tell you plainly now that I don't think it will be necessary for me to resign, and the sooner you find my successor the better for the party. The Lords are in a corner ; they've got to fight now or never, and I think they will throw out the Budget. Then they will go on fighting. It is a fight that will last for years. They have a sort of social discipline, and you haven't. You Liberals will find yourselves with a country behind you, vaguely indignant perhaps, but totally unprepared with any ideas whatever in the matter, face to face with the problem of bringing the British constitution up-to-date. Anything may happen, provided only that it is sufficiently absurd. If the King backs the Lords – and I don't see why he shouldn't – you have no Republican movement whatever to fall back upon. You lost it during the Era of Good Taste. The country, I say, is destitute of ideas, and you have no ideas to give it. I don't see what you will do. . . . For my own part, I mean to spend a year or so between a window and my writing-desk.'

I paused. 'I think, gentlemen,' began Parvill, 'that we hear all this with very great regret. . . .'


4

My estrangement from Margaret stands in my memory now as something that played itself out within the four walls of our house in Radnor Square, which was, indeed, confined to those limits. I went to and fro between my house and the House of Commons, and the dining-rooms and clubs and offices in which we were preparing our new developments, in a state of aggressive and energetic dissociation, in the nascent state, as a chemist would say. I was free now, and greedy for fresh combination. I had a tremendous sense of released energies. I had got back to the sort of thing I could do, and to the work that had been shaping itself for so long in my imagination. Our purpose now was plain, bold, and extraordinarily congenial. We meant no less than to organize a new movement in English thought and life, to resuscitate a Public Opinion and prepare the ground for a revised and renovated ruling culture.

For a time I seemed quite wonderfully able to do whatever I wanted to do. Shoesmith responded to my first advances. We decided to create a weekly paper as our nucleus, and Crupp and I set to work forthwith to collect a group of writers and speakers, including Esmeer, Britten, Lord Gane, Neal, and one or two younger men, which should constitute a more or less definite editorial council about me, and meet at a weekly lunch on Tuesday to sustain our general co-operations. We marked our claim upon Toryism even in the colour of our wrapper, and spoke of ourselves collectively as the Blue Weeklies. But our lunches were open to all sorts of guests, and our deliberations were never of a character to control me effectively in my editorial decisions. My only influential counsellor at first was old Britten, who became my sub-editor. It was curious how we two had picked up our ancient intimacy again and resumed the easy give and take of our speculative dreaming schoolboy days.

For a time my life centred altogether upon this journalistic work. Britten was an experienced journalist, and I had most of the necessary instincts for the business. We meant to make the paper right and good down to the smallest detail, and we set ourselves at this with extraordinary zeal. It wasn't our intention to show our political motives too markedly at first, and through all the dust-storm and tumult and stress of the political struggle of 1910 we made a little intellectual oasis of good art criticism and good writing. It was the firm belief of nearly all of us that the Lords were destined to be beaten badly in 1910, and our game was the longer game of reconstruction that would begin when the shouting and tumult of that immediate conflict were over. Meanwhile we had to get into touch with just as many good minds as possible.

As we felt our feet, I developed slowly and carefully a broad-

294

ly conceived and consistent political attitude. As I will explain later, we were feminist from the outset, though that caused Shoesmith and Gane great searchings of heart ; we developed Esmeer's House of Lords reform scheme into a general cult of the aristocratic virtues, and we did much to humanize and liberalize the narrow excellencies of that Break-up of the Poor Law agitation which had been organized originally by Beatrice and Sidney Webb. In addition, without any very definite explanation to any one but Esmeer and Isabel Rivers, and as if it was quite a small matter, I set myself to secure a uniform philosophical quality in our columns.

That, indeed, was the peculiar virtue and characteristic of the *Blue Weekly*. I was now very definitely convinced that much of the confusion and futility of contemporary thought was due to the general need of metaphysical training. . . . The great mass of people – and not simply common people, but people active and influential in intellectual things – are still quite untrained in the methods of thought and absolutely innocent of any criticism of method ; it is scarcely a caricature to call their thinking a crazy patchwork, discontinuous and chaotic. They arrive at conclusions by a kind of accident, and do not suspect any other way may be found to their attainment. A stage above this general condition stands that minority of people who have at some time or other discovered general terms and a certain use for generalizations. They are – to fall back on the ancient technicality – Realists of a crude sort. Such are the Baileys ; such, to take their great prototype, was Herbert Spencer (who couldn't read Kant) ; such are whole regiments of prominent and entirely self-satisfied contemporaries. They go through queer little processes of definition and generalization and deduction with the completest belief in the validity of the intellectual instrument they are using. They are Realists – Cocksurists – in matter of fact ; sentimentalists in behaviour. The Baileys having got to this glorious stage in mental development – it is glorious because it has no doubts – were always talking about training 'Experts' to apply the same simple process to all the affairs of mankind. Well, Realism isn't the last word of human wisdom. Modest-minded people, doubtful people, subtle people, and the like – the kind of people William James writes of as 'tough-minded', go on beyond this methodical

295

happiness, and are forever after critical of premisses and terms. They are truer – and less confident. They have reached scepticism and the artistic method. They have emerged into the new Nominalism.

Both Isabel and I believe firmly that these differences of intellectual method matter profoundly in the affairs of mankind, that the collective mind of this intricate complex modern state can only function properly upon neo-Nominalist lines. This has always been her side of our mental co-operation rather than mine. Her mind has the light movement that goes so often with natural mental power; she has a wonderful art in illustration, and, as the reader probably knows already, she writes of metaphysical matters with a rare charm and vividness. So far there has been no collection of her papers published; they are to be found not only in the *Blue Weekly* columns, but scattered about the monthlies; many people must be familiar with her style. It was an intention we did much to realize before our private downfall, that we would use the *Blue Weekly* to maintain a stream of suggestion against crude thinking, and at last scarcely a week passed but some popular distinction, some large imposing generalization, was touched to flaccidity by her pen or mine. . . .

I was at great pains to give my philosophical, political, and social matter the best literary and critical backing we could get in London. I hunted sedulously for good descriptive writing and good criticism; I was indefatigable in my readiness to hear and consider, if not to accept advice; I watched every corner of the paper, and had a dozen men alert to get me special matter of the sort that draws in the unattached reader. The chief danger on the literary side of a weekly is that it should fall into the hands of some particular school, and this I watched for closely. It seems almost impossible to get vividness of apprehension and breadth of view together in the same critic. So it falls to the wise editor to secure the first and impose the second. Directly I detected the shrill partizan note in our criticism, the attempt to puff a poor thing because it was 'in the right direction', or damn a vigorous piece of work because it wasn't, I tackled the man and had it out with him. Our pay was good enough for that to matter a good deal. . . .

Our distinctive little blue-and-white poster kept up its neat

296

persistent appeal to the public eye, and before 1911 was out the *Blue Weekly* was printing twenty pages of publishers' advertisements, and went into all the clubs in London and three-quarters of the country houses where week-end parties gather together. Its sale by newsagents and bookstalls grew steadily. One got more and more the reassuring sense of being discussed and influencing discussion.

5

Our office was at the very top of a big building near the end of Adelphi Terrace ; the main window beside my desk, a big undivided window of plate glass, looked out upon Cleopatra's Needle, the corner of the Hotel Cecil, the fine arches of Waterloo Bridge, and the long sweep of south bank with its shot towers and chimneys, past Bankside to the dimly seen piers of the great bridge below the Tower. The dome of St Paul's just floated into view on the left against the hotel façade. By night and day, in every light and atmosphere, it was a beautiful and various view, alive as a throbbing heart ; a perpetual flow of traffic ploughed and splashed the streaming silver of the river, and by night the shapes of things became velvet black and grey, and the water, a shining mirror of steel, wearing coruscating gems of light. In the foreground the Embankment trams sailed glowing by, across the water advertisements flashed and flickered, trains went and came and a rolling drift of smoke reflected unseen fires. By day that spectacle was sometimes a marvel of shining wet and wind-cleared atmosphere, sometimes a mystery of drifting fog, sometimes a miracle of crowded details, minutely fine.

As I think of that view, so variously spacious in effect, I am back there, and this sunlit paper might be lamp-lit and lying on my old desk. I see it all again, feel it all again. In the foreground is a green-shaded lamp and crumpled galley slips and paged proofs and letters, two or three papers in manuscript, and so forth. In the shadows are chairs and another table bearing papers and books, a rotating bookcase dimly seen, a long window-seat black in the darkness, and then the cool unbroken spectacle of the window. How often I would watch some tram-car, some string of barges, go from me slowly out of sight. The people were black animalculae by day, clustering, collecting, dispersing ; by night they were phantom face-specks coming, vanishing, stirring obscurely between light and shade.

I recall many hours at my desk in that room before the crisis came, hours full of the peculiar happiness of effective strenuous work. Once some piece of writing went on, holding me intent and forgetful of time until I looked up from the warm circle of my electric lamp to see the eastward sky above the pale silhouette of the Tower Bridge, flushed and banded brightly with the dawn.

# Chapter the Fourth

# The Besetting of Sex

## 1

Art is selection and so is most autobiography. But I am concerned with a more tangled business than selection, I want to show a contemporary man in relation to the state and social usage, and the social organism in relation to that man. To tell my story at all I have to simplify. I have given now the broad lines of my political development, and how I passed from my initial liberal-socialism to the conception of a constructive aristocracy. I have tried to set that out in the form of a man discovering himself. Incidentally that self-development led to a profound breach with my wife. One has read stories before of husband and wife speaking severally two different languages and coming to an understanding. But Margaret and I began in her dialect, and, as I came more and more to use my own, diverged.

I had thought when I married that the matter of womankind had ended for me. I have tried to tell all that sex and women had been to me up to my married life with Margaret and our fatal entanglement, tried to show the queer, crippled, embarrassed and limited way in which these interests break upon the life of a young man under contemporary conditions. I do not think my lot was a very exceptional one. I missed the chance of sisters and girl playmates, but that is not an uncommon misadventure in an age of small families; I never came to know any woman at all intimately until I was married to Margaret. My earlier love affairs were encounters of sex, under conditions of furtiveness and adventure that made them things in themselves, restricted and unilluminating. From a boyish disposition to be mystical and worshipping towards women I had passed into a disregardful attitude, as though women were things inferior or irrelevant, disturbers in great affairs. For a time Margaret had blotted out all other women; she was so different and so near; she was like a person who stands suddenly in front of a little window through which one has been surveying a crowd. She didn't become womankind for me so much as eliminate womankind from my world. . . . And then came this secret separation. . . .

Until this estrangement and the rapid and uncontrollable development of my relations with Isabel which chanced to follow it, I seemed to have solved the problem of women by marriage and disregard. I thought these things were over. I went about my career with Margaret beside me, her brow slightly knit, her manner faintly strenuous, helping; and if we had not altogether abolished sex we had at least so circumscribed and isolated it that it would not have affected the general tenor of our lives in the slightest degree if we had.

And then, clothing itself more and more in the form of Isabel and her problems, this old, this fundamental obsession of my life returned. The thing stole upon my mind so that I was unaware of its invasion and how it was changing our long intimacy. I have already compared the lot of the modern publicist to Machiavelli writing in his study: in his day women and sex were as disregarded in these high affairs as, let us say, the chemistry of air or the will of the beasts in the fields; in ours the case has altogether changed, and woman has come now to stand beside the tall candles, half in the light, half in the mystery of the shadows, besetting, interrupting, demanding unrelentingly an altogether unprecedented attention. I feel that in these matters my life has been almost typical of my time. Woman insists upon her presence. She is no longer a mere physical need, an aesthetic by-play, a sentimental background; she is a moral and intellectual necessity in a man's life. She comes to the politician and demands, Is she a child or a citizen? Is she a thing or a soul? She comes to the individual man, as she came to me, and asks, Is she a cherished weakling or an equal mate, an unavoidable helper? Is she to be tried and trusted or guarded and controlled, bond or free? For if she is a mate, one must at once trust more and exact more, exacting toil, courage, and the hardest, most necessary thing of all, the clearest, most shameless explicitness of understanding. . . .

# 2

In all my earlier imaginings of statecraft I had tacitly assumed either that the relations of the sexes were all right or that anyhow they didn't concern the state. It was a matter they, whoever 'they' were, had to settle among themselves. That sort of disregard was possible then. But even before 1906 there were endless intimations that the dams holding back great reservoirs of discussion were crumbling. We political schemers were ploughing wider than any one had ploughed before in the field of social reconstruction. We had also, we realized, to plough deeper. We had to plough down at least to the passionate elements of sexual relationship and examine and decide upon them.

The signs multiplied. In a year or so half the police of the metropolis were scarce sufficient to protect the House from one clamorous aspect of the new problem. The members went about Westminster with an odd, new sense of being beset. A good proportion of us kept up the pretence that the Vote for Women was an isolated fad, and the agitation an epidemic madness that would presently pass. But it was manifest to any one who sought more than comfort in the matter that the streams of women and sympathizers and money forthcoming marked far deeper and wider things than an idle fancy for the franchise. The existing laws and conventions of relationship between Man and Woman were just as unsatisfactory a disorder as anything else in our tumbled confusion of a world, and that also was coming to bear upon statecraft.

My first parliament was the parliament of the Suffragettes. I don't propose to tell here of that amazing campaign, with its absurdities and follies, its courage and devotion. There were aspects of that unquenchable agitation that were absolutely heroic and aspects that were absolutely pitiful. It was unreasonable, unwise, and, except for its one central insistence, astonishingly incoherent. It was amazingly effective. The very incoherence of the demand witnessed, I think, to the forces that lay behind it. It wasn't a simple argument based on a simple assumption ; it was the first crude expression of a great mass and mingling of convergent feelings, of a widespread, confused persuasion among modern educated women that the conditions of their relations with men were oppressive, ugly, dishonouring, and had to be altered. They had not merely adopted the Vote as a symbol of equality; it was fairly manifest to me that, given it, they meant to use it, and to use it perhaps even vindictively and blindly, as a weapon against many things they had every reason to hate. . . .

I remember, with exceptional vividness, that great night early in the session of 1909, when – I think it was – fifty or sixty women went to prison. I had been dining at the Brahams', and Lord Braham and I came down from the direction of St James's Park into a crowd and a confusion outside the Caxton Hall. We found ourselves drifting with an immense multitude towards Parliament Square and parallel with a slight, closely-packed column of girls and women, for the most part white-faced and intent. I still remember the effect of their faces upon me. It was quite different from the general effect of staring about and divided attention one gets in a political procession of men. There was an expression of heroic tension.

There had been a pretty deliberate appeal on the part of the women's organizers to the Unemployed, who had been demonstrating throughout that winter, to join forces with the movement, and the result was shown in the quality of the crowd upon the pavement. It was an ugly, dangerous-looking crowd, but as yet good-tempered and sympathetic. When at last we got within sight of the House the square was a seething sea of excited people, and the array of police on horse and on foot might have been assembled for a revolutionary outbreak. There were dense masses of people up Whitehall, and right on to Westminster Bridge. The scuffle that ended in the arrests was the poorest explosion to follow such stupendous preparations. . . .


3

Later on in that year the women began a new attack. Day and night, and all through the long nights of the Budget sittings, at all the piers of the gates of New Palace Yard and at St Stephen's Porch, stood women pickets, and watched us silently and reproachfully as we went to and fro. They were women of all sorts, though, of course, the independent worker-class predominated. There were grey-headed old ladies standing there, sturdily charming in the rain; battered-looking, ambiguous women, with something of the desperate bitterness of battered women showing in their eyes; north-country factory girls; cheaply-dressed suburban women; trim, comfortable mothers of families; valiant-eyed girl graduates and undergraduates; lank, hungry-looking creatures, who stirred one's imagination; one very dainty little woman in deep mourning, I recall, grave and steadfast, with eyes fixed on distant things. Some of those women looked defiant, some timidly aggressive, some full of the stir of adventure, some drooping with cold and fatigue. The supply never ceased. I had a mortal fear that somehow the supply might halt or cease. I found that continual siege of the legislature extraordinarily impressive – infinitely more impressive than the feeble-forcible 'ragging' of the more militant section. I thought of the appeal that must be going through the country, summoning the women from countless scattered homes, rooms, colleges, to Westminster.

I remember too the petty little difficulty I felt, whether I should ignore these pickets altogether, or lift a hat as I hurried past with averted eyes, or look them in the face as I did so. Towards the end the House evolved an etiquette of salutation.

## 4

There was a tendency, even on the part of its sympathizers, to treat the whole suffrage agitation as if it were a disconnected issue, irrelevant to all other broad developments of social and political life. We struggled, all of us, to ignore the indicating finger it thrust out before us. 'Your schemes, for all their bigness,' it insisted to our reluctant, averted minds, 'still don't go down to the essential things. . . .'

We have to go deeper, or our inadequate children's insufficient children will starve amidst harvests of earless futility. That conservatism which works in every class to preserve in its essentials the habitual daily life is all against a profounder treatment of political issues. The politician, almost as absurdly as the philosopher, tends constantly, in spite of magnificent preludes, vast intimations, to specialize himself out of the reality he has so stupendously summoned – he bolts back to

303

littleness. The world has to be moulded anew, he continues to admit, but without, he adds, any risk of upsetting his week-end visits, his morning cup of tea. . . .

The discussion of the relations of men and women disturbs everyone. It reacts upon the private life of everyone who attempts it. And at any particular time only a small minority have a personal interest in changing the established state of affairs. Habit and interest are in a constantly recruited majority against conscious change and adjustment in these matters. Drift rules us. The great mass of people, and an overwhelming proportion of influential people, are people who have banished their dreams and made their compromise. Wonderful and beautiful possibilities are no longer to be thought about. They have given up any aspirations for intense love, for splendid off-spring, for keen delights, have accepted a cultivated kindliness and an uncritical sense of righteousness as their compensation. It's a settled affair with them, a settled, dangerous affair. Most of them fear, and many hate, the slightest reminder of those abandoned dreams. As Dayton once said to the Pentagram Circle, when we were discussing the problem of a universal marriage and divorce law throughout the Empire, 'I am for leaving all these things alone.' And then, with a groan in his voice, 'Leave them alone! Leave them all alone!'

That was his whole speech for the evening, in a note of suppressed passion, and presently, against all our etiquette, he got up and went out.

For some years after my marriage, I too was for leaving them alone. I developed a dread and dislike for romance, for emotional music, for the human figure in art – turning my heart to landscape. I wanted to sneer at lovers and their ecstasies, and was uncomfortable until I found the effective sneer. In matters of private morals these were my most uncharitable years. I didn't want to think of these things any more for ever. I hated the people whose talk or practice showed they were not of my opinion. I wanted to believe that their views were immoral and objectionable and contemptible, because I had decided to treat them as at that level. I was, in fact, falling into the attitude of the normal decent man.

And yet one cannot help thinking! The sensible moralized man finds it hard to escape the stream of suggestion that there are still dreams beyond these commonplace acquiescences, – the appeal of beauty suddenly shining upon one, the mothlike stirrings of serene summer nights, the sweetness of distant music. . . .

It is one of the paradoxical factors in our public life at the present time, which penalizes abandonment to love so abundantly, so heavily, that power and influence and control fall largely to unencumbered people and sterile people and people who have married for passionless purposes, people whose very deficiency in feeling has left them free to follow ambition, people beauty-blind, who don't understand what it is to fall in love, what it is to desire children or have them, what it is to feel in their blood and bodies the supreme claim of good births and selective births above all other affairs in life, people almost of necessity averse from this most fundamental aspect of existence. . . .


5

It wasn't, however, my deepening sympathy with and understanding of the position of women in general, or the change in my ideas about all these intimate things my fast friendship with Isabel was bringing about, that led me to the heretical views I have in the last five years dragged from the region of academic and timid discussion into the field of practical politics. Those influences, no doubt, have converged to the same end, and given me a powerful emotional push upon my road, but it was a broader and colder view of things that first determined me in my attempt to graft the Endowment of Motherhood in some form or other upon British Imperialism. Now that I am exiled from the political world, it is possible to estimate just how effectually that grafting has been done.

I have explained how the ideas of a trained aristocracy and a universal education grew to paramount importance in my political scheme. It is but a short step from this to the question of the quantity and quality of births in the community, and from that again to those forbidden and fear-beset topics of marriage, divorce, and the family organization. A sporadic discussion of these aspects had been going on for years, a Eugenic society existed, and articles on the Falling Birth Rate

305

and the Rapid Multiplication of the Unfit were staples of the monthly magazines. But beyond an intermittent scolding of prosperous childless people in general – one never addressed them in particular – nothing was done towards arresting those adverse processes. Almost against my natural inclination, I found myself forced to go into these things. I came to the conclusion that under modern conditions the isolated private family, based on the existing marriage contract, was failing in its work. It wasn't producing enough children, and children good enough and well trained enough for the demands of the developing civilized state. Our civilization was growing outwardly, and decaying in its intimate substance, and unless it was presently to collapse, some very extensive and courageous reorganization was needed. The old haphazard system of pairing, qualified more and more by worldly discretions, no longer secures us a young population numerous enough or good enough for the growing needs and possibilities of our Empire. Statecraft sits weaving splendid garments, no doubt, but with a puny, ugly, insufficient baby in the cradle.

No one so far has dared to take up this problem as a present question for statecraft, but it comes unheralded, unadvocated, and sits at every legislative board. Every improvement is provisional except the improvement of the race, and it became more and more doubtful to me if we were improving the race at all! Splendid and beautiful and courageous people must come together and have children, women with their fine senses and glorious devotion must be freed from the net that compels them to be celibate, compels them to be childless and useless, or to bear children ignobly to men whom need and ignorance and the treacherous pressure of circumstances have forced upon them. We all know that, and so few dare even to whisper it for fear that they should seem, in seeking to save the family, to threaten its existence. It is as if a party of pygmies in a not too capacious room had been joined by a carnivorous giant – and decided to go on living happily by cutting him dead. . . .

The problem the developing civilized state has to solve is how it can get the best possible increase under the best possible conditions. I became more and more convinced that the independent family unit of today, in which the man is master of the wife and owner of the children, in which all are dependent upon him, subordinated to his enterprises and liable to follow his fortunes up or down, does not supply anything like the best conceivable conditions. We want to modernize the family footing altogether. An enormous premium both in pleasure and competitive efficiency is put upon voluntary childlessness, and enormous inducements are held out to women to subordinate instinctive and selective preferences to social and material considerations.

The practical reaction of modern conditions upon the old tradition of the family is this: that beneath the pretence that nothing is changing, secretly and with all the unwholesomeness of secrecy everything is changed. Offspring fall away, the birth rate falls and falls most among just the most efficient and active and best adapted classes in the community. The species is recruited from among its failures and from among less civilized aliens. Contemporary civilizations are in effect burning the best of their possible babies in the furnaces that run the machinery. In the United States the native Anglo-American strain has scarcely increased at all since 1830, and in most Western European countries the same is probably true of the ablest and most energetic elements in the community. The women of these classes still remain legally and practically dependent and protected, with the only natural excuse for their dependence gone. . . .

The modern world becomes an immense spectacle of unsatisfactory groupings; here childless couples bored to death in the hopeless effort to sustain an incessant honeymoon, here homes in which a solitary child grows unsocially, here small two- or three-child homes that do no more than continue the culture of the parents at a great social cost, here numbers of unhappy educated but childless married women, here careless, decivilized fecund homes, here orphanages and asylums for the heedlessly begotten. It is just the disorderly proliferation of Bromstead over again, in lives instead of in houses.

What is the good, what is the common sense, of rectifying boundaries, pushing research and discovery, building cities, improving all the facilities of life, making great fleets, waging wars, while this aimless decadence remains the quality of the biological outlook? . . . .

It is difficult now to trace how I changed from my early

aversion until I faced this mass of problems. But so far back as 1910 I had it clear in my mind that I would rather fail utterly than participate in all the surrenders of mind and body that are implied in Dayton's snarl of 'Leave it alone; leave it all alone!' Marriage and the begetting and care of children are the very ground substance in the life of the community. In a world where everything changes, in which fresh methods, fresh adjustments, and fresh ideas perpetually renew the circumstances of life, it is preposterous that we should not even examine into these matters, should rest content to be ruled by the uncriticized traditions of a barbaric age.

## 6

Now, it seems to me that the solution of this problem is also the solution of the woman's individual problem. The two go together, are right and left of one question. The only conceivable way out from our *impasse* lies in the recognition of parentage, that is to say of adequate mothering, as no longer a chance product of individual passions, but a service rendered to the State. Women must become less and less subordinated to individual men, since this works out in a more or less complete limitation, waste, and sterilization of their essentially social function; they must become more and more subordinated as individually independent citizens to the collective purpose. Or, to express the thing by a familiar phrase, the highly organized, scientific state we desire must, if it is to exist at all, base itself, not upon the irresponsible man-ruled family, but upon the matriarchal family, the citizenship and freedom of women and the public endowment of motherhood.

After two generations of confused and experimental revolt, it grows clear to modern women that a conscious, deliberate motherhood and mothering is their special function in the State, and that a personal subordination to an individual man with an unlimited power of control over this intimate and supreme duty is a degradation. No contemporary woman of education put to the test is willing to recognize any claim a man can make upon her but the claim of her freely given devotion to him. She wants the reality of her choice and she means 'family' while a man too often means only possession. This alters the spirit of the family relationships fundamentally. Their form remains just what it was when woman was esteemed a pretty, desirable, and incidentally a child-producing, chattel. Against these time-honoured ideas the new spirit of womanhood struggles in shame, astonishment, bitterness, and tears. . . .

I confess myself altogether feminist. I have no doubts in the matter. I want this coddling and brow-beating of women to cease. I want to see women come in, free and fearless, to a full participation in the collective purpose of mankind. Women, I am convinced, are as fine as men ; they can be as wise as men ; they are capable of far greater devotion than men. I want to see them citizens, with a marriage law framed primarily for them and for their protection and the good of the race, and not for men's satisfactions. I want to see them bearing and rearing good children in the State as a generously rewarded public duty and service, choosing their husbands freely and discerningly, and in no way enslaved by or subordinated to the men they have chosen. The social consciousness of women seems to me an unworked, an almost untouched mine of wealth for the constructive purpose of the world. I want to change the respective values of the family group altogether, and make the home indeed the woman's kingdom and the mother the owner and responsible guardian of her children.

It is no use pretending that this is not novel and revolutionary ; it is. The Endowment of Motherhood implies a new method of social organization, a rearrangement of the social unit, untried in human experience – as untried as electric traction was or flying in 1800. Of course, it may work out to modify men's ideas of marriage profoundly. To me that is a secondary consideration. I do not believe that particular assertion myself, because I am convinced that a practical monogamy is a psychological necessity to the mass of civilized people. But even if I did believe it I should still keep to my present line, because it is the only line that will prevent a highly organized civilization from ending in biological decay. The public Endowment of Motherhood is the only possible way which will ensure the permanently developing civilized state at which all constructive minds are aiming. A point is reached in the life-history of a civilization when either this reconstruction must be effected or the quality and *morale* of the population prove insufficient for the needs of the developing organization. It is not so much moral decadence that will destroy us as moral inadaptability. The old code fails under the new needs. The only alternative to this profound reconstruction is a decay in human quality and social collapse. Either this unprecedented rearrangement must be achieved by our civilization, or it must presently come upon a phase of disorder and crumble and perish, as Rome perished, as France declines, as the strain of the Pilgrim Fathers dwindles out of America. Whatever hope there may be in the attempt, therefore, there is no alternative to the attempt.

## 7

I wanted political success now dearly enough, but not at the price of constructive realities. These questions were no doubt monstrously dangerous in the political world; there wasn't a politician alive who didn't look scared at the mention of 'The Family,' but if raising these issues were essential to the social reconstructions on which my life was set, that did not matter. It only implied that I should take them up with deliberate caution. There was no release because of risk or difficulty.

The question of whether I should commit myself to some open project in this direction was going on in my mind concurrently with my speculations about a change of party, like bass and treble in a complex piece of music. The two drew to a conclusion together. I would not only go over to Imperialism, but I would attempt to biologize Imperialism.

I thought at first that I was undertaking a monstrous uphill task. But as I came to look into the possibilities of the matter, a strong persuasion grew up in my mind that this panic fear of legislative proposals affecting the family basis was excessive; that things were much riper for development in this direction than old, experienced people out of touch with the younger generation imagined; that, to phrase the thing in a parliamentary fashion, 'something might be done in the constituencies' with the Endowment of Motherhood forthwith, provided only that it was made perfectly clear that anything a sane person could possibly intend by 'Morality' was left untouched by these proposals.

I went to work very carefully. I got Roper of the *Daily Telephone* and Burkett of the *Dial* to try over a silly-season discussion of State Help for Mothers, and I put a series of articles on eugenics, upon the fall in the birth rate, and similar topics in the *Blue Weekly*, leading up to a tentative and generalized advocacy of the public endowment of the nation's children. I was more and more struck by the acceptance won by a sober and restrained presentation of this suggestion.

And then, in the fourth year of the *Blue Weekly*'s career, came the Handitch election, and I was forced by the clamour of my antagonist, and very willingly forced, to put my convictions to the test. I returned triumphantly to Westminster with the Public Endowment of Motherhood as part of my open profession and with the full approval of the party press. Applauding benches of Imperialists cheered me on my way to the table between the whips.

That second time I took the oath I was not one of a crowd of new members, but salient, an event, a symbol of profound changes and new purposes in the national life.

Book the Fourth
# Isabel

# Love and Success

## 1

And now I come to the most evasive and difficult part of my story, which is to tell how Isabel and I have made a common wreck of our joint lives.

It is not the telling of one simple disastrous accident, but of a vein in our nature, and how gradually and at this point it crept to the surface. A thing so pervasive has necessarily a thousand aspects and a thousand values. One may indeed see it in the form of a catastrophe as disconnected and conclusive as a meteoric stone falling out of heaven upon two friends and crushing them both. But I do not think that is true to our situation or ourselves. We were not taken by surprise. The thing was in us and not from without, it was akin to our way of thinking and our habitual attitudes ; it had, for all its impulsive effect, a certain necessity. We might have escaped, no doubt, as two men at a hundred yards may shoot at each other with pistols for a considerable time and escape. But it isn't particularly reasonable to talk of the contrariety of fate if they both get hit.

Isabel and I were dangerous to each other for several years of friendship, and not quite unwittingly so.

In writing this, moreover, there is a very great difficulty in steering my way between two equally undesirable tones in the telling. In the first place, I do not want to seem to confess my sins with a penitence I am very doubtful if I feel. Now that I have got Isabel we can no doubt reckon the cost and feel unquenchable regrets, but I am not sure, if we could be put back now into such circumstances as we were in a year ago, or two years ago, whether with my eyes fully open I should not do over again very much as I did. And on the other hand, I do not want to justify. We are two bad people, we have acted badly, and quite apart from any other considerations we've largely wasted our own very great possibilities. But it is part of a queer humour that underlies all this, that I find myself

315

slipping again and again into a sentimental treatment of our case that is as unpremeditated as it is insincere. It seems almost the natural way of telling of irregular love. It is certainly the easiest way, and when I am a little tired after a morning's writing I find getting into every other sentence the faint suggestion that our blunders and misdeeds embodied, after the fashion of the prophet Horsea, profound moral truths. Indeed, I feel so little confidence in my ability to keep this altogether out of my book that I must warn the reader here that in spite of anything he may read elsewhere in the story, intimating however shyly an esoteric and exalted virtue in our proceedings, the plain truth of this business is that Isabel and I wanted each other with a want entirely formless, inconsiderate, and overwhelming. And though I could tell you countless delightful and beautiful things about Isabel, were this a book in her praise, I cannot either analyze that want or account for its extreme intensity.

I will confess that in my mind is a belief in a sort of wild rightness about any love that is fraught with beauty, but that eludes me and vanishes again, and is not, I feel, to be put with the real veracities and righteousnesses and virtues, into the paddocks and menageries of human reason. . . .

We have already a child, and Margaret was childless, and I find myself particularly prone to insist upon that as if it was a justification. But, indeed, when we became lovers there was small thought of Eugenics between us. Ours was a mutual and not a philoprogenitive passion. Old Nature behind us may have had such purposes with us, but it is not for us to annex her intentions by a moralizing afterthought. There isn't, in fact, any decent justification for us whatever – at that the story must stand.

But if there is no justification there was at least a very effective excuse in the mental confusedness of our time. The evasion of that passionately thorough exposition of belief and of the grounds of morality, which is the outcome of the mercenary religious compromises of the late Victorian period, the stupid suppression of anything but the most timid discussion of sexual morality in our literature and drama, the pervading cultivated and protected muddle-headedness, leaves mentally vigorous people with relatively enormous powers of destruction and

316

little effective help. They find themselves confronted by the habits and prejudices of manifestly commonplace people, and by that extraordinary patched-up Christianity, the cult of that 'Bromsteadized' deity, diffused, scattered, and aimless, which hides from examination and any possibility of faith behind the plea of good taste. A god about whom there is delicacy is far worse than no god at all. We are *forced* to be laws unto ourselves and to live experimentally. It is inevitable that a considerable fraction of just that bolder, more initiatory section of the intellectual community, the section that can least be spared from the collective life in a period of trial.and change demanding the utmost versatility, will drift into such emotional crises and such disaster as overtook us. Most perhaps will escape, but many will go down, many more than the world can spare. It is the unwritten law of all our public life, and the same holds true of America, that an honest open scandal ends a career. England in the last quarter of a century has wasted half a dozen statesmen on this score; she would, I believe, reject Nelson now if he sought to serve her, she would turn her back upon Wellington.

Is it wonderful that to us fretting here in exile this ostracism should seem the cruellest as well as the most foolish waste of necessary social elements? It destroys no vice ; for vice hides by nature. It not only rewards dullness as if it were positive virtue, but sets an enormous premium upon hypocrisy. That is my case, and that is why I am telling this side of my story with so much explicitness.

2

Ever since the Kinghamstead election I had maintained what seemed a desultory friendship with Isabel. At first it was rather Isabel kept it up than I. Whenever Margaret and I went down to that villa, with its three or four acres of garden and shrubbery about us, which fulfilled our election promise to live at Kinghamstead, Isabel would turn up in a state of frank cheerfulness, rejoicing at us, and talk all she was reading and thinking to me, and stay for all the rest of the day. In her shameless liking for me she was as natural as a savage. She would exercise me vigorously at tennis, while Margaret lay and rested her back in the afternoon, or guide me for some long ramble that dodged the suburban and congested patches of the constituency with amazing skill. She took possession of me in that unabashed, straightminded way a girl will sometimes adopt with a man, chose my path or criticized my game with a motherly solicitude for my welfare that was absurd and delightful. And we talked. We discussed and criticized the stories of novels, scraps of history, pictures, social questions, socialism, the policy of the Government. She was young and most unevenly informed, but she was amazingly sharp and quick and good. Never before in my life had I known a girl of her age, or a woman of her quality. I had never dreamt there was such talk in the world. Kinghamstead became a lightless place when she went to college. Heaven knows how much that may not have precipitated my abandonment of the seat!

At that time I think we neither of us suspected the possibility of passion that lay like a coiled snake in the path before us. It seemed to us that we had the quaintest, most delightful friendship in the world; she was my pupil, and I was her guide, philosopher, and friend. People smiled indulgently – even Margaret smiled indulgently – at our attraction for one another.

Such friendships are not uncommon nowadays – among easygoing, liberal-minded people. For the most part there's no sort of harm, as people say, in them. The two persons concerned are never supposed to think of the passionate love that hovers so close to the friendship, or it they do, then they banish the thought. I think we kept the thought as permanently in exile as any one could do. If it did in odd moments come into our heads, we pretended elaborately it wasn't there.

Only we were both very easily jealous of each other's attention, and tremendously insistent upon each other's preference.

I remember once during the college days an intimation that should have set me thinking and I suppose discreetly disentangling myself. It was one Sunday afternoon, and it must have been about May, for the trees and shrubs were gay with blossom, and fresh with the new sharp greens of spring. I had walked talking with Isabel and a couple of other girls through the wide gardens of the place, seen and criticized the new brick pond, nodded to the daughter of this friend and that in the hammocks under the trees, and picked a way among the scat-

318

tered tea-parties on the lawn to our own circle on the grass under a Siberian crab near the great bay window. There I sat and ate great quantities of cake, and discussed the tactics of the Suffragettes. I had made some comments upon the spirit of the movement in an address to the men in Pembroke, and it had got abroad, and a group of girls and women dons were now having it out with me.

I forget the drift of the conversation or what it was made Isabel interrupt me. She did interrupt me. She had been lying prone on the ground at my right hand, chin on fists, listening thoughtfully, and I was sitting beside old Lady Evershead on a garden seat. I turned to Isabel's voice, and saw her face uplifted, and her dear cheeks and nose and forehead all splashed and barred with sunlight and the shadows of the twigs of the trees behind me. And something – an infinite tenderness, stabbed me. It was a keen physical feeling, like nothing I had ever felt before. For the first time in my narrow and concentrated life another human being had really thrust into my being and gripped my very heart.

Our eyes met perplexed for an extraordinary moment. Then I turned back and addressed myself a little stiffly to the substance of her intervention. For some time I couldn't look at her again.

From that time forth I knew I loved Isabel beyond measure.

Yet it is curious that it never occurred to me for a year or so that this was likely to be a matter of passion between us. I have told how definitely I put my imagination into harness in those matters at my marriage, and I was living now in a world of big interests, where there is neither much time nor inclination for deliberate love-making. I suppose there is a large class of men who never meet a girl or a woman without thinking of sex, who meet a friend's daughter and decide: 'Mustn't get friendly with her – wouldn't *do*,' and set invisible bars between themselves and all the wives in the world. Perhaps that is the way to live. Perhaps there is no other method than this effectual annihilation of half – and the most sympathetic and attractive half – of the human beings in the world, so far as any frank intercourse is concerned. I am quite convinced, anyhow, that such a qualified intimacy as ours, such a drifting into the sense of possession, such untrammelled conversation with an invisible, implacable limit set just where the intimacy glows, is no kind of tolerable compromise. If men and women are to go so far together, they must be free to go as far as they may want to go, without the vindictive destruction that has come upon us. On the basis of the accepted code, the jealous people are right and the liberal-minded ones are playing with fire. If people are not to love, then they must be kept apart. If they are not to be kept apart, then we must prepare for an unprecedented toleration of lovers.

Isabel was as unforeseeing as I to begin with, but sex marches into the life of an intelligent girl with demands and challenges far more urgent than the mere call of curiosity and satiable desire that comes to a young man. No woman yet has dared to tell the story of that unfolding. She attracted men, and she encouraged them, and watched them, and tested them, and dismissed them, and concealed the substance of her thoughts about them in the way that seems instinctive in a natural-minded girl. There was even an engagement – amidst the protests and disapproval of the college authorities. I never saw the man, though she gave me a long history of the affair, to which I listened with a forced and insincere sympathy. She struck me oddly as taking the relationship for a thing in itself, and regardless of its consequences. After a time she became silent about him, and then threw him over ; and by that time, I think, for all that she was so much my junior, she knew more about herself and me than I was to know for several years to come.

We didn't see each other for some months after my resignation, but we kept up a frequent correspondence. She said twice over that she wanted to talk to me, that letters didn't convey what one wanted to say, and I went up to Oxford pretty definitely to see her – though I combined it with one or two other engagements – somewhen in February. Insensibly she had become important enough for me to make journeys for her.

But we didn't see very much of one another on that occasion. There was something in the air between us that made a faint embarrassment ; the mere fact, perhaps, that she had asked me to come up.

A year before she would have dashed off with me quite un-

320

scrupulously to talk alone, carried me off to her room for an hour with a minute of chaperonage to satisfy the rules. Now there was always some one or other near us that it seemed impossible to exorcise.

We went for a walk on the Sunday afternoon with old Fortescue, K.C., who'd come up to see his two daughters, both great friends of Isabel's, and some mute inglorious don whose name I forget, but who was in a state of marked admiration for her. The six of us played a game of conversational entanglements throughout, and mostly I was impressing the Fortescue girls with the want of mental concentration possible in a rising politician. We went down Carfax, I remember, to Folly Bridge, and inspected the Barges, and then back by way of Merton to the Botanic Gardens and Magdalen Bridge. And in the Botanic Gardens she got almost her only chance with me.

'Last months of college,' she said.

'And then?' I asked.

'I'm coming to London,' she said.

'To write?'

She was silent for a moment. Then she said abruptly, with that quick flush of hers and a sudden boldness in her eyes: 'I'm going to work with you. Why shouldn't I?'

3

Here, again, I suppose I had a fair warning of the drift of things. I seem to remember myself in the train to Paddington, sitting with a handful of papers – galley proofs for the *Blue Weekly*, I suppose – on my lap, and thinking about her and that last sentence of hers, and all that it might mean to me.

It is very hard to recall even the main outline of anything so elusive as a meditation. I know that the idea of working with her gripped me, fascinated me. That my value in her life seemed growing filled me with pride and a kind of gratitude. I was already in no doubt that her value in my life was tremendous. It made it none the less, that in those days I was obsessed by the idea that she was transitory, and bound to go out of my life again. It is no good trying to set too fine a face upon this complex business; there is gold and clay and sunlight and savagery in every love-story, and a multitude of elvish elements peeped out beneath the fine rich curtain of affection that masked our future. I've never properly weighed how immensely my vanity was gratified by her clear preference for me. Nor can I for a moment determine how much deliberate intention I hide from myself in this affair.

Certainly I think some part of me must have been saying in the train: 'Leave go of her. Get away from her. End this now.' I can't have been so stupid as not to have had that in my mind. . . .

If she had been only a beautiful girl in love with me, I think I could have managed the situation. Once or twice since my marriage and before Isabel became of any significance in my life, there had been incidents with other people, flashes of temptation – no telling is possible of the thing resisted. I think that mere beauty and passion would not have taken me. But between myself and Isabel things were incurably complicated by the intellectual sympathy we had, the jolly march of our minds together. That has always mattered enormously. I should have wanted her company nearly as badly if she had been some crippled old lady ; we would have hunted shoulder to shoulder, as two men. Only two men would never have had the patience and readiness for one another we two had. I had never for years met any one with whom I could be so carelessly sure of understanding or to whom I could listen so easily and fully. She gave me, with an extraordinary completeness, that rare, precious effect of always saying something fresh, and yet saying it so that it filled into and folded about all the little recesses and corners of my mind with an infinite, soft familiarity. It is impossible to explain that. It is like trying to explain why her voice, her voice heard speaking to any one – heard speaking in another room – pleased my ears.

She spent the summer in Scotland and Yorkshire, writing to me continually of all she now meant to do, and stirring my imagination. She came to London for the autumn session. For a time she stayed with old Lady Colbeck, but she fell out with her hostess when it became clear she wanted to write, not novels, but journalism, and then she set every one talking by taking a flat near Victoria and installing as her sole protector an elderly German governess she had engaged through a scholastic agency. She began writing, not in that copious flood the undisciplined young woman of gifts is apt to produce, but in exactly the manner of an able young man, experimenting with forms, developing the phrasing of opinions, taking a definite line. She was, of course, tremendously discussed. She was disapproved of, but she was invited out to dinner. She got rather a reputation for the management of elderly distinguished men. It was an odd experience to follow Margaret's soft rustle of silk into some big drawing-room and discover my snub-nosed girl in the blue sack transformed into a shining creature in the soft splendour of pearls and ivory-white and lace, and with a silver band about her dusky hair.

For a time we did not meet very frequently, though always she professed an unblushing preference for my company, and talked my views and sought me out. Then her usefulness upon the *Blue Weekly* began to link us closelier. She would come up to the office, and sit by the window and talk over the proofs of the next week's articles, going through my intentions with a keen investigatory scalpel. Her talk always puts me in mind of a steel blade. Her writing became rapidly very good ; she had a wit and a turn of phrase that was all her own. We seemed to have forgotten the little shadow of embarrassment that had fallen over our last meeting. Everything seemed natural and easy between us in those days ; a little unconventional, but that made it all the brighter.

We developed something like a custom of walks, about once a week or so, and letters and notes became frequent. I won't pretend things were not keenly personal between us, but they had an air of being innocently mental. She used to call me 'Master' in our talks, a monstrous and engaging flattery, and I was inordinately proud to have her as my pupil. Who wouldn't have been? And we went on at that distance for a long time – until within a year of the Handitch election.

After Lady Colbeck threw her up as altogether too 'intellectual' for comfortable control, Isabel was taken up by the Balfes in a less formal and compromising manner, and week-ended with them and their cousin Leonora Sparling, and spent large portions of her summer with them in Hertfordshire. There was a lover or so in that time, men who came a little timidly at this brilliant young person with the frank manner and the Amazonian mind, and, she declared, received her kindly refusals with manifest relief. And Arnold Shoesmith struck up a sort of friendship that oddly imitated mine. She took a liking to him because he was clumsy and shy and inexpressive ; she embarked upon the dangerous interest of helping him to find his soul. I had some twinges of jealousy about that. I didn't see the necessity of him. He invaded her time, and I thought that might interfere with her work. If their friendship stole some hours from Isabel's writing, it did not for a long while interfere with our walks or our talks, or the close intimacy we had together.

4

Then suddenly Isabel and I found ourselves passionately in love.

The change came so entirely without warning or intention that I find it impossible now to tell the order of its phases. What disturbed pebble started the avalanche I cannot trace. Perhaps it was simply that the barriers between us and this masked aspect of life had been wearing down unperceived.

And there came a change in Isabel. It was like some change in the cycle of nature, like the onset of spring – a sharp brightness, an uneasiness. She became restless with her work; little encounters with men began to happen,. encounters not quite the quality of the earlier proposals ; and then came the odd incident of which she told me, but somehow, I felt, didn't tell me completely. She told me all she was able to tell me. She had been at a dance at the Ropers', and a man, rather well known in London, had kissed her. The thing amazed her beyond measure. It was the sort of thing immediately possible between any man and any woman, that one never expects to happen until it happens. It had the surprising effect of a judge generally known to be bald suddenly whipping off his wig in court. No absolutely unexpected revelation could have quite the same quality of shock. She went through the whole thing to me with a remarkable detachment, told me how she had felt – and the odd things it seemed to open to her.

'I *want* to be kissed, and all that sort of thing,' she avowed. 'I suppose every woman does.'

She added after a pause : 'And I don't want any one to do it.'

This struck me as queerly expressive of the woman's attitude to these things. 'Some one presently will – solve that,' I said.

'Some one will, perhaps.'

I was silent.

'Some one will,' she said, almost viciously. 'And then we'll have to stop these walks and talks of ours, dear Master. . . . I'll be sorry to give them up.'

'It's part of the requirements of the situation,' I said, 'that he should be – oh, very interesting! He'll start, no doubt, all sorts of new topics, and open no end of attractive vistas. . . . You can't, you know, always go about in a state of pupilage.'

'I don't think I can,' said Isabel. 'But it's only just recently I've begun to doubt about it.'

I remember these things being said, but just how much we saw and understood, and just how far we were really keeping opaque to each other then, I cannot remember. But it must have been quite soon after this that we spent nearly a whole day together at Kew Gardens, with the curtains up and the barriers down, and the thing that had happened plain before our eyes. I don't remember we ever made any declaration. We just assumed the new footing. . . .

It was a day early in the year – I think in January, because there was thin, crisp snow on the grass, and we noted that only two other people had been to the Pagoda that day. I've a curious impression of greenish colour, hot, moist air and huge palm fronds about very much of our talk, as though we were nearly all the time in the Tropical House. But I also remember very vividly looking at certain orange and red spraylike flowers from Patagonia, which could not have been there. It is a curious thing that I do not remember we made any profession of passionate love for one another; we talked as though the fact of our intense love for each other had always been patent between us. There was so long and frank an intimacy between us that we talked far more like brother and sister or husband and wife than two people engaged in the war of sexes. We wanted to know what we were going to do, and whatever we did we meant to do in the most perfect concert. We both felt an extraordinary accession of friendship and tenderness then, and, what again is curious, very little passion. But there was also, in spite of the perplexities we faced, an immense satisfaction about that day. It was as if we had taken off something that had hindered our view of each other, like people who unvizard to talk more easily at a masked ball.

I've had since to view our relations from the standpoint of the ordinary observer. I find that vision in the most preposterous contrast with all that really went on between us. I suppose there I should figure as a wicked seducer, while an unprotected girl succumbed to my fascinations. As a matter of fact, it didn't occur to us that there was any personal inequality between us. I knew her for my equal mentally ; in so many things she was beyond comparison cleverer than I; her courage outwent mine. The quick leap of her mind evoked a flash of joy in mine like the response of an induction wire ; her way of thinking was like watching sunlight reflected from little waves upon the side of a boat, it was so bright, so mobile, so variously and easily true to its law. In the back of our minds we both had a very definite belief that making love is full of joyous, splendid, tender, and exciting possibilities, and we had to discuss why we shouldn't be to the last degree lovers.

Now, what I would like to print here, if it were possible, in all the screaming emphasis of red ink, is this: that the circumstances of my upbringing and the circumstances of Isabel's upbringing had left not a shadow of belief or feeling that the utmost passionate love between us was in itself intrinsically *wrong*. I've told with the fullest particularity just all that I was taught or found out for myself in these matters, and Isabel's reading and thinking, and the fierce silences of her governesses and the breathless warnings of teachers, and all the social and religious influences that had been brought to bear upon her, had worked out to the same void of conviction. The code had failed with us altogether. We didn't for a moment consider anything but the expediency of what we both, for all our quiet faces and steady eyes, wanted most passionately to do.

Well, here you have the state of mind of whole brigades of people, and particularly of young people, nowadays. The current morality hasn't gripped them ; they don't really believe in it at all. They may render it lip-service, but that is quite another thing. There are scarcely any tolerable novels to justify its prohibitions ; its prohibitions do, in fact, remain unjustified

326

amongst these ugly suppressions. You may, if you choose, silence the admission of this in literature and current discussion; you will not prevent it working out in lives. People come up to the great moments of passion crudely unaware, astoundingly unprepared, as no really civilized and intelligently planned community would let any one be unprepared. They find themselves hedged about with customs that have no organic hold upon them, and mere discretions all generous spirits are disposed to despise.

Consider the infinite absurdities of it! Multitudes of us are trying to run this complex modern community on a basis of 'Hush' without explaining to our children or discussing with them anything about love and marriage at all. Doubt and knowledge creep about in enforced darknesses and silences. We are living upon an ancient tradition which everybody doubts and nobody has ever analyzed. We affect a tremendous and cultivated shyness and delicacy about imperatives of the most arbitrary appearance. What ensues? What did ensue with us, for example? On the one hand was a great desire, robbed of any appearance of shame and grossness by the power of love, and on the other hand the possible jealousy of so and so, the disapproval of so and so, material risks and dangers. It is only in the retrospect that we have been able to grasp something of the effectual case against us. The social prohibition lit by the intense glow of our passion presented itself as preposterous, irrational, arbitrary, and ugly, a monster fit only for mockery. We might be ruined! Well, there is a phase in every love-affair when death and ruin are agreeable additions to the prospect. It gives the business a gravity, a solemnity. Timid people may hesitate and draw back with a vague instinctive terror of the immensity of the oppositions they challenge, but neither Isabel nor I are timid people.

We weighed what was against us. We decided just exactly as scores of thousands of people have decided in this very matter, that if it were possible to keep this thing to ourselves, there was nothing against it. And so we took our first step. With the hunger of love in us, it was easy to conclude we might be lovers, and still keep everything to ourselves. That cleared our minds of the one persistent obstacle that mattered to us – the haunting presence of Margaret.

We took that step at last – with all the tremulous joy, the clean abandon, of lovers in Paradise.

And then we found, as all those scores of thousands of people scattered about us have found, that we could not keep it to ourselves. Love will out. All the rest of this story is the chronicle of that. Love with sustained secrecy cannot be love. It is just exactly the point people do not understand.

## 5

But before things came to that pass, some months and many phases and a sudden journey to America intervened.

'This thing spells disaster,' I said. 'You are too big and I am too big to attempt this secrecy. Think of the intolerable possibility of being found out! At any cost we have to stop – even at the cost of parting.'

'Just because we may be found out!'

'Just because we may be found out.'

There followed a struggle of immense insincerity between us. It is hard to tell who urged and who resisted.

I fled absurdly. That is the secret of the futile journey to America that puzzled all my friends.

I ran away from Isabel. I took hold of the situation with all my strength, put in Britten with sketchy, hasty instructions to edit the paper, and started headlong and with luggage, from which, among other things, my shaving things were omitted, upon a tour round the world.

Preposterous flight that was! I remember as a thing almost farcical my explanations to Margaret, and how frantically anxious I was to prevent the remote possibility of her coming with me, and how I crossed in the *Tuscan*, a bad, wet boat, and mixed seasickness and ungovernable sorrow. I wept – tears. It was inexpressibly queer and ridiculous – and, good God! how I hated my fellow-passengers!

New York inflamed and excited me for a time, and when things slackened, I whirled westward to Chicago – eating and drinking, I remember, in the train from shoals of little dishes, with a sort of desperate voracity. I did the queerest things to distract myself – no novelist would dare to invent my mental and emotional muddle. Chicago also held me at first, amazing lapse from civilization that the place is! and then abruptly, with hosts expecting me, and everything settled for some days in Denver, I found myself at the end of my renunciations, and turned and came back headlong to London.

Let me confess it wasn't any sense of perfect and incurable trust and confidence that brought me back, or any idea that now I had strength to refrain. It was a sudden realization that after all the separation might succeed; some careless phrasing in one of her jealously read letters set that idea going in my mind – the haunting perception that I might return to London and find it empty of the Isabel who had pervaded it. Honour, discretion, the careers of both of us, became nothing at the thought. I couldn't conceive my life resuming there without Isabel. I couldn't, in short, stand it.

I don't even excuse my return. It is inexcusable. I ought to have kept upon my way westward – and held out. I couldn't. I wanted Isabel, and I wanted her so badly now that everything else in the world was phantom-like until that want was satisfied. Perhaps you have never wanted anything like that. I went straight to her.

But here I come to untellable things. There is no describing the reality of love. The shapes of things are nothing, the actual happenings are nothing, except that somehow there falls a light upon them and a wonder. Of how we met, and the thrill of the adventure, the curious bright sense of defiance, the joy of having dared, I can't tell – I can but hint of just one aspect, of what an amazing *lark* – it's the only word – it seemed to us. The beauty which was the essence of it, which justifies it so far as it will bear justification, eludes statement.

What can a record of contrived meetings, of sundering difficulties evaded and overcome, signify here? Or what can it convey to say that one looked deep into two dear, steadfast eyes, or felt a heart throb and beat, or gripped soft hair softly in a trembling hand? Robbed of encompassing love, these things are of no more value than the taste of good wine or the sight of good pictures, or the hearing of music, – just sensuality and no more. No one can tell love – we can only tell the gross facts of love and its consequences. Given love – given mutuality, and one has effected a supreme synthesis and come to a new level of life – but only those who know can know. This business has brought me more bitterness and sorrow than I had ever expected to bear, but even now I will not say that I regret that wilful home-coming. We loved – to the uttermost. Neither of us could have loved any one else as we did and do love one another. It was ours, that beauty; it existed only between us when we were close together, for no one in the world ever to know save ourselves.

My return to the office sticks out in my memory with an extreme vividness, because of the wild eagle of pride that screamed within me. It was Tuesday morning, and though not a soul in London knew of it yet except Isabel, I had been back in England a week. I came in upon Britten and stood in the doorway.

'*God!*' he said at the sight of me.

'I'm back,' I said.

He looked at my excited face with those red-brown eyes of his. Silently I defied him to speak his mind.

'Where did you turn back?' he said at last.

6

I had to tell what were, so far as I can remember, my first positive lies to Margaret in explaining that return. I had written to her from Chicago and again from New York, saying that I felt I ought to be on the spot in England for the new session, and that I was coming back – presently. I concealed the name of my boat from her, and made a calculated prevarication when I announced my presence in London. I telephoned before I went back for my rooms to be prepared. She was, I knew, with the Bunting Harblows in Durham, and when she came back to Radnor Square I had been at home a day.

I remember her return so well.

My going away and the vivid secret of the present had wiped out from my mind much of our long estrangement. Something too, had changed in her. I had had some hint of it in her letters, but now I saw it plainly. I came out of my study upon the landing when I heard the turmoil of her arrival below, and she came upstairs with a quickened gladness. It was a cold March, and she was dressed in unfamiliar dark furs that suited her extremely and reinforced the delicate flush of her sweet face.

She held out both hands to me, and drew me to her unhesitatingly and kissed me.

'So glad you are back, dear,' she said. 'Oh! so very glad you are back.'

I returned her kiss with a queer feeling at my heart, too undifferentiated to be even a definite sense of guilt or meanness. I think it was chiefly amazement – at the universe – at myself.

'I never knew what it was to be away from you,' she said.

I perceived suddenly that she had resolved to end our estrangement. She put herself so that my arm came caressingly about her.

'These are jolly furs,' I said.

'I got them for you.'

The parlourmaid appeared below, dealing with the maid and the luggage cab.

'Tell me all about America,' said Margaret. 'I feel as though you'd been away six years.'

We went arm-in-arm into her little sitting room, and I took off the furs for her and sat down upon the chintz-covered sofa by the fire. She had ordered tea, and came and sat by me. I don't know what I had expected, but of all things I had certainly not expected this sudden abolition of our distances.

'I want to know all about America,' she repeated, with her eyes scrutinizing me. 'Why did you come back?'

I repeated the substance of my letters rather lamely, and she sat listening.

'But why did you turn back – without going to Denver?'

'I wanted to come back. I was restless.'

'Restlessness,' she said, and thought. 'You were restless in Venice. You said it was restlessness took you to America.'

Again she studied me. She turned a little awkwardly to her tea-things, and poured needless water from the silver kettle into the teapot. Then she sat still for some moments looking at the equipage with expressionless eyes. I saw her hand upon the edge of the table tremble slightly. I watched her closely. A vague uneasiness possessed me. What might she not know or guess?

She spoke at last with an effort. 'I wish you were in Parliament again,' she said. 'Life doesn't give you events enough.'

'If I was in Parliament again, I should be on the Conservative side.'

'I know,' she said, and was still more thoughtful.

'Lately,' she began, and paused. 'Lately I've been reading – you.'

I didn't help her out with what she had to say. I waited.

'I didn't understand what you were after. I had misjudged. I didn't know. I think perhaps I was rather stupid.' Her eyes were suddenly shining with tears. 'You didn't give me much chance to understand.'

She turned upon me suddenly with a voice full of tears.

'Husband,' she said abruptly, holding her two hands out to me, 'I want to begin over again!'

I took her hands, perplexed beyond measure. 'My dear!' I said.

'I want to begin over again.'

I bowed my head to hide my face, and found her hand in mine and kissed it.

'Ah!' she said, and slowly withdrew her hand. She leant forward with her arm on the sofa-back, and looked very intently into my face. I felt the most damnable scoundrel in the world as I returned her gaze. The thought of Isabel's darkly shining eyes seemed like a physical presence between us. . . .

'Tell me,' I said presently, to break the intolerable tension, 'tell me plainly what you mean by this.'

I sat a little away from her, and then took my teacup in hand, with an odd effect of defending myself. 'Have you been reading that old book of mine?' I asked.

'That and the paper. I took a complete set from the beginning down to Durham with me. I have read it over, thought it over. I didn't understand – what you were teaching.'

There was a little pause.

'It all seems so plain to me now,' she said, 'and so true.'

I was profoundly disconcerted. I put down my tea-cup, stood up in the middle of the hearthrug, and began talking. 'I'm tremendously glad, Margaret, that you've come to see I'm not altogether perverse,' I began. I launched out into a rather trite and windy exposition of my views, and she sat close to me on the sofa, looking up into my face, hanging on my words, a deliberate and invincible convert.

'Yes,' she said, 'yes'. . . .

I had never doubted my new conceptions before; now I doubted them profoundly. But I went on talking. It's the grim irony in the lives of all politicians, writers, public teachers, that once the audience is at their feet, a new loyalty has gripped them. It isn't their business to admit doubts and imperfections. They have to go on talking. And I was now so accustomed to Isabel's vivid interruptions, qualifications, restatements, and confirmations. . . .

Margaret and I dined together at home. She made me open out my political projects to her. 'I have been foolish,' she said. 'I want to help.'

And by some excuse I have forgotten she made me come to her room. I think it was some book I had to take her, some American book I had brought back with me, and mentioned in our talk. I walked in with it, and put it down on the table and turned to go.

'Husband!' she cried, and held out her slender arms to me. I was compelled to go to her and kiss her, and she twined them softly about my neck and drew me to her and kissed me. I disentangled them very gently, and took each wrist and kissed it, and the backs of her hands.

'Good night,' I said. There came a little pause. 'Good night, Margaret,' I repeated, and walked very deliberately and with a kind of sham preoccupation to the door.

I did not look at her, but I could feel her standing, watching me. If I had looked up, she would, I knew, have held out her arms to me. . . .

At the very outset that secret, which was to touch no one but Isabel and myself, had reached out to stab another human being.


# 7

The whole world had changed for Isabel and me; and we tried to pretend that nothing had changed except a small matter between us. We believed quite honestly at that time that it was possible to keep this thing that had happened from any reaction at all, save perhaps through some magically enhanced vigour in our work, upon the world about us! Seen in retrospect, one can realize the absurdity of this belief; within a week I realized it; but that doesn't alter the fact that we did believe as much, and that people who are deeply in love and unable to marry will continue to believe so to the very end of time. They will continue to believe out of existence every consideration that separates them until they have come together. Then they will count the cost, as we two had to do.

I am telling a story, and not propounding theories in this book; and chiefly I am telling of the ideas and influences and emotions that have happened to me – me as a sort of sounding-board for my world. The moralist is at liberty to go over my conduct with his measure and say, 'At this point or that you went wrong, and you ought to have done' – so-and-so. The point of interest to the statesman is that it didn't for a moment occur to us to do so-and-so when the time for doing it came. It amazes me now to think how little either of us troubled about the established rights or wrongs of the situation. We hadn't an atom of respect for them, innate or acquired. The guardians of public morals will say we were very bad people; I submit in defence that they are very bad guardians – provocative guardians. . . . And when at last there came a claim against us that had an effective validity for us, we were in the full tide of passionate intimacy.

I had a night of nearly sleepless perplexity after Margaret's return. She had suddenly presented herself to me like something dramatically recalled, fine, generous, infinitely capable of feeling. I was amazed how much I had forgotten her. In my contempt for vulgarized and conventionalized honour I had forgotten that for me there was such a reality as honour. And here it was, warm and near to me, living, breathing, unsuspecting. Margaret's pride was my honour, that I had had no right even to imperil.

I do not now remember if I thought at that time of going to Isabel and putting this new aspect of the case before her. Perhaps I did. Perhaps I may have considered even then the possibility of ending what had so freshly and passionately begun. If I did, it vanished next day at the sight of her. Whatever regrets came in the darkness, the daylight brought an obstinate confidence in our resolution again. We would, we declared, 'pull the thing off'. Margaret must not know. Margaret should not know.

334

If Margaret did not know, then no harm whatever would be done. We tried to sustain that. . . .

For a brief time we had been like two people in a magic cell, magically cut off from the world and full of a light of its own, and then we began to realize that we were not in the least cut off, that the world was all about us and pressing in upon us, limiting us, threatening us, resuming possession of us. I tried to ignore the injury to Margaret of her unreciprocated advances. I tried to maintain to myself that this hidden love made no difference to the now irreparable breach between husband and wife. But I never spoke of it to Isabel or let her see that aspect of our case. How could I? The time for that had gone. . . .

Then in new shapes and relations came trouble. Distasteful elements crept in by reason of our unavoidable furtiveness ; we ignored them, hid them from each other, and attempted to hide them from ourselves. Successful love is a thing of abounding pride, and we had to be secret. It was delightful at first to be secret, a whispering, warm conspiracy, then presently it became irksome and a little shameful. Her essential frankness of soul was all against the masks and falsehoods that many women would have enjoyed. Together in our secrecy we relaxed, then in the presence of other people again it was tiresome to have to watch for the careless, too easy phrase, to snatch back one's hand from the limitless betrayal of a light, familiar touch.

Love becomes a poor thing, at best a poor beautiful thing, if it develops no continuing and habitual intimacy. We were always meeting, and most gloriously loving and beginning – and then we had to snatch at remorselessly ticking watches, hurry to catch trains, and go back to this or that. That is all very well for the intrigues of idle people, perhaps, but not for an intense personal relationship. It is like lighting a candle for the sake of lighting it, over and over again, and each time blowing it out. That, no doubt, must be very amusing to children playing with the matches, but not to people who love warm light, and want it in order to do fine and honourable things together. We had achieved – I give the ugly phrase that expresses the increasing discoloration in my mind – 'illicit intercourse'. To end at that, we now perceived, wasn't in our style. But where were we to end? . . .

Perhaps we might at this stage have given it up. I think if we could have seen ahead and around us we might have done so. But the glow of our cell blinded us. . . . I wonder what might have happened if at that time we had given it up? . . . We propounded it, we met again in secret to discuss it, and our overpowering passion for one another reduced that meeting to absurdity. . . .

Presently the idea of children crept between us. It came in from all our conceptions of life and public service; it was, we found, in the quality of our minds that physical love without children is a little weak, timorous, more than a little shameful. With imaginative people there very speedily comes a time when it is impossible for that to go on. We hadn't thought of that before – it isn't natural to think of that before. We hadn't known. There is no literature in English dealing with such things.

There is a necessary sequence of phases in love. These came in their order, and with them, unanticipated tarnishings on the first bright perfection of our relations. For a time these developing phases were no more than a secret and private trouble between us, little shadows spreading by imperceptible degrees across that vivid and luminous cell.


8

The Handitch election flung me suddenly into prominence.

It is still only two years since that struggle, and I will not trouble the reader with a detailed history of events that must be quite sufficiently present in his mind for my purpose already. Huge stacks of journalism have dealt with Handitch and its significance. For the reader very probably, as for most people outside a comparatively small circle, it meant my emergence from obscurity. We obtruded no editor's name in the *Blue Weekly*; I had never as yet been on the London hoardings. Before Handitch I was a journalist and writer of no great public standing; after Handitch, I was definitely a person, in the little group of persons who stood for the Young Imperialist movement. Handitch was, to a very large extent, my affair. I realized then, as a man comes to do, how much one can still grow after seven and twenty. In the second election I was a man taking hold of things; at Kinghamstead I had been simply a young candidate, a party unit, led about the constituency,

336

told to do this and that, and finally washed in by the great Anti-Imperialist flood, like a starfish rolling up a beach.

My feminist views had earnt the mistrust of the party, and I do not think I should have got the chance of Handitch or indeed any chance at all of Parliament for a long time, if it had not been that the seat with its long record of Liberal victories and its Liberal majority of 3642 at the last election, offered a hopeless contest. The Liberal dissensions and the belated but by no means contemptible Socialist candidate were providential interpositions. I think, however, the conduct of Gane, Crupp, and Tarville in coming down to fight for me did count tremendously in my favour. 'We aren't going to win, perhaps,' said Crupp, 'but we are going to talk.' And until the every eve of victory, we treated Handitch not so much as a battlefield as a hoarding. And so it was the Endowment of Motherhood as a practical form of Eugenics got into English politics.

Plutus, our agent, was scared out of his wits when the thing began.

'They're ascribing all sorts of queer ideas to you about the Family,' he said.

'I think the Family exists for the good of the children,' I said ; 'is that queer?'

'Not when you explain it – but they won't let you explain it. And about marriage –?'

'I'm all right about marriage – trust me.'

'Of course, if *you* had children,' said Plutus, rather inconsiderately. . . .

They opened fire upon me in a little electioneering rag called the *Handitch Sentinel,* with a string of garbled quotations and misrepresentations that gave me an admirable text for a speech. I spoke for an hour and ten minutes with a more and more crumpled copy of the *Sentinel* in my hand and I made the fullest and completest exposition of the idea of endowing motherhood that I think had ever been made up to that time in England. Its effect on the press was extraordinary. The Liberal papers gave me quite unprecedented space under the impression that I had only to be given rope to hang myself; the Conservatives cut me down or tried to justify me ; the whole country was talking. I had had a pamphlet in type upon the subject, and I revised this carefully and put it on the bookstalls

337

within three days. It sold enormously and brought me bushels of letters. We issued over three thousand in Handitch alone. At meeting after meeting I was heckled upon nothing else. Long before polling day Plutus was converted.

'It's catching on like old age pensions,' he said. 'We've dished the Liberals! To think that such a project should come from our side!'

But it was only with the declaration of the poll that my battle was won. No one expected more than a snatch victory, and I was in by over fifteen hundred. At one bound Cossington's papers passed from apologetics varied by repudiation to triumphant praise. 'A renascent England, breeding men,' said the leader in his chief daily on the morning after the polling, and claimed that the Conservatives had been ever the pioneers in sanely bold constructive projects.

I came up to London with a weary but rejoicing Margaret by the night train.

## Chapter the Second

# The Impossible Position

## 1

To any one who did not know of that glowing secret between Isabel and myself, I might well have appeared at that time the most successful and enviable of men. I had recovered rapidly from an uncongenial start in political life; I had become a considerable force through the *Blue Weekly*, and was shaping an increasingly influential body of opinion ; I had re-entered Parliament with quite dramatic distinction, and in spite of a certain faltering on the part of the orthodox Conservatives towards the bolder elements in our propaganda, I had loyal and unenvious associates who were making me a power in the party. People were coming to our group, understandings were developing. It was clear we should play a prominent part in the next general election, and that, given a Conservative victory, I should be assured of office. The world opened out to me brightly and invitingly. Great schemes took shape in my mind, always more concrete, always more practicable ; the years ahead seemed falling into order, shining with the credible promise of immense achievement.

And at the heart of it all, unseen and unsuspected, was the secret of my relations with Isabel – like a seed that germinates and thrusts, thrusts relentlessly.

From the onset of the Handitch contest onward, my meetings with her had been more and more pervaded by the discussion of our situation. It had innumerable aspects. It was very present to us that we wanted to be together as much as possible – we were beginning to long very much for actual living together in the same house, so that one could come as it were carelessly – unawares – upon the other, busy perhaps about some trivial thing. We wanted to feel each other in the daily atmosphere. Preceding our imperatively sterile passion, you must remember, outside it, altogether greater than it so far as our individual lives were concerned, there had grown and still grew an enormous affection and intellectual sympathy between us. We brought all our impressions and all our ideas to each other, to see them in each other's light. It is hard to convey that quality of intellectual unison to any one who has not experienced it. I thought more and more in terms of conversation with Isabel; her possible comments upon things would flash into my mind, oh! – with the very sound of her voice.

I remember, too, the odd effect of seeing her in the distance going about Handitch, like any stranger canvasser; the queer emotion of her approach along the street, the greeting as she passed. The morning of the polling she vanished from the constituency. I saw her for an instant in the passage behind our Committee rooms.

'Going?' said I.

She nodded.

'Stay it out. I want you to see the fun. I remember – the other time.'

She didn't answer for a moment or so, and stood with face averted.

'It's Margaret's show,' she said abruptly. 'If I see her smiling there like a queen by your side –! She did – last time. I remember.' She caught at a sob, and dashed her hand across her face impatiently. 'Jealous fool, mean and petty, jealous fool! . . . Good luck, old man, to you! You're going to win. But I don't want to see the end of it, all the same. . . .'

'Good-bye!' said I, clasping her hand as some supporter appeared in the passage. . . .

I came back to London victorious, and a little flushed and coarse with victory; and so soon as I could break away I went to Isabel's flat and found her white and worn, with the stain of secret weeping about her eyes. I came into the room to her and shut the door.

'You said I'd win,' I said, and held out my arms.

She hugged me closely for a moment.

'My dear,' I whispered, 'it's nothing – without you – nothing!'

We didn't speak for some seconds. Then she slipped from my hold. 'Look!' she said, smiling like winter sunshine. 'I've had in all the morning papers – the pile of them, and you – resounding.'

'It's more than I dared hope.'

'Or I.'

She stood for a moment still smiling bravely, and then she was sobbing in my arms. 'The bigger you are – the more you show,' she said – 'the more we are parted. I know, I know –'

I held her close to me, making no answer.

Presently she became still. 'Oh, well,' she said, and wiped her eyes and sat down on the little sofa by the fire ; and I sat down beside her.

'I didn't know all there was in love,' she said, staring at the coals, 'when we went love-making.'

I put my arm behind her and took a handful of her dear soft hair in my hand and kissed it.

'You've done a great thing this time,' she said. 'Handitch will make you.'

'It opens big chances,' I said. 'But why are you weeping, dear one?'

'Envy,' she said, 'and love.'

'You're not lonely?'

'I've plenty to do – and lots of people.'

'Well?'

'I want you.'

'You've got me.'

She put her arm about me and kissed me. 'I want you,' she said, 'just as if I had nothing of you. You don't understand – how a woman wants a man. I thought once if I just gave myself to you it would be enough. It was nothing – it was just a step across the threshold. My dear, every moment you are away I ache for you – ache! I want to be about when it isn't love-making or talk. I want to be doing things for you, and watching you when you're not thinking of me. All those safe, careless, intimate things. And something else –' she stopped. 'Dear, I don't want to bother you. I just want you to know I love you. . . .

She caught my head in her hands and kissed it, then stood up abruptly.

I looked up at her, a little perplexed.

'Dear heart,' said I, 'isn't this enough? You're my counsellor, my colleague, my right hand, the secret soul of my life —'

'And I want to darn your socks,' she said, smiling back at me.

'You're insatiable.'

She smiled. 'No,' she said. 'I'm not insatiable, Master. But I'm a woman in love. And I'm finding out what I want, and want is necessary to me – and what I can't have. That's all.'

'We get a lot.'

'We want a lot. You and I are greedy people for the things we like. It's very evident we've got nearly all we can ever have of one another – and I'm not satisfied.'

'What more is there?'

'For you – very little. I wonder. For me – everything. Yes – everything. You didn't mean it; you didn't know any more than I did when I began, but love between a man and a woman is sometimes very one-sided. Fearfully one-sided! That's all. . . .'

'Don't *you* ever want children?' she said abruptly.

'I suppose I do.'

'You don't!'

'I haven't thought of them.'

'A man doesn't, perhaps. But I have. . . . I want them – like hunger. *Your* children, and home with you. Really, continually you! That's the trouble. . . . I can't have 'em, and I can't have you.'

She was crying, and through her tears she laughed.

'I'm going to make a scene,' she said, 'and get this over. I'm so discontented and miserable; I've got to tell you. It would come between us if I didn't. I'm in love with you, with every-thing – with all my brains. I'll pull through all right. I'll be good, never you fear. But today I'm crying out with all my being. This election – You're going up; you're going on. In these papers – you're a great big fact. It's suddenly come home to me. At the back of my mind I've always had the idea I was going to have you somehow presently for myself – I mean to have you to go long tramps with, to keep house for, to get meals for, to watch for of an evening. It's a sort of habitual background to my thought of you. And it's nonsense – utter nonsense!' She stopped. She was crying and choking. 'And the child, you know – the child!'

I was troubled beyond measure, but Handitch and its intimations were clear and strong.

'We can't have that,' I said.

'No,' she said, 'we can't have that.'

'We've got our own things to do.'

'*Your* things,' she said.

'Aren't they yours too?'

'Because of you,' she said.

'Aren't they your very own things?'

'Women don't have that sort of very own thing. Indeed, it's true! And think! You've been down there preaching the goodness of children, telling them the only good thing in a state is happy, hopeful children, working to free mothers and children –'

'And we give our own children to do it?' I said.

'Yes,' she said. 'And sometimes I think it's too much to give – too much altogether. . . . Children get into a woman's brain – when she mustn't have them, especially when she must never hope for them. Think of the child we might have now! – the little creature with soft, tender skin, and little hands and little feet! At times it haunts me. It comes and says, Why wasn't I given life? I can hear it in the night. . . . The world is full of such little ghosts, dear lover – little things that asked for life and were refused. They clamour to me. It's like a little fist beating at my heart. Love children, beautiful children. Little cold hands that tear at my heart! Oh, my heart and my lord!' She was holding my arm with both her hands and weeping against it, and now she drew herself to my shoulder and wept and sobbed in my embrace. 'I shall never sit with your child on my knee and you beside me – never, and I am a woman and your lover! . . .'

2

But the profound impossibility of our relation was now becoming more and more apparent to us. We found ourselves seeking justification, clinging passionately to a situation that was coldly, pitilessly impossible and fated. We wanted quite intensely to live together and have a child, but also we wanted very many other things that were incompatible with these

343

desires. It was extraordinarily difficult to weigh our political and intellectual ambitions against those intimate wishes. The weights kept altering according as one found oneself grasping this valued thing or that. It wasn't as if we could throw everything aside for our love, and have that as we wanted it. Love such as we bore one another isn't altogether, or even chiefly, a thing in itself – it is for the most part a value set upon things. Our love was interwoven with all our other interests; to go out of the world and live in isolation seemed to us like killing the best parts of each other; we loved the sight of each other engaged finely and characteristically, we knew each other best as activities. We had no delusions about material facts; we didn't want each other alive or dead, we wanted each other fully alive. We wanted to do big things together, and for us to take each other openly and desperately would leave us nothing in the world to do. We wanted children indeed passionately, but children with every helpful chance in the world, and children born in scandal would be handicapped at every turn. We wanted to share a home and not a solitude.

And when we were at this stage of realization, began the intimations that we were found out, and that scandal was afoot against us. . . .

I heard of it first from Esmeer, who deliberately mentioned it, with that steady grey eye of his watching me, as an instance of the preposterous falsehoods people will circulate. It came to Isabel almost simultaneously through a married college friend, who made it her business to demand either confirmation or denial. It filled us both with consternation. In the surprise of the moment Isabel admitted her secret, and her friend went off 'reserving her freedom of action.'

Discovery broke out in every direction. Friends with grave faces and an atmosphere of infinite tact invaded us both. Other friends ceased to invade either of us. It was manifest we had become – we knew not how – a private scandal, a subject for duologues, an amazement, a perplexity, a vivid interest. In a few brief weeks it seemed London passed from absolute unsuspiciousness to a chattering exaggeration of its knowledge of our relations.

It was just the most inappropriate time for that disclosure. The long smouldering antagonism to my endowment of motherhood ideas had flared up into an active campaign in the *Expurgator*, and it would be altogether disastrous to us if I should be convicted of any personal irregularity. It was just because of the manifest and challenging respectability of my position that I had been able to carry the thing as far as I had done. Now suddenly my fortunes had sprung a leak, and scandal was pouring in. . . . It chanced, too, that a wave of moral intolerance was sweeping through London, one of those waves in which the bitterness of the consciously just finds an ally in the panic of the undiscovered. A certain Father Blodgett had been preaching against social corruption with extraordinary force, and had roused the Church of England people to a kind of competition in denunciation. The old methods of the Anti-Socialist campaign had been renewed and had offered far too wide a scope and too tempting an opportunity for private animosity to be restricted to the private affairs of the Socialists. I had intimations of an extensive circulation of 'private and confidential' letters. . . .

I think there can be nothing else in life quite like the unnerving realization that rumour and scandal are afoot about one. Abruptly one's confidence in the solidity of the universe disappears. One walks silenced through a world that one feels to be full of inaudible accusations. One cannot challenge the assault, get it out into the open, separate truth and falsehood. It slinks from you, turns aside its face. Old acquaintances suddenly evaded me, made extraordinary excuses; men who had presumed on the verge of my world and pestered me with an intrusive enterprise, now took the bold step of flat repudiation. I became doubtful about the return of a nod, retracted all those tentacles of easy civility that I had hitherto spread to the world. I still grow warm with amazed indignation when I recall that Edward Crampton, meeting me full on the steps of the Climax Club, cut me dead. 'By God!' I cried, and came near catching him by the throat and wringing out of him what, of all good deeds and bad, could hearten him, a younger man than I and empty beyond comparison, to dare to play the judge to me. And then I had an open slight from Mrs Millingham, whom I had counted on as one counts upon the sunrise. I had not expected things of that sort; they were disconcerting beyond measure; it was as if the world were giving way beneath my feet, as though something failed in the essential confidence of life, as though a hand of wet ice had touched my heart. Similar things were happening to Isabel. Yet we went on, working, visiting, meeting, trying to ignore this gathering of im-implacable forces against us.

For a time I was perplexed beyond measure to account for this campaign. I went about watchful, alert, raging internally. I suspected everyone. For a time, I will confess, I turned my thoughts to Altiora Bailey. There was a certain reason in that. The Baileys had never forgiven me my abandonment of the Young Liberal group they had done so much to inspire and organize ; their dinner-table had long been a scene of hostile depreciation of the *Blue Weekly* and all its allies ; week after week Altiora proclaimed that I was 'doing nothing,' and found other causes for our by-election triumphs ; I counted Chambers Street a dangerous place for me. Always I had been a wasp in their spider's web, difficult to claim as a tool, critical, antag-onistic. I admired their work and devotion enormously, but I had never concealed my contempt for a certain childish vanity they displayed, and for the frequent puerility of their political intrigues. Yet it scarcely seemed consistent with a certain gal-lantry in Altiora's character that she should use a private scandal against me.

Then with a real feeling of relief towards her, I came upon the culprits, the Booles, those queer rivals and allies and under-studies of the Baileys. It was odd I didn't think of the Booles from the outset, but I didn't. Counting on a certain physical resemblance to Altiora, Mrs Boole had set herself quite deliber-ately to plagiarize her success, and had contrived the oddest duplication. It is one of the penalties of success, this usurpation of a personality, and Mrs Boole managed to carry it even to a similarity of intonation and a travesty of Altiora's relations to her husband. But she had none of that largeness of mind one admired in Altiora ; she was a vulgar careerist aiming only at prominence, and perhaps her best quality was a real unreason-ing devotion to what she imagined were her great exemplar's interests. She felt no doubt that what injured Altiora must necessarily injure her. And these Booles, more galled by my manifest disregard of Baileyism than the Baileys could ever have been, set themselves industriously with all the loyalty of parasites to disseminate a highly coloured scandal against me. It was almost entirely their doing, I am persuaded; at the worst the Baileys were guilty only of a passive acquiescence. But the Booles certainly needed no help. Boole, I found, was warning fathers of girls against me as a 'reckless libertine,' and his wife, flushed, roguish, and dishevelled, was sitting on her fender curb after dinner, and pledging little parties of five or six women at a time with infinite gusto not to let the matter go further. Our cell was open to the world, and a bleak, distressful daylight streaming in.

I had a gleam of a more intimate motive in Mrs Boole from the reports that came to me. Isabel had been doing a series of five or six articles in the *Political Review* in support of our campaign, the *Political Review* which had hitherto been loyally Baileyite. Quite her best writing up to the present, at any rate, is in those papers, and no doubt the Baileyites had had not only to read her in those invaded columns, but listen to her praises in the mouths of the tactless influential. Mrs Boole is a person of literary ambitions herself, but she writes a poor and slovenly prose and handles an argument badly ; the literary gift even of Altiora is not above criticism, and Isabel has her University training behind her and wrote from the first with the stark power of a clear-headed man. 'Now we know,' said Mrs Boole on her curb, with just a gleam of malice showing through her brightness, 'now we know who helps with the writing !'

She revealed astonishing knowledge.

For a time I couldn't for the life of me discover her sources. I had, indeed, a desperate intention of challenging her, and then I bethought me of a youngster named Curmain, who had been my supplementary typist and secretary for a time, and whom I had sent on to her before the days of our breach. 'Of course !' said I, 'Curmain !' He was a tall, drooping, sidelong youth with sandy hair, a little forward head, and a long thin neck. He stole stamps, and, I suspected, rifled my private letter drawer, and I found him one day on a turn of the stairs looking guilty and ruffled with a pretty Irish housemaid of Margaret's manifestly in a state of hot indignation. I saw nothing, but I felt everything in the air between them. I hate this pestering of servants, but at the same time I didn't want Curmain wiped out of existence, so I had packed him off without unnecessary discussion to Mrs Boole. I had intended him for Altiora at first. Mrs Boole came in as an afterthought. He was quick and cheap, anyhow, and I thought Altiora's general austerity ought to redeem him if anything could ; the Chambers Street housemaid wasn't for any man's kissing and showed it, and the stamps and private letters were looked after with an efficiency altogether surpassing mine. But alas! he fell to Mrs Boole – I didn't reflect on what the difference meant – and she, I've no doubt left now whatever, pumped this young undesirable about me, and scenting a story, had him to dinner alone one evening to get to the bottom of the matter. She got quite to the bottom of it, – it must have been a queer duologue. She read Isabel's careless, intimate letters to me, so to speak, by this proxy, and she wasn't ashamed to use this information in the service of the bitterness that had sprung up in her since my political breach with the people to whom she had attached herself. It was essentially a personal bitterness ; it helped no public purpose of theirs to get rid of me. My downfall in any public sense was sheer waste, – the loss of a man. She knew she was behaving badly, and so, when it came to remonstrance, she behaved worse. She'd got names and dates and places; the efficiency of her information was irresistible. And she set to work at it marvellously. Never, in all her pursuit of efficient ideals, had Altiora achieved such levels of efficiency as her understudy attained in this pursuit. I wrote a protest that was perhaps ill-advised and angry. I went to her and tried to stop her. The woman wouldn't listen, she wouldn't think, she denied and lied, she behaved like a naughty child of six years old which has made up its mind to be hurtful. It wasn't only, I think, that she couldn't bear our political and social influence ; she also – I realized at that interview – couldn't bear our loving. It seemed to her the sickliest thing, – a thing quite unendurable. While such things were, the virtue had gone out of her world.

'I've the vividest memory of that call of mine. She'd just come in and taken off her hat, and she was grey and dishevelled and tired, and in a business-like dress of black and crimson, a frank adoption of Altiora's colours, that didn't suit her and was muddy about the skirts. She'd a cold in her head and sniffed

348

penetratingly; she avoided my eye as she talked and interrupted everything I had to say; she kept stabbing fiercely at the cushions of her sofa with a long hat-pin and pretending she was overwhelmed with grief at the *débâcle* she was deliberately organizing.

'Then part,' she cried, 'part. If you don't want a smashing up, – part! You two have got to be parted. You've got never to see each other ever, never to speak.' There was a zest in her voice. 'We're not circulating stories,' she denied. 'No! And Curmain never told us anything – Curmain is an *excellent* young man ; oh! a quite excellent young man. You misjudged him altogether.' . . .

I was equally unsuccessful with Boole. I caught the little wretch in the League Club, and he wriggled and lied. He tried to get past me as though he hadn't seen me. He wouldn't say where he had got his facts, he wouldn't admit he had told any one. When I gave him the names of two men who had come to me astonished and incredulous, he attempted absurdly to make me think they had told *him*. He did his horrible little best to suggest that honest old Quackett, who had just left England for the Cape, was the real scandal-monger. That struck me as mean, even for Boole. I've still the odd vivid impression of his fluting voice, excusing the inexcusable, his big, shifty face evading me, his perspiration-beaded forehead, the shrugging shoulders, and the would-be exculpatory gestures – Houndsditch gestures – of his enormous ugly hands.

'I can assure you, my dear fellow,' he lisped ; 'I can assure you we've done everything to shield you – everything.' . . .

3

Isabel came after dinner one evening and talked in the office. She made a white-robed, dusky figure against the deep blues of my big window. I sat at my desk and tore a quill pen to pieces as I talked.

'The Booles don't intend to let this drop,' I said. 'They mean that everyone in London is to know about it.'

'I know.'

'Well!' I said.

'Dear heart,' said Isabel, facing it, 'it's no good waiting for things to overtake us; we're at the parting of the ways.'

'What are we to do?'

'They won't let us go on.'

'Damn them! To be separated by people like that!'

'They are *organizing* scandal.'

'It's no good waiting for things to overtake us,' I echoed; 'they have overtaken us.' I turned on her. 'What do you want to do?'

'Everything,' she said. 'Keep you and have our work. Aren't we Mates?'

'We can't.'

'And we can't!'

'I've got to tell Margaret,' I said.

'Margaret!'

'I can't bear the idea of anyone else getting in front with it. I've been wincing about Margaret secretly—'

'I know. You'll have to tell her. Yes. . . .'

She leant back against the bookcases under the window.

'We've had some good times, Master,' she said, with a sigh in her voice.

And then for a long time we stared at one another in silence.

'We haven't much time left,' she said.

'Shall we bolt?' I said.

'And leave all this?' she asked, with her eyes going round the room. 'And that?' And her head indicated Westminster. 'No!'

I said no more of bolting.

'We've got to screw ourselves up to surrender,' she said.

'Something.'

'A lot.'

'Master,' she said, 'it isn't all sex and stuff between us?'

'No!'

'I can't give up the work. Our work's my life.'

We came upon another long pause.

'No one will believe we've ceased to be lovers – if we simply do,' she said.

'We shouldn't.'

'We've got to do something more parting than that. We've got to part – part thoroughly, openly, finally.'

350

I nodded, and again we paused. She was coming to something.

'I could marry Shoesmith,' she said abruptly.

'But—' I objected.

'He knows. It wasn't fair. I told him.'

'Oh, that explains,' I said. 'There's been a kind of sulkiness—But – you told him?'

She nodded. 'He's rather badly hurt,' she said. 'He's been a good friend to me. He's curiously loyal. But something, something he said one day – forced me to let him know. . . . That's been the beastliness of all this secrecy. That's the beastliness of all secrecy. You have to spring surprises on people. But he keeps on. He's steadfast. He'd already suspected. He wants me very badly to marry him. . . .'

'But you don't want to marry him?'

'I'm forced to think of it.'

'But does he want to marry you at that? Take you as a present from the world at large? – against your will and desire? . . . I don't understand him.'

'He cares for me.'

'How?'

'He thinks this is a fearful mess for me. He wants to pull it straight.'

We sat for a time in silence, with imaginations that obstinately refused to take up the realities of this proposition.

'I don't want you to marry Shoesmith,' I said at last.

'Don't you like him?'

'No.'

'He's a very clever and sturdy person – and very generous and devoted to me.'

'And me?'

'You can't expect that. He thinks you are wonderful – and, naturally, that you ought not to have started this.'

'I've a curious dislike to anyone thinking that but myself. I'm quite ready to think it myself.'

'He'd let us be friends – and see each other at times.'

'Let us be friends!' I cried, after a long pause. 'You and me!'

'He wants me to be engaged soon. He wants our parting to be clear and conclusive. Then, he says, he can go round fighting these rumours, defending us both -- and force a quarrel on the Booles.'

'I don't understand him,' I said, and added, 'I don't understand you.'

I was staring at her face. It seemed white and set in the dimness.

'Do you really mean this, Isabel?' I asked.

'What else is there to do, my dear? – what else is there to do at all? I've been thinking day and night. You can't go away with me. You can't smash youself suddenly in the sight of all men. I'd rather die than that should happen. Look what you are becoming in the county! Look at all you've built up! – me helping. I wouldn't let you do it if you could. I wouldn't let you – if it were only for Margaret's sake. *This* . . . closes the scandal, closes everything.'

'It closes all our life together,' I cried.

She was silent.

'It never ought to have begun,' I said.

She winced. Then abruptly she was on her knees before me, with her hands upon my shoulder and her eyes meeting mine.

'My dear,' she said very earnestly, 'don't misunderstand me! Don't think I'm retreating from the things we've done! Our love is the best thing I could ever have had from life. Nothing can ever equal it ; nothing could ever equal the beauty and delight you and I have had together. Never! You have loved me ; you do love me. . . .

'No one could ever know how to love you as I have loved you ; no one could ever love me as you have loved me, my king. And it's just because it's been so splendid, dear ; it's just because I'd die rather than have a tithe of all this wiped out of my life again – for it's made me, it's all I am – dear, it's years since I began loving you – it's just because of its goodness that I want not to end in wreckage now, not to end in the smashing up of all the big things I understand in you and love in you. . . .

'What is there for us if we keep on and go away?' she went on. 'All the big interests in our lives will vanish – everything. We shall become specialized people – people overshadowed by a situation. We shall be an elopement, a romance – all our breadth and meaning gone! People will always think of it first when they think of us ; all our work and aims will be warped by it and subordinated to it. Is it good enough, dear? Just to specialize. ... I think of you. We've got a case, a passionate case, the best of cases, but do we want to spend all our lives defending it and justifying it? And there's that other life. I know now you care for Margaret – you care more than you think you do. You have said fine things of her. I've watched you about her. Little things have dropped from you. She's given her life for you ; she's nothing without you. You feel that to your marrow all the time you are thinking about these things. Oh, I'm not jealous, dear. I love you for loving her. I love you in relation to her. But there it is, an added weight against us, another thing worth saving.'

Presently, I remember, she sat back on her heels and looked up into my face. 'We've done wrong – and parting's paying. It's time to pay. We needn't have paid, if we'd kept to the track. ... You and I, Master, we've got to be men.'

'Yes,' I said ; 'we've got to be men.'


4

I was driven to tell Margaret about our situation by my intolerable dread that otherwise the thing might come to her through some stupid and clumsy informant. She might even meet Mrs Boole, and have it from her.

I can still recall the feeling of sitting at my desk that night in that large study of mine in Radnor Square, waiting for Margaret to come home. It was oddly like the feeling of a dentist's reception-room ; only it was for me to do the dentistry with clumsy, cruel hands. I had left the door open so that she would come in to me.

I heard her silken rustle on the stairs at last, and then she was in the doorway. 'May I come in?' she said.

'Do,' I said, and turned round to her.

'Working?' she said.

'Hard,' I answered. 'Where have *you* been?'

'At the Vallerys'. Mr Evesham was talking about you. They were all talking. I don't think everybody knew who I was. Just Mrs Mumble I'd been to them. Lord Wardenham doesn't like you.'

'He doesn't.'

'But they all feel you're rather big, anyhow. Then I went on to Park Lane to hear a new pianist and some other music at Eva's.'

'Yes.'

'Then I looked in at the Brabrants' for some midnight tea before I came here. They'd got some writers – and Grant was there.'

'You *have* been flying round. . . .'

There was a little pause between us.

I looked at her pretty, unsuspecting face, and at the slender grace of her golden-robed body. What gulfs there were between us! 'You've been amused,' I said.

'It's been amusing. You've been at the House?'

'The Medical Education Bill kept me.' . . .

After all, why should I tell her? She'd got to a way of living that fulfilled her requirements. Perhaps she'd never hear. But all that day and the day before I'd been making up my mind to do the thing.

'I want to tell you something,' I said. 'I wish you'd sit down for a moment or so.' . . .

Once I had begun, it seemed to me I had to go through with it.

Something in the quality of my voice gave her an intimation of unusual gravity. She looked at me steadily for a moment and sat down slowly in my armchair. 'What is it?' she said.

I went on awkwardly. 'I've got to tell you – something extraordinarily distressing,' I said.

She was manifestly altogether unaware.

'There seems to be a good deal of scandal abroad – I've only recently heard of it – about myself – and Isabel.'

'Isabel!'

I nodded.

'What do they say?' she asked.

It was difficult, I found, to speak.

'They say she's my mistress.'

'Oh! How abominable!'

She spoke with the most natural indignation. Our eyes met.

'We've been great friends,' I said.

'Yes. And to make *that* of it. My poor dear! But how can they?' She paused and looked at me. 'It's so incredible. How can anyone believe it? I couldn't.'

She stopped, with her distressed eyes regarding me. Her expression changed to dread. There was a tense stillness for a second, perhaps.

I turned my face towards the desk, and took up and dropped a handful of paper fasteners.

'Margaret,' I said, 'I'm afraid you'll have to believe it.'

## 5

Margaret sat very still. When I looked at her again, her face was very white, and her distressed eyes scrutinized me. Her lips quivered as she spoke. 'You really mean – *that*?' she said.

I nodded.

'I never dreamt.'

'I never meant you to dream.'

'And that is why – we've been apart?'

I thought. 'I suppose it is.'

'Why have you told me now?'

'Those rumours. I didn't want anyone else to tell you.'

'Or else it wouldn't have mattered?'

'No.'

She turned her eyes from me to the fire. Then for a moment she looked about the room she had made for me, and then quite silently, with a childish quivering of her lips, with a sort of dismayed distress upon her face, she was weeping. She sat weeping in her dress of cloth of gold, with her bare slender arms dropped limp over the arms of her chair, and her eyes averted from me, making no effort to stay or staunch her tears. 'I am sorry, Margaret,' I said. 'I was in love. . . . I did not understand. . . .'

Presently she asked: 'What are you going to do?'

'You see, Margaret, now it's come to be your affair – I want to know what you – what you want.'

'You want to leave me?'

'If you want me to, I must.'

'Leave Parliament – leave all the things you are doing, – all this fine movement of yours?'

'No.' I spoke sullenly. 'I don't want to leave anything. I want to stay on. I've told you, because I think we – Isabel and I, I mean – have got to drive through a storm of scandal anyhow.

I don't know how far things may go, how much people may feel, and I can't, I can't have you unconscious, unarmed, open to any revelation –'

She made no answer.

'When the thing began – I knew it was stupid, but I thought it was a thing that wouldn't change, wouldn't be anything but itself, wouldn't unfold – consequences. . . . People have got hold of these vague rumours. . . . Directly it reached anyone else but – but us two – I saw it had to come to you.'

I stopped. I had that distressful feeling I have always had with Margaret, of not being altogether sure she heard, of being doubtful if she understood. I perceived that once again I had struck at her and shattered a thousand unsubstantial pinnacles. And I couldn't get at her, to help her, or touch her mind! I stood up, and at my movement she moved. She produced a little dainty handkerchief, and made an effort to wipe her face with it, and held it to her eyes. 'Oh, my Husband!' she sobbed.

'What do you mean?' she said with her voice muffled by her handkerchief.

'We're going to end it,' I said.

Something gripped me tormentingly as I said that. I drew a chair beside her and sat down. 'You and I, Margaret, have been partners,' I began. 'We've built up this life of ours together; I couldn't have done it without you. We've made a position, created a work –'

She shook her head. 'You,' she said.

'You helping. I don't want to shatter it – if you don't want it shattered. I can't leave my work. I can't leave you. I want you to have – all that you have ever had. I've never meant to rob you. I've made an immense and tragic blunder. My character and accident have conspired – We'll pay – in ourselves, not in our public service.'

I halted again. Margaret remained very still.

'I want you to understand that the thing is at an end. It is definitely at an end. We – we talked – yesterday. We mean to end it altogether.' I clenched my hands. 'She's – she's going to marry Arnold Shoesmith.'

I wasn't looking now at Margaret any more, but I heard the rustle of her movement as she turned on me.

'It's all right,' I said, clinging to my explanation. 'We're do-

356

ing nothing shabby. He knows. He will. It's all as right – as things can be now. We're not cheating anyone, Margaret. We're doing things straight – now. Of course, you know. . . . We shall – we shall have to make sacrifices. Give things up pretty completely. . . . We shall have not to see each other for a time, you know. Perhaps not for a long time. Or write – or just any of that sort of thing ever –'

Some subconscious barrier gave way in me. I found myself crying uncontrollably – as I have never cried since I was a little child. I was amazed and horrified at myself. And wonderfully, Margaret was on her knees beside me, with her arms about me, mingling her weeping with mine. 'Oh, my husband!' she cried, 'my poor Husband! Does it hurt you so? I would do anything! Oh, the fool I am! Dear, I love you. I love you over and away and above all these jealous little things!'

She drew down my head to her as a mother might draw down the head of a son. She caressed me, weeping bitterly with me. 'Oh! my dear,' she sobbed, 'my dear! I've never seen you cry! I've never seen you cry. Ever! I didn't know you could. Oh! my dear! Can't you have her, my dear, if you want her? I can't bear it! Let me help you, dear. Oh! my Husband! My Man! I can't bear to have you cry!' For a time she held me in silence. 'I've thought this might happen, I dreamt it might happen. You two, I mean. It was dreaming put it into my head. When I've seen you together, so glad with each other. . . . Oh! Husband mine, believe me! believe me! I'm stupid, I'm cold, I'm only beginning to realize how stupid and cold, but all I want in all the world is to give my life to you.' . . .

6

'We can't part in a room,' said Isabel.

'We'll have one last talk together,' I said, and planned that we should meet for half a day between Dover and Walmer and talk ourselves out. I still recall that day very well, recall even the curious exaltation of grief that made our mental atmosphere distinctive and memorable. We had seen so much of one another, had become so intimate, that we talked of parting even as we parted with a sense of incredible remoteness. We went together up over the cliffs, and to a place where they fall towards the sea, past the white, quaint-lanterned lighthouses of the South Foreland. There, in a kind of niche below the crest, we sat talking. It was a spacious day, serenely blue and warm, and on the wrinkled water remotely below a black tender and six hooded submarines came presently, and engaged in mysterious manoeuvres. Shrieking gulls and chattering jackdaws circled over us and below us, and dived and swooped; and a skerry of weedy, fallen chalk appeared, and gradually disappeared again, as the tide fell and rose.

We talked and thought that afternoon on every aspect of our relations. It seems to me now we talked so wide and far that scarcely an issue in the life between man and woman can arise that we did not at least touch upon. Lying there at Isabel's feet, I have become for myself a symbol of all this world-wide problem between duty and conscious, passionate love the world has still to solve. The sky, the wide horizon, seemed to lift us out of ourselves until we were something representative and general. She was womanhood become articulate, talking to her lover.

'I ought,' I said, 'never to have loved you.'

'It wasn't a thing planned,' she said.

'I ought never to have let our talk slip to that, never to have turned back from America.'

'I'm glad we did it,' she said. 'Don't think I repent.'

I looked at her.

'I will never repent,' she said. 'Never!' as though she clung to her life in saying it.

I remember we talked for a long time of divorce. It seemed to us then and it seems to us still, that it ought to have been possible for Margaret to divorce me, and for me to marry without the scandalous and ugly publicity, the taint and ostracism that follow such a readjustment. We went on to the whole perplexing riddle of marriage. We criticized the current code, how muddled and conventionalized it had become, how modified by subterfuges and concealments and new necessities, and the increasing freedom of women. 'It's all like Bromstead when the building came,' I said; for I had often talked to her of that early impression of purpose dissolving again into chaotic forces. 'There is no clear right in the world any more. The world is Byzantine. The justest man today must practise a tainted goodness.'

These questions need discussion – a magnificent frankness of discussion – if any standards are again to establish an effective hold upon educated people. Discretions, as I have said already, will never hold anyone worth holding – longer than they held us. Against every 'shalt not' there must be a 'why not' plainly put, – the 'why not' largest and plainest, the law deduced from its purpose. 'You and I, Isabel,' I said, 'have always been a little disregardful of duty, partly at least because the idea of duty comes to us so ill-clad. Oh! I know there's an extravagant insubordinate strain in us, but that wasn't all. I wish humbugs would leave duty alone. I wish all duty wasn't covered with slime. That's where the real mischief comes in. Passion can always contrive to clothe itself in beauty, strip itself splendid. That carried us. But for all its mean associations there *is* this duty. . . .'

'Don't we come rather late to it?'

'Not so late that it won't be atrociously hard to do.'

We talked for a long time of Margaret, and I told Isabel of my new impressions of her quality. 'I used in a manner to despise her,' I confessed. 'But, Isabel, she's so much better than we, so much cleaner and finer . . . not simply because she's simpler – but in grain. Think of her away there in London, knowing perhaps we are here. She *must* know we are here. The pride of her! Think of the sort of courage she shows, the conquest of jealousy – and mortification. She's been cheated, slighted. . . . Never once has she been, for a second, base.'

'It's queer to think of now,' said Isabel. 'Who could believe we did all we have done honestly? Well, in a manner honestly. Who could believe we thought this might be hidden? Who could trace it all step by step from the time when we found that a certain boldness in our talk was pleasing? We talked of love. . . . Master, there's not much for us to do in the way of Apologia that anyone will credit. And yet if it were possible to tell the very heart of our story . . .

'Does Margaret really want to go on with you?' she asked – 'shield you – knowing of . . . *this?*'

'I'm certain. I don't understand – just as I don't understand Shoesmith, but she does. These people walk on solid ground which is just thin air to us. They've got something we haven't got. Assurances? I wonder. . . .'

Then it was, or later, we talked of Shoesmith, and what her life might be with him.

'He's good,' she said ; 'he's kindly. He's everything but magic. He's the very image of the decent, sober, honourable life. You can't say a thing against him or I – except that something – something in his imagination, something in the tone of his voice – fails for me. Why don't I love him? – he's a better man than you! Why don't you? *Is* he a better man than you? He's usage, he's honour, he's the right thing, he's the breed and the tradition, – a gentleman. You're your erring, incalculable self. I suppose we women will trust his sort and love your sort to the very end of time. . . .'

We spent a long time talking of laws and customs, and how they might change in the coming years. We lay side by side and nibbled at grass stalks as we talked. It seemed enormously unreasonable to us that two people who had come to the pitch of easy and confident affection and happiness that held between us should be obliged to part and shun one another, or murder half the substance of their lives. We felt ourselves crushed and beaten by an indiscriminating machine which destroys happiness in the service of jealousy. 'The mass of people don't feel these things in quite the same manner as we feel them,' she said. 'Is it because we're different in grain, or educated out of some primitive instinct?'

'It's because we've explored love a little, and they know no more than the gateway,' I said. 'Lust and then jealousy ; their simple conception – and we have gone a little beyond that. . . .'

I remember that for a time we watched two of that larger sort of gull, whose wings are brownish-white, circle and hover against the blue. And then we lay and looked at a band of water mirror-clear far out to sea, and wondered why the breeze that rippled all the rest should leave it so serene.

'And in this State of ours,' I resumed.

'Eh!' said Isabel, rolling over into a sitting posture and looking out at the horizon. 'Let's talk no more of things we can never see. Talk to me of the work you are doing and all we shall do – after we have parted. We've said too little of that. We've had our red life, and it's over. Thank Heaven! – though we stole it! Talk about your work, dear, and the things we'll go on doing – just as though we were still together. We'll still be together in a sense – through all these things we have in common.'

And so we talked about politics and our outlook. We were interested to the pitch of self-forgetfulness. We weighed persons and forces, discussed the probabilities of the next general election, the steady drift of public opinion in the north and west away from Liberalism towards us. It was very manifest that in spite of Wardenham and the *Expurgator*, we should come into the new Government strongly. The party had no one else, all the young men were formally or informally with us; Esmeer would have office, Lord Tarville, I . . . and very probably there would be something for Shoesmith. 'And for my own part,' I said, 'I count on a backing on the Liberal side. For the last two years we've been forcing competition in constructive legislation between the parties. The Liberals have not been long in following up our Endowment of Motherhood lead. They'll have to give votes and lip service anyhow. Half the readers of the *Blue Weekly*, they say, are Liberals. . . .

'I remember talking about things of this sort with old Willersley,' I said, 'ever so many years ago. It was some place near Locarno, and we looked down the lake that shone weltering – just as now we look over the sea. And then we dreamt in an indistinct featureless way of all that you and I are doing now.'

'I!' said Isabel, and laughed.

'Well, of some such thing,' I said, and remained for awhile silent, thinking of Locarno.

I recalled once more the largeness, the release from small personal things that I had felt in my youth; statecraft became real and wonderful again with the memory, the gigantic handling of gigantic problems. I began to talk out my thoughts, sitting up beside her, as I could never talk of them to anyone but Isabel; began to recover again the purpose that lay under all my political ambitions and adjustments and anticipations. I saw the State, splendid and wide as I had seen it in that first travel of mine, but now it was no mere distant prospect of spires and pinnacles, but populous with fine-trained, bold-thinking, bold-doing people. It was as if I had forgotten for a long time and now remembered with amazement.

At first, I told her, I had been altogether at a loss how I could do anything to battle against the aimless muddle of our world; I had wanted a clue – until she had come into my life questioning, suggesting, unconsciously illuminating. 'But I have done nothing,' she protested. I declared she had done everything in growing to education under my eyes, in reflecting again upon all the processes that had made myself, so that instead of abstractions and blue-books and bills and devices, I had realized the world of mankind as a crowd needing before all things fine women and men. We'd spoilt ourselves in learning that, but anyhow we had our lesson. Before her I was in a nineteenth-century darkness, dealing with the nation as if it were a crowd of selfish men, forgetful of women and children and that shy wild thing in the hearts of men, love, which must be drawn upon as it has never been drawn upon before, if the State is to live. I saw now how it is possible to bring the loose factors of a great realm together, to create a mind of literature and thought in it, and the expression of a purpose, to make it self-conscious and fine. I had it all clear before me, so that at a score of points I could presently begin. The *Blue Weekly* was a centre of force. Already we had given Imperialism a criticism, and leavened half the press from our columns. Our movement consolidated and spread. We should presently come into power. Everything moved towards our hands. We should be able to get at the schools, the services, the universities, the church; enormously increase the endowment of research, and organize what was sorely wanted, a criticism of research; contrive a closer contact between the press and creative intellectual life; foster literature, clarify, strengthen the public consciousness, develop social organization and a sense of the State. Men were coming to us every day, brilliant young peers like Lord Dentonhill, writers like Carnot and Cresswell. It filled me with pride to win such men. 'We stand for so much more than we seem to stand for,' I said. I opened my heart to her, so freely that I hesitate so to open my heart even to the reader, telling of projects and ambitions I cherished, of my consciousness of great powers and widening opportunities. . . .

Isabel watched me as I talked.

She too, I think, had forgotten these things for a while. For it is curious and I think a very significant thing that since we had become lovers, we had talked very little of the broader things that had once so strongly gripped our imaginations.

'It's good,' I said, 'to talk like this to you, to get back to youth and great ambitions with you. There have been times lately when politics has seemed the pettiest game played with mean souls for mean ends – and none the less so that the happiness of three hundred million people might be touched by our follies. I talk to no one else like this. . . . And now I think of parting, I think but of how much more I might have talked to you.' . . .

Things drew to an end at last, but after we had spoken of a thousand things.

'We've talked away our last half-day,' I said, staring over my shoulder at the blazing sunset sky behind us. 'Dear, it's been the last day of our lives for us. . . . It doesn't seem like the last day of our lives. Or any day.'

'I wonder how it will feel?' said Isabel.

'It will be very strange at first – not to be able to tell you things.'

'I've a superstition that after – after we've parted – if ever I go into my room and talk, you'll hear. You'll be – somewhere.'

'I shall be in the world – yes.'

'I don't feel as though these days ahead were real. Here we are, here we remain.'

'Yes, I feel that. As though you and I were two immortals, who didn't live in time and space at all, who never met, who couldn't part, and here we lie in Olympus. And those two poor creatures who did meet, poor little Richard Remington and Isabel Rivers, who met and loved too much and had to part, they part and go their ways, and we lie here and watch them, you and I. She'll cry, poor dear.'

'She'll cry. She's crying now!'

'Poor little beasts! I think he'll cry too. He winces. He could – for tuppence. I didn't know he had lachrymal glands at all until a little while ago. Poor mites! Silly little pitiful creatures! How we have blundered! Think how we must look to God! Well, we'll pity them, and then we'll inspire him to stiffen up again – and do as we're determined he shall do. We'll see it through, – we who lie here on the cliff. They'll be mean at times, and horrid at times; we know them! Do you see her, a poor little fine lady in a great house, – she sometimes goes to her room and writes.'

363

'She writes for his *Blue Weekly* still.'

'Yes. Sometimes – I hope. And he's there in the office with a bit of her copy in his hand.'

'Is it as good as if she still talked it over with him before she wrote it? Is it?'

'Better, I think. Let's play it's better – anyhow. It may be that talking over was rather mixed with love-making. After all, love-making is joy rather than magic. Don't let's pretend about that even. . . . Let's go on watching him. (I don't see why her writing shouldn't be better. Indeed I don't.) See! There he goes down along the Embankment to Westminster just like a real man, for all that he's smaller than a grain of dust. What is running round inside that speck of a head of his? Look at him going past the policemen, specks too – selected large ones from the country. I think he's going to dinner with the Speaker – some old thing like that. Is his face harder or commoner or stronger? – I can't quite see. . . . And now he's up and speaking in the House. Hope he'll hold on to the thread. He'll have to plan his speeches to the very end of his days – and learn the headings.'

'Isn't she up in the women's gallery to hear him?'

'No. Unless it's by accident.'

'She's there,' she said.

'Well, by accident it happens. Not too many accidents, Isabel. Never any more adventure for us, dear, now. . . . They play the game, you know. They've begun late, but now they've got to. You see it's not so very hard for them since you and I, my dear, are always here, always faithfully here on this warm cliff of love accomplished, watching and helping them under high heaven. It isn't so *very* hard. Rather good in some ways. Some people *have* to be broken a little. Can you see Altiora down there, by any chance?'

'She's too little to be seen,' she said.

'Can you see the sins they once committed?'

'I can only see you here beside me, dear – for ever. For all my life, dear, till I die. Was that – the sin?' . . .

I took her to the station, and after she had gone I was to drive to Dover and cross to Calais by the night boat. I couldn't, I felt, return to London. We walked over the crest and down to the little station of Martin Mill side by side, talking at first in broken fragments, for the most part of unimportant things.

'None of this,' she said abruptly, 'seems in the slightest degree real to me. I've got no sense of things ending.'

'We're parting,' I said.

'We're parting – as people part in a play. It's distressing. But I don't feel as though you and I were really never to see each other again for years. Do you?'

I thought. 'No,' I said.

'After we've parted I shall look to talk it over with you.'

'So shall I.'

'That's absurd.'

'Absurd.'

'I feel as if you'd always be there, just about where you are now. Invisible perhaps, but there. We've spent so much of our lives joggling elbows.' . . . .

'Yes. Yes. I don't in the least realize it. I suppose I shall begin to when the train goes out of the station. Are we wanting in imagination, Isabel?'

'I don't know. We've always assumed it was the other way about.'

'Even when the train goes out of the station —! I've seen you into so many trains.'

'I shall go on thinking of things to say to you – things to put in your letters. For years to come. How can I ever stop thinking in that way now? We've got into each other's brains.'

'It isn't real,' I said; 'nothing is real. The world's no more than a fantastic dream. Why are we parting, Isabel?'

'I don't know. It seems now supremely silly. I suppose we have to. Can't we meet? – don't you think we shall meet even in dreams?'

'We'll meet a thousand times in dreams,' I said.

'I wish we could dream at the same time,' said Isabel. . . . 'Dream walks. I can't believe, dear, I shall never have a walk with you again.'

'If I'd stayed six months in America,' I said, 'we might have walked long walks and talked long talks for all our lives.'

'Not in a world of Baileys,' said Isabel. 'And anyhow –'

She stopped short. I looked interrogation.

'We've loved, dear one,' she said.

I took her ticket, and stood by the door of the compartment. 'Good-bye,' I said a little stiffly, conscious of the people upon the platform. She bent above me, white and dusky, looking at me very steadfastly.

'Come here,' she whispered. 'Never mind the porters. What can they know? Just one time more – I must.'

She rested her hand against the door of the carriage and bent down upon me, and put her cold, moist lips to mine.

# Chapter the Third

# The Breaking Point

## 1

And then we broke down. We broke our faith with both Margaret and Shoesmith, flung career and duty out of our lives, and went away together.

It is only now, almost a year after these events, that I can begin to see what happened to me. At the time it seemed to me I was a rational, responsible creature, but indeed I had not parted from her two days before I became a monomaniac to whom nothing could matter but Isabel. Every truth had to be squared to that obsession, every duty. It astounds me to think how I forgot Margaret, forgot my work, forgot everything but that we two were parted. I still believe that with better chances we might have escaped the consequences of the emotional storm that presently seized us both. But we had no foresight of that and no preparation for it, and our circumstances betrayed us. It was partly Shoesmith's unwisdom in delaying his marriage until after the end of the session – partly my own amazing folly in returning within four days to Westminster. But we were all of us intent upon the defeat of scandal and the complete restoration of appearances. It seemed necessary that Shoesmith's marriage should not seem to be hurried, still more necessary that I should not vanish inexplicably. I had to be visible with Margaret in London just as much as possible ; we went to restaurants, we visited the theatre ; we could even contemplate the possibility of my presence at the wedding. For that, however, we had schemed a week-end visit to Wales, and a fictitious sprained ankle at the last moment which would justify my absence. . . .

I cannot convey to you the intolerable wretchedness and rebellion of my separation from Isabel. It seemed that in the past two years all my thoughts had spun commissures to Isabel's brain, and I could think of nothing that did not lead me surely to the need of the one intimate I had found in the world. I came back to the House and the office and my home, I filled all my days with appointments and duty, and it did not save me in the least from a lonely emptiness such as I had never felt before in all my life. I had little sleep. In the daytime I did a hundred things, I even spoke in the House on two occasions, and by my own low standards spoke well, and it seemed to me that I was going about in my own brain like a hushed survivor in a house whose owner lies dead upstairs.

I came to a crisis after that wild dinner of Tarville's. Something in that stripped my soul bare.

It was an occasion made absurd and strange by the odd accident that the house caught fire upstairs while we were dining below. It was a men's dinner – 'A dinner of all sorts,' said Tarville, when he invited me ; 'everything from Evesham and Gane to Wilkins the author, and Heaven knows what will happen!' I remember that afterwards Tarville was accused of having planned the fire to make his dinner a marvel and a memory. It was indeed a wonderful occasion, and I suppose if I had not been altogether drenched in misery, I should have found the same wild amusement in it that glowed in all the others. There were one or two university dons, Lord George Fester, the racing man, Panmure, the artist, two or three big City men, Weston Massinghay and another prominent Liberal whose name I can't remember, the three men Tarville had promised and Esmeer, Lord Wrassleton, Waulsort, the member for Monckton, Neal, and several others. We began a little coldly, with dualogues, but the conversation was already becoming general – so far as such a long table permitted – when the fire asserted itself.

It asserted itself first as a penetrating and emphatic smell of burning rubber, – it was caused by the fusing of an electric wire. The reek forced its way into the discussion of the Peking massacres that had sprung up between Evesham, Waulsort, and the others at the end of the table. 'Something burning,' said the man next to me.

'Something must be burning,' said Panmure.

Tarville hated undignified interruptions. He had a particularly imperturbable butler with a cadaverous sad face and an eye of rigid disapproval. He spoke to this individual over his

368

shoulder. 'Just see, will you?' he said, and caught up the pause in the talk to his left.

Wilkins was asking questions, and I, too, was curious. The story of the siege of the Legations in China in the year 1900 and all that followed upon that is just one of those disturbing interludes in history that refuse to join on to that general scheme of protestation by which civilization is maintained. It is a break in the general flow of experience as disconcerting to statecraft as the robbery of my knife and the scuffle that followed it had been to me when I was a boy at Penge. It is like a tear in a curtain revealing quite unexpected backgrounds. I had never given the business a thought for years ; now this talk brought back a string of pictures to my mind ; how the reliefs arrived and the plundering began, how section after section of the International Army was drawn into murder and pillage, how the infection spread upward until the wives of Ministers were busy looting, and the very sentinels stripped and crawled like snakes into the Palace they were set to guard. It did not stop at robbery, men were murdered, women, being plundered, were outraged, children were butchered; strong men had found themselves with arms in a lawless defenceless city, and this had followed. Now it was all recalled.

'Respectable ladies addicted to district visiting at home were as bad as anyone,' said Panmure. 'Glazebrook told me of one – flushed like a woman at a bargain sale, he said – and when he pointed out to her that the silk she'd got was bloodstained, she just said,'Oh bother ! ' and threw it aside and went back. . . .'

We became aware that Tarvrille's butler had returned. We tried not to seem to listen.

'Beg pardon, m'lord,' he said. 'The house *is* on fire, m'lord.'

'Upstairs, m'lord.'

'Just overhead, m'lord.'

'The maids are throwing water, m'lord, and I've telephoned *fire*.'

'No, m'lord, no immediate danger.'

'It's all right,' said Tarvrille to the table generally. 'Go on ! It's not a general conflagration, and the fire brigade won't be five minutes. Don't see that it's our affair. The stuff's insured. They say old Lady Paskershortly was dreadful. Like a harpy. The Dowager Empress had shown her some little things of hers. Pet things – hidden away. Susan went straight for them – used to take an umbrella for the silks. Born shoplifter.'

It was evident he didn't want his dinner spoilt, and we played up loyally.

'This is recorded history,' said Wilkins, – 'practically. It makes one wonder about unrecorded history. In India, for example.'

But nobody touched that.

'Thompson,' said Tarvrille to the imperturbable butler, and indicating the table generally, 'champagne. Champagne. Keep it going.'

'M'lord,' and Thompson marshalled his assistants.

Some man I didn't know began to remember things about Mandalay. 'It's queer,' he said, 'how people break out at times'; and told his story of an army doctor, brave, public-spirited, and, as it happened, deeply religious, who was caught one evening by the excitement of plundering – and stole and hid, twisted the wrist of a boy until it broke, and was afterwards overcome by wild remorse.

I watched Evesham listening intently. 'Strange,' he said, 'very strange. We are such stuff as thieves are made of. And in China, too, they murdered people – for the sake of murdering. Apart, so to speak, from mercenary considerations. I'm afraid there's no doubt of it in certain cases. No doubt at all. Young soldiers – fresh from German high schools and English homes!'

'Did *our* people?' asked some patriot.

'Not so much. But I'm afraid there were cases . . . Some of the Indian troops were pretty bad.'

Gane picked up the tale with confirmations.

It is all printed in the vividest way as a picture upon my memory, so that were I a painter I think I could give the deep rich browns and warm greys beyond the brightly lit table, the various distinguished faces, strongly illuminated, interested and keen, above the black and white of evening dress, the alert men-servants with their heavier, clean-shaven faces indistinctly seen in the dimness behind. Then this was coloured emotionally for me by my aching sense of loss and sacrifice, and by the chance trend of our talk to the breaches and unrealities of the civilized scheme. We seemed a little transitory circle of light

370

in a universe of darkness and violence; an effect to which the diminishing smell of burning rubber, the trampling of feet overhead, the swish of water, added enormously. Everybody – unless, perhaps, it was Evesham – drank rather carelessly because of the suppressed excitement of our situation, and talked the louder and more freely.

'But what a flimsy thing our civilization is!' said Evesham; 'a mere thin net of habits and associations!'

'I suppose those men came back,' said Wilkins.

'Lady Paskershortly did!' chuckled Evesham.

'How do they fit it in with the rest of their lives?' Wilkins speculated. 'I suppose there's Peking-stained police officers, Peking-stained J.P.s – trying petty pilferers in the severest manner.' . . .

Then for a time things became preposterous. There was a sudden cascade of water by the fireplace, and then absurdly the ceiling began to rain upon us, first at this point and then that. 'My new suit!' cried some one. 'Perrrrrr-up pe-rr' – a new vertical line of blackened water would establish itself and form a spreading pool upon the gleaming cloth. The men nearest would arrange catchment areas of plates and flower-bowls. 'Draw up!' said Tarvrille, 'draw up. That's the bad end of the table!' He turned to the imperturbable butler. '"Take round bath towels,' he said; and presently the men behind us were offering – with inflexible dignity – 'Port wine, Sir. Bath towel, Sir!' Waulsort, with streaks of blackened water on his forehead, was suddenly reminded of a wet year when he had followed the French army manoeuvres. An animated dispute sprang up between him and Neal about the relative efficiency of the new French and German field guns. Wrassleton joined in, and a little drunken shrivelled Oxford don of some sort with a black-splashed shirt front who presently silenced them all by the immensity and particularity of his knowledge of field artillery. Then the talk drifted to Sedan and the effect of dead horses upon drinking-water, which brought Wrassleton and Weston Massinghay into a dispute of great vigour and emphasis. 'The trouble in South Africa,' said Weston Massinghay, 'wasn't that we didn't boil our water. It was that we didn't boil our men. The Boers drank the same stuff we did. *They* didn't get dysentery.'

That argument went on for some time. I was attacked across the table by a man named Burshort about my Endowment of Motherhood schemes, but in the gaps of that debate I could still hear Weston Massinghay at intervals repeat in a rather thickened voice: '*They* didn't get dysentery.'

I think Evesham went early. The rest of us clustered more and more closely towards the drier end of the room, the table was pushed along, and the area beneath the extinguished conflagration abandoned to a tinkling, splashing company of pots and pans and bowls and baths. Everybody was now disposed to be hilarious and noisy, to say startling and aggressive things; we must have sounded a queer clamour to a listener in the next room. The devil inspired them to begin baiting me. 'Ours isn't the Tory party any more,' said Burshort. 'Remington has made it the Obstetric Party.'

'That's good!' said Weston Massinghay, with all his teeth gleaming ; 'I shall use that against you in the House!'

'I shall denounce you for abusing private confidences if you do,' said Tarvrille.

'Remington wants us to give up launching Dreadnoughts and launch babies instead,' Burshort urged. 'For the price of one Dreadnought –'

The little shrivelled don who had been omniscient about guns joined in the baiting, and displayed himself a venomous creature. Something in his eye told me he knew of Isabel and hated me for it. 'Love and fine thinking,' he began, a little thickly, and knocking over a wine-glass with a too easy gesture 'Love and fine thinking. Two things don't go together. No ph'losophy worth a damn ever came out of excesses of love. Salt Lake City – Pigott – Ag – Agapamone again – no works to matter.'

Everybody laughed.

'Got to rec'nize these facts,' said my assailant. 'Love and fine think'n pretty phrase – attractive. Suitable for P'litical dec'rations. Postcard, Christmas, gilt lets, in a wreath of white flow's. Not oth'wise valu'ble.'

I made some remark, I forgot what, but he overbore me.

'Real things we want are Hate – Hate and *coarse* think'n. I b'long to the school of Mrs F's Aunt –'

'What?' said someone, intent.

'In "Little Dorrit," ' explained Tarvrille; 'go on!'

'Hate a fool,' said my assailant.

Tarvrille glanced at me. I smiled to conceal the loss of my temper.

'Hate,' said the little man, emphasizing his point with a clumsy fist. 'Hate's the driving force. What's m'rality? – hate of rotten goings on. What's patriotism? – hate of int'loping foreigners. What's Radicalism? – hate of lords. What's Tory-ism? – hate of disturbance. It's all hate – hate from top to bottom. Hate of a mess. Remington owned it the other day, said he hated a – mu'll. There you are! If you couldn't get hate into an election, damn it (hic) people wou'n't poll. Poll for love! – no' me!'

He paused, but before any one could speak he had resumed.

'Then this about fine thinking. Like going into a bear pit armed with a tagle – talgent – talgent galv'nometer. Like going to fight a mad dog with Shasepear and the Bible. Fine thinking –what we want is the thickes' thinking we can get. Thinking that stands up alone. Taf Reform means work for all, – thas-sort of thing.'

The gentleman from Cambridge paused. '*You* a flag!' he said. 'I'd as soon go to ba'ell und' wet tissue paper!'

My best answer on the spur of the moment was: 'The Japan-ese did.' Which was absurd.

I went on to some other reply, I forget exactly what, and the talk of the whole table drew round me. It was an extraordinary revelation to me. Every one was unusually careless and out-spoken, and it was amazing how manifestly they echoed the feeling of this old Tory spokesman. They were quite friendly to me, they regarded me and the *Blue Weekly* as valuable party assets for Toryism, but it was clear they attached no more im-portance to what were my realities than they did to the re-markable therapeutic claims of Mrs Eddy. They were flushed and amused, perhaps they went a little too far in their resolves to draw me, but they left the impression on my mind of men irrevocably set upon narrow and cynical views of political life. For them the political struggle was a game, whose counters were human hate and human credulity; their real aim was just everyone's aim, the preservation of the class and way of living to which their lives were attuned. They did not know how tired I was, how exhausted mentally and morally, or how cruel their convergent attack on me chanced to be. But my temper gave way, I became tart and fierce, perhaps my replies were a trifle absurd, and Tarvrille, with that quick eye and sympathy of his, came to the rescue. Then for a time I sat silent and drank port wine while the others talked. The disorder of the room, the still dripping ceiling, the noise, the displaced ties and crumpled shirts of my companions, jarred on my tormented nerves. . . .

It was long past midnight when we dispersed. I remember Tarvrille coming with me into the hall, and then suggesting we should go upstairs to see the damage. A manservant carried up two flickering candles for us. One end of the room was gutted, curtains, hangings, several chairs and tables were completely burnt, the panelling was scorched and warped, three smashed windows made the candles flare and gutter, and some scraps of broken china still lay on the puddled floor.

As we surveyed this, Lady Tarvrille appeared, back from some party, a slender, white-cloaked, satin-footed figure with amazed blue eyes beneath her golden hair. I remember how stupidly we laughed at her surprise.

2

I parted from Panmure at the corner of Aldington Street, and went my way alone. But I did not go home; I turned westward and walked for a long way, and then struck northward aimlessly. I was too miserable to go to my house.

I wandered about that night like a man who has discovered his Gods are dead.

I do not feel now the logical force of the process that must have convinced me then that I had made my sacrifice and spent my strength in vain. At no time had I been under any illusion that the Tory party had higher ideals than any other party, yet it came to me like a thing newly discovered that the men I had to work with had for the most part no such dreams, no sense of any collective purpose, no atom of the faith I held. They were just as immediately intent upon personal ends, just as limited by habits of thought, as the men in any other group or party. Perhaps I had slipped unawares for a time into the delusions of a party man – but I do not think so.

No, it was the mood of profound ·despondency that had followed upon the abrupt cessation of my familiar intercourse with Isabel, that gave this fact that had always been present in my mind its quality of devastating revelation. It seemed as though I had never seen before nor suspected the stupendous gap between the chaotic aims, the routine, the conventional acquiescences, the vulgarizations of the personal life, and that clearly conscious development and service of a collective thought and purpose at which my efforts aimed. I had thought them but a little way apart, and now I saw they were separated by all the distance between earth and heaven. I saw now in myself and everyone around me, a concentration upon interests close at hand, an inability to detach oneself from the provocations, tendernesses, instinctive hates, dumb lusts, and shy timidities that touched one at every point ; and, save for rare exalted moments, a regardlessness of broader aims and remoter possibilities that made the white passion of statecraft seem as unearthly and irrelevant to human life as the story an astronomer will tell, half proven but altogether incredible, of habitable planets and answering intelligences, suns' distances uncounted across the deep. It seemed to me I had aspired too high and thought too far, had mocked my own littleness by presumption, had given the uttermost dear reality of life for a theorizer's dream.

All through that wandering agony of mine that night a dozen threads of thought interwove; now I was a soul speaking in protest to God against a task too cold and high for it, and now I was an angry man, scorned and pointed upon, who had let life cheat him of the ultimate pride of his soul. Now I was the fool of ambition, who opened his box of gold to find blank emptiness, and now I was a spinner of flimsy thoughts, whose web tore to rags at a touch. I realized for the first time how much I had come to depend upon the mind and faith of Isabel, how she had confirmed me and sustained me, how little strength I had to go on with our purposes now that she had vanished from my life. She had been the incarnation of those great abstractions, the saving reality, the voice that answered back. There was no support that night in the things that had been.

We were alone together on the cliff for evermore! – that was very pretty in its way, but it had no truth whatever that could help me now, no ounce of sustaining value. I wanted Isabel that night, no sentiment or memory of her, but Isabel alive, – to talk to me, to touch me, to hold me together. I wanted unendurably the dusky gentleness of her presence, the consolation of her voice.

We were alone together on the cliff! I startled a passing cabman into interest by laughing aloud at that magnificent and characteristic sentimentality. What a lie it was! That was just where we shouldn't remain. We of all people had no distinction from that humanity whose lot is to forget. We should go out to other interests, new experiences, new demands. That tall and intricate fabric of ambitious understandings we had built up together in our intimacy would be the first to go; and last perhaps to endure with us would be a few gross memories of sights and sounds, and trivial incidental excitements. . . .

I had a curious feeling that night that I had lost touch with life for a long time, and had now been reminded of its quality. That infernal little don's parody of my ruling phrase, 'Hate and coarse thinking,' stuck in my thoughts like a poisoned dart, a centre of inflammation. Just as a man who is debilitated has no longer the vitality to resist an infection, so my mind, slackened by the crisis of my separation from Isabel, could find no resistance to his emphatic suggestion. It seemed to me that what he had said was overpoweringly true, not only of contemporary life, but of all possible human life. Love is the rare thing, the treasured thing; you lock it away jealously and watch, and well you may; hate and aggression and force keep the streets and rule the world. And fine thinking is, in the rough issues of life, weak thinking, is a balancing indecisive process, discovers with disloyal impartiality a justice and a defect on each disputing side. 'Good honest men,' as Dayton calls them, rule the world, with a way of thinking out decisions like shooting cartloads of bricks, and with a steadfast pleasure in hostility. Dayton liked to call his antagonists 'blaggards and scoundrels' – it justified his opposition – the Lords were 'scoundrels', all people richer than he were 'scoundrels', all Socialists, all troublesome poor people; he liked to think of jails and justice being done. His public spirit was saturated with the sombre joys of conflict and the pleasant thought of condign punishment for all recalcitrant souls. That was the way of it, I perceived. That had survival value, as the biologists say. He was fool enough in politics to be a consistent and happy politician. . . .

Hate and coarse thinking; how the infernal truth of the phrase beat me down that night! I couldn't remember that I had known this all along, and that it did not really matter in the slightest degree. I had worked it all out long ago in other terms, when I had seen how all parties stood for interests inevitably, and how the purpose in life achieves itself, if it achieves itself at all, as a by-product of the war of individuals and classes. Hadn't I always known that science and philosophy elaborate themselves in spite of all the passions and narrowness of men, in spite of the vanities and weakness of their servants, in spite of all the heated disorder of contemporary things? Wasn't it my own phrase to speak of 'that greater mind in men, in which we are but moments and transitorily lit cells'? Hadn't I known that the spirit of man still speaks like a thing that struggles out of mud and slime, and that the mere effort to speak means choking and disaster? Hadn't I known that we who think without fear and speak without discretion will not come to our own for the next two thousand years?

It was the last was most forgotten of all that faith mislaid. Before mankind, in my vision that night, stretched new centuries of confusion, vast stupid wars, hastily conceived laws, foolish temporary triumphs of order, lapses, set-backs, despairs, catastrophes, new beginnings, a multitudinous wilderness of time, a nigh plotless drama of wrong-headed energies. In order to assuage my parting from Isabel we had set ourselves to imagine great rewards for our separation, great personal rewards, we had promised ourselves success visible and shining in our lives. To console ourselves in our separation we had made out of the *Blue Weekly* and our young Tory movement preposterously enormous things – as though those poor fertilizing touches at the soil were indeed the germinating seeds of the millennium, as though a million lives such as ours had not to contribute before the beginning of the beginning. That poor pretence had failed. That magnificent proposition shrivelled to nothing in the black loneliness of that night.

I saw that there were to be no such compensations. So far as my real services to mankind were concerned, I had to live an unrecognized and unrewarded life. If I made successes it would be by the way. Our separation would alter nothing of that. My scandal would cling to me now for all my life, a thing affecting relationships, embarrassing and hampering my spirit. I should follow the common lot of those who live by the imagination, and follow it now in infinite loneliness of soul; the one good comforter, the one effectual familiar, was lost to me for ever; I should do good and evil together, no one caring to understand; I should produce much weary work, much bad spirited work, much absolute evil; the good in me would be too often ill-expressed and missed or misinterpreted. In the end I might leave one gleaming flake or so amidst the slag heaps for a moment of post-mortem sympathy. I was afraid beyond measure of my derelict self. Because I believed with all my soul in love and fine thinking, that did not mean that I should necessarily either love steadfastly or think finely. I remember how I fell talking to God – I think I talked out loud. 'Why do I care for these things,' I cried, 'when I can do so little? Why am I set apart from the jolly thoughtless fighting life of men? These dreams fade to nothingness, and leave me bare!'

I scolded. 'Why don't you speak to a man, show yourself? I thought I had a gleam of you in Isabel, – and then you take her away. Do you really think I can carry on this game alone, doing your work in darkness and silence, living in muddled conflict, half living, half dying?'

Grotesque analogies arose in my mind. I discovered a strange parallelism between my now tattered phrase of 'Love and fine thinking' and the 'Love and the Word' of Christian thought. Was it possible the Christian propaganda had at the outset meant just that system of attitudes I had been feeling my way towards from the very beginning of my life? Had I spent a lifetime making my way back to Christ? It mocks humanity to think how Christ has been overlaid. I went along now, recalling long-neglected phrases and sentences; I had a new vision of that great central figure preaching love with hate and coarse thinking even in the disciples about Him,

378

rising to a tidal wave at last in that clamour for Barabbas, and the public satisfaction in His fate. . . .

It's curious to think that hopeless love and a noisy disordered dinner should lead a man to these speculations, but they did. 'He *did* mean that!' I said, and suddenly thought of what a bludgeon they'd made of His Christianity. Athwart that perplexing, patient enigma sitting inaudibly among publicans and sinners, danced and gibbered a long procession of the champions of orthodoxy. 'He wasn't human,' I said, and remembered that last despairing cry, 'My God! My God! why hast Thou forsaken Me?'

'Oh, *He* forsakes every one,' I said, flying out as a tired mind will, with an obvious repartee. . . .

I passed at a bound from such monstrous theology to a towering rage against the Booles. In an instant and with no sense of absurdity I wanted – in the intervals of love and fine thinking – to fling about that strenuously virtuous couple ; I wanted to kick Keyhole of the *Peepshow* into the gutter and make a common massacre of all the prosperous rascaldom that makes a trade and rule of virtue. I can still feel that transition. In a moment I had reached that phase of weakly decisive anger which is for people of my temperament the concomitant of exhaustion.

'I will have her,' I cried. 'By Heaven! I *will* have her! Life mocks me and cheats me. Nothing can be made good to me again. . . . Why shouldn't I save what I can? I can't save myself without her. . . .'

I remember myself – as a sort of anti-climax to that – rather tediously asking my way home. I was somewhere in the neighbourhood of Holland Park. . . .

It was then between one and two. I felt that I could go home now without any risk of meeting Margaret. It had been the thought of returning to Margaret that had sent me wandering that night. It is one of the ugliest facts I recall about that time of crisis, the intense aversion I felt for Margaret. No sense of her goodness, her injury and nobility, and the enormous generosity of her forgiveness, sufficed to mitigate that. I hope now that in this book I am able to give something of her silvery splendour, but all through this crisis I felt nothing of that. There was a triumphant kindliness about her that I found

379

intolerable. She meant to be so kind to me, to offer unstinted consolation, to meet my needs, to supply just all she imagined Isabel had given me.

When I left Tarville's I felt I could anticipate exactly how she would meet my homecoming. She would be perplexed by my crumpled shirt front, on which I had spilt some drops of wine ; she would overlook that by an effort, explain it sentimentally, resolve it should make no difference to her. She would want to know who had been present, what we had talked about, show the alertest interest in whatever it was – it didn't matter what. . . . No, I couldn't face her.

So I did not reach my study until two o'clock.

There, I remember, stood the new and very beautiful old silver candlesticks that she had set there two days since to please me – the foolish kindliness of it! But in her search for expression, Margaret heaped presents upon me. She had fitted these candlesticks with electric lights, and I must, I suppose, have lit them to write my note to Isabel. 'Give me a word – the world aches without you,' was all I scrawled, though I fully meant that she should come to me. I knew, though I ought not to have known, that now she had left her flat, she was with the Balfes – she was to have been married from the Balfes – and I sent my letter there. And I went out into the silent square and posted the note forthwith, because I knew quite clearly that if I left it until morning I should never post it at all.

3

I had a curious revulsion of feeling that morning of our meeting. (Of all places for such a clandestine encounter she had chosen the Bridge opposite Buckingham Palace.) Overnight I had been full of self-pity, and eager for the comfort of Isabel's presence. But the ill-written scrawl in which she had replied had been full of the suggestion of her own weakness and misery. And when I saw her, my own selfish sorrows were altogether swept away by a wave of pitiful tenderness. Something had happened to her that I did not understand. She was manifestly ill. She came towards me wearily, she who had always borne herself so bravely ; her shoulders seemed bent, and her eyes were tired, and her face white and drawn. All my life has been a narrow self-centred life; no brothers, no sisters or children or weak things had ever yet made any intimate appeal to me, and suddenly – I verily believe for the first time in my life! – I felt a great passion of protective ownership; I felt that here was something that I could die to shelter, something that meant more than joy or pride or splendid ambitions or splendid creation to me, a new kind of hold upon me, a new power in the world. Some sealed fountain was opened in my breast. I knew that I could love Isabel broken, Isabel beaten, Isabel ugly and in pain, more than I could love any sweet or delightful or glorious thing in life. I didn't care any more for anything in the world but Isabel, and that I should protect her. I trembled as I came near her, and could scarcely speak to her for the emotion that filled me. . . .

'I had your letter,' I said.

'I had yours.'

'Where can we talk?'

I remember my lame sentences. 'We'll have a boat. That's best here.'

I took her to the little boat-house, and there we hired a boat, and I rowed in silence under the bridge and into the shade of a tree. The square grey stone masses of the Foreign Office loomed through the twigs, I remember, and a little space of grass separated us from the pathway and the scrutiny of passers-by. And there we talked.

'I had to write to you,' I said.

'I had to come.'

'When are you to be married?'

'Thursday week.'

'Well?' I said. 'But – can we?'

She leant forward and scrutinized my face with eyes wide open. 'What do you mean?' she said at last in a whisper.

'Can we stand it? After all?'

I looked at her white face. 'Can you?' I said.

She whispered. 'Your career?'

Then suddenly her face was contorted, – she wept silently, exactly as a child tormented beyond endurance might suddenly weep. . . .

'Oh! I don't care,' I cried, 'now. I don't care. Damn the whole system of things. Damn all this patching of the irrevocable! I want to take care of you, Isabel! and have you with me.'

'I can't stand it,' she blubbered.

'You needn't stand it. I thought it was best for you. . . . I thought indeed it was best for you. I thought even you wanted it like that.'

'Couldn't I live alone – as I meant to do?'

'No,' I said, 'you couldn't. You're not strong enough. I've thought of that. I've got to shelter you.

'And I want you,' I went on. 'I'm not strong enough – I can't stand life without you.'

She stopped weeping, she made a great effort to control herself, and looked at me steadfastly for a moment. 'I was going to kill myself,' she whispered. 'You don't know all. . . . I was going to kill myself quietly – somehow. I meant to wait a bit and have an accident. I thought – you didn't understand. You were a man, and couldn't understand. . . .'

'People can't do as we thought we could do,' I said. 'We've gone too far together.'

'Yes,' she said, and I stared into her eyes.

'The horror if it,' she whispered. 'The horror of being handed over. It's just only begun to dawn upon me, seeing him now as I do. He tries to be kind to me. . . . I didn't know. I felt adventurous before. . . . It makes me feel like all the women in the world who have ever been owned and subdued. . . . It's not that he isn't the best of men, it's because I'm a part of you. . . . I can't go through with it. If I go through with it, I shall be left – robbed of pride – outraged – a woman beaten. . . .'

'I know,' I said, 'I know.'

'I want to live alone. . . . I don't care for anything now but just escape. If you can help me. . . .'

'I must take you away. There's nothing for us but to go away together.'

'But your work,' she said; 'your career! Margaret! Our promises!'

'We've made a mess of things, Isabel – or things have made a mess of us. I don't know which. Our flags are in the mud, anyhow. It's too late to save those other things! They have to go. You can't make terms in a rout. I thought it was Margaret needed me most. But it's you. And I need you. I didn't think of that either. I haven't a doubt left in the world now. We've got to leave everything rather than leave each other. I'm sure of it. Now we have gone so far. We've got to go right down to earth and begin again. . . . Dear, I *want* disgrace with you. . . .'

So I whispered to her as she sat crumpled together on the faded cushions of the boat, this white and weary young woman who had been so valiant and careless a girl. 'I don't care,' I said. 'I don't care for anything, if I can save you out of the wreckage we have made together.'

4

The next day I went to the office of the *Blue Weekly* in order to get as much as possible of its affairs in working order before I left London with Isabel. I just missed Shoesmith in the lower office. Upstairs I found Britten amidst a pile of outside articles, methodically reading the title of each and sometimes the first half-dozen lines, and either dropping them in a growing heap on the floor for a clerk to return, or putting them aside for consideration. I interrupted him, squatted on the window-sill of the open window, and sketched out my ideas for the session.

'You're far-sighted,' he remarked at something of mine which reached out ahead.

'I like to see things prepared,' I answered.

'Yes,' he said, and ripped open the envelope of a fresh aspirant.

I was silent while he read.

'You're going away with Isabel Rivers,' he said abruptly.

'Well!' I said, amazed.

'I know,' he said, and lost his breath. 'Not my business. Only –'

It was queer to find Britten afraid to say a thing.

'It's not playing the game,' he said.

'What do you know?'

'Everything that matters.'

'Some games,' I said, 'are too hard to play.'

There came a pause between us.

'I didn't know you were watching all this,' I said.

'Yes,' he answered, after a pause, 'I've watched.'

'Sorry – sorry you don't approve.'

'It means smashing such an infernal lot of things, Remington.'

I did not answer.

'You're going away, then?'

'Yes.'

'Soon?'

'Right away.'

'There's your wife.'

'I know.'

'Shoesmith – whom you're pledged to in a manner. You've just picked him out and made him conspicuous. Everyone will know. Oh! of course – it's nothing to you. Honour –'

'I know.'

'Common decency.'

I nodded.

'All this movement of ours. That's what *I* care for most. . . . It's come to be a big thing, Remington.'

'That will go on.'

'We have a use for you – no one else quite fills it. No one. . . . I'm not sure it will go on.'

'Do you think I haven't thought of all these things?'

He shrugged his shoulders, and rejected two papers unread.

'I knew,' he remarked, 'when you came back from America. You were alight with it.' Then he let his bitterness gleam for a moment. 'But I thought you would stick to your bargain.'

'It's not so much a choice as you think,' I said.

'There's always a choice.'

'No,' I said.

He scrutinized my face.

'I can't live without her – I can't work. She's all mixed up with this – and everything. And besides, there's things you can't understand. There's feelings you've never felt. . . . You don't understand how much we've been to one another.'

Britten frowned and thought.

'Some things one's *got* to do,' he threw out.

'Some things one can't do.'

'These infernal institutions –'

'Some one must begin,' I said.

He shook his head. 'Not *you*,' he said. 'No!'

He stretched out his hands on the desk before him, and spoke again.

'Remington,' he said, 'I've thought of this business day and night too. It matters to me. It matters immensely to me. In a way – it's a thing one doesn't often say to a man – I've loved you. I'm the sort of man who leads a narrow life. . . . But you've been something fine and good for me, since that time, do you remember? when we talked about Mecca together.'

I nodded.

'Yes. And you'll always be something fine and good for me anyhow. I know things about you, – qualities – no mere act can destroy them. . . . Well, I can tell you, you're doing wrong. You're going on now like a man who is hypnotized and can't turn round. You're piling wrong on wrong. It was wrong for you two people ever to be lovers.'

He paused.

'It gripped us hard,' I said.

'Yes! – but in your position! And hers! It was vile!'

'You've not been tempted.'

'How do you know? Anyhow – having done that, you ought to have stood the consequences and thought of other people. You could have ended it at the first pause for reflection. You didn't. You blundered again. You kept on. You owed a certain secrecy to all of us! You didn't keep it. You were careless. You made things worse. This engagement and this publicity –! Damn it, Remington!'

'I know,' I said, with smarting eyes. 'Damn it! – with all my heart! It came of trying to patch. . . . You *can't* patch.'

'And now, as I care for anything under heaven, Remington, you two ought to part. Other people have to stand things! Other people have to part. You ought to. You say – what do you say? It's loss of so much life to lose each other. So is losing a hand or a leg. But it's what you've incurred. Amputate. Take your punishment – After all, you chose it.'

'Oh, damn!' I said, standing up and going to the window.

'Damn by all means. I never knew a topic so full of justifiable damns. But you two did choose it. You ought to stick to your undertaking.'

I turned upon him with a snarl in my voice. 'My dear Britten!' I cried. 'Don't I *know* I'm doing wrong? Aren't I in a net? Suppose I don't go! Is there any right in that? Do you think we're going to be much to ourselves or anyone after this parting? I've been thinking all last night of this business, trying it over and over again from the beginning. How was it we went wrong? Since I came back from America – I grant you *that* – but *since*, there's never been a step that wasn't forced, that hadn't as much right in it or more, as wrong. You talk as though I was a thing of steel that could bend this way or that and never change. You talk as though Isabel was a cat one could give to any kind owner. . . . We two are things that change and grow and alter all the time. We're – so interwoven that being parted now will leave us just misshapen cripples. . . . You don't know the motives, you don't know the rush and feel of things, you don't know how it was with us, and how it is with us. You don't know the hunger for the mere sight of one another; you don't know anything.'

Britten looked at his finger-nails closely. His red face puckered to a wry frown. 'Haven't we all at times wanted the world put back?' he grunted, and looked hard and close at one particular nail.

There was a long pause.

'I want her,' I said, 'and I'm going to have her. I'm too tired for balancing the right or wrong of it any more. You can't separate them. I saw her yesterday. . . . She's ill. . . . I'd take her now, if death were just outside the door waiting for us.'

'Torture?'

I thought. 'Yes.'

'For her?'

'There isn't,' I said.

'If there was?'

I made no answer.

'It's blind Want. And there's nothing ever been put into you to stand against it. What are you going to do with the rest of your lives?'

'No end of things.'

'Nothing.'

'I don't believe you are right,' I said. 'I believe we can save something –'

Britten shook his head. 'Some scraps of salvage won't excuse you,' he said.

386

His indignation rose. 'In the middle of life!' he said. 'No man has a right to take his hand from the plough!'

He leant forward on his desk and opened an argumentative palm. 'You know, Remington,' he said, 'and I know, that if this could be fended off for six months – if you could be clapped in prison, or got out of the way somehow, – until this marriage was all over and settled down for a year, say – you know then you two could meet, curious, happy, as friends. Saved! You *know* it.'

I turned and stared at him. 'You're wrong, Britten,' I said. 'And does it matter if we could?'

I found that in talking to him I could frame the apologetics I had not been able to find for myself alone.

'I am certain of one thing, Britten. It is our duty not to hush up this scandal.'

He raised his eyebrows.

'It's our duty,' I went on, 'to smash now openly in the sight of everyone. I've got that as clean and plain – as prison white-wash. I am convinced that we have got to be public to the uttermost now – I mean it – until every corner of our world knows this story, knows it fully, adds it to the Parnell story and the Ashton Dean story and the Carmel story and the Witterslea story, and all the other stories that have picked man after man out of English public life, the men with active imaginations, the men of strong initiative. To think this tottering old-woman-ridden Empire should dare to waste a man on such a score! You say I ought to be penitent –'

Britten shook his head and smiled very faintly.

'I'm boiling with indignation,' I said. 'I lay in bed last night and went through it all. What in God's name was to be expected of us but what has happened? I went through my life bit by bit last night, I recalled all I've had to do with virtue and women, and all I was told and how I was prepared. I was born into cowardice and debasement. We all are. Our generation's grimy with hypocrisy. I came to the most beautiful things in life – like peeping Tom of Coventry. I was never given a light, never given a touch of natural manhood by all this dingy, furtive, canting, humbugging English world. Thank God! I'll soon be out of it! The shame of it! The very savages in Austra-lia initiate their children better than the English do today.

387

Neither of us was ever given a view of what they call morality
that didn't make it show as shabby subservience, as the meanest
discretion, an abject submission to unreasonable prohibitions!
Meek surrender of mind and body to the dictation of pedants
and old women and fools. We weren't taught – we were
mumbled at!'

'Yes,' said Britten. 'That's all very well –'

I interrupted him. 'I know there's a case – I'm beginning to
think it a valid case against us; but we never met it! There's a
steely pride in self-restraint, a nobility of chastity, but only for
those who see and think and act – untrammelled and unafraid.'
I put my foot in a chair, and urged my case upon him. 'This is a
dirty world, Britten, simply because it is a muddled world, and
the thing you call morality is dirtier now than the thing you call
immorality. Why don't the moralists pick their stuff out of the
slime if they care for it, and wipe it? – damn them! I am burning now to say: "Yes, we did this and this," to all the world.
All the world! . . . I will!'

Britten rubbed the palm of his hand on the corner of his
desk. 'That's all very well, Remington,' he said. 'You mean to
go.'

He stopped and began again. 'If you didn't know you were in
the wrong you wouldn't be so damned rhetorical. You're in the
wrong. It's as plain to you as it is to me. You're leaving a big
work, you're leaving a wife who trusted you, to go and live with
your jolly mistress. . . . You won't see you're a statesman that
matters, that no single man, maybe, might come to such influence as you in the next ten years. You're throwing yourself
away and accusing your country of rejecting you.'

He swung round upon his swivel at me. 'Remington,' he said,
'have you forgotten the immense things our movement means?'

I thought. 'Perhaps I *am* rhetorical,' I said.

'But the things we might achieve! If you'd only stay now –
even now! Oh! you'd suffer a little socially, but what of that?
You'd be able to go on – perhaps all the better for hostility of
the kind you'd get. You know, Remington – you *know*.'

I thought and went back to his earlier point. 'If I am rhetorical, at any rate it's a living feeling behind it. Yes, I remember
all the implications of our aims – very splendid, very remote.
But just now it's rather like offering to give a freezing man the

sunlit Himalayas from end to end in return for his camp-fire. When you talk of me and my jolly mistress, it isn't fair. That misrepresents everything. I'm not going out of this – for delights. That's the sort of thing men like Snuffles and Keyhole imagine – that excites them! When I think of the things these creatures think! Ugh! But *you* know better! You know that physical passion that burns like a fire – ends clean. I'm going for love, Britten – if I sinned for passion. I'm going, Britten, because when I saw her the other day she *hurt* me. She hurt me damnably, Britten. . . . I've been a cold man – I've had a rhetorical life – you hit me with that word! – I put things in a windy way, I know, but what has got hold of me at last is her pain. She's ill. Don't you understand? She's a sick thing – a weak thing. She's no more a goddess than I'm a god. . . . I'm not in love with her now ; I'm *raw* with love for her. I feel like a man that's been flayed. I have been flayed. . . . You don't begin to imagine the sort of helpless solicitude. . . . She's not going to do things easily; she's ill. Her courage fails. . . . It's hard to put things when one isn't rhetorical, but it's this, Britten – there are distresses that matter more than all the delights or achievements in the world. . . . I made her what she is – as I never made Margaret. I've made her – I've broken her. . . . I'm going with my own woman. The rest of my life and England, and so forth, must square itself to that.'

For a long time, as it seemed, we remained silent and motionless. We'd said all we had to say. My eyes caught a printed slip upon the desk before him, and I came back abruptly to the paper.

I picked up this galley proof. It was one of Winter's essays. 'This man goes on doing first rate stuff,' I said. 'I hope you will keep him going.'

He made no answer. He sat back in his chair with his chin in his collar and his hands deep in his trouser pockets.


5

I have a letter Margaret wrote me within a week of our flight. I cannot resist transcribing some of it here, because it lights things as no words of mine can do. It is a string of nearly inconsecutive thoughts written in pencil in a fine, tall, sprawling hand. Its very inconsecutiveness is essential. Many words are underlined. It was in answer to one from me ; but what I wrote has passed utterly from my mind. . . .

'Certainly,' she says, 'I want to hear from you, but I do not want to see you. That's a sort of abstract *you* that I want to go on with. Something I've made *out* of you. . . . I want to know things about you – but I don't want to see or feel or imagine. When some day I have got rid of my intolerable sense of proprietorship, it may be different. Then perhaps we may meet again. I think it is even more the loss of our political work and dreams that I am feeling than the loss of your presence. Aching loss. I thought so much of the things we were *doing* for the world – had given myself so unreservedly. You've left me with nothing to *do*. I am suddenly at loose ends. . . .

'We women are trained to be so dependent on a man. I've got no life of my own at all. It seems now to me that I wore my clothes even for you and your schemes. . . .

'After I have told myself a hundred times why this has happened, I ask again, "Why did he give things up? Why did he give things up?" . . .

'It is just as though you were wilfully dead. . . .

'Then I ask again and again whether this thing need have happened at all, whether if I had had a warning, if I had understood better, I might not have adapted myself to your restless mind and made this catastrophe impossible. . . .

'Oh, my dear! why hadn't you the pluck to hurt me at the beginning, and tell me what you thought of me and life? You didn't give me a chance ; not a chance. I suppose you couldn't. All these things you and I stood away from. You let my first repugnances repel you. . . .

'It is strange to think after all these years that I should be asking myself, do I love you? have I loved you? In a sense I think I *hate* you. I feel you have taken my life, dragged it in your wake for a time, thrown it aside. I am resentful. Unfairly resentful, for why should I exact that you should watch and understand my life, when clearly I have understood so little of yours? But I am savage – savage at the wrecking of all you were to do.

'Oh, why – why did you give things up?

'No human being is his own to do what he likes with. You

390

were not only pledged to my tiresome, ineffectual companion-
ship, but to great purposes. They *are* great purposes. . . .

'If only I could take up your work as you leave it, with the
strength you had – then indeed I feel I could let you go – you
and your young mistress. . . . All that matters so little to me. . . .

'Yet I think I must indeed love you yourself in my slower
way. At times I am mad with jealousy at the thought of all I
hadn't the wit to give you. . . . I've always hidden my tears
from you – and what was in my heart. It's my nature to hide –
and you, you want things brought to you to see. You are so
curious as to be almost cruel. You don't understand reserves.
You have no mercy with restraints and reservations. You are
not really a *civilized* man at all. You hate pretences – and not
only pretences but decent coverings. . . .

'It's only after one has lost love and the chance of loving that
slow people like myself find what they might have done. Why
wasn't I bold and reckless and abandoned? It's as reasonable to
ask that, I suppose, as to ask why my hair is fair. . . .

'I go on with these perhapses over and over again here when
I find myself alone. . . .

'My dear, my dear, you can't think of the desolation of things
– I shall never go back to that house we furnished together,
that was to have been the laboratory (do you remember calling
it a laboratory?) in which you were to forge so much of the
new order. . . .

'But, dear, if I can help you – even now – in any way –
help both of you, I mean. . . . It tears me when I think of you
poor and discredited. You will let me help you if I can – it will
be the last wrong not to let me do that. . . .

'You had better not get ill. If you do, and I hear of it – I
shall come after you with a troupe of doctors and nurses. If I
am a failure as a wife, no one has ever said I was anything but
a success as a district visitor. . . .'

There are other sheets, but I cannot tell whether they were
written before or after the ones from which I have quoted.
And most of them have little things too intimate to set down.
But this oddly penetrating analysis of our differences must, I
think, be given.

'There are all sorts of things I can't express about this and
want to. There's this difference that has always been between

us, that you like nakedness and wildness, and I, clothing and restraint. It goes through everything. You are always *talking* of
order and system, and the splendid dream of the order that
might replace the muddled system you hate, but by a sort of
instinct you seem to want to break the law. I've watched you
so closely. Now *I* want to obey laws, to make sacrifices, to follow
rules. I don't want to make, but I do want to keep. You are at
once makers and rebels, you and Isabel too. You're bad people
– criminal people, I feel, and yet full of something the world
must have. You're so much better than me, and so much viler.
It may be there is no making without destruction, but it seems
to me sometimes that it is nothing but an instinct for lawless-
ness that drives you. You remind me – do you remember? – of
that time we went from Naples to Vesuvius, and walked over
the hot new lava there. Do you remember how tired I was? I
know it disappointed you that I was tired. One walked there in
spite of the heat because there was a crust ; like custom, like
law. But directly a crust forms on things, you are restless to
break down to the fire again. You talk of beauty, both of you,
as something terrible, mysterious, imperative. *Your* beauty is
something altogether different from anything I know or feel.
It has a pain in it. Yet you always speak as though it was
something I ought to feel and am dishonest not to feel. *My*
beauty is a quiet thing. You have always laughed at my feeling
for old-fashioned chintz and blue china and Sheraton. But I
like all these familiar *used* things. My beauty is *still* beauty,
and yours is excitement. I know nothing of the fascination of
the fire, or why one should go deliberately out of all the decent
fine things of life to run dangers and be singed and tormented
and destroyed. I don't understand. . . .'


6

I remember very freshly the mood of our departure from
London, the platform of Charing Cross with the big illuminated
clock overhead, the bustle of porters and passengers with
luggage, the shouting of newsboys and boys with flowers and
sweets, and the groups of friends seeing travellers off by the
boat train. Isabel sat very quiet and still in the compartment,
and I stood upon the platform with the door open, with a curi-

ous reluctance to take the last step that should sever me from London's ground. I showed our tickets, and bought a handful of red roses for her. At last came the guards crying: 'Take your seats,' and I got in and closed the door on me. We had, thank Heaven! a compartment to ourselves. I let down the window and stared out.

There was a bustle of final adieux on the platform, a cry of 'Stand away, please, stand away!' and the train was gliding slowly and smoothly out of the station.

I looked out upon the river as the train rumbled with slowly gathering pace across the bridge, and the bobbing black heads of the pedestrians in the footway, and the curve of the river and the glowing great hotels, and the lights and reflections and blacknesses of that old, familiar spectacle. Then with a common thought, we turned our eyes westward to where the pinnacles of Westminster and the shining clock tower rose hard and clear against the still, luminous sky.

'They'll be in Committee on the Reformatory Bill tonight,' I said, a little stupidly.

'And so,' I added, 'good-bye to London!'

We said no more, but watched the south-side streets below – bright gleams of lights and movement, and the dark, dim, monstrous shapes of houses and factories. We ran through Waterloo Station, London Bridge, New Cross, St John's. We said never a word. It seemed to me that for a time we had exhausted our emotions. We had escaped, we had cut our knot, we had accepted the last penalty of that headlong return of mine from Chicago a year and a half ago. That was all settled. That harvest of feelings we had reaped. I thought now only of London, of London as the symbol of all we were leaving and all we had lost in the world. I felt nothing now but an enormous and overwhelming regret. . . .

The train swayed and rattled on its way. We ran through old Bromstead, where once I had played with cities and armies on the nursery floor. The sprawling suburbs with their scattered lights gave way to dim tree-set country under a cloud-veiled, intermittently shining moon. We passed Cardcaster Place. Perhaps old Wardingham, that pillar of the old Conservatives, was there, fretting over his unsuccessful struggle with our young Toryism. Little he recked of this new turn of the wheel and how it would confirm his contempt of all our novelties. Perhaps some faint intimation drew him to the window to see, behind the stems of the young fir trees that bordered his domain, the little string of lighted carriage windows gliding southward. . . .

Suddenly I began to realize just what it was we were doing.

And now, indeed, I knew what London had been to me, London where I had been born and educated, the slovenly mother of my mind and all my ambitions, London and the empire! It seemed to me we must be going out to a world that was utterly empty. All our significance fell from us – and before us was no meaning any more. We were leaving London; my hand, which had gripped so hungrily upon its complex life, had been forced from it, my fingers left their hold. That was over. I should never have a voice in public affairs again. The inexorable unwritten law which forbids overt scandal sentenced me. We were going out to a new life, a life that appeared in that moment to be a mere shrivelled remnant of life, a mere residuum of sheltering and feeding and seeing amidst alien scenery and the sound of unfamiliar tongues. We were going to live cheaply in a foreign place, so cut off that I meet now the merest stray tourist, the commonest tweed-clad stranger with a mixture of shyness and hunger. . . . And suddenly all the schemes I was leaving appeared fine and adventurous and hopeful as they had never done before. How great was this purpose I had relinquished, this bold and subtle remaking of the English will! I had doubted so many things, and now suddenly I doubted my unimportance, doubted my right to this suicidal abandonment. Was I not a trusted messenger, greatly trusted and favoured, who had turned aside by the way? Had I not, after all, stood for far more than I had thought; was I not filching from that dear great city of my birth and life some vitally necessary thing, a key, a link, a reconciling clue in her political development, that now she might seek vaguely for in vain? What is one life against the State? Ought I not to have sacrificed Isabel and all my passion and sorrow for Isabel, and held to my thing – stuck to my thing?

I heard as though he had spoken it in the carriage Britten's 'It *was* a good game. No end of a game.' And for the first time I imagined the faces and voices of Crupp and Esmeer and Gane when they learnt of this secret flight, this flight of which they were quite unwarned. And Shoesmith might be there in the house, – Shoesmith who was to have been married in four days – the thing might hit him full in front of any kind of people. Cruel eyes might watch him. Why the devil hadn't I written letters to warn them all? I could have posted them five minutes before the train started. I had never thought to that moment of the immense mess they would be in; how the whole edifice would clatter about their ears. I had a sudden desire to stop the train and go back for a day, for two days, to set that negligence right. My brain for a moment brightened, became animated and prolific of ideas. I thought of a brilliant line we might have taken on that confounded Reformatory Bill....

That sort of thing was over....

What indeed wasn't over? I passed to a vaguer, more multitudinous perception of disaster, the friends I had lost already since the campaign of scandal began, the ampler remnant whom now I must lose. I thought of people I had been merry with, people I had worked with and played with, the companions of talkative walks, the hostesses of houses that had once glowed with welcome for us both. I perceived we must lose them all. I saw life like a tree in late autumn that had once been rich and splendid with friends – and now the last brave dears would be hanging on doubtfully against the frosty chill of facts, twisting and tortured in the universal gale of indignation, trying to evade the cold blast of the truth. I had betrayed my party, my intimate friend, my wife, the wife whose devotion had made me what I was. For a while the figure of Margaret, remote, wounded, shamed, dominated my mind, and the thought of my immense ingratitude. Damn them! they'd take it out of her too. I had a feeling that I wanted to go straight back and grip someone by the throat, someone talking ill of Margaret. They'd blame her for not keeping me, for letting things go so far.... I wanted the whole world to know how fine she was. I saw in imagination the busy, excited dinner-tables at work upon us all, rather pleasantly excited, brightly indignant, merciless.

Well, it's the stuff we are! ...

Then suddenly, stabbing me to the heart, came a vision of Margaret's tears and the sound of her voice saying, 'Husband mine! Oh! husband mine! To see you cry!' ...

I came out of a cloud of thoughts to discover the narrow compartment, with its feeble lamp overhead, and our rugs and hand-baggage swaying on the rack, and Isabel, very still in front of me, gripping my wilting red roses tightly in her bare and ringless hand.

For a moment I could not understand her attitude, and then I perceived she was sitting bent together with her head averted from the light to hide her tears that were streaming down her face. She had not got her handkerchief out for fear that I should see this, but I saw her tears, dark drops of tears, upon her sleeve. . . .

I suppose she had been watching my expression, divining my thoughts.

For a time I stared at her and was motionless, in a sort of still and weary amazement. Why had we done this injury to one another? Why? Then something stirred within me.

'Isabel!' I whispered.

She made no sign.

'Isabel!' I repeated, and then crossed over to her and crept closely to her, put my arm about her, and drew her wet cheek to mine.